THE LAST FAREWELL

BY THE SAME AUTHOR

Featuring Lieutenant St. Vincent Halfhyde, RN
Beware, Beware the Bight of Benin
Halfhyde's Island
The Guns of Arrest
Halfhyde to the Narrows
Halfhyde for the Queen
Halfhyde Ordered South
Halfhyde and the Flag Captain
Halfhyde on Zanaru
Halfhyde Outward Bound
The Halfhyde Line
Halfhyde and the Chain Gangs
Halfhyde Goes to War
Halfhyde on the Amazon
Halfhyde and the Admiral

Featuring Donald Cameron
Cameron Comes Through
Lieutenant Cameron, RNVR
Cameron's Convoy
Cameron in the Gap
Orders for Cameron
Cameron in Command
Cameron and the Kaiserhof
Cameron's Raid
Cameron's Chase
Cameron's Troop Lift
Cameron's Commitment

Featuring Commodore John Mason Kemp RD, RNR:
The Convoy Commodore
Convoy North
Convoy South
Convoy East
Convoy of Fear

Philip McCutchan

THE LAST
FAREWELL

A novel

St. Martin's Press
New York

Library of Congress Cataloging-in-Publication Data

McCutchan, Philip.
    The last farewell : a novel / Philip McCutchan.
        p.   cm.
    ISBN 0-312-05458-0
    I. Title.
PR6063.A167L37   1991
823′.914—dc20   90-49227
                                                     CIP

First published in Great Britain by George Weidenfeld and Nicolson Limited.

First U.S. Edition: March 1991
10 9 8 7 6 5 4 3 2 1

*To my wife Elizabeth,
my son Donald
and my daughter Rosemary,
with my love*

AUTHOR'S NOTE

I WOULD LIKE TO THANK MY FRIEND FRANK
LEOCADI OF NEW YORK AND WORTHING FOR
HIS INVALAUABLE HELP IN RESEARCHING THE
CONTEMPORARY AMERICAN SCENE IN 1915
AND FOR THE VERY GREAT TROUBLE HE WENT
TO ON MY BEHALF.

THE LAST FAREWELL

I

SOME three to four weeks earlier, before the ordeal of the man at the Court of Inquiry presided over in Westminster by Lord Mersey, the bodies had started to come ashore on the tides that washed the shores of south-west Ireland, around Garretstown Strand and Courtmacsherry Bay. Those bodies had been gathered in by the beachcombers, the Irish peasantry from their white-washed, thatched cottages with the turf fires smoking in the single living-rooms that served also as bedrooms and for most other purposes. Poor men and women, living on the brink of starvation largely, they had pounced like vultures on the dead. Rich and poor, male and female, young and old (many were children), first class, second and third classes – British and American and many other nationalities caught in the cruel web of war by the German torpedoes. One tide after another brought more pickings . . . at Schull, and Bantry Bay, all around the inhospitable, tricky promontories of County Kerry. The pickings were well worth while: the relatives of the dead wanted their loved ones back for decent burial ashore. The PanAtlantic Line had offered inducements: a British body was worth a pound; and two pounds would be paid for a citizen of the United States of America.

The rich, the famous, the men in the news earned much more; up to a thousand pounds per well-heeled body. In death as in life.

Coming away from Central Buildings in Westminster the man walked fast, with long strides, unseeingly. He was tall and of heavy build; the face beneath the bowler hat was square, weather-beaten, strong but kindly, though now it was drawn into an expression combining worry and anger in equal measure. The look was of the sea; but of the Merchant Service rather than the RN. There was a lack of starchiness though there was plenty of assurance and self-reliance – the face of a man whose orders had never been backed by the iron hand of formal RN discipline but had always been obeyed because of his strength of personality and because he knew his job and was known to be capable of carrying out himself any order he gave.

The fast walk, the long strides, carried the man towards Whitehall and a search for a taxi. Before he found one he was approached by a

I

young woman wearing a long coat with a fur collar, and a flowery hat on her fair hair.

She spoke to the man, her voice icily contemptuous. She said, 'I followed you from the Inquiry. I have this for you.' She produced a white feather and with the speed of movement of a snake stuck it in his button-hole. The man turned away; a taxi had drawn up in response to his raised arm. He got in. 'Waterloo,' he said abruptly. The young lady looked put out, baulked of something.

The taxi went along Whitehall, the man sitting rigid in the back. He was bound now for Southsea, the residential suburb of Portsmouth, where he had been brought up as a child, where he lived still. Portsmouth and his father, who had been an Admiralty pilot, had given him his love of the sea that had become his life, his whole interest, his ambition to become what he had become: a master mariner. Now he felt the sea had let him down. Or if not the sea itself, then some of the men who made their careers upon it. And the politicians, notably Winston Churchill, First Lord of the Admiralty. And the lawyers, who knew nothing of the sea, nothing of the many strains laid upon a shipmaster, nothing of the war at sea.

The month was the June of 1915, and the man was Captain William Pacey, lately Master of the PanAtlantic liner *Laurentia*, until a few weeks earlier the pride of the North Atlantic run, now lying on the seabed off the Old Head of Kinsale after German submarine attack. 1201 souls had perished with her, among them 139 United States citizens, men, women and children.

Laurentia's passenger list on her final voyage from New York had been a very varied one. There were so many different social backgrounds and income groups to fill the three classes. There were diplomats and politicians, Englishmen returning to war-bound Britain to join in the fight against the Kaiser and the German Empire. There was a Swedish couple returning across the North Atlantic with a six-year-old son who had gone to the United States for life-saving treatment, an operation performed successfully by a top American surgeon. There was a fading stage and movie star getting the hell out from a husband who no longer cared. There were the socialites, leaders of New York society, rich men and women. There was a French general who had been conducting a military mission to President Wilson, returning to Paris to report a signal lack of success and who was to spend the homeward voyage alternating between concocting a lengthy written document proving that failure had not been his fault but the President's and bedding a fairly recent introduction, an attractive and very willing widowed American lady who had intended visiting her late English husband's family in Stratford-on-

Avon but was thrilled at the promise, made a few days before, of being taken to Paris by French brass – and a 'de' at that – even though the German Army was so close. 'Me, I shall protect you,' the general had sworn in excellent English soon after sailing.

And there were many, many others. A mix of nationalities in the third class, that area of crowded cabins, some of them containing twelve wooden bunks apiece, these multi-bunk cabins being of one sex so that husbands and wives were separated, a state of berthing that necessitated a good deal of bargaining to secure a clear cabin when nature called.

Frederick Jones fitted none of these catogeries. He was by profession an architect; he was a British citizen married to an American wife from upstate New York, whom, four days before embarkation, he had murdered. A couple of years before the outbreak of war he had been sent by his firm to study American construction methods. During this time he had defected, gaining employment with a New York company at the age of forty-six; he had also married Maggie Holroyd who was twenty-four years younger than himself. She was attractive enough but had a shrill laugh that men had found irritating. In Frederick Jones Maggie had not seen a romantic figure, for he was short and skinny and wore high stand-up starched collars and gold-rimmed spectacles, but a man who was destined – he said and she believed – to become 'a big shot' in his line, a man who now had experience in the US as well as in London, England, and had so impressed his New York employers, a noted firm, that he had been offered a partnership. Now he was going back to Britain, not to remain for long, but to visit his old mother, a widow of just on eighty who was sick and not expected to live.

'Let's hope she doesn't,' Maggie had said.

'What a thing to say!' Frederick Jones was shocked.

'I'll want to get back fast to the good old USA, Fred. Guess I won't like Britain. All that war – and all those lords.' She'd given her shrill laugh; Frederick tried to block his ears but it was no use. He knew why she wanted to get back to New York as soon as possible. He also knew why he'd insisted on her accompanying him. The reason was the same in each case: she had lovers. Frederick Jones was himself not capable of much sexual activity and some of Maggie's desires revolted him. But there were plenty of other men who were more than willing, despite the laugh, to indulge the whims and fancies of a young woman with whom no question of marriage could arise. The married ones were always safer.

All this Frederick Jones knew though Maggie did not know he knew. Consumed with jealousy, consumed with his own inadequacy, angry about the remark concerning his old mother, irritated beyond endurance by the shrill laugh, he had come to a decision and had plotted. It should be quite simple. In the event, it was. He had suggested borrowing an automobile from a friend and taking Maggie on a mid-week visit prior to embarkation aboard the *Laurentia*, a run up to Arlington, Massachusetts where her married sister lived. Maggie had agreed; Frederick Jones knew she would – not on account of her sister, whom she visited often enough anyway, but because she had a lover in Arlington and was well able to meet him because the sister, who was a nurse, was out a lot, as was the husband on account of his own job.

They went to Arlington in a big, heavy automobile with cans of gasoline secured to the running-boards and with a lockable boot like a big, square, black box stuck on the back. During their short stay Maggie managed to slip away for an hour or so saying she had some girlie shopping to do and didn't want Fred around. That apart, they had themselves a period that Frederick was determined should look to his sister-in-law a time of much love and domestic bliss, so that she could say so if ever the body was discovered.

On the way back home they passed through hilly country and conifer woods. Frederick stopped the automobile in the woods; it was a lovely day and they might as well have a stroll, he said. In the automobile's big boot was an axe wrapped in a blanket. Frederick brought this out.

'So what's the idea?' Maggie laughed, shrilly. 'Going to do me in, or what, Fred?'

He hated being called Fred; he had been christened Frederick and his old mother had always called him that, in full. But he gave a jolly laugh, seeing the joke as she did not. 'You never know,' he said, still laughing. 'No – I just thought a nice log fire. . . .'

'In May?'

'For when we come back from England, dear.'

'Silly,' she said crossly.

'It's nice and cheerful, a log fire.'

'All that smoke . . .' She moved conveniently ahead of him. They walked in the depths of the trees.

'Well, yes,' he said. 'There's that.' He used the axe, splitting her skull neatly in two halves with a shrewdly placed blow. There was no sound but there was a lot of blood, more so as Frederick Jones went to work and messily dismembered the corpse, which he first undressed. He severed the limbs with the axe, like a butcher, and then went back to the automobile for a spade. Returning to the scene he began to dig a hole in ground that was hard with tree roots. As he paused in his work he heard the sound of running water ahead. He went on and came to a river. He believed it was the Wappinger. By the water's edge the ground might be softer. It was. He dug five separate graves – legs, arms, torso. Not as deep as he would have wished, but he managed. He went back to the dismembered body and dragged the segments bloodily to the graves. Before the torso was interred he smashed the face a little more with the spade so that the jawbone was split into many pieces and the teeth came out. These he placed in his pocket: dentists could tell tales, not that Maggie had often visited a dentist. Then he began the burial. During it a leg rolled down into the water and floated off downstream. Frederick cursed but didn't worry unduly; it would doubtless get caught somewhere and be eaten by fish. He went on with the other burials. This done, he fetched a rake from the automobile's boot. He raked the grave-tops and the area where the axe had been used, drawing a clean layer of pine needles over the earth. It did stand out a bit, it was true, since the rest of the wood was unraked, but in a day or so nature would have done its work and the earth would look neither disturbed nor overneedled.

There was blood on his clothing and body and on Maggie's apparel but he had provided for this as well. A resourceful man, he had brought a change of clothing, a length of rope and a couple of large bottles of water, the latter now rendered redundant by the river's proximity. He stripped, sluiced water over his naked body, removed the teeth from the discarded suit and put them in the pocket of the fresh one, bundled all the bloody garments, his and hers, into an old mackintosh from which all labels had been removed as they had been removed from his discarded suit, and now from Maggie's dress, washed again, put on the fresh clothing, carried the roped mackintosh back to the borrowed automobile and drove off. Some miles farther along he came again to the river. There was no one around. He stopped the motor and threw the bundle of clothing into the river, a fast-flowing one that, even if the bundle, nicely anonymous, should be found, would have washed it clean of Maggie's blood. Then he threw in the axe, the spade, the rake.

He drove back to New York and returned the vehicle to his friend.

'Have a good trip?' the friend asked.

'Sure. Very good.'

'Maggie enjoy it?'

'Very much,' Frederick Jones said. The automobile delivered, he walked to his apartment, soon to be vacated for the *Laurentia*. It was only after he'd been back for a few hours that the snags began to occur to him. He'd been buoyed up, euphoric really, by the thought of being free of a whore with a shrill laugh who called him Fred and never mind his protests. A whore who said unkind things about his old mother. He and his mother had been close once, until divided by the waste of seas. She was going to be so pleased to see him again. But those possible snags . . . he'd been on a high, of course. Now he was thinking there could be animals in those woods, animals who might smell out flesh and start scraping with their claws, and there coud be rangers to see the result. On the other hand, the animals might eat Maggie's remains, in which case all would be well.

Another spectrum of the forthcoming embarkation across a sea at war: the lush Fifth Avenue apartment of a big-time New York banker, Patrick Haggerty, whose forebears had emigrated from County Galway in Ireland's west some seventy-five years earlier, driven out by the failure of the potato crop and the subsequent famine, which the Haggertys of the day had put down to the absentee landlords, the Protestant Ascendancy.

With Haggerty was a man from the White House. Haggerty was embarking for Britain in connexion with a loan being sought by the British Government to help pay for the war. The man from the White House was Ralph K. Butz, a big name in the US administration. They were enjoying an excellent dinner and fine wine, waited on by a manservant. While this servant was in the room, a big one richly furnished – and while Haggerty's wife was there as well – the talk was innocuous. The latest show was discussed, and some pictures in the Metropolitan Museum of Art, and the books of some American and British authors; that sort of thing. When Mrs Haggerty withdrew and the manservant had poured brandy and left the decanter, the talk shifted.

'You know one thing,' Butz stated.

'Go on.'

'The President won't stand for it. He's hedging, that's Wilson's way, but he'll never agree finally.'

'I know that,' Haggerty said with a smile.

'Then why waste your time, Patrick? Why go?'

Haggerty smiled again. 'I'm going *because* Wilson will say no. Do you think I'd help bring off a deal to help the goddam English off the hook?' He hastened to add, 'That's not to go beyond these four walls, Ralph, okay?'

'Okay,' Butz agreed. 'But you mean you're going across to foul up Asquith's request, backed by King George in person?'

'I didn't say that, Ralph. I didn't say that at all and you know it.'

Butz kept silent. It had been a most excellent meal and Haggerty was an influential man. The brandy had given Butz a feeling of mellowness, though he happened not to like his host. And he believed there was a lot more to Haggerty's mission than had appeared on the surface. He even believed that the President might have chosen Haggerty to go to the British War Cabinet precisely so that he could foul it all up while at the same time leaving the President himself with the appearance of having

6

done his best to be co-operative with Mr Asquith, the British Prime Minister. Certainly it was true that President Wilson wouldn't sanction the loan, a very big one indeed – in the region of a billion dollars in fact. At the war's start, Secretary of State William Jennings Bryan had, with Presidential authority, affirmed that the United States Government believed that for American bankers to make loans to any belligerents was not consistent with neutrality. That was the way it was; yet President Wilson didn't like to say no, blatantly. In Butz's view he could be using Haggerty, relying on him to insist on conditions so harsh that the British Government would be obliged to reject them. Wheels within wheels, and duplicity in high places, were facts of life in government all over the world. But Wilson, now: blind eyes and deaf ears had been turned to various arms deals in the past, without a doubt. Cargoes of munitions that were virtually contraband whilst Britain was in a state of war had crossed the Atlantic on numerous occasions. Wilson – if he had known – had been one of those who turned a blind eye to such. But times had changed a little now. The loan was desperately needed by Mr Asquith and King George; also by Mr Winston Churchill. And the pressures from across the North Atlantic had been a shade too much for a President determined to maintain his country's neutrality. There had been times, as Butz knew, when the President had remarked bitterly that Winston Churchill at all events would stop at nothing to drag the United States into the war. For the intervention of the enormous power of America would be the salvation of the embattled British nation, its army bogged down interminably in the Flanders mud, and its ships being sunk daily by the German U-boats.

When Butz had left the Fifth Avenue apartment, Patrick Haggerty sat with his wife in front of a big window looking out over Manhattan, across towards the Hudson River and beyond it the lights of New Jersey. It was to New Jersey that the original Haggertys had come from County Galway. Patrick Haggerty liked to look across to his origins. His wife Lois knew this; when her husband looked pensive as he did now, she forbore to speak. She was a comfortable woman, at fifty-five four years younger than her husband; and she was an inveterate knitter. She was knitting now, something for a grandchild. Her mind went ahead to their embarkation aboard the *Laurentia*. She looked forward to seeing London again; unlike her husband, she admired the British and she liked the elegance of London and the aura of royalty in the capital. The colourful prewar scenes of the changing of the guard at Buckingham Palace, or at the Horse Guards, and the ceremony of beating retreat that she had once seen carried out by a Scottish regiment, the Royal

Highland Regiment, known, she had been told, as the Black Watch from the dark hue of their kilts and the fact that they had been formed in Aberfeldy in Perthshire for the purpose of maintaining a watch on the Highlands to prevent any gathering of subversive clans. Lois Haggerty had adored the sound of the pipes and drums and had said so.

'British hypocrisy,' her husband had growled, and had gone on to mutter about Butcher Cumberland who had slaughtered the Scots at the whim of the English king, and then he'd spoken of the later clearances when the Scottish lairds, imbued by then with English ideas, had burned the crofters out of their homes to make way for the herds of sheep whose wool and flesh were going to be much more profitable than the rents collected from the half-starved Highlanders. Just like Ireland, Patrick Haggerty had said.

Lois knew he was thinking of Ireland now. Once, not so long ago, they had been across to Ireland and to County Galway. The original Haggertys had lived some three miles north of Galway City, in a village called Newcastle. They had occupied a thatched cottage with white-washed walls containing the one room where all the family had lived and slept and eaten. There had been a turf fire and a beaten floor, and a hole in the thatch above the fire for the smoke to escape, though this it did not always do. They had lived in the shadow of a big house known as Glenlo Abbey because there were the remains of an abbey in the grounds that ran down to Lough Corrib. The Haggertys had lived a wretched existence while – so said Patrick Haggerty on that occasion – the big house was occupied by the scions of the Protestant Ascendancy who ran the country and ran over the native Irish at the same time, while the English monarch's Lord Lieutenant ruled the roost in Dublin. One day, he said, it would all change.

Patrick Haggerty had tried to identify the cottage but without success; it seemed that despite long Irish memories no one now remembered the Haggertys. He had been told of a Haggerty who lived in a cottage in the Claddagh in Galway City, a fisherman who scraped his living off Aran Island outside Galway Bay, but when he found this man he appeared to be no relation: none of his family, he said, had ever gone to America so far as he knew.

They had seen as much as time allowed of the west of Ireland, going out from Galway City in a sidecar that the English called a jaunting car, into the wild mountains of Connemara reaching into the mists, wet with the interminable Irish rain; past the dark bogs where the turf was being cut for the fires. There had been a particular smell about the whole place, and it came largely from the burning of the turf, a never-to-be-forgotten smell.

Lois found she could understand her husband's feelings though she believed him to be over obsessed with something that had gone for ever.

There were the other passengers-to-be, very soon now as the days went by. They were, of course, not all from New York. From Annapolis in Maryland an English youth in American exile was preparing to say goodbye to his family and take the train for Grand Central station and a taxi to the PanAtlantic pier on Manhattan. His name was John Holmes and he was eighteen years of age. He was going to Britain, which he had last seen nine years before, to join the Britsh Navy and fight under Jellicoe, or Beatty, or some other admiral. His hero had been Rear-Admiral Sir Christopher Cradock, who had met a vastly superior German squadron under von Spee off Coronel in South America some months earlier and had refused to run. Cradock had gone down to glory with his flagship, HMS *Good Hope*. John Holmes had discovered that there was to be a memorial to Cradock in York Minster and he hoped he would have the time and opportunity to see it whilst in England, once it was in place on the age-old walls.

The night before he left home was somewhat fraught. His mother was unable to hold back her tears. His father was gruff, his two sisters, younger than himself, were silent.

'You'll go and see your grandmother,' his father said, not for the first time, clearing his throat as he said it.

'Of course, dad.'

'Try to persuade her to come across, h'm?'

'Yes, I will, but she won't listen, dad. You know that.'

His father nodded. 'Obstinate. The old are, of course.' Mrs Holmes senior had refused to accompany then when they'd left Liverpool aboard the *Carmania* back in 1906: she was British to the core, stiffbacked and adamant. The Americans, she said, were all very well but they were loud and brash and they'd rebelled against the Crown. She wouldn't forgive them for that and there had been an unspoken rebuke in her face when her son had first announced his intention. He was a doctor of philosophy and had had a very good offer from an American university. The silent rebuke had become vocal.

'Money,' his mother had said, and sniffed. There was a wealth of meaning in the sniff alone, summing up her whole opinion of America.

John's father smiled now and said, 'You won't change her, I do realize . . . but she'll be delighted to see you, John. She missed you badly when we left, you know. Missed all of us,' he added, not wanting to stress that John had been the favourite.

Also from Annapolis as it happened was Elizabeth Kent, a shorthand-typist who had come out to the USA on holiday in early 1914 aboard the *Laurentia*, and after the outbreak of war had been unable to return, finance being one of the reasons: she had lost her return ticket and had overspent herself. In addition she had been having a good time and hadn't wanted it to end. She was an attractive girl and used her charms to get herself a work permit. Bed had been involved in this and she had been distraught when after a few months the man, an official in the State Department, had admitted to having a wife, but she had quickly recovered her spirits, found a job in Annapolis which she preferred to New York, and also found someone else whom she hoped to marry in due course, when the young man in question had established himself as an attorney. This was not yet. Now she had had a telegram saying her father was desperately ill and was asking for her.

By this time she had saved some money and her fiancé kind-heartedly made up the rest.

'You'll come back won't you?' he asked on the last night.

'Sure I will, hon.'

'Not get right back in the English scene?'

'No.'

'Promise?' There was much anxiety in his tone: he knew what mothers at any rate could be like, especially when they could be facing widowhood and loneliness. Elizabeth was an only child and she'd told him her father was as possessive as a mother. He dreaded sailing day of the *Laurentia*.

She said, 'Promise. I'll be back. Just as soon as ... everything's worked out.'

'I love you, Liz.' He sounded so dejected. They kissed. That was all. Just a kiss. He didn't know she was no longer a virgin and he wouldn't take risks. A pure young man and a sincere one, he believed in waiting for the ceremony in any case.

After the passage of two full days had raised neither query nor the resurrection of the flesh, Frederick Jones found another aspect nagging at his mind, his frugal mind: he regretted having paid the passage money for two. On embarkation, to take another aspect, there might be a demand for explanations by some officious purser. Of course, the paying of the money had secured him a double berth cabin with only himself now to be in it and that was a good thing. He believed that during the night after the deed he had talked in his sleep. He had come awake very suddenly and believed he had heard his own voice, the tail end of something or other that could possibly have been about Maggie. That would have been most dangerous in a shared cabin, of course, and he intended to use every subterfuge in order to ensure that no one was foisted on him when he turned up without Maggie. If the *Laurentia* should be fully booked there might be a number of disappointed would-be passengers waiting for a berth to become vacant, people willing to accept a pierhead jump. . . . In the meantime Mr Jones went about his normal routine and kept a composed exterior. He cleared his desk at the office of work that had piled up during his leave of absence at Arlington. He answered questions about his wife: yes, she was well but of course she wasn't really looking forward to the voyage, what with all the war scares, though certainly the *Laurentia*, a peaceful liner, should be safe from attack. The Germans would never attack a liner filled with civilians, many of them neutral American citizens.

His colleague disagreed. 'Not read the papers?'

Mr Jones had, very keenly just recently, but he'd had other things on his mind than the war, and his reading had concentrated on the possible finding of things best left hidden. 'In what respect?' he asked.

'Quote from the *Desmoines Register*, April 23rd. Today's *Sun*. The German Embassy's announced that British flag ships are liable to destruction once they're in the war zone. Since April 23rd that's not been new, but the *Sun*'s highlighted it again.'

Frederick Jones nodded. Maggie had been on about that, he remembered. Too risky, she'd said. He had taken no notice; his old mother was liable to peg out and he genuinely didn't believe for one moment that the Germans would risk bringing the United States into the war by attacking a ship carrying US citizens, and Washington had not been slow to make it plain that US citizens were perfectly free to use British ships if they so wished and would continue so to be. So the Germans had been warned. They were not fools. Mr Jones was unworried.

Captain William Pacey was far from unworried. He had very many lives, passengers and crew, to worry about – fewer certainly than the *Laurentia* had been originally designed to carry, for by this stage of hostilities the Admiralty had gutted a good deal of the third class accommodation for possible war use of its own. But still very many, more than 1200 passengers plus 663 crew, would be sailing under the Captain's orders. For many months now Pacey had sailed the seas in war; back and forth across the North Atlantic he had carried that enormous responsibility for lives and ship and cargo. He knew the dangers, was well aware that some German U-boat captain, finding a big British liner in his periscope, might be unable to resist temptation. The U-boats of the German Emperor, congregating off the western approaches to Great Britain, had made innumerable attacks, sinking ships of the Emperor's cousin King George . . . an Imperial Majesty against one who preferred to call himself a plain one even though King George was as much an Emperor as His Imperial Majesty of Germany.

Pacey, two days before he was due to take his ship out through the Narrows and take his departure from the Ambrose Light for Liverpool, was in his day cabin together with a senior man from the Line's New York offices, a small and pedantic man with a shrewd eye and a mouth like a clam. This man was Isaac Jackson, bane of all PanAtlantic masters for some years past.

'So what's worrying you, Captain?'

'This.' Captain Pacey held up the newspaper that carried the proclamation of the Germany Embassy. This stated, in full, that travellers intending to embark on the Atlantic voyage were reminded that a state of war existed between Germany and her allies and Great Britain and her allies; that the zone of war included the waters adjacent to the British Isles; that, in accordance with formal notice given by the Imperial German Government, vessels flying the flag of Great Britain, or any of her allies, were liable to destruction in those waters and that travellers sailing in the war zone on ships of Great Britain or her allies did so at their own risk.

'So?' Jackson asked sardonically.

Pacey threw down the newspaper. 'Obvious, isn't it? We're a very big target and a prestigious one for any U-boat captain, I'd have thought.'

'Nonsense.' Isaac Jackson echoed, unconsciously, the thoughts of Frederick Jones and many others. 'No one but a lunatic would take the risk of bringing in the United States.'

'Lunatics exist,' Pacey said. 'And I'll be carrying a large number of women and children.'

'So what do you suggest, Captain?'

'What I've suggested before, a warship escort to meet us by the time we reach 40 degrees west latitude.'

'The British Admiralty won't do it, Captain. You'll be met in the Western Approaches and that's as far as they'll go.'

'I wonder,' Pacey said in a tone tinged with bitterness, 'if they appreciate the risks – this time.' He paused, looking hard at Jackson. 'If Berlin should get word about what's in my cargo, they could have a legitimate excuse to attack.'

'You have no guns now,' Jackson said.

'That's beside the point. My cargo – '

'We'll not talk about that, Captain. It's by way of being a *fait accompli*. In other words, my friend, you're stuck with it. What I was going to say was this: the Germans have no damn excuse in all the world to attack an unarmed, defenceless ship.' The mouth clamped tight; there was no more to be said. Pacey would have liked to suggest that all women and children be taken off the embarkation list and their passage money repaid, but he recognized that this was unrealistic and that indeed those who sailed did so at their own risk – the Germans had undoubtedly given fair warning. Captain Pacey believed in his heart that they had had the sailing of the *Laurentia* specifically in mind.

The Swedish couple with the now cured six-year-old son were the Lundkvists, Torsten and Alva. The boy's name was Olof. They came from Karlskrona on the Baltic, in the far south of their country. Torsten Lundkvist was in marine insurance. They were not poor. They were both in their late twenties and Olof was their only son; there was a daughter in Karlskrona currently being cared for by her grandmother, Alva's mother. The family were members of the Evangelical Lutheran Church and were deeply religious. They believed in prayer and they had prayed continually that Olof should be made well.

They prayed now, as the time of embarkation drew near – prayed for the safety of the great *Laurentia* against the power of the sea and against German torpedoes and mines. Little Olof had not come through a difficult operation and a harrowing period after it while he grew well, just to be sunk beneath the waves of the North Atlantic.

They had read the German Embassy's warnings.

They were spending the few days before embarkation in New York, at the Waldorf Astoria Hotel. New York was normal, a great city in a country at peace, a blaze of lights at night with everyone enjoying themselves. Nobody seemed concerned about that distant war; it couldn't touch them. President Wilson would see to that: he was all for keeping out of conflict, having his country's interests at heart, though he was friendlily disposed towards Great Britain and had often said as much in his public addresses. He admired the British greatly, but he wasn't going to fight for them. So in America there would be safety for the Lundkvists; for little Olof in particular. If they stayed there. . . .

When Olof, tucked up in bed asleep under the care of a chambermaid who had volunteered for the duty, being a mother herself, the Lundkvists went down for dinner. Alva Lundkvist was strikingly beautifully: tall and fair and with a straight back and a swing to her shoulders that set men looking at her as she passed by. Torsten was very different: short and stout, with heavy spectacles, but with a cheerful and honest face; a kindly man, devoted to his beautiful wife and his son, who showed signs of taking after his mother rather than his father.

At dinner Alva broached the question that had been on her mind ever since reading the proclamation. 'Do you think it is wise, Torsten?'

'Is what?'

'You know very well what I mean. To go back to Sweden.'

'Because of the Germans?'

'The sea is so dangerous, Torsten. There is Olof to be thought of.'

Torsten Lundkvist broke a bread roll. 'That I know, dearest.'

'Here in America we would all be so safe.'

'I would have no work here, Alva.'

She shrugged it off. 'Money can be sent through.'

'And there's Christina. And your mother, who – '

'As against Olof, I do not worry about my mother. And Christina will be well cared for until the war is over.' She leaned across the table, her face taut, her eyes beseeching. 'Please, Torsten. I do not wish to go on the *Laurentia*.'

Torsten pursed his lips. 'It will be safe, dearest. I know this.' He repeated what so many people had been saying, laughing in some cases at the German proclamation. 'The Germans will not *dare* to attack the ship! With Americans aboard we shall be quite safe, I promise.' He paused, then went on in a voice of strong conviction. 'There are many Americans who disagree with President Wilson, many who believe that the United States should enter the war as soon as possible, and help England before it is too late and the Kaiser turns his attention across the Atlantic. There is in fact a powerful lobby for declaring war on Germany at once. Wilson is resisting this . . . and this being so, any U-boat commander who attacks the *Laurentia* and thus gives ammunition to the war lobby and forces Wilson's hand – he would be shot by the Kaiser as not only a blatant fool but also as a traitor. This he would know.' Torsten took her hand. 'I assure you of this, Alva.'

She shook her head. There was a glint of tears; she was very distressed and Torsten patted her hand. He said, 'Then there is a simple solution. We shall ask God.'

After dinner, on their knees in their bedroom, they did so. But God was deaf that night, or had other preoccupations while half his world was at war. He gave no answer either way. It was left to Torsten to decide.

Fatefully, he did so.

In another part of New York, not so far from the Waldorf Astoria, the stage star whose fame was dimming had words with the husband she was leaving behind. Words were something that Livia Costello didn't mince.

'Risking the Germans is a darn sight better than staying anywhere where you are.'

Her husband lifted an eyebrow. 'Have I said something to detain you, darling?'

He hadn't; she said crisply, 'You can drop the darling, you rotten little rat. Save it for your fancy bit after I've gone.' She examined herself in the mirror, adjusted her hair. 'If you want to know, I've heard the talk about the risks. I guess that doesn't matter to you.'

He laughed. 'Guess you're dead right at that, *darling*.'

She flared up at him, her face suddenly ugly. She been beautiful, but at close on forty the hothouse world of the stage had caught up and overtaken her. Hard work, late nights, too much drink, nights of passion with glamorous fellow stars: Larry wasn't the only one who had strayed. A string of obscenities came from a mouth that had once been soft. Larry got up from the sofa where he'd been sitting.

'Bitch,' he said flatly. 'Go to hell. Sink or swim, do I have to care any more?'

He left the apartment, slamming the outer door behind him, hard. Livia Costello took a deep breath, then lit a cigarette which she inserted into a gold holder. She was trembling all over. God, she thought, what have things come to?

The night before embarkation the Holmeses went with John to the railroad station at Annapolis. It was the usual departure scene so familiar across the seas in Britain, though not as yet familiar in the United States. Waiting for the train to pull along the track in its clouds of steam, the cow-catcher coming into view beneath the depot lights. Inconsequential talk: you had to keep on saying something. Heart-wrench had to be covered; and mothers mustn't cry. Each minute like an hour, and relief when the engine appeared.

A handshake between father and son, a mother's kiss. 'Oh Johnny. . . .'

'Goodbye, mum. Goodbye, dad.' John reached out and ruffled his sisters' hair. 'I'm going to be okay, you know that? It's going to be fun.'

'Well, let's hope so,' his father said sombrely. 'Tell you something: I guess it's not going to be so long before Uncle Sam's in the war.' Holmes, as an Englishman still though like all of them he had picked up the American idiom to some extent, was one of those who wanted President Wilson to act decisively.

'Maybe, dad.' John hesitated. 'I'll be sure to go and see gran.'

'You do that, John. But don't talk American or she'll bite your head off.'

John grinned and embarked, hung from the window. Down along the train a grey-eyed girl kissed a man in his early twenties, a man who clung to her as long as possible and then turned away as the train moved off as though he couldn't bear actually to see her vanish into the steam-filled dark beyond the lights.

Annapolis dwindled.

John moved along the train, seeking a seat. The grey-eyed girl moved towards him on a similar errand. They met: each saw the labels on the other's hand baggage: PanAtlantic Line S.S. *Laurentia*. They smiled. 'You too,' John said.

'Um-h'm.'

They found seats next to each other. There was an immediate link, a companionship in that both were British. They talked of England and each revealed the purpose of their passage aboard the *Laurentia*. They talked of the German threat. Elizabeth Kent asked if the threat bothered him, and he laughed.

'I guess not! The British Navy . . . they'll see off the U-boats.'

She smiled at his intensity, his total assurance. 'You reckon?' she asked.

'Dead cert, Miss. . . ?'

'Elizabeth,' she said.

'I'm John.' They shook hands sideways on, very formal. Each was glad to have met the other, to ease the parting. John had already decided he would get to know her on board the ship, maybe try to see her again after the *Laurentia* reached the UK. That was, if the British Navy allowed him the time. That came first.

At 1100 on the day before sailing, the *Laurentia*'s Master made rounds, accompanied by his Staff Captain, Chief Officer, Chief Engineer, Purser, Ship's Surgeon, and Chief and Second Stewards. Ahead Of Captain Pacey, in the lead of the procession, was the senior of the two masters-at-arms, Bill Warner, ex-RN and smart as a button. A full inspection of all compartments was efficiently carried out, the leading hands of sections standing at their stations ready to answer any query put by the Captain or the senior officers. A liner was a city; a floating city. In her crew list she carried a remarkable cross-section of callings: there were – apart from those one would expect such as seamen, engineers and stewards – bakers, barbers and bank staff; butchers, boilermakers, buglers, bandsmen; carpenters, chefs, confectioners; a dispenser, an interpreter, joiners, gardeners, librarians, ladies' hairdressers, a manicurist, printers, painters, typists, wireless operators and many others. All their departments, their spheres of work, had to be inspected prior to sailing and again throughout the voyage on Captain's rounds. Today Pacey and his Chief Officer, Mr Arkwright, paid particular attention to the watertight doors, the fire hoses and, on deck, the condition of the forty-eight lifeboats, twenty-six of these being collapsible with a hollow wooden base and canvas sides. Pacey cast an eye over the sites of the gun-rings fore and aft intended to take the six-inch quick-firing armament, over the girders and beams set in place as strengthening for the guns that had been installed in 1914 but later removed. Below in the engine-room, kingdom of Chief Engineer Hackett with his junior engineer officers, his trimmers, firemen and greasers, Pacey deferred to the god of the lower regions.

'All well, Mr Hackett?'

'All well, sir.'

Hackett's word could be taken for that: there was no better chief engineer in the Line. Like a mother he looked after the steam turbines that provided the power that drove the shafts of the quadruple-bladed screws that could drive the *Laurentia*'s 31,550 tons and 700-foot length through the water at twenty-four knots.

As the long inspection drew to a close at the foot of the companion-way leading up to the Master's accommodation and the bridge, Pacey turned to face his retinue. He said, 'Carry on, gentlemen.' Salutes were exchanged; Pacey buttonholed his Staff Captain and Chief Officer. 'My day cabin,' he said.

The two senior officers followed the master up the stairway. In the day cabin they were invited to sit. 'Gin?' Pacey asked.

Gin it was; small ones. A silver salver with the drinks was brought by Mullins, the Captain's steward. When Mullins had left the cabin, Captain Pacey voiced his anxieties.

'That announcement from the German Embassy.'

'Wind, sir.' This was Staff Captain Morgan. He went on to say what so many people had been saying. 'They'd never dare. The whole civilized world. . . .'

Pacey grunted. 'The world's not so civilized sometimes, Morgan. There's always an eye to the main chance. Sink the *Laurentia* and what do you get? Condemnation, yes, but the stink wouldn't last. You also get the fear of the Hun put up all Allied and neutral merchant shipping, with the result that the UK would lose one hell of a number of much needed ships' bottoms to keep her fed. And not only with food. Oil fuel, munitions.'

Morgan said, 'You also get America into the war.'

'Yes, that's the theory. The Kaiser may not believe it. Wilson's been leaning over backwards to stay neutral. He may have convinced the German High Command. Besides, there's the other aspect. Your pigeon, Arkwright,' he added, turning to the Chief Officer.

'The cargo, sir, yes. Tricky – or could be.' The *Laurentia* was carrying some of that 'contraband' that the US customs had let through without comment, or anyway without action to prevent it: in her holds the ship carried 173 tons of small-arms ammunition in 4200 cases, plus 1259 cases of steel shrapnel shells; and all cargo holds had in fact been requisitioned for possible use by the British Admiralty.

'Tricky,' Captain Pacey repeated in a flat tone. 'I'd go further,

Arkwright. If anything's leaked, if the German High Command has got to hear, then as I've already said to Jackson we become a legitimate target. At any rate in German eyes.'

'Nothing we can do about it, sir.'

'I know, Arkwright. Just the one thing: extra vigilance throughout the voyage, more so once we've passed forty west. Lookouts to be changed more frequently than usual. Boat stations to be exercised daily, likewise fire drill. I'll issue other orders later as we make our easting . . . and I'll not be breathing easy until we've picked up our escort in the Western Approaches.'

When the others had left to go about their various duties, Captain Pacey stood staring through the big square ports that gave on to his foredecks, the fore cargo hold and fo'c'sle with the anchor cables that after clearing away from the land would be secured for sea, the anchors themselves drawn up tight to the hawse-pipes and the Blake slips and bottlescrew slips taking the strain of the heavy links of the cable. Beyond the ship he looked away towards the great sky-scrapers that dominated Manhattan: the Singer Tower, 618 feet in height, forty storeys; the Woolworth building, 750 feet of it, with foundations going down some 130 feet into the earth. America was a land of bigness in all things. Captain Pacey hoped that one day President Wilson would come to think big about the threat from across the sea. America could surely not stand aloof indefinitely. Thinking of the President, Pacey's mind went to another anxiety: among his passengers was to be a US diplomat, Henry Sayers Grant, going to London to relieve Mr Ambassador Page as the United States representative at the Court of St James.

2

Eyes of grey – a sodden quay,
Driving rain and falling tears,
As the steamer puts to sea
In a parting storm of cheers. . . .

Rudyard Kipling, *The Lovers' Litany*

THERE was as it happened no rain as the great *Laurentia* was taken by the harbour tugs and eased off her berth at the PanAtlantic pier. But there were many Godspeeders to send her off and wish her well, and there was that storm of cheering as the gap of water widened slowly at first then faster. The gloomy blare of her steam whistle seemed to hold foreboding; and many tears were shed as loved ones pulled away into the channel, heading out for the open sea and the war zone. The bereft ashore were largely the spouses or fiancées of those going on business to Britain: there were pickings to be had in a country at war, a country growing short of all manner of things that astute money-makers could provide. But there were also the fringe relatives of the holidaymakers, complete family units; even in the midst of war many Americans, the wealthier ones, were going across for the London season, or what remained of it in a time of austerity. They were not particularly expectant of seeing taxi-loads of debutantes queuing across the forecourt of Buckingham Palace to be presented to His Majesty King George V. The scene would be sterner now; the King, mainly dressed these days in the uniform of an Admiral of the Fleet, would doubtless be more concerned with the giving of decorations for gallantry to the heroes returning from the horrors of Flanders or from the bitter, U-boat-infested seas around his island kingdom.

Earlier, shortly before the time of departure, Captain Pacey had been summoned personally to the office of a retired British general, Sir Courtenay Bennett who, curiously perhaps, had been appointed to perform the duties of Senior Naval Officer in New York. The reason for this was that an actual appointment of SNO could not in fact be made in a neutral port. Pacey was surprised at the telephone summons. Normally a staff member would have brought all necessary documents and orders. Pacey's thought was that his sailing orders were to be cancelled, or at least delayed pending further consideration of the German Embassy's announcement so publicly made.

This was not to be.

Asking for the route orders, Pacey was told that nothing had been received from the British Admiralty and that therefore he should follow a course similar to his last eastbound track. A warship escort would make the rendezvous south of the Fastnet off Cape Clear in County Cork when the *Laurentia* stood forty miles to the westward. This escort would accompany the liner up St George's Channel into Liverpool Bay. There was a strong degree of secrecy about Sir Courtenay – almost an embarrassed furtiveness. This secrecy was presumably the reason for Pacey's being summoned to a personal briefing, if it could be called a briefing. Pacey was again surprised; there was precious little secrecy elsewhere. The whole world was aware of the sailing of the *Laurentia* from New York. And, significantly as it was to turn out, Captain Pacey was not informed of the latest Admiralty advice that, following RN routine, merchant ships should henceforward employ the zig-zag when in suspect waters.

Passengers milled around the Purser's office below decks. They were mostly out of their depth aboard a ship, the seasoned travellers apart, bewildered by strange surroundings, by the hum of generators and the ventilation system, by the close, confined spaces in which they found themselves.

Many were now, at the last moment, fearful. To some extent this fear had been instilled by the presence on the quay of a large number of newspaper reporters plus a newsreel team with cameras and naphtha lights. These persons were present largely because of the sailing of the Ambassador-to-be, Henry Sayers Grant, and of banker Haggerty. But to the passengers the interest of the press and film-makers had seemed more like a presage of doom, the last shots and words of those who would not return.

A bedroom steward reported to the Deputy Purser. 'Scared as mice that's seen the cat, sir. Some of 'em 'ave asked us not to unpack their cabin baggage. Just in case, like.'

Inside the Purser's office where the saloon table seating was organized – each of the passengers being given a table number – the names for the Captain's table were being typed out for the information of the first-class head waiter, a job that should have been done earlier but had succumbed to the general rush and bustle of any ship approaching departure, on this voyage even more pronounced.

Two days before, Pacey had run through the passenger list. Certain names had stood out.

'Mr Grant, of course. This French general – de Gard. Mr Paul Descartes – partner in Alfred Booth, is he not?'

'Yes, sir.' Alfred Booth and Company owned a large parcel of shares in PanAtlantic. 'And wife, of course.'

'Of course.'

'And six children, sir?'

'Don't be funny, Purser. Nursery.' Pacey paused, thrust his big frame back from his desk at arm's length. 'Age of oldest?'

'Eighteen.'

'Boy or girl?'

'Boy, sir.'

'All right, then. May as well have some young blood, though I doubt if any of them will see much of me this voyage.' He paused again. 'Anyone else? Company's recommendations?'

There were: one was a Lady Barlow. Banker Haggerty was another, with his wife. Another was a US senator on a fact-finding mission to Britain. The Purser made a suggestion: Livia Costello was a big name in the entertainment world. Or had been.

'Who the devil's she?' Pacey asked.

Purser Matthews told him.

'No,' he said.

'But she'll expect some sort of – of star treatment, sir.'

'Will she? She'll not get it from me, Matthews.'

'But if the Board – '

'It's my table, Matthews, not the directors'. You can wish her on to the Staff Captain if you like. Or yourself.'

Purser Matthews made a mental note: she might be worth giving the once-over. Morals were notoriously loose in the film industry. And Matthews was something of a womanizer.

The list was completed with two blanks. Captain Pacey had always liked to make sure of an option after he had had an opportunity of surveying a few faces, looking for interesting ones.

On sailing day, with the ship moving out into the stream, Purser Matthews when approaching the door into his private office was waylaid by a big woman in a flowery hat, with a black velvet band doing its best to contain her sagging chins. In a loud voice the woman demanded, 'Tell me, are you the Purser?'

She had been looking at the three gold rings around Matthews' cuff, the gold interspersed with the white distinction cloth that indicated the Purser and his staff.

Matthews confirmed that he was the Purser. 'Can I help you?' he asked.

'Yes. I am Lady Barlow. Kindly tell me what is the price of a two-cent postage stamp?'

Matthews had been many years at sea. He remained unruffled and unsurprised. Passengers were always curious animals; it was said that on embarking they marked their brains NOT WANTED ON VOYAGE and consigned them to the hold. He answered the query. 'Precisely the same as it is ashore, Lady Barlow.'

'Which is?'

'Two cents.'

'Thank you. Perhaps you'll sell me one.'

Matthews said, 'There'll be no more mail leaving the ship now, Lady Barlow. The next mail will be landed in Liverpool, and for that you'll need a British postage stamp.'

'I call that *very* inconvenient.' She clicked her tongue. 'Cannot a hexception be made? I do not see 'ow – how – '

'I'm sorry,' Matthews said. 'The ship is turning in the stream for the Narrows.'

'But the Captain, surely – I'm *Lady Barlow.*'

'I'm afraid not.'

Lady Barlow scowled angrily and turned with a sweeping motion of her ankle-length dress. Behind her an uncertain-looking man in his thirties hovered and was collected up and told to follow. Matthews ran his mind over the embarkation list. Lady Barlow. A son – the collected young man? Lady Barlow, whose diction and accent seemed a little uncertain, was a widow and her booking form had been accompanied by a medical note from a clinic in Virginia. She had come from England for treatment – Matthews couldn't recall what for. Going into his private office he walked through to the main office for a word with his deputy. After a while there was something of a commotion in the foyer beyond the grilles of the main office: a bunch of pressmen with camera crews who'd got left behind as the liner came off the pier, notwithstanding the broadcast that the ship was about to sail. It turned out that they'd been imbibing free liquor in the main dispense bar, the place below in the working alleyways where the chief barkeeper kept his stocks. They could go ashore with the pilot, but the Captain would not be pleased.

They made their excuses to the Purser. They had come aboard to interview Miss Livia Costello but she'd evaded them. They knew all about her matrimonial affairs.

'Which,' Matthew said sardonically, 'is no doubt why she kept her head down.'

The pressman shook his head. 'Actresses, they just love the press.'

'Not when the press is all set to invent what they don't get told.' Matthews turned away. He heard a loud remark about stuffed-shirt limeys. He used his telephone and rang Staff Captain Morgan, who would arrange for the pilot boat to take off the press. Leaving the office again, he saw a curious sight.

Leon Fielding was a singer, not a renowned one. He was in his middle seventies. He did not attract the press; and that despite his odd appearance. He wore a very large straw hat with an undulating brim, a high-crowned affair coloured red. Also a floppy cravat. He himself had a lot of white hair that bushed out sideways beyond the brim of the straw hat. He had a chubby baby-face. And he was propelling a small perambulator, a doll's pram. No doll. He had waylaid the Chief Steward, who was being polite but was a very busy man.

'It's Ming,' the singer said sadly.

'Ming, sir?'

'My little Pekinese, don't you know.'

'Oh, yes, sir?'

'I push her everywhere in her perambulator, you see. Or I did until now. She suffers from paralysis, poor little scrap. In her hind feet.'

The Chief Steward was showing signs of alarm. He darted an appealing glance towards Matthews, who was grinning. 'The little dog, sir. He doesn't appear to be in the pram. Is he. . . ?'

'She. No, she's not aboard at all. I feared she might suffer from *mal-de-mer*, you see. Also, there was the question of her not being allowed to stay in my cabin.'

'Company regulations, sir, do state – '

'Yes, I do realize, and then there might have been quarantine I suppose. So I was forced to leave her with mummy. She *so* wanted to come with daddy, but there we are. The authorities are so unfeeling, don't you find?'

'Well, sir.' The Chief Steward gave a cough. 'The pram, sir – '

'It reminds me of Ming. Mummy has another for her, so she's perfectly all right. I'm sorry.' Leon Fielding broke off to apologize to an elderly man who had all but fallen over the doll's pram. He removed his straw hat politely, then replaced it and turned back to the Chief Steward, only to find that the man had gone. He looked disappointed, but shrugged and began talking to the empty pram just as though Ming was in it still. 'You needn't worry, darling, the sea may be rough and dangerous but daddy will look after you, rest assured. No nasty Germans.'

The elderly man who had fallen foul of the doll's pram turned to his wife. 'Dreadful feller,' he said in a hoarse old voice. 'Damned if I know what things are coming to. God knows what the Americans must think.' Leon Fielding's voice was very English.

* * *

23

Apprehension came early to the *Laurentia*'s passengers.

As Captain Pacey, to the pilot's advices though he had no need of them, brought the *Laurentia* between the Battery and Ellis Island into New York Bay for the Narrows, a report reached the Staff Captain and was immediately reported by Morgan to the Captain: the two masters-at-arms had carried out their routine post-sailing inspection of the decks, looking for stowaways and such who, like the press, could be disembarked with the pilot. On the port side of the shelter deck, in a stewards' pantry, they had found two men. The men had with them a camera. And the men were Germans. They were searched, various camera plates were removed, and they were locked in cells.

Captain Pacey, once outside the port, altered course towards the British cruiser on station at the three-mile limit, acting as blockading vessel. A seaboat was lowered and the camera and plates, together with a report of the incident, were sent across. Not the Germans. On the Captain's decision they were to be taken on to Britain for questioning.

Laurentia proceeded out into the North Atlantic. Word about the Germans spread. The result was unease.

Insidiously, the spectre of fear grew larger along the many decks of the great liner.

The ship's company and the passengers began in many cases to count the days to safety. Or the other thing. *Laurentia* was due to enter Liverpool Bay on the a.m. tide on Saturday 8 May. Today was 1 May: seven days of anxiety and uncertainty as the liner covered the 2943 sea miles from the Ambrose Channel Light Vessel to the Fastnet on her summer track.

Mr Jones's anxieties and uncertainties were not to do with the sea or the Germans. He had those others. On embarkation, up the gangway past the masters-at-arms, Mr Jones had got away with it. He'd mumbled something about the other half, as it were, of his ticket – Maggie – coming aboard behind him. The ship's staff seemed to be too busy to bother much. Mr Jones breathed easy: first hurdle over. He'd not wanted to say, for instance, that his wife was ill or had changed her mind: he still wanted the sanctity of an unshared cabin.

So far he'd got it.

A steward escorted him down a few decks: Mr Jones was travelling second class. Alone in the cabin he sat for a while on the lower bunk while his heart palpitated. He unscrewed a flask from his pocket and took a little brandy: he was no toper, and he 'took' rather than drank. In the same pocket as the flask were Maggie's teeth. He didn't know, really, why he'd kept them. Not sentimentality, that was for sure. Security? Yes, maybe. Teeth were indestructible, unlike flesh. But perhaps he would cast them overboard so they would sink forever to safety.

Meanwhile he took them out and arranged them on the chest of drawers. Somehow they fascinated him. Past those teeth had come Maggie's shrill, infuriating laugh. No more now. There were twenty-eight of them. Mr Jones did a quick calculation. Near enough two per lover, give or take an incisor: he had elucidated by stealth lovers numbering thirteen. There could well have been more for all he knew. He gathered up the teeth when he heard a rattle at his cabin door and thrust them back into his pocket before a man entered.

'Bedroom steward, sir. Name of Hawley. There's this.' He thrust two printed forms into Frederick Jones's hand. There were spaces to be filled in.

'What are these for?' Mr Jones asked.

'Interrogatory forms, sir. Needed by HM Customs and Immigration on arrival in UK. One for you, one for madam.' The steward looked around the cabin. 'Madam not come aboard, sir?'

'Oh, yes. She's – er.'

Steward Hawley seemed to understand: madam was answering a call of nature no doubt. He left, saying he would collect the completed forms later. Mr Jones shook: now he had committed himself to having his wife aboard as booked. There could be, would be, complications. He examined the forms as they shook in his hand. Full name, Mr, Mrs, Miss or title, nationality, last address in USA, future address in UK . . . age, profession or occupation, marital status . . . Mr Jones began to sweat. He should have remembered there had been similar forms when he'd arrived in the USA. The Captain or Purser or somebody would check up and his answers (for both himself and Maggie?) would be read by the British officials in Liverpool.

What was he to do?

He took a little more brandy.

With the Battery and the East River and the Ambrose Channel light now well behind, the *Laurentia* pushed her great stem into a heavy sea. Pacey was still on the bridge. The ship was, as seaman say, 'lively'. This had been the case ever since the Admiralty's structured alterations that had taken away a good deal of the weight from the ship's lowest sections. At the same time the strengthening of C deck, the shelter deck, had added weight to her top hamper. Also, much of the vessel's forward area was empty, under that requisition order from the Admiralty. The second-class smoking room and the third-class dining saloon had been closed off; one result of this was that the normally strict regulations as to the use of the public rooms had been relaxed and the three classes would mingle more or less freely, the third class having the use of the second-class public rooms and deck space while the second class shared with the first class. Another result was that the ship rode light for'ard and was subject to a nasty corkscrew motion in anything of a sea. The passengers would be unhappy, with queasy stomachs at the start.

Pacey spoke to the First Officer, who had the bridge watch.

'Usual first night in the saloon, no doubt, Mr Main.'

'Yes, sir. All that waste!'

Pacey glanced sideways. 'The food? Yes. In wartime that's very bad. But it can't be helped.'

'I suppose not, sir.'

It wouldn't be all that great: the chef was used to first-night stomachs. Pacey walked up and down his bridge, backwards and forwards along the strip of coir matting. Already spray was flinging up over the bows, dropping down on the anchors and cables now secured for the North Atlantic passage, the slips drawn down hard, the cables running close along the chafing plates. Food: the menu would be up to peacetime standards. The passengers had paid their fares and no matter the war they were entitled to their money's worth and their gluttony, while the British troops pigged it in the terrible mud of the trenches all along the Western Front. Scenes of horror entered Pacey's mind: he had had the trenches described to him by his son James, who at twenty-three had been a subaltern in Flanders. James had gone in for estate management and on the outbreak of war had been working for the Duchy of Cornwall in Launceston. He had joined up almost at once, as a private in the Duke of Cornwall's Light Infantry in Bodmin. He had proved a good soldier and when most of the regular Second Battalion had been wiped out at the Marne and the other battles in the first few months of the war he had been commissioned and after leave had been sent back to the trenches, the graveyard of so many second lieutenants, those very junior officers who had to be first 'over the top', leading their men in the suicidal dash into the German machine-guns.

James had, on being pressed, told his father some of the facts: the everlasting mud, the shelling, day and night sometimes before a push, the whizz-bangs, the lice. The menu: two hard biscuits and half a tin of bully beef a day. Tea perhaps once a week. Always plenty of cigarettes – all the fighting governments and all the senior officers recognized the value of the part played by the tobacco manufacturers in sustaining morale. It was the fags that kept them going; that, and news from home so long as it was good news. But already spirits were sagging under the constant bombardment and the wet of Flanders, and in winter the biting cold that the ragged uniforms could never keep out. And of course the casualties. Men mown down in swathes, friends left hanging on the barbed wire as the infantry made their abortive raids and sometimes took a sector of the German front-line trenches, only to lose it again the next day. Corpses everywhere, half buried in the collapsed mud of the trench walls. James had spoken of a corporal who used a protruding leg as a handy anchorage for his tin hat: if the leg had been shifted, the firestep would have collapsed inwards. The leg had become an integral part of the structure. And the stench: the decaying flesh.

And the rats; and again the all-pervading lice and the resultant filthy feeling, and the scratching. And seldom any washing facilities for clothes or body.

It was inhuman. Pacey was thankful for the sea's cleanliness. At least until the torpedo hit came, or the mine. Then there could be an inferno of red-hot metal, and shattered bulkheads, and burning flesh, and the inrush of the waters to batter men to their deaths in the lower compartments of the ship.

Pacey reflected that it could go on for ever. The Germans were proving very determined fighters and their army was superb. The drain on British manpower was intense and alarming, while the hidebound generals committed division after division in an attempt to win a war that was fast becoming one of attrition.

And James had been one of the unlucky subalterns. Pacey had just got home on leave the voyage before last when the War Office telegram had come, and some deep part of him had died with his son.

There was another son, the eldest of the two sons and two daughters: Harry, who had gone to sea and was now a lieutenant of the Royal Naval Reserve serving under Admiral Beatty in the Battle-Cruiser Squadron.

Captain Pacey had very personal reasons for wishing that President Wilson would bring in the enormous power of the United States – before it was too late for Europe and then the world.

3

Am informed by reliable authority that Laurentia will be attacked by German submarines. Advise you cancel forthwith. So had run a telegram addressed to an important intending passenger. It was signed by the French word for death.

There had been other similar warnings to individual passengers.

Memo in early February, three months before the sailing of the *Laurentia* from New York, from Mr Winston Churchill, First Lord of the Admiralty, to Mr Walter Runciman, President of the Board of Trade: it was 'most important to attract neutral shipping to our shores, in the hopes especially of embroiling the United States with Germany ... the more the better; *and if some of it gets into trouble, better still. ...*'

Mr Churchill was not the only highly placed person to plan for the enforced entry of the United States into the war. Jackie Fisher –Admiral of the Fleet Lord Fisher, the First Sea Lord, was another. Fisher was in the view of many of his contemporaries becoming more and more unbalanced; always a fiery and temperamental man he had many years before, when he was on his way up the ladder of naval promotion, divided the Service into pro- and anti-Fisher men. His views had always been controversial, always unconventional. A gunnery specialist, he had revolutionized the whole concept of naval gunnery both as regards tactics and the actual weaponry. Many heads had fallen before him. He was no respecter of persons either senior or junior to him. He was intensely single minded. A dictum he relished was one of his own invention: *favouritism is the keynote of efficiency.* It was no idle saying. Fisher had joined the Navy in the days of the Sail Training Squadron under Rear-Admiral the Earl of Clanwilliam; that training had been hard and it made Fisher hard in his turn. He had no patience with inefficiency and he had no patience with those who disagreed with him; Fisher was always right. He surrounded himself with, and recommended for promotion, those who believed this. Also he had no time for those senior officers whom he considered to have declined into bumbledom; or with those who clung tenaciously to old ideas; or those whom he considered to have their priorities wrong. He had sailed in the ironclads under captains whose first aim had been sheer smartness of ships and men. Such officers had in some cases ordered the burnishing of the cable as it lay on the fo'c'sle with the anchor down and the links riding on the slips and the brake of the capstan. To Fisher, this was a ridiculous waste of seamen's time when they could be exercised on the guns. Such senior officers had been known even to have the watertight doors burnished to the extent that they were no longer watertight. And gunnery officers entering requests for practice shoots to be carried out were rebuffed with the reply that such reverberating endeavours ruined the paintwork.

Fisher had changed all this. He had been a human dynamo. Now he was beginning to burn himself out into a final fiery fizz. He had become more and more forthright, more and more extreme in his utterances and his actions.

And now, as the Navy's professional head under Mr Churchill, he had a war to win. A war to win at sea.

Mr Churchill, returning to the Admiralty from a Cabinet meeting in Downing Street, was waylaid by his First Sea Lord. Fisher was in an excited mood, almost stamping his feet. He accompanied Mr Churchill to the First Lord's room. 'They have to be brought in,' he said, almost in a snarl.

There was no need to specify who 'they' were. 'I agree,' Mr Churchill said. Cigar smoke was already filling the opulent room with its polished mahogany and Regency chairs.

'You have American connections, Winston. For God's sake, *use 'em*!'

Mr Churchill smiled chubbily but said nothing. Fisher went on. He said, 'Any methods. *Any methods!* Most of 'em *want* to fight! It's only Wilson! His hand has to be forced!' Fisher seemed always to underline half his words and to speak, as it were, in exclamation marks.

Eyes half closed against the wreathing cigar smoke, Mr Churchill murmured, 'The sinking of an American ship. Or casualties to US citizens . . . aboard a British ship?'

Fisher, scarcely listening, was fuming away, his voice full of scorn. 'Wilson's out of touch! Damned hesitancy – doesn't fit the times! The man's determined to go down in history as the one who kept America out of the war!' He simmered down, then said, 'You spoke of a sinking, Winston. Or American casualties.'

Churchill nodded. 'The *Laurentia* has left New York, Jackie.'

'I know that. My job to know.'

'U-boat reports. I've seen them – so have you.'

Fisher stared at the politician, studying the expression. 'Are you suggesting something, Winston?'

The baby face was enigmatic. Churchill smiled again. 'The hand of providence,' he said. That was all. He looked at the clock on the mantelpiece. He had, he said, much work to do.

As Captain Pacey had forecast, the attendance at dinner in the saloon was scanty on the first night. Few of the passengers were there to appreciate the splendours still left from the days of peace, the part of the ship left untouched by the hand of the Admiralty. The *Laurentia*'s first-class dining room was immense. It occupied two decks and was topped with a domed gallery. It was panelled throughout in the style of Louis XVI; the carving was by John Crawford of Glasgow, gilding by Messrs Waring and Gillow. The first-class lounge, where General François de Gard sat after dinner with Adeline Scott-Mason, the attractive American widow of an English husband, was also intact as in peacetime. It was panelled in inlaid mahogany, Georgian style. It was upholstered in green – green carpeting, furniture supplied by the ubiquitous Waring and Gillow. The Edwardian glass skylight consisted of twelve panes of stained glass to the design of Oscar Patterson, each one representing a month of the year. At each end of the room were vast marble fireplaces overhung by enamelled panels.

'It certainly is great,' Adeline Scott-Mason said. 'The British know how to do it, don't you agree?'

'Ah, but you have not seen Paris! Soon you will.'

'Providing the Germans don't get there first.'

'They will not. They will never reach Paris. The glorious Army of France will never permit.' General de Gard's tone was passionate. He believed what he said. Paris was La France, and La France was deep in every Frenchman's and Frenchwoman's heart. This had been instilled into François de Gard first by his parents and the other mentors of his childhood, then by his military officer's training at St Cyr, then by his regiment of cuirassiers. Finally by his own standing in the hierarchy that was leading the fight for La France. The fact that he was currently not militarily engaged but on a semi-diplomatic mission was, he felt, beside the point.

'There are Germans aboard, François,' Adeline Scott-Mason said. 'You know that?'

'I know it, yes.' The general's reply was brief and cautious. The two German nationals, with camera, had been brought before the Captan for questioning and Captain Pacey had requested the attendance of himself to represent the French interest and ask more pointed questions than a sailor might think of. Nothing had emerged. The Germans were polite but had refused to answer any of the questions other than to give their names, which were not in fact believed. General de Gard had conferred afterwards with Captain Pacey, who had seemed to believe the Germans had been put aboard to take photographs of the guns that were not there any more. If this was the case, and it could well be, then it pointed in the one direction: the German Admiralty wished to establish the presence of armament, to provide the excuse for attack.

General de Gard said nothing of this to Mrs Scott-Mason. Captain Pacey had, unnecessarily in the general's view, made much of the point that he didn't wish his passengers to be worried. In any case there were other matters on the mind of a Frenchman travelling without his wife. General de Gard began to broach them.

'Your cabin, it is comfortable?'

'Oh, yes, I guess so . . . could be better, could be worse. Could be bigger.' She added, 'The exigencies of war. It was a stateroom, once, I guess. Now I share it.'

'Ah.' A hand strayed. 'Not so very comfortable, then. My accommodation is superb. Spacious. A suite. And I have champagne.'

'Do you?' She smiled, looked across the lounge at an elderly couple coming in and taking it very carefully on account of the roll of the ship, the deck lurching now and again as the liner met a sea. They looked frail; frail and aristocratic. De Gard's hand moved again. Adeline knew precisely what was in his mind. She'd known François de Gard for some weeks only but there was no doubt that an affair had started; though it had not reached its culmination. For one thing, the general's wife had been in New York with him. Now she was not; he had elected to leave her behind in peace and safety.

And now they were at sea, in a strange world, a world entirely of its own, compact upon the waters, with no one ashore knowing what went on afloat.

'We can be alone,' François de Gard murmured into her ear. He was a very good-looking man and well preserved. Tall and with only the suggestion of a stomach. He had charming manners and was very attentive. And he was a General. Paris would be fun, something not to be missed. There would, of course, be strings attached. Naturally.

'Not a bad idea at that,' she said. 'This lounge is pretty dreary.'

He got to his feet and gave her an arm. *Accompli.*

The old couple whom Adeline Scott-Mason had observed across the lounge were the Rickardses. Mr and Mrs Rickards, both in their seventies. On the first night at sea, it was not customary to dress for dinner; the old man more a shabby but well-kept suit of smooth cloth, dark, with short lapels and three widely spaced buttons, all done up so that his lean body had a straitjacketed appearance of extreme discomfort. The starched white collar was high, biting into the neck immediately below the ears as he sat stiffly on a settee with his wife. Mrs

31

Rickards wore an ankle-length dress, also dark, with an arrangement of net covering her neck and with boned high points rising, like her husband's collar, to just beneath her ears, which were decorated with long earrings. Her hair, fair once and now white, was piled on top of her head. Like her husband, she walked with the aid of a walking-stick. The sticks were now placed together between them.

Into the lounge as they sat came Leon Fielding with his doll's pram. He was still wearing his curious straw hat.

'Appalling feller.'

'Yes, Jeffrey.'

'Don't attract his attention.'

'As though I would.'

'You know what you are,' he said testily.

'Yes, Jeffrey.' Mrs Rickards was inclined to be gregarious; her husband was not. But she never went against him. She knew her place as a wife. The result was often loneliness. Much as she loved Jeffrey there were other people, interesting people, in the world. Leon Fielding looked interesting and kindly. And lonely too, talking to something – or nothing – in the doll's pram. He was perhaps a little – well, eccentric. There was no harm in that. Leon Fielding caught her eye, smiled, and doffed his straw hat. Mrs Rickards looked away quickly; Jeffrey would not like any forwardness, naturally.

Rickards growled in her ear. 'Did you see that? Fancy wearing the damn thing in the first-class lounge! After dinner! Didn't see him in the saloon.'

'No, Jeffrey.'

'Feller's a lunatic, obviously. That perambulator.'

Mrs Rickards didn't respond. Her mind had gone to something that always worried her in hotels, in taxis, and now aboard ship: tips. Everyone expected a tip, palms always ready. She hated to appear mean. But the fact was she and Jeffrey had no money. Just enough to keep up their standards and appearances. Nothing left over. Every penny had to be watched. Poverty was why they were Mr and Mrs Rickards. That was how they appeared in the passenger list. Their passport told a different story: the truth.

Purser Matthews had spoken of this to the Captain after the passengers had embarked.

'Mr and Mrs Rickards, sir.'

'Yes?' Pacey had reflected for a moment. 'I seem to know the name, Purser. Why?'

'Major-General Lord Rickards, sir. He was Chief of Staff to Lord Roberts in South Africa. Now retired.'

'Good heavens! Why the Mr and Mrs?'

'Probably no money, sir. They look as poor as church mice. Can't afford to keep up that kind of style. They prefer not to let the past down, if you follow.'

'Yes, I think I do. Well?'

'I was wondering . . . they're travelling second class, but your table in the saloon – '

'Oh no. I'd like to have them, of course – somebody who's done something in the world. Not some popinjay who's simply made money. But no. We must respect their wishes, Purser. So keep it dark, you understand?'

'Yes, sir.'

'If I can find the time, I'll ask them up to my cabin for afternoon tea – I'll let you know.'

This night, while the Rickardses and Leon Fielding sat in mutual isolation in the near-empty first-class lounge, Captain Pacey was standing on the Master's deck outside the big square ports of his accommodation. He was staring out for'ard, into the wind and sea; and he was thinking about Major-General Lord Rickards and his lady. Following the Purser's report, he had found time before sailing to contact the PanAtlantic offices in New York by telephone and had delivered a broadside: as Captain, he should have been informed by the shore and he had not been. The shore excuse was as ever: pressure of work, a pressure much increased by the war. There had been a slip-up. The shore officials confirmed the story as told, or theorized, by Matthews: the Rickardses were on their beam ends and wanted no fuss. Had it been otherwise, they would have gone aboard as Recommended Passengers, which automatically meant the Captain's table and a number of other privileges. They were known to the PanAtlantic management in New York, which made the omission all the worse.

Pacey was given the background story.

On retiring from the army, Lord Rickards had commuted his pension and had gone to Canada. The commuted pension and most of the rest of the capital went into the purchase of a small gold mine, not at the time of purchase said to have been almost worked out. At first it had produced a little gold. With the mine, Lord Rickards had also purchased virtually the entire community: the general store, the dwellings of the miners and so on. Then the gold had stopped. The mine was done for and so were the Rickardses and the greater part of the work force. Lord Rickards had recompensed the workers out of what was left of his capital and had had very little left for himself and his wife. It was believed that he was now mostly dependent upon the three sons, all of whom were in the army and had been left a fair competence in the will of an uncle. What

33

the uncle, a brother of Lord Rickards, had left to Lord Rickards, had joined the commuted pension in the sunken gold mine. The Rickardses were now going home to England to be near the sons, who in fact were all fighting in France. All of them were lieutenant-colonels.

Pacey found it a sad story. He didn't like to see people come down in the world. Especially when they had served their country well. It would be very hard for them. Pacey knew what hardship meant, if in a different way. As the wind and sea buffeted at him, and the *Laurentia* rolled and pitched to the makings of a fresh gale, and the water from the fo'c'sle streamed aft to wash against the fore superstructure, he thought back to his early days at sea.

He had served his four-year apprenticeship in sail, in the old square-riggers, the windjammers that were now almost all gone from the world's great oceans. Four years of real sailoring and grim conditions on the long run from Liverpool or the London River to Australia for wool or grain cargoes. Seven years before he could sit the Board of Trade examination for his Master's certificate. Beating into the never-ending westerlies off the pitch of Cape Horn, beating sometimes for weeks as the Master sought the shift of wind that would carry him round into the calm waters of the South Pacific. Days and nights when the cry was constantly for All Hands to go aloft and take in sail. Iced-up footropes and ratlines. Nails torn from frozen fingers as they scrabbled at ice-hard canvas. Over all the tearing scream of the wind that tugged hard at oilskins . . . it was a case of one hand for the ship and one for yourself. If a man fell from aloft into the surging greybeards of the Horn he was gone forever, nothing to be done about it. If he fell to the deck and broke limbs or back he was likely to die before the ship could reach her far-off port. He would be medically attended by the steward under the supervision of the Master assisted by a publication called The Ship Captain's Medical Guide. Some masters were prepared to amputate, using a carving knife from the galley or a carpenter's axe. The patient, or victim, would be anaesthetized by the application of the neck of a bottle of rum between his lips. Survival was problematic. An appendicitis meant automatic death.

Other things happened at sea. Sometimes things that could not be explained.

One such: Pacey remembered an occasion when, now second mate aboard a windjammer heading down past the Falkland Islands for Cape Horn, he had been officer of the watch – the midnight to 4 am, known to seamen as the graveyard watch.

Pacing the poop deck he had heard the Master's voice coming to him from the hatch leading down to the after cabin and the saloon. He heard it clearly.

'Alter course, steer east-south-east.'

Pacey had repeated back the order: 'Steer east-south-east, sir.'

The order was passed to the man at the wheel. This was eased over until the compass needle showed the new course. Pacey watched the set of the sails closely: the weather was fair, the wind was astern, it should not be necessary to send the watch aloft. The canvas could be hauled on the braces if necessary.

The windjammer moved on. But the alteration had caused a heel, a slant of the deck, and there had been a rattle of deck gear and new creakings of woodwork in the cabins and saloon below. The Captain appeared on the poop. Captain Thomas was a small man, sparrow-like, and currently was almost extinguished by the immense woollen nightcap knitted by his wife. Many years previously he had taken to religion and was known on the Australian coast as Testament Thomas.

'Well now, Mister. What's going on? I see you've altered course. It's not the province of any damned second mate to alter without permission and well you know it. Eh?'

'Your orders, sir – '

'Be damned to that, Mister! I gave no order.'

'It was your voice, sir. I heard it clearly, from the hatch. The order was steer east-south-east.'

Testament Thomas was angry, his voice harsh. 'I think you've taken leave of your senses, Mr Pacey. As God's my judge, I do! Resume course immediately, d'you hear me?'

'Aye, aye, sir.'

Pacey had obeyed the order. The windjammer swung back to her original track. The Master went below, muttering to himself. The sea was calm, the wind still light from astern – light, but enough to fill the sails and maintain some six knots of speed through the water. The foul weather as yet lay ahead. Half an hour later the Master's voice came again, this time with urgency.

'Steer east-south-east!'

Pacey opened his mouth to respond then shut it again. He would not be caught a second time. He went to the hatch and down the ladder. Testament Thomas was sleeping. Pacey woke him. He said what he had heard. He insisted that he was not hearing things that had not been said: the order had been loud and clear and in the Master's voice.

'I'll be damned,' Testament Thomas said wonderingly. He sat up in his bunk. In the light from the candle lantern that Pacey had brought in from the alleyway he shook his head, then stared at his second mate suspiciously. 'I'll smell your breath, if you please, Mister.'

Pacey bent and puffed.

'No drink. Well, I'll be damned,' the Captain said again. He pulled at his chin, thoughtfully. Then he said, 'I'll turn out and come on deck. Back to the poop, Mister.'

Pacey went up the ladder. Four minutes later he was joined by Testament Thomas, now dressed. 'It seems somebody wishes us to comply. It's very strange. You are sure about the voice?'

'Absolutely certain, sir.'

Testament Thomas nodded. 'Very well, then. We shall steer east-south-east. Just until the dawn, and see what happens. After that, I must alter back for the Horn.'

They steered east-south-east.

Just before the dawn they came upon a ship's lifeboat, dead ahead of their track. The lifeboat was filled with exhausted men; some were dead. A windjammer had caught fire – a self-combustible cargo – and had burned to the waterline.

Testament Thomas said it had been the hand of God – the *voice* of God, using him as His instrument.

Now, so many years later, as Captain Pacey stared for'ard from the *Laurentia*'s spray-covered deck, he saw that lifeboat again. With its dead and its barely living. He gave a sudden shiver. There could be so many more lifeboats if things went wrong with this voyage. Worse: there could be none. Torpedoes could blow very big holes in a liner; and a liner was not so compartmented as a warship, not so many watertight divisions in her hull. She could go down very fast, and the explosions could cause considerable damage to her lifeboats if the blast went upwards. They would be unlikely to get them all away.

The questionnaires had been completed and collected by the bedroom stewards for handing in to the Purser's office. Frederick Jones had completed one for himself but not for his wife. He could not spend the entire voyage making excuses to Steward Hawley for Maggie's absence. Maggie apart, he had entered the truth, more or less, on the questionnaire. Name, date of birth, last address in New York – that could be checked – occupation architect. Married, no children. Address in the United Kingdom not yet known but he gave a London hotel where in fact he would not be staying.

In London, he would get lost, give himself some time by going to ground. Time to think and plan once he was back in Britain and had become reabsorbed into the British scene. Currently he seemed unable to think straight; he was very confused and worried and scared stiff.

Hawley asked about his wife. 'Not seen sight nor sound of the lady, sir.'

'No. It's quite all right, though. My wife – she went back ashore. Just before sailing. She . . . lost her nerve, you know. That German warning.'

'Yes, sir, very understandable, like, sir. Nasty buggers, them Germans, if you'll pardon the expression, sir.'

Hawley had gone away presumably satisfied. Mr Jones's fingers, in his pocket, once again made contact with Maggie's teeth. They must be got rid of. Mr Jones went up top and out on deck, into the wind's buffet. He lurched up and down the boat deck. He went aft, moving at a staggering run when the bows lifted, to be brought up all standing when the bows dipped and the stern came up instead. He clutched at the rails and the lifeboats for support. He saw seagulls circling astern, with mournful cries, waiting for the galley to discharge the uneaten food and general galley waste. They must have come all the way from New York, Mr Jones fancied. He'd seen gulls before, on the voyage when he'd first gone to America. Even in mid-Atlantic they had followed the ship.

Thoughtfully, Mr Jones went below again. The ocean would be receptive, but he must not risk being seen to cast teeth into it.

At luncheon in the saloon he managed to stow a large piece of bread in his pockets without being seen. He went to his cabin. He brought out Maggie's teeth and kneaded each one into a small bread ball, like a pill. These – twenty-eight with teeth, about a dozen without – he put into a paper bag that had held toffees.

He went on deck again.

The seagulls were there still, wheeling and crying their plaintive, somewhat squawkingly plaintive, note.

He cast a pill. It went into the sea. He cast another; a seagull swooped and took it and hovered for more. The bird was joined by others. Mr Jones cast again. Then he felt a tug at his sleeve.

He looked down. There was a small boy, a rather sickly looking small boy with big, pleading eyes. He didn't appear to be either British or American. 'Me feed?' the boy asked, smiling up at Mr Jones.

'No.'

'Please – '

Mr Jones grew terrified. Small boys were unpredictable. This one might run off to his mother with the pellet. He might eat it himself, and then what?

Mr Jones's voice rose and he shouted, 'Go away can't you, you little pest?' He raised a hand, threateningly.

The small boy's face fell, the small mouth went into a sad shape. He flinched away from Mr Jones. Tears came. Mr Jones, in a great hurry now, threw the remainder of the teeth into the sea. A woman came towards him, a young woman with a troubled, anxious face that was now angry.

'There was no need to be so unkind,' Alva Lundkvist said. 'My little boy, he was not really being a nuisance.'

37

Mr Jones mopped at his face but said nothing. The mother held the boy close to her skirt. 'Come away, Olof. Do not let the man make you unhappy.' She said this in her own language. Mr Jones hoped the remark was not to do with teeth. He didn't believe the small boy had cottoned on. It was only as he was going back to his cabin that Mr Jones wondered about the seagulls. The teeth might stick in their gullets and kill them. He would be sorry about that; he had no quarrel with the birds. On the other hand, they might live and follow the ship to Liverpool, and one day die, and Maggie's teeth might be discovered in a rotting carcase. The British detectives had a reputation for leaving no stone unturned . . . but Mr Jones told himself that this was being much too fanciful, much too fearful altogether.

The next day was Sunday: first day out but Captain Pacey decided to follow Sunday routine and hold Divine Service in the first-class lounge, which was set up by the stewards for the purpose, the chairs and settees pushed into some semblance of pews in a church ashore and evidence of drinking and smoking removed. By five minutes to eleven the passengers, or those who wished to attend, and a large number did, were in their seats or crowding the screened deck beside the big lounge windows. The Purser reported to the Staff Captain, who reported to Pacey.

On the stroke of 1100, Pacey entered the lounge and strode towards the lectern. He wore his best uniform, the four gold stripes on either cuff standing out below the starch of his white shirt, his gold-oak-leaved cap beneath his left arm.

He started the service in a carrying voice, bidding his passengers to prayer in an abbreviated form of morning service. He read a short lesson after the singing of a psalm and then, to the music of the ship's orchestra, the time-honoured hymn of the sea was sung.

> Eternal Father, strong to save
> Whose arm doth bind the mighty wave . . .
> Oh hear us when we cry to Thee
> For those in peril on the sea.

After that, a special prayer for use at sea, read by Pacey, a seaman's voice that fitted the words. 'Oh Lord, be pleased to receive into Thy most gracious protection the persons of us Thy servants and the ship in which we sail . . . that we may pass upon the seas on our lawful occasions and return in peace to enjoy the blessings of the land with the fruits of our labours. . . .'

It was very impressive, with the clamour of the Atlantic waves outside, and the salt spray lashing against the windows of the lounge, and the sense of danger that had gripped most of the passengers from the moment of clearing away from the land. The German proclamation was much in the minds of them all.

One man was disgruntled: this was a florid man of large stature, an American citizen wearing a clerical collar.

He buttonholed the Purser.

'Say, Purser. I guess it would have been a courtesy of the skipper to ask me to take Divine Service. Isn't it kind of customary?'

Matthews said, 'Captain Pacey always perfers to take the service himself. He'll have intended no offence.'

'No, but I reckon – like I said, Purser, it's a courtesy I always thought.'

Matthews made a gesture of negation. 'I'm sorry, but it's entirely up to the Captain. For one thing, there are other clergymen aboard and to make any distinction would be invidious.' He added, 'Of course, if say a bishop of the Church of England happened to be aboard – well, then the Line would expect. . . .'

'OK, I get you. Say no more, Purser.'

The cleric went off in a huff. The Purser had sounded stuffy. It was, the cleric thought, typically British. The British were so class conscious it wasn't true. Or anyway, rank conscious.

The cleric encountered Pacey, coming down from the bridge to the boat deck. 'Say, Captain?'

Pacey halted. 'Yes, Mr – ?'

'Divine. Reverend Divine. Say, can you tell me, I hear this ship is the fastest in the world. I've heard it said, no German submarine could ever catch up with her. Is this correct?'

Pacey hesitated, then said, 'That statement is perfectly true, Mr Divine.' There seemed no point in going on to say that U-boats were not in the habit of chasing their prey; they waited for it to cross their tracks. Passengers were always best reassured.

For dinner that second night, Captain Pacey reluctantly attended his table in the first-class saloon. His steward, a linen napkin over his arm, pulled back his chair at the head of the table.

'Thank you, Mullins. I apologize,' Captain Pacey added to his passengers, 'for being a little late. I plead the exigencies of the bridge. Please sit down, gentlemen.' Led by Mr Ambassador-to-be Henry Sayers Grant, all the men had risen at the Captain's approach. Pacey had already met Grant, had been at the embarkation gangway to welcome him aboard. Now, Grant was at his right hand. At his left was

Lady Barlow. Next to Lady Barlow was General François de Gard. Next to the Frenchman was the Barlow son, his face twitching with some nervous tic. At Pacey's right, next to Grant, was the wife of Paul Descartes of the Albert Booth company; next to him, the US senator from Wyoming, Melvin Manderton. Next to him, Paul Descartes. At the end of the table, the New York banker, Patrick Haggerty. There were three empty places; Captain Pacey had not yet made his further choice of table companions, and one of his original list, Mrs Haggerty, had not turned up. Probably, he thought, fallen foul of the weather.

General de Gard, a man who liked to talk about himself, had already established that Paul Descartes had French ancestry.

'Way back, General. Lost in the mists of time, I guess.' Descartes smiled; he was a cheery man in his fifties, rotund without being fat.

De Gard nodded courteously; he was wishing Adeline Scott-Mason had found table-favour with the Captain. Pacey was glad to find they had all made the mutual introductions; he was a taciturn man when it came to anyone he didn't know well and with whom he might find nothing in common. Now, however, he began a conversation with Henry Sayers Grant, his most important passenger. Grant was an urbane man, tall, distinguished, with thick grey hair and very direct blue eyes. To Pacey he looked more like a soldier than a diplomat. He had an ability to put people at ease straight away. He said, 'Sir, you have a heavy responsibility in time of war. So many passengers and crew. It's good of you to take the time to come down to the saloon.'

'A pleasure, sir,' Pacey said.

'Well – maybe. I hope it is. Anyway, so far as we're concerned, it's very reassuring, sir. If the Captain's below, there can't be anything wrong up top.'

That was one reason for Pacey being there. Reassurance, confidence in those who carried their lives in their hands, was important to all passengers. Henry Sayers Grant spoke of the war raging in Europe: a tragedy, he said, that so many young men had died and would go on dying. Pacey kept all expression from his face, saying nothing of his own recent loss. General de Gard made his contribution, stiffly.

'M'sieur Grant, if your President Wilson could be persuaded to bring in your great country, perhaps fewer would die.'

That was tactless and provocative. Before Pacey could engineer a change of subject the senator from Wyoming said in a loud, rather hectoring voice, 'More American boys would, sure. And I don't see why they should. Right, Mr Ambassador?'

Grant smiled. 'You're a little premature, Melvin. Ambassador Page is still in office right now.'

'Sure. But Americans dying. What's your view?'

'I think you know it well enough, Melvin. I deplore all killing, but I guess America's place now is beside Great Britain.'

Senator Melvin Manderton gave a snort. Pacey noticed that the New York banker, Haggerty, had given a slight nod of approval at the Senator's reaction. He steered the talk away from the war, asking if all present were comfortable aboard his ship. Except for Lady Barlow, they were. Lady Barlow had found her cabin noisy. There was, she said, a person, a woman, berthed opposite her, across the passage as she called it, whom she believed to be addicted to strong drink and caused disturbance as a result.

'I'm sorry to hear that, Lady Barlow. I shall speak to the Purser.'

'The man 'oo – who refused to post a letter for me?'

Like Purser Matthews himself, Captain Pacey had encountered this sort of thing before, not once but a thousand times. He asked, 'When was this, Lady Barlow?'

'Shortly after sailing.'

'Ah, yes. *After* sailing.'

'I said you would probably take the ship back to the pier. If you'd been told.'

Pacey smiled. 'Unlikely, I'm afraid. Schedules are there to be kept to, and tugs and pilots have much to do, for other ships as well as the *Laurentia*.' Before she could get another word in, Pacey asked, 'What takes you to Britain at such a time, Lady Barlow?'

'Because it's my 'ome, that's what,' she answered sharply. 'I went to America for health reasons, don't you know. I'm glad to be leaving.' She swept a look around the table at the US citizens. 'It's all so different from England, not at all British.'

'I dare say not,' Pacey said quickly. He went on, addressing the son farther down the table. 'Mr Barlow, are you going home to join one of the services?'

It was not the son who answered; it was Lady Barlow. 'My son has a weak heart. He certainly can't fight the Germans. Of course, he would if he could, make no mistake. He would join the Brigade of Guards. Eustace?' The use of the name was peremptory.

'Yes, mama?'

'Am I not right?'

Eustace Barlow swallowed soup. An Adam's apple prominent in a long, thin neck moved up and down above the wing collar. Wiping his lips with his napkin he said. 'Yes, dearest mama, quite right.'

Pacey failed to see Barlow as being the right material for the Brigade of Guards. Also, he doubted the weak heart; the man, in his early thirties, looked fit enough, if wet. But there was something about Lady Barlow with her many loose chins and her flouncy evening dress that said she would fight tooth and nail to keep Eustace away from the Germans. Even after conscription came in, which one day it would have to: the losses were mounting wickedly. The day before sailing – indeed every day the ship had been in port – the New York press had reported the same stories. The German Army was a wonderfully efficient machine and the Fatherland's manpower seemed inexhaustible. The British and French, under General Sir John French and General Joffre respectively, were making no net gains of ground. It was a case of advance at appalling cost, and then retreat, over and over again. The mud of Flanders grew deeper and bloodier every day, famous regiments with long histories of valour in war were being cut to pieces and re-formed with raw recruits from Kitchener's Army. The German Emperor called them, dismissingly, 'that contemptible little army'. Years later, those men were to call themselves, with pride, The Old Contemptibles.

Before dinner was finished, before Captain Pacey went to the first-class lounge to drink coffee with Henry Sayers Grant and General de Gard – who didn't stay long and was seen shortly after by a night steward creeping along one of the passenger alleyways – the talk had turned to Ireland and the trouble Britain was having in John Bull's Other Island. In Ireland trouble and insurrection was the order of the day. The Irish Republican Brotherhood under its hotheads was flaunting the orange, green and white tricolour in the faces of the British garrison in Dublin. In the north Sir Edward Carson was busily castigating the home government for any small concession that it was suggested might be made to the rebels. Religion again, Pacey reflected, always religion, Catholic against Protestant . . . right back to the Crusades, more people had been killed in the name of religion than anything else. With, of course, the exception of the war with Germany. The British and Germans were, basically, Protestants together. Each side held its drumhead services behind the front line, each side at home filled its great cathedrals and churches with its citizens bending the ear of God in their favour. God had to be on two sides at once, a very uncomfortable position.

By this time the homeward-bound *Laurentia* was the subject of important discussions between the German Emperor and his admirals. The U-boat commanders at sea in the Western Approaches, in the sectors of the North Atlantic closest to the shores of Great Britain, had had certain orders in regard to unarmed merchant vessels and all neutral shipping. And *Unterzeebooten* 120 currently at sea was commanded by a very ambitious young officer, keen for promotion and keen also to impress his wife: *Kapitanleutnant* Klaus Eppler. Eppler was held in high regard by the German Admiralty. Certain plans involving Eppler were under discussion in Berlin.

4

KAPITANLEUTNANT Eppler, U-boat commander at the age of twenty-five, was professionally very competent. All reports upon him had been good since the day he had joined the naval academy as a young cadet, scarcely more than a child. He was loyal to his Emperor, to his Fatherland, and to the Imperial Navy. He was a first-class seaman and ship-handler. He had specialized, once his training and his big-ship time was over, in the submarine service. He had no fear in him; always – once the war had burst upon the Fatherland over the so stupid business of Belgian neutrality – he could be relied upon to search zealously for the enemy and then to press home his attack. In recent months he had made a number, not large it was true, of killings. A 2000-ton collier, the *Hartlepool*; the 3200-ton freighter *Weston* and a few others, small fry mostly. He had disabled a British cruiser in the German Ocean that the British called the North Sea. He had attacked an oil-tanker off the Scilly Isles, his gunnery on this occasion causing no more than superficial damage. When Eppler had seen that the oil-tanker was flying the American flag he had broken off his attack.

Very right and proper.

Yet despite all this there was unfortunately one small doubt in the minds of certain senior officers and this doubt was expressed in the German Admiralty by a rear-admiral under whom Eppler had served a year earlier.

'There is a reserve about Eppler.'

An eyebrow was lifted: a full admiral, Commander-in-Chief of the Imperial Navy. 'Kindly elabrate, von Schrader.'

'A certain hesitation over certain targets.' Schrader, frowning, fiddled with a pencil. 'That is not quite right . . . Eppler has always attacked when he has found a target. But he has wasted time – time in which the British destroyers could have picked him up – in allowing the merchant crews to take to their boats. On occasions he has taken them aboard. There is . . . a chivalry that we cannot this time afford against the British.'

'Chivalry. An over-compensation, von Schrader?'

'Perhaps.' Von Schrader understood the reference very well. He had had a number of conversations with Eppler, and Eppler's background was naturally known to the High Command here in Berlin. Eppler did not fit easily into the German officer corps concept, into the concept of the elite, a concept similar to that of the old Prussian officers of the German Army. Eppler's father was a minor official in the War Department, a clerk, an estimable and loyal man but not the proper parentage for the usual naval officer. Eppler, von Schrader agreed, could be leaning over backwards to show the chivalry that was innate to the German upper class. Von Schrader said, 'It's hard to fault him for that, of course. But just at this particular moment. . . .'

'Precisely.' The Commander-in-Chief had snapped the word out. 'Eppler's command is the one most handily placed for the attack. It would take too much time for another to be sent into the area. We must rely upon Eppler now. Such a prestigious target!'

'A dangerous one,' another of the admirals remarked. 'One that could bring America into the war against us. The liner's carrying American citizens – this has been confirmed.'

'I know, I know. We all know, but the decision has been taken.' A shaft of sunlight penetrated the gloom of the room in which the high-ranking officers sat round the long, polished mahogany table, lit on the dark brown of the leather chairs, on the heavy furnishings, on the many gold rings on the cuffs of the admirals, on orders and decorations. 'Now it is not the fact of the attack we are discussing, gentlemen. It is *Kapitanleutnant* Eppler, the one who is to carry out that attack.' The Commander-in-Chief turned again to von Schrader. 'What will his reaction be, to attacking a huge liner with passengers, women and children amongst them?'

Von Schrader shrugged. 'He will be aware of the penalty for refusal. Or for bungling.'

'That does not fully answer my question, von Schrader. There is that hesitation you spoke of. The chivalry.' The Commander-in-Chief paused, then said, 'The British Lord Nelson had a blind eye that failed to see the signal at Copenhagen. Eppler could fail to see properly through his periscope, could he not? He could fail to find the target.'

'But the penalty – he is a keen. . . .'

'Yes, yes! But chivalry, or in his case perhaps a tendency to overplay the chivalry – this could override reason. Afterwards, when the liner has been sunk, there will be much antagonism. Eppler could be – and will be no doubt – portrayed as an inhuman monster by the British, especially so by the man Churchill and his henchman Lord Fisher. So a way for Eppler must, I think, be found.'

'A way, Admiral?'

'A salve for his conscience. He must see that he is acting for Germany and nothing else. For the Fatherland and its glory.' The Commander-in-Chief got to his feet and walked across to the window. He stood there for a while, looking down at the traffic moving along the Unter den Linden and the lime trees that had given it its name, down towards the great Brandenburg Gate at the entry to the Tiergarten. Then he swung round.

'A wireless signal will be made to Eppler. He will be informed that the *Laurentia* is armed with six-inch guns, that – '

Von Schrader interrupted. 'I have not heard of this, Admiral?'

'No. Neither have I! But the information will help to salve Eppler's conscience, I think, and afterwards the signal log will be destroyed. Eppler will be informed that she is no unarmed merchantman on a peaceful voyage . . . that she truly carries munitions of war in great quantities and that she is therefore a very legitimate target for his torpedoes. Both the British and Americans have been guilty of duplicity in supplying and carrying arms destined for use against Germany under the protection of the merchant flag. That will deal in advance with America as well as with Eppler. President Wilson will be seen to have sullied hands . . . and His Imperial Majesty does not in any case believe that Wilson will ever declare war on the German Empire. It is all bluff, gentlemen. All bluff!'

The decoded transcript of the wireless message had been handed to U-120's commander whilst surfaced earlier. Now Eppler handed the message form to his First Lieutenant.

'What do you make of that, Dirnecker?'

Leutnant Dirnecker's reply was stiff. 'We have been given our duty, sir.'

'Our duty. Yes. Yes, you're quite right, Dirnecker.'

'Which, of course, we shall carry out?'

It had been phrased as a question and Eppler answered it quietly. 'Yes, we shall carry it out, Dirnecker.'

The First Lieutenant gave a nod and turned away, leaving the control room and moving aft towards the engine conpartment of the boat. Eppler stood by his periscope, tapping the message form against his hand, frowning, not seeing the many dials and gauges that loomed from the close-set bulkhead inside the pressure hull, the U-boat's outer skin. Not aware of the ratings sitting at their various control stations, the steering gear, the hydroplanes, the torpedo tubes. Always in enemy waters the boat was ready for action. Not at full action stations all the time, but every man not on watch dressed and ready to close-up the instant the order was given.

Eppler looked at the brassbound clock ahead of him. Time yet before he would need to blow tanks and once again surface under cover of the night in order to charge his batteries and to allow fresh air to blow down through the conning-tower hatch to clear away the terrible fug of the submerged boat, the fug that resulted in all aboard a submarine developing colds soon after the start of each patrol.

He spoke to his Officer of the Watch, who was keeping a constant sweep of the surface through the raised periscope.

'I shall be in my cabin, Forster.'

'*Ja, mein Kapitan.*'

Eppler moved through the boat's close constriction, bending his head away from projections in the deckhead, pipes and cables and the gear for bringing the spare torpedoes to the tubes. He went to what he euphemistically spoke of as his cabin. This was no more than a bunk outside the wardroom entry, a bunk that on account of his position as captain was enclosed by a curtain. Fully dressed, he lay on the bunk, the curtain drawn around him. He listened to the hum of the electric motors and once again he read the message from Berlin.

A passenger liner was at his mercy. But she was armed; any armed ship was his legitimate prey. That was, of course, a fact. So was war a fact. So was his great responsibility a fact. But he knew the *Laurentia*, greyhound of the seas, the pride of the PanAtlantic fleet. As a youth Eppler had visited England with his father, a once-in-a-lifetime holiday abroad with a father who could ill afford such luxuries. The highlight of that holiday, so looked forward to by both of them, had been a journey by train to Liverpool to watch the first sailing of the great *Laurentia*. That had been on 7 September 1907. The Epplers, father and son, had been two of more than 200,000 people who had been there at the quayside and on other vantage points to see the great 31,550-ton monster move to sea. The cheering had been tumultuous. All the shipping in the Mersey River had blown their steam sirens as the great bulk of the *Laurentia* had moved off the Landing Stage with her 2300 passengers embarked, the well-dressed maiden voyagers leaning over the rails of the many decks to wave goodbye. To attend upon these passengers 900 crew were carried. Eppler senior had been ready with this information, informing his son that the liner would cross the Atlantic at a probable speed of twenty-four knots. As the huge bulk, its ports and lounge brightly lit, vanished into the gathering darkness to head out into Liverpool Bay for Queenstown in Ireland, the young Eppler had felt a lump come into his throat. Always there was some romance about the sailing of a ship, leaving the safety of the land to venture out across great waters, carrying so many people, some for pleasure, some to begin a new life in a new country, leaving family and old associations behind as the great adventure began.

Romance and sadness.

It had been a most wonderful and memorable holiday. Both the Epplers had looked back upon it with nostalgia. And the young Eppler knew that some of the sadness, the poignancy, he had felt as the gap of water had widened between that British liner and the Liverpool Landing Stage had been to do with his father. His father had always wanted to go to sea himself. His health had not permitted. Young Eppler that evening had watched his father's face. It had been transformed. There had been envy there, but not envy alone. There had been a sort of oneness with the men who sailed her. His father's spirit had sailed with the *Laurentia*, the world's biggest and fastest ship. When the liner had captured the Blue Riband on her next voyage from Liverpool to the Ambrose Light Eppler senior had been pleased; proud almost, even though he was a loyal German and the British ship had eclipsed the *Kaiser Wilhelm II*, proud because he had been present to wish her Godspeed on her maiden voyage.

In some curious and indefinable way, even after the outbreak of war, the *Laurentia* had in Eppler's mind been bound up with his father.

And now?

Kapitanleutnant Eppler once again read the message from Berlin. It was unequivocal. The *Laurentia* was an armed and legitimate target of war. His duty was to locate, intercept and sink. His duty for the Fatherland was to destroy grace and beauty and the lives of passengers.

Eppler thought of his puny boat – puny in size but with a mighty punch. Hundreds of people in the water, women and children among them. To attempt rescue would be ridiculous, ludicrous.

Eppler's mind went to his wife Ilse. Born Ilse von Neuburg she was the daughter of an admiral of the old shcool. She was aristocratic and high spirited and usually had a disdainful look. Her family, perhaps surprisingly, had not objected to the marriage; the Admiral had seen much good in Klaus Eppler and knew he had a good future in the Imperial Navy. But after two years of marriage, during which Eppler had spent many months away at sea both in peace and war, Ilse had appeared to look down on him, and especially upon his father, the ministry clerk. She had taunted him with his background, comparing him unfavourably with other naval officers. There had been no children; she had taunted him with this as well. He had begun to suspect affairs with other officers, ones of good breeding. Before Eppler had left Wilhelmshavn at the start of U-120's current patrol, there had been a scene, an unpleasant one.

'If there are to be children one day,' Ilse had said, 'they will have a clerk for a grandfather. Also, of course, an admiral. This will be bad for them, so perhaps it is as well you have not fathered any.'

'Why bad?' Eppler had asked.

She made an angry gesture. 'The mixture of classes. They will not know who or what they are.'

'That's rubbish, Ilse, and you know it.'

'I do not know it.' She had stormed at him, hands on hips like a fishwife despite her breeding that she set so much store by. 'Go to sea in your tin-pot *unterzeebooten* and think about it, my good Klaus! Think about it well. And so shall I.'

After that the leave-taking had been frigid. Klaus Eppler knew that his wife was contemptuous of his war record to date. A few coasters sunk, a cruiser damaged only slightly. Ashore in Bremerhavn and Hamburg and Wilhelmshavn, and in the social circles of Berlin, there were many senior naval officers who had not set foot aboard a seagoing ship since the start of the war but who had many decorations to fill their chests, and much money to entertain wives whose husbands were slogging wearily around the war-torn seas, or beneath them in their smelly tin cans that could shatter in minutes under the impact of the British depth charges or mines. Ilse von Neuburg, as was, wanted her husband to be a war hero. That might redress the balance of his unoffending father, still working in his ministry and wishing he could be at sea like his son.

The *Laurentia*?

For Ilse, yes. Not, Eppler believed, for his father-in-law the Admiral, now retired. Old Admiral von Neuburg would never have been the man to send women and children to their deaths. He would stand by the old Prussian code of military honour. He would not despatch a torpedo into the bowels of an unarmed, helpless ship.

But the *Laurentia* was not unarmed.

Or so Berlin said.

And his own father? The act would be a betrayal of that day in Liverpool, of all that wonderful and well-remembered holiday. Eppler's father was a gentle man. He was, of course, loyal to the Kaiser and the Fatherland; but he would never condone murder.

Was duty murder?

Duty was duty. Wives, fathers, fathers-in-law and all their thoughts must of course defer to the concept of duty.

Kapitanleutnant Eppler gave a deep sigh and looked at his wristwatch. It was night now, and time to bring the boat to the surface for recharging batteries. Eppler thrust a leg out of his bunk, pulled the curtain aside, stood up and made his way to the control room.

'All clear above?' he asked.

The officer at the periscope said, 'All clear, *mein Kapitan*.'

'Blow tanks,' Eppler said crisply. The routine swung into action as the compressed air was fed into the ballast tanks. U-120 canted upwards.

Soon her bows broke through the surface. She steadied, and Eppler went to the conning-tower hatch. He moved briskly, or as briskly as was possible in the confined space, and the set of his mouth was firm. There was one personal rule above all for any Captain, more so for the Captain of a U-boat where all hands lived in such close proximity: the Captain must never show doubt. His inner thoughts and feelings, unlike the boat herself, must never come to the surface.

As the liner came below the Newfoundland Banks, word was passed from the bridge that an iceberg would shortly be sighted. Soon, away to the north, it loomed grotesquely beneath a watery sun coming through the overcast. The sun's rays lit on a great edifice – a double edifice, twin towers joined by low-lying ice. With memories of the *Titanic*'s one and only voyage across the Atlantic, it was an awesome sight. The passengers crowded the decks. Leon Fielding was impressed with what he saw.

'Most magnificent,' he said to Chief Officer Arkwright, who was nearby on the boat deck supervising the overhauling of one of the lifeboats' falls. 'A splendid sight, splendid! But I imagine the Captain will take us no nearer?'

Arkwright laughed. 'No, he'll not do that, Mr Fielding. I agree it's a great sight, but – '

'Is it not unusual, to have icebergs so far south?'

'Not really, though it's true only a few do get this far down. They come, or some of them do, across from Iceland and East Greenland, brought around Cape Farewell by the East Greenland current . . . then they join forces with thousands of others and get swept up into Baffin Bay. From there, the Labrador current brings them down south of the Banks. Usually not more than about fifty get this far, though. So long as there's no fog, they're not hard to stand clear of.'

'Yes, I see.' Fielding clutched at his immense straw hat, holding it against the wind. 'Do you get any warning of them in advance?'

'Yes, we do, thanks to the US Coastguard. They maintain two vessels on constant ice patrol. They keep track of the most southerly bergs and issue warnings where necessary. Frankly, I don't know how we ever managed without them.'

Fielding nodded; a sailor's life with its many dangers and uncertainties would never have been for him. He wondered about the *Titanic* . . . and the Chief Officer went on to say that it was that disaster that had brought the initial setting up of the ice patrol in 1912, following which, in 1913, an international conference on safety of life at sea was held in London, resulting in an international service of ice observation and patrol, which had become a United States responsibility to manage.

Fielding continued looking at the iceberg, fascinated by its great size and beauty, until gradually it drew away astern as the *Laurentia* proceeded safely on her course for the Old World. Still many days to the westward of U-120's position, the liner steamed on for Liverpool Bay unescorted and unarmed.

Captain Pacey spent most of his time on his bridge, even though his ship was as yet far from the U-boat zones. You never knew what might happen in war. A master had to be watchful all the time. There could be no taking for granted at sea. Pacey, like Klaus Eppler, kept his anxieties out of his face. There was the same need to appear confident before both crew and passengers. Sometimes it was very difficult. But Pacey believed that his passengers were reasonably unworried. Earlier he had spoken to them in the main first-class lounge, telling them that as soon as they made their approach to home waters, they would come under the protection of the British Navy.

That seemed to have reassured them.

But, below the bridge in the passenger accommodation, there were other worries.

'That wretched man,' Alva Lundkvist said bitterly.

'What wretched man, my dearest?'

'Oh, Torsten, you know very well who I mean! The man who was throwing bread to the seagulls. Olof was so upset and it has put him back, I think.' Alva Lundkvist patted at her hair, her face drawn with worry. They had been through so much and Olof had been so much better. Now he had been crying and was very listless and disinclined to go on deck. The specialist in America had stressed the need for fresh air and Alva had done her best to carry out doctor's orders. Until now she had succeeded. She said, 'I shall send for the doctor, Torsten.'

She rang for the cabin steward. The ship's surgeon attended. Dr Fellowes was an elderly man, stringy and haggard, with a lined, yellowish face. Gin had affected his liver over the years. First-class and second-class passengers were charged a fee for a cabin visit, so he came. In the third class they would be expected to come to him in the surgery.

'What seems to be the matter with the boy?'

Alva told him, explaining about the specialist they had crossed the Atlantic to consult, and his recommended treatment after Olof had been discharged from hospital. Dr Fellowes took Olof's temperature.

'H'm. A little up.'

'Yes. He has been so much upset, Doctor.' She told him about the man casting bread balls to the seagulls.

Fellowes gave a short laugh. 'My dear young woman, that sort of thing doesn't lead to temperatures. The boy must learn to take his small knocks.' He paused. 'Keep the child in his bunk. I'll send along a physic, two dollars the bottle, and I'll call again tomorrow.' He added, 'It's no more than a passing chill.'

'Thank you, Doctor,' she said. Dr Fellowes left the cabin, looking grumpy. Alva Lundkvist made a face behind the departing back. She sensed that the old man was out of touch, had no feeling for children and no knowledge of them either. He would have spent his sea life attending old ladies for seasickness and imaginary diseases.

In accordance with the Captain's order, boat drill for all hands and all passengers was held each afternoon. The drill was supervised by Chief Officer Arkwright. The passengers were mustered at their stations on the embarkation deck and the lifeboats were lowered on the falls from the davits, descending from their stowed positions on the boat deck above. There were scared faces among some of the passengers. Mrs Rickards was apprehensive; she had travelled before.

'It's not usual, Jeffrey,' she said to her husband.

'Nothing to worry about, Emmy.'

'But usually boat drill's only held just after leaving port.'

'Yes. The Captain's merely taking precautions, my dear. Very sensible and very proper.' He held her hand for a moment, protectively. 'We shall be perfectly all right. The Captain spoke of the naval escort later. We can depend on the Navy. No one at the Admiralty's going to let the *Laurentia* come under attack. Stands to reason. Good God, there's that man again!'

'Who?'

'That appalling feller. With that perambulator.'

Leon Fielding was approaching along the deck. He was talking to the empty conveyance. Something along the lines of what Rickards had been saying: he was going to be all right and Ming in New York mustn't fuss about daddy's safety, the ship's Captain would look after him. Catching, for the second time, Mrs Rickards' eye he broke off and raised his straw hat.

'Good morning, dear lady.'

'Good morning . . . er.'

'Fielding, dear lady. Leon Fielding of whom you may perhaps have heard?'

'Er. . . .'

'A tenor. I have sung at the Albert Hall.' He bowed, he removed his straw hat again and swept it across his body. Jeffrey Rickards gave a snort like a cavalry horse but said nothing. At that moment the First Officer came along with Chief Officer Arkwright. He took charge.

'Into line, please, ladies and gentlemen, and put on your lifejackets.'

It was a very definite command and it expected obedience. It got it.

The passengers shuffled into line and the First Officer walked along the ranks like a general inspecting troops, adjusting the set of lifejackets to his satisfaction. He reminded his charges, as he did at every boat drill, that if the alarm should sound they were to proceed as quickly as possible but without panic to where they now were. They would then await orders from the officers or senior ratings. They would not embark in the lifeboats until told to do so. And he stressed that the rule at sea was always women and children first, at which Rickards nodded his approval. Whatever might happen, he would ensure that Emmy got away to safety.

The routine was being repeated all round the embarkation deck, each boat station being under the orders of one or other of the deck officers or the Purser's staff. Purser Matthews himself had a boat station. In this responsibility he was assisted by a junior member of his staff, for when an alarm came his first duty would be to ensure the embarkation of the ship's documents and, if possible, cash.

One of his passengers was Livia Costello. She was looking drawn and there was an aura of gin. Captain Pacey, always meticulous, had acted on his promise to Lady Barlow. He had acted via Staff Captain Morgan, who had approached Matthews. Matthews had had words with the star; he'd been glad to do so. It was an introduction and he made use of it. He spoke in an easy fashion, half-laughing at the foibles of a tiresome old titled woman with an army of servants at home.

Livia referred to her as an old bag, but had been co-operative. 'I'll be good,' she promised, 'if I can.'

'Fine. How good is good?' Matthews had asked with a particular look in his eye.

'Depends,' she said. She had returned the look. The signs had been fair. Matthews was a fast worker. He had spent that night, last night now, in Livia's cabin. At least it had kept her quiet to Lady Barlow's satisfaction.

This morning at boat drill Matthews adjusted Livia's lifejacket with a proprietorial air. She giggled as his hand caressed her breast. 'Naughty boy,' she said a shade too loudly. Matthews realized that she had already been in attendance at the lounge bar. He gave her a dirty look: Captain Pacey had strict standards, as had the Line. Do what you liked ashore but never, never bring the Line into disrepute with the passengers.

Later that morning Livia Costello was back in the lounge bar. She was thinking of Larry back in the New York apartment. He wouldn't be thinking of her, of course; he would be engaged elsewhere, the lousy worm. The trouble was, she still loved him, deep down. It was crazy really. Lousy worm was the right term for Larry if you thought about him in cold blood. If you could. She drowned her sorrows with grim determination. She became befuddled. She thought about last night. Matthews was very British, thought a hell of a lot of himself because he was British. The impression he'd given, even if he hadn't exactly meant to, was that an American woman ought be flattered by an Englishman's attentions and that, of course, was crap. Still, he was a port in a storm.

She got to her feet unsteadily. She wove her way through the lounge, which was full of people. The Rickardses, Leon Fielding. Elizabeth Kent sitting with John Holmes from Annapolis, Frederick Jones unaccustomedly indulging in whisky and looking haunted, Patrick Haggerty the New York banker, Senator Melvin Manderton from Wyoming, the French general and his mistress. Many others.

Fossils, largely. That old Rickards. . . .

They needed a shot in the arm, something solid to carry on about.

At the forward end of the lounge, each side of the big observation windows that gave onto the fo'c'sle and the flung spray from the heaving waters, were large portraits of King George V and Queen Mary. The King was in naval uniform; the Queen was wearing a diamond tiara and a fine dress with the broad blue ribbon of the Garter across her breasts. All very regal, with what Livia took to be looks down noses at Americans.

She approached the portrait of the King.

Loudly she said, 'Hiya, King. Hope it keeps fine for you in Buckingham Palace. And bloody safe.' Then she lifted two fingers and jerked them towards the portrait. That done, she turned to watch the effect. It was very satisfactory. She allowed herself to be led away by a horrified first-class lounge steward.

Just before her act the US Ambassador-to-be had entered the lounge. His face was like thunder as he joined Haggerty and Senator Manderton. 'Disgraceful,' he said. 'Makes one ashamed to be a US citizen . . . that sort of thing.'

'Nothing to be ashamed of, being a US citizen.'

'I didn't say there was, Senator. Don't you misquote me. But what sort of impression of us do filthy manners like that give the British? Let's hope Captain Pacey doesn't get to hear of it.'

'He will,' Haggerty said. He didn't seem displeased; nor did Senator Manderton. 'There'll be plenty that'll see that he does.'

'If that's so, I shall apologize on behalf of our country.'

'You do that,' Haggerty said. He was thinking of his Irish forebears, who had cocked a collective snook at the then King of England when they'd crossed the North Atlantic to be free of his sway. He couldn't feel too badly about Livia Costello, though he regretted the handle it gave the British to criticize the USA.

* * *

'Ought to be horsewhipped.' Rickards spoke in a flat fury, spoke, in that single utterance, as Major-General Lord Rickards, one-time Chief of Staff in South Africa who as a younger man had fought with distinction along the terrible mountain passes of the North-West Frontier of India.

'Drastic, that, sir,' a voice said from a nearby chair, 'for a woman.'

Rickards glared. 'May I ask who you are?'

'Why, sure you can. Elmer Houston Pousty.'

'I see.'

Pousty, a hefty-looking man in his middle twenties, was prepared to be talkative: he hadn't met many British and none of the British upper class, so he indulged his fancy and never mind Rickards' wooden look, though after a while he addressed his remarks to the old boy's wife, calling her ma'am. It emerged that he was going to Britain to help out. He didn't like the way President Wilson was holding back.

Rickards thawed a little. 'Army?' he asked.

'No, *sir*. Though I guess you might call it that. But not the way you mean. My folks, they've been Quakers from way back. You've heard of Pousty Incorporated?'

'No, never.'

'We're big employers, sir, very big. Meat canners in Chicago. But we employ only Quakers. So me, I guess I don't exactly fight.'

'Ha.'

'I'm going across to become a medical corpsman. More precisely, I aim to be a stretcher-bearer, maybe drive an ambulance.'

Mrs Rickards glanced quickly at her husband's face and said quietly, 'Mr Pousty, if I were a man I'd take off my hat to you. Jeffrey?'

'What? Oh – yes, yes. Most certainly.'

It had not been long before word of the exhibition in the first-class lounge had reached the Master. It was brought to Pacey by Staff Captain Morgan.

'Very deplorable,' Pacey said. 'I take it the woman had been drinking?'

'Very much so.'

'Then a word with the Purser, Morgan. The bar staff are to be on the lookout. I'll not have obvious drinking during a wartime passage. If the bar staff can't cope, I'll turn off her tap.'

'Yes, sir.' Morgan paused. 'I was thinking . . . a short, sharp lesson to impress her that you don't insult the King aboard a British ship?'

'You mean, have her up before me?'

'Yes, sir. I think –'

'No, Morgan. I'm not going to make too much of it – too much of drink talking. We have the usual mix of Americans and British and I don't want what you might call domestic trouble. I doubt if she'll repeat that performance – if she does, then it's a different matter.' Pacey paused, ran a hand over eyes tired from looking out over the heaving grey waters. 'By the way, I've got that US senator coming up after the noon sight's been taken. A pre-lunch gin. If you can spare the time I'd like you to come along and help me out.'

One of the people who had witnessed Livia Costello's indiscretion had been the *Laurentia*'s bosun, Andrew MacFarlane, known to the deck department, though never to his face, as Grandad. MacFarlane had been passing along the leeward side of A deck and some of the big square windows had been open. He had heard the words and seen the gesture. Bosun MacFarlane had been at sea for fifty-three years, thirty-five of them in sail. Sail had taken him to all parts of the world – Australia and New Zealand, South America, Japan and China and the Scandinavian countries, the USA and Canada . . . He had gone from sail to the PanAtlantic Line, signing as bosun from the start. He had sailed in the *Laurentia* continually from her maiden voyage. He had never taken leave; he had no home to go to. The *Laurentia* was his home and he didn't want to leave her. But soon he would have to: he was due for pension when the ship berthed in Liverpool. He was an old man. Too old, the Marine Superintendent of the Line had said.

Not too old to be shaken to the core by what he had heard a first-class passenger say. Loyalty had always been his watchword. To his captain, the Line, his country and his monarch. When the young MacFarlane had first gone to sea, slipping down the Clyde from the Broomielaw and into the Firth past Greenock and Dunoon for the Cumbraes, Arran Island and Ailsa Craig, Queen Victoria had just gone into mourning for her beloved Albert, the Prince Consort. The whole of Britain had grieved. MacFarlane, scarcely more than a child really, had sworn an oath to himself. He would be a Queen's man until he died.

The oath was very much alive now. He went on his way for'ard. He went down the hatch alongside the windlass, down to his cabin in the seamen's accommodation below the fo'c'sle. This was a place of noise when the sea was running high. The thud of green water dropping onto the anchor-cables and the slips and other deck gear, the constant rattle of the cables' links in the navel pipes on either side. Also a place of smells: the paint shop, the bosun's store with its cordage and its grease and tallow, the close-set seamen's berths with the pervading stench of sweaty bodies and socks worn too long. A far cry from the passengers' luxurious surroundings. But home. A much loved place, even though today, as ever since they had cleared the Ambrose Channel, a home that rose and fell and heaved sideways and made the din worse.

In his cabin Andrew MacFarlane, muttering to himself, brought a sheet of paper from a drawer. He also equipped himself with a red crayon. On the paper he draw a representation of the woman in the first-class lounge. Then he struck a match. He set light to the woman. While she was burning away nicely he lit his pipe. And a knock came at the door. His senior bosun's mate came in.

'What's up, Bose?'

MacFarlane told him in full. 'Yon wicked woman's fit only for hell fire.'

'American. . . ?'

'Aye, American, aye. And bad cess to 'em all.'

The bosun's mate grinned. 'You're not blaming the whole of America for one daft woman, are you, Bose?'

'I am, yes.'

The bosun's mate shook his head. Grandad really was getting old. There was nothing wrong with Americans. The majority of them understood what Britain was facing from the Kaiser. and that majority wanted to come into the war and teach the Huns a lesson. They had a fine army, eager enough to go over and finish off the Kaiser's aspirations. One day, the bosun's mate believed, they would.

A shoeless and stockingless leg had arrived in New York. To be exact, in the Hudson River. The New York Police Department was at first stymied. No identification had been on the leg. Forensic had said the leg was female, age middle-twenties, not dead long – a matter of days though they couldn't be precise.

The routines swung into action. There had been plenty of murders and plenty of persons reported missing. New York was a vast place, teeming with life and death, teeming with mobsters, protection racketeers, anything you cared to name. But the leg could have come downstream into the Hudson River, perhaps, from some tributary. If it had, that widened the scope of the enquiry. Or might. The murderer could have done his deed in the big city and then carried the leg upstate. Carried the whole body. There had obviously been dismemberment; but where had it taken place? Forensic had no theories on that but did suggest the use of an axe or carving knife, or both, which was fairly obvious really and not of much help.

The Police Captain in charge of the precinct where the leg had come ashore knew he was in for a long slog. The lists of missing female persons in their twenties were gone through; or anyway, a start was made on them. It all took time; and nothing seemed to fit. Not at first. There were so many possibilities. A jealous lover, or a sudden attack say in Central Park, a sex maniac maybe . . . and there were any number of single young women living alone in New York and its environs. It could be a long while before they were missed. Especially of course if they had no job. No regular job.

The leg could have come from an abandoned woman, a prostitute.

The Captain's wish was his command but Staff Captain Morgan had asked to be excused from meeting Senator Manderton: a crisis, a domestic one, had blown up, had been referred to him and needed prompt attention. A British couple with a spoiled and precocious child, a boy of nine, had complained about Leon Fielding. Fielding had encountered the boy on a sheltered deck in the second-class accommodation. The boy had been sitting in a deck chair on the leeward side and had been alone. The singer had got into conversation with him and had talked about his dog, Ming the Pekinese. The boy had asked if the dog was in the perambulator. Fielding had said no, she wasn't. The boy had then said she must be because he'd seen Fielding talking to her. Fielding had told the boy to look for himself. When the boy's head was down in the perambulator, the father had come along and had seen, or so he insisted, Fielding caress the boy's buttocks. The boy had corroborated this. Fielding had denied it. The father said the man was an obvious oddity, with his straw hat and floppy cravat and his perambulator with non-existent dog and was likely enough to be a pervert. Staff Captain Morgan, who believed Fielding's protestations, was doing his best to sort it out but the father was a narrow-faced bigot and was set to make trouble.

So in the Master's quarters Pacey's steward poured only two drinks: a small gin and a rather large Bourbon, the latter for Senator Manderton. Manderton hadn't said, 'Fine, thanks,' until his glass had been very well filled.

Steward Mullins then departed, a clean napkin over his arm, his white jacket starched and spotless. Manderton looked over the furnishings and said, 'They do you people well, I'll say that, Captain.'

'PanAtlantic's a good line, Senator.'

'Sure. But easy drinks and comfort in wartime and all – you know?'

Pacey said nothing. Manderton certainly hadn't held back on the Bourbon, wartime or not. Manderton went on, 'It's going to be interesting, seeing Britain at war. Seeing how you're coping.'

'Have you visited Britain in peacetime, Senator?'

'Why no, I guess not. Always been too goddam busy –'

'H'm.'

'That's why I'm going over *now*. To get acquainted.'

'A fact-finding mission, as I understand.'

'Right.'

'Is this for Washington, Senator? Or are you freelancing?'

58

'Well now, I guess it's a little bit of both.' Manderton raised a hand and scratched beneath his left armpit. He was a coarse man, Pacey thought, red-faced and beefy, with a truculent way of speaking. A very different sort from Henry Sayers Grant. 'I'm doing this on my own. But what I report to Washington when I get back . . . well, it's going to be listened to.'

Pacey nodded. He was aware that US senators were important people. People with a lot of influence. People that politicians in the United States didn't wish to cross. They could be useful; they could be deadly to the career prospects of an enemy. So you didn't make enemies. Pacey, however, was outside their scope and he didn't like the way Senator Manderton was reclining in the armchair, with a leg raised carelessly over the arm and a foot dangling in space. And a hand behind the neck, scratching now and again. He hadn't liked the way the senator had produced a cigar from his top pocket and lit it.

He asked, 'What are you going to give them to listen to, Senator?'

'How's that again?'

'What sort of facts do you propose to dig out?'

Manderton shrugged, but narrowed his eyes. 'Facts are facts, right? What I dig, I find.'

'That's precisely what I meant,' Pacey said, but accompanied the words with a smile. 'If you –'

'Okay, okay, I get the point. You're saying I dig what I want to find . . . that I'm going into this with a prejudiced mind, right?' He didn't wait for the Captain to answer. 'I guess we all do that in our own way. And boy, am I . . .' Pacey believed he'd been about to add the word 'prejudiced' but it didn't come. Instead Manderton went on, 'Look, Captain. I'm going to observe the scene, that's all. Talk and listen. To your Prime Minister. To your Mr Churchill. To Lord Kitchener. Get their views on how the war's going for your country. Maybe I'll get to see King George. If I do, I'll say, "King, you've got yourself a problem. And now you want the United States to come in and help you out of a darn big hole." I'll say that to his face. Also, I want to meet the people, the ordinary people. See what they think. Right?'

Pacey, his face expressionless, asked a question. 'What's your own view, Senator, as to whether or not America should come in?'

'Not up to me, Captain.'

'But you have a view?'

Manderton laughed. 'Sure, I have a view! I don't want to see one single American boy die for Britain. And so long as President Wilson holds firm, that won't happen.'

'I see,' Pacey said evenly. 'I respect your concern for American lives. But there is a rider to that. Lives lost now, while there's still time, may save thousands, even millions, later on. Because it's as sure as tomorrow's dawn that if the Kaiser destroys the British and French Armies, America's turn will come next. And you'll find yourselves without an ally.' He was going to say more when an interruption came. The voice-pipe from the bridge. Pacey reached out a hand and took the earpiece from its hook by his desk. 'Captain here.'

'Officer of the Watch, sir. Would you come to the bridge, sir, please?'

'Right away.' Pacey had almost said, 'Gladly.' He excused himself from Senator Manderton, who drained his glass and left the cabin, leaving his cigar. Pacey climbed to the bridge. His face was angry; Manderton, unlike most Americans whom Pacey had met over the years, had left a nasty taste. Americans in Pacey's experience had been happy, outgoing, generous people with a zest for life and getting the best of it along the way. Enthusiastic people without chips on their shoulders; hardworking and largely self-made, and interesting to meet. Not Manderton, with his closed mind – closed as it seemed against Britain. Pacey sighed. Perhaps it was the war itself, putting everything normal out of focus, polarizing opinion.

Reaching the bridge he was told that a wireless message had been received from the Admiralty in London. The Officer of the Watch had not wanted to say this down the voice-pipe when the Captain was entertaining a passenger.

'Quite right,' Pacey said. 'What's the message?'

A signal form was handed over. Pacey read: MASTER LAURENTIA REPEATED C-IN-C GRAND FLEET, DIRECTOR TRADE DIVISION AND SNO QUEENSTOWN FROM ADMIRALTY. CRUISER FORCE E REPORTS TWO U-BOATS SAILED HELIGOLAND BELIEVED ON COURSE FOR VICINITY OF CAPE CLEAR. The time of origin of the signal was given as 0836 that morning.

The *Laurentia* was not in possession of the naval code. The signal had been sent in plain language. Since all the world knew where the *Laurentia* was and where she was bound, this was not considered important.

The Officer of the Watch was looking expectantly at the Captain. Pacey said, 'We have plenty of time yet. I'll not alarm the passengers.'

Cape Clear was inshore of the Fastnet Rock at the south-western tip of County Cork. The *Laurentia* would stand well to the eastward for entry to St George's Channel. But of course the exact destination, or later position, of the U-boats was not currently forecast.

Pacey said reassuringly, 'The naval escort will meet us in good time. There's no cause for alarm. None at all.'

5

No cause for alarm; but the Admiralty's signal was a warning that before very much longer the exigencies of war would wrap themselves around the luxury of a great liner.

Captain Pacey called a conference, unobtrusively, of his senior officers. He informed them of the contents of the signal. 'From now on, extra vigilance throughout the ship, below decks as well as on the bridge. The night stewards and the masters-at-arms to be ready instantly to take control of the passengers if anything should happen while they're sleeping. The worst thing we can face after torpedoing is panic.'

They were all aware that a liner was a very different kettle of fish from a warship. A warship's company was trained for emergency, every man knowing his place and his duty in any eventuality from fire and striking a rock to attack by a determined enemy. Passengers were not so trained and had never expected or until now needed to be. The one thing they had been exercised in had been their abandon ship stations. Above anything else Pacey dreaded what would happen to his ship if upwards of a thousand passengers, men, women and children, took fright and stampeded the close alleyways and cabin corridors with the vessel perhaps sinking around them. He had heard the stories from the *Titanic* after she had hit the iceberg many years earlier. Stories of men fighting for a place in the lifeboats, women being pushed out of the way, the ship's company losing control in some instances. Boats' falls jamming on the blocks, lowered boats coming up-and-down as one set of falls ran out before the other, tipping the survivors into the sea. That would not happen to Pacey's boats, or it shouldn't: they'd been exercised enough. . . .

The six children of Paul Descartes, partner in Albert Booth, were high spirited and playful. Four boys, two girls, ages ranging from four to eighteen. The eighteen-year-old son stood aloof. The others roamed the ship, going where they were permitted and where they were not permitted. Rickards found them a confounded nuisance in the first-class writing room, where he was composing a letter to one of his sons, to be posted when the mail went ashore in Liverpool. A small girl thundered in, arms spread like an aeroplane. She zoomed round the compartment ahead of a small boy.

She bumped into Rickards' chair. 'Ooh!' she said in her small voice. 'Sorry!'

Rickards sighed. 'What's the idea – hey?'

'I was told to be a torpedo.'

'I see. By whom?'

'Timmy.'

'Timmy?'

'My brother.' She pointed. 'There.'

'And what's he?'

'A torpedo-boat destroyer. And you're the *Laurentia*.' She giggled. 'You weren't meant to be but you were in the way. Anyway, I've sunk you so there.'

She pirouetted away, holding her skirts out sideways, like a ballet dancer, pursued by the torpedo-boat destroyer. And by a lounge steward who had just appeared. He shooed them out of the writing room and then approached Rickards.

'Sorry I'm sure, sir. Not allowed in here, sir, the children aren't, little 'orrors.'

'It's all right.' Rickards said. 'The parents should have more control over them, of course.' He added, 'I thought their game was a tactless one.'

'What was that, sir?'

'They were torpedoing the ship.'

'This ship, sir?'

Rickards nodded. He was thinking: there's many a true word said in jest. He was far from being a superstitious man but he didn't like it. However, they were only children. The lounge steward took it differently, with all a seaman's superstition. He had a word later with Second Steward Parker.

'It's not right, Mr Parker. Tempting providence I call it. If I hear 'em at it, I'll give 'em a clip round the lug-'ole.'

'Don't you,' Parker said, and meant it. 'Passengers is passengers. Never lay a hand on 'em. There's going to be enough troubles over that Mr Fielding.' Word of that had spread fast. 'Not been long at sea, have you? Tact's the watchword. Tact at all times, with the ship's officers as well as the loafers. Ever hear the story of the officers' steward – not in PanAtlantic – who found the Chief Officer in 'is bunk with a woman, against all Company's regulations, when 'e took in the morning tea?'

'No . . .'

'That steward had been well trained in tact. Didn't blink an eyelid. Just said, "Beg pardon, gentlemen," and left the tea and went out.'

Chief Engineer Hackett had been one of the senior officers summoned to the Captain's conference and he was thoughtful as he left the Master's deck and went below to the starting-platform in his engine room. With his senior second engineer he went through all the engine spaces, the great boiler-rooms included, the furnaces that consumed nearly 900 tons of coal daily. Firemen and trimmers smartened up as the Chief approached: old Hackett was a stickler and prickly with it. He examined everything, leaving nothing to chance. If an attack came, the bridge, the whole ship, all its passengers and crew, would be dependent on swift reactions from the engine-room staff. Immediate answering of the bridge telegraphs, immediate response from well-maintained machinery, could make all the difference between a hit and a miss, if Captain Pacey was in the business of dodging a well-aimed tin fish — which, if the trail had been spotted, he would be.

Hackett hadn't so far met the enemy. He had never seen the result of a torpedo hit, one that could strike the ship in the vicinity of the engine spaces.

His brother had. His brother was in the RN, an engine-room artificer recently promoted to the rank of Engineer Lieutenant. He'd been second in charge of the engines aboard a light cruiser that had taken a tin fish slap into one of her boiler rooms, followed closely by a second that had gone into the engine room itself.

His brother had described it. The chaos in total darkness as the ring main had gone; the escaping steam under high pressure that had flayed men's bodies as they fought to reach the network of ladders, now shattered into a broken spider's web, that ran up to the air-lock at the top, the air-lock that was the only escape from hell. The screams of burned and lacerated men, the stumbling over the remains of the many bodies that had been cut to ribbons by the explosion itself. The appalling stench of cordite mixed with burning flesh.

Not many had got out. Hackett's brother had been one of the lucky ones. Knocked out cold, he'd been carried out by a leading stoker. After survivors' leave — the cruiser had subsequently gone down — he was back at sea, back in another engine room.

'Anything wrong, Chief?' the senior second engineer asked.

Hackett lifted an eyebrow. 'No. Does something show?'

'Just thought you looked pensive, that's all!'

'I was. No real reason.'

There was nothing to be gained from spreading his personal fears. Mr Hackett carried on with his close inspection, knowing that if the ship should go down he would have been wasting his time. Nevertheless, he nit-picked: some Brasso was needed here and there. Some grease wanted cleaning away from where it shouldn't have been. That sort of thing. If the Chief was seen to be worrying over trivia, then it was proof that he wasn't worried about anything more than having a top-line engine room when the superintending chief engineer came aboard for his inspection in Liverpool. It was a simple but quite effective psychology. Like Pacey, Hackett had to inspire confidence.

Faster than they had thought possible, the New York Police Department got some information. It was, the Police Captain had to admit, sheer luck, but there it was. To his precinct came a man, a friend of a Mr Frederick Jones currently a passenger aboard the *Laurentia*. Four or five days before the liner had sailed, this man had lent his automobile to Mr and Mrs Jones for a trip upstate. The automobile had been returned as promised. The day after, the man had found a purse belonging to Mrs Jones. It had been beneath a rug on the back seat. The man had taken it round to his friend's apartment but there had been no answer to his ring, and no answer either on subsequent visits.

Then the liner had sailed.

The man had gone round to the PanAtlantic offices and had handed over the purse against a receipt. It would be sent by the next boat for the United Kingdom. Then the official to whom the purse had been handed checked a list. The name of Mrs Maggie Jones had been deleted; it had not been checked at the gangway and thus she had been struck from the list that had gone back ashore. The man had visited the Jones apartment again but still no luck. No Maggie Jones.

'Did the Line confirm positively that this Mrs Jones was not aboard?' the man was asked.

'Not positively, no. It would only be possible to confirm for sure after the ship had left and certain other forms had been handed in to the Purser, as far as I can gather.'

'Um-h'm.'

It wasn't much of a lead. But then something else came in: a woman in Arlington, Massachusetts, sister of Mrs Jones, had reported to the local police that she had tried to contact her sister before the latter had gone aboard the *Laurentia* but had failed to connect. She was worried because she had been aware of strained relations when the Joneses had been staying in her home. Also, she had never trusted her brother-in-law. Mr Jones's ploy to establish love and domestic bliss had failed.

'Okay,' the Police Captain had said. 'So we send a wireless message to the liner.'

'New York Police Department, sir,' a clerk reported to Purser Matthews. 'Inquiry re a Mrs Jones.' The message had come down from the Marconi operators in the ship's wireless room and the clerk had done some checking. 'There's a Frederick Jones aboard, sir, but no wife. On the other hand, he's occupying a double cabin and Mrs Jones was in fact booked.'

'But didn't embark?'

'Apparently not, sir.'

'Sure you have the right Jones?'

'Yes, sir. We have quite a few Joneses but these are the only Frederick and Maggie Jones, according to the original passenger list.'

Matthews sighed; the Purser was always a busy man. 'Better have him along,' he said.

There was unpleasant trouble elsewhere as well: Staff Captain Morgan was trying to sort out the Fielding affair. He had first interviewed the complaining father, a British citizen named Craigson, a man of the artisan class who had got Morgan's back up by saying constantly, 'Now look here,' and waving a hand in front of Morgan's face. His mind was impermeable: he'd seen what he'd seen and that was that. He said his boy would corroborate; when asked, the boy did. Morgan formed the impression that he'd been told to do so by his father. He also formed the impression that the father had it in for anyone who looked as odd as Fielding and when he'd seen the disputed gesture he'd jumped at once to a conclusion. Ridding himself of Craigson with a promise that the affair would be investigated further, he sent a request to Fielding that he would come to his cabin at the for'ard end of B deck in the first-class accommodation.

Fielding, who had been awaiting such a summons fearfully, came with his perambulator and Staff Captain Morgan stated the facts as reported.

'Oh, dear me.' Fielding's face was contorted with misery. 'I most certainly did no such thing. What a very *wicked* little boy.'

Morgan said noncommittally, 'Please describe what *did* happen, Mr Fielding.'

'By all means.' Fielding did so, speaking of the boy's interest in Ming. Morgan had already heard about Ming so no question was necessary. 'I think I did touch his back, in passing as it were. Quite accidentally . . . the boy was bent over the perambulator, you see.'

'Yes. You can assure me that that was all that took place?'

'Yes. My word of honour,' Fielding said with a curious dignity. 'I would *never* . . .'

'Are you married, Mr Fielding?'

'Oh yes. Mummy's in New York. She –'

'Mummy?'

'My wife – Ming's mummy as she thinks of herself. I'm her daddy. Ming's daddy,' he added as he saw the look of bewilderment on Morgan's face. 'That's how we regard ourselves. You see, much to our regret, we never had any children.' He brought out a vast silk handkerchief of a startling red and wiped his face and brow. He was obviously very distressed. 'This is a most terrible thing. I don't know what Ming will think, I really don't.'

'I understand Ming's in New York? In which case . . . I doubt if she'll know. I really wouldn't worry, Mr Fielding –'

'No, perhaps not. Yes, you're quite right, Captain Morgan. But my position is scarcely tenable now. There has already been talk. I am being cold-shouldered, ostracized. People move away when I approach, you know. It's all so terribly unfair. Just because of poor little Ming really.' The handkerchief was in play again, and Fielding's hands shook as he mopped at his face. Morgan was anxious: a man in his state could act drastically. The charge, if it came to that in the end, and Craigson showed every sign of seeing to it that it would, was certainly a terrible one, about the worst a man, especially if innocent, could be faced with. Currently, Fielding seemed in a state to do almost anything. As Morgan pondered, Fielding asked, 'What is to happen now, Captain?'

Morgan said, 'I shall have to make a report to Captain Pacey. In the meantime, I advise you to try not to worry – easier said than done, I know. If I may make a suggestion, I'd send your steward to the main dispense bar for a bottle of whisky. And then remain in your cabin.'

'Do you mean I'm under arrest?'

Morgan laughed kindly. 'By no means. But you might find that easier – to remain in your cabin, rather than . . . you did say there's been a reaction from the other passengers, Mr Fielding.' Then he added, 'I'm sure it will all have been worked out by the time we reach Liverpool.'

When Fielding had left, dispiritedly dragging the perambulator behind him, Staff Captain Morgan telephoned through to the surgery. He had a word with Dr Fellowes, suggesting a sedative. He said he feared a possible suicide attempt, so easily done at sea. Putting down the telephone he thought ahead to Liverpool: the man Craigson would probably press charges ashore. He had that right if he so wished.

Morgan went back over Fielding's final remark before leaving his cabin, a remark in reference to Morgan's about everything being settled by the time the ship reached Liverpool. Fielding had said, 'If ever we do reach Liverpool.'

'We'll reach Liverpool, all right,' Morgan had said with confidence.

'The ship is not to reach Liverpool.'

The statement was firm, as was the expression of the high-ranking Admiral who had uttered it. The Admiral was speaking in the German Admiralty. In front of him, spread out over a much-polished mahogany table, were charts of the North Atlantic and the Western Approaches to

66

Britain. The current position, as estimated, of the *Laurentia* was marked with a neatly pencilled cross. This position was brought up to date each four hours. 'There will be no difficulty,' the Admiral said, another firm statement that brooked no argument. 'I am sure we can reply upon Eppler.' Suddenly he laughed. 'Not upon Eppler alone!'

One of the officers present, von Schrader, lifted an eyebrow. 'Not, Admiral?'

The Admiral jabbed at the chart. 'We have been able to pinpoint the ship with very great accuracy. I ask, why? No, no, I shall myself answer. It is because we have picked up so many British signals, some in their naval cypher, some in plain language. Also, we know that no warship escort is being provided until the liner reaches *there*.' He laid the tip of a pair of divides on a spot a little to the west of Cape Clear in the south of Ireland. 'The British are being stupid, I think. Or perhaps clever. Too clever for their own good.'

'Perhaps there is a trap, some –'

'No, no. Or perhaps yes, but not the sort of trap I think you have in mind, von Schrader. Always when dealing with the man Churchill one is bound to suspect a trap, an intrigue, something Machiavellian. Churchill is a man of twisted mind . . . the flamboyant cigar, the baby face, so chubby with smiles, mendacious smiles . . . also, remember he is half-American. He is said much to regret his mother's country not coming to his aid in the war. It has become a personal matter. Do you understand, von Schrader?'

'Perhaps.'

Von Schrader left the meeting very thoughtfully. The Admiral's meaning had been clear enough. In his view Mr Churchill, First Lord of the British Admiralty, was setting the scene for the sinking of the *Laurentia*, the act that so many people on both sides of the Atlantic but not in Germany believed would draw the United States into the war.

6

PATRICK Haggerty pushed aside a sheaf of documents that he had been studying in his state-room, removed his spectacles and rubbed at his eyes.

'Tired, dear?' his wife asked.

'Yes.'

'Why not leave it?'

He answered impatiently. 'I can't leave it, Lois. I have to have all the angles covered.'

'To block Mr Churchill?'

'I didn't say that.' Haggerty got up from his chair, crossed the state-room towards the port. The sea was restless still. The spray spattered the glass of the port from time to time. The ends of the curtains, their middles held by a tie-back, swayed outwards as the liner rolled to starboard. A pencil moved across the table-top and fell to the deck. This sort of weather, Haggerty had gathered in conversation at the Captain's table in the saloon, was not propitious for the German U-boats. They would remain submerged. Long may it continue, Haggerty thought. Attack would play right into the hands of those in his own country who wished to push the United States into the war, to say nothing of those in Britain with the same objective. But Haggerty's worry was that President Wilson's hand would be forced somehow or other and never mind a safe arrival in Liverpool of the *Laurentia*. The British were wily and America had its hotheads in plenty. America, unfortunately in Haggerty's view, was or had been a fighting nation. They had beaten the British in the War of Independence more than a century before; more recently north had fought south in the Civil War. And over the years of building themselves into a nation, their pioneers moving west had fought nature to establish great communities through much hardship, the covered wagons rolling inexorably from the old states to found the new. And they had fought the Indians with immense courage. The US Cavalry had established a world-wide reputation. It was not so long since General Custer's last stand at Little Big Horn. There were those in America who wanted to show their mettle once again.

Patrick Haggerty's private view, never in fact uttered, was that if America wished to fight she should come in on the side of the Germans.

There were very many people of German extraction in the United States, the descendants of incoming Germans years ago, men who had emigrated in their thousands as had the Irish. There was nothing special to United States citizens about the high and mighty British Empire and its dominance over a quarter of the world's population.

Lois was saying something.

'What was that, dear?'

'Oh, nothing really. I was just saying . . . about that woman. Livia Costello. And King George.'

'Just showed her feelings, that's all.'

'She shouldn't have done. I thought it was appalling. Such insulting manners in a British ship.'

'No need to harp on it, Lois.' This wasn't the first time his wife had said something similar. She'd been really upset about the incident. He could see her point a little way – as he'd thought at the time, it gave the British a handle to lambast Americans. Not that any comments had been passed in his hearing: the British were like that, all diplomatic smiles and charm to your face, and pull you to pieces amongst themselves after. Haggerty did not like the British one little bit.

He said now, 'I'm going out on deck. Coming?'

Lois Haggerty shook her head: she was, as usual, knitting. The grandson's birthday would be soon after the *Laurentia*'s arrival in Liverpool and she wanted to put the little woolly garment in the post as soon as she got to London. Along with a nice fat cheque, of course, to be saved against the child's future. But she had always thought something personal should go with a money gift. She said, biting off a strand of wool, 'You go, Patrick. Fresh air. You've stuffed down below long enough.'

He nodded and went out into the alleyway. He climbed the big main stairway leading from the foyer, up towards the boat deck. He went out on the windward side and met the gale. His hair blew around; it was cold and wet but the wind, he guessed, was coming from Ireland – from the east anyway.

He breathed deep, began to imagine the distinctive smell of Ireland, the turf burning in the fires of what had been his forebears' homeland, green and lush, with purple mountains and great blue loughs beneath ever-changing skies. He could see again, as he had seen on that visit with Lois some years before, the cleanly whitewashed cottages under their roofs of thatch.

It went deep with Patrick Haggerty.

Years before, his maternal grandfather, by name Hannibal O'Hara, had been one of the so-called 'Rebels of 48', a group of Irish exiles who had assembled in Paris to plan a rising in Munster against the English.

When the 'Phoenix Conspiracy', as the Munster rising was known, had failed, Hannibal O'Hara had crossed the Atlantic to America and had become one of the founding fathers of the Fenian movement whose objective had been to establish an independent Republic of Ireland; the Fenians had found many a follower among those who had left Ireland after the failure of the potato crop and the resulting famine that had killed so many of those who had remained in their own land. Feelings were immensely bitter against the English absentee landlords who had done nothing for their tenants. The Fenians in those days had had grandiose plans, and their numbers had swelled after the Civil War that had cast adrift large numbers of Irishmen with a fighting spirit that longed for further adventure: even an invasion of Canada had been planned and to a small and limited extent carried out.

Parick Haggerty had memories of Hannibal O'Hara in his extreme old age. Grandfather O'Hara had lost no opportunity of indoctrinating the boy in the cause of Ireland and the grand concept of Ourselves Alone, or Sinn Fein. Young Patrick had listened to stories of how the patriots had suborned the English soldiers serving at the Curragh and other English military stations in Ireland. The doctrine of a desirable war against the Saxon was preached to him and he had grown up with the memories of it. A cousin, another grandson of Hannibal O'Hara, had become active in forming new and more vigorous Fenian societies, because the old movement had failed to spread far in Ireland, chiefly as the result of the Catholic priesthood setting its face against violence so that the peasantry, the great mass of the Irish people, had held aloof.

The two main new factions had been the Clan-na-Gael and the United Irish Brotherhood. Both were directed from America; from America killings of the English in Ireland were organized, as were ambushes of English soldiers. Patrick Haggerty had supported these movements with money, paid over in cash. And secretly. Not even Lois knew of this; she would not have supported him had she known.

Haggerty's cousin did his work for him. The relationship was not known. For the sake of his career, Patrick Haggerty kept his hands clean. In public. And never could he or would he voice his innermost wish that President Wilson might one day declare for Germany. That would be far from popular with the great majority. In Ireland a man called Sir Roger Casement was organizing the supply of German arms to disaffected Irishmen for use when the time was right against the English. That had become known through various clandestine sources. Most of those who knew about it in America condemned it.

Patrick Haggerty, his tall frame bent against the wind, walked for'ard and stared through big windows looking out over the fore hatch and the fo'c'sle. The glass was misted with salt spray; the very air was salty. He

70

could taste it on his lips. The *Laurentia* butted through the seas towards Great Britain, bringing with her a British hope: Patrick Haggerty, the chief US negotiator for the loan which was to be used to buy arms and munitions of war, the sinews that Britain, running out of money and shells and guns, ships and aeroplanes and men, needed so desperately.

'Much depends on this man Haggerty.'

Sandringham: King George's study on a fine, clear day when His Majesty, weary of London's smoke, would have wished nothing better than to be free to tramp around his Norfolk estate, acting, as he had once described his role when in retreat at Sandringham, the simple country squire.

Not today.

Mr Asquith had sought and had been granted an audience: the King did not refuse his Prime Minister. But Mr Asquith had brought his First Lord of the Admiralty with him. And Mr Churchill had been accompanied by the First Sea Lord, Admiral of the Fleet Lord Fisher, that unruly man.

It was Fisher who had spoken. The First Sea Lord's tone had been pugnacious and derogatory. He went on, 'Finance is not my province, sir. I am merely a seaman.' This was a statement that the King knew to be untrue; Fisher was anything but a mere seaman. He was an intriguer, and a hothead who had inflamed half the Navy against himself by his dictatorial manner and his utter ruthlessness.

'Then speak as a seaman,' the King suggested, tongue in cheek. 'You have your audience.'

'Thank you, sir.' Fisher's red face went a deeper shade as he smacked a fist into his palm and spoke with his usual forcefulness. 'We need more ships! Our yards are working to capacity and yet we cannot produce ships fast enough! We have lost cruisers, TBDs, minelayers, mine-sweepers. We have an empire to police along extended sea lanes. If America won't see fit to come into the war, then at least they'll accept money to build ships for us. That is, if we *have* the money. They're a money-minded nation, sir!'

The King said mildly, 'But a friendly one.'

'Friendly!' Fisher spat the words out, his lips twisting in a sneer. 'Only when money is forthcoming, sir! And Asquith says we have no money left!'

'An exaggeration,' Mr Asquith said. 'Though it's true enough the coffers are running out. An American loan would –'

'A loan, Prime Minister, to be used to buy war materials from the lender! A wonderful deal for them! Financiers are all sharks! Their machinations are above my head but below my sense of – of *gentlemanliness*. If I were asked –'

Mr Asquith held up a hand: Fisher grated upon him. The King took the opportunity to turn to the First Lord. 'Mr Churchill, you're well acquainted with America. Do you know anything of Mr Haggerty?'

Mr Churchill removed his cigar from his lips and pouted thoughtfully as he blew smoke. The cigar was one of his own: when offered one by His Majesty he had asked politely to be excused. He had, he said, his own supply sent to him from Havana. Now, he said, 'I know nothing of Mr Haggerty, sir, beyond two plain facts: he is an eminent banker, well thought of by Washington and by the President. And that he is of Irish extraction – which is obvious, of course. Patrick Haggerty. I –'

'I don't trust *any* damn Irishman!' Lord Fisher announced. 'This one will have something up his sleeve I don't doubt for an instant!'

'What are you suggesting, Lord Fisher?'

'Why, sir, that the damn loan won't be forthcoming!'

'Which,' Mr Churchill put in quickly to the King, 'is why we have come to see you, sir. You spoke of my acquaintance with the United States. It as, as you know, sir, a very close acquaintance.' Winston Spencer Churchill's mother had been Jennie Jerome from New York; his maternal, and American, grandfather had been a wealthy financier – Mr Churchill was related to the Vanderbilts. He had much time for the United States and knew the country intimately. Now his tone become sonorous as he launched himself into a speech. King George stirred restlessly after a while: a foot had gone to sleep. He shook it. The King's grandmother, Queen Victoria, had once complained of her own Prime Minister, Mr Gladstone, that he tended to address her as though she were a public meeting. Mr Churchill's voice was neither harsh nor hectoring; nor was it overloud. But it was a voice that knew it spoke well and knew that it was appreciated by its producer. Mr Churchill had much to say in rolling phrases about the mutual respect between Great Britain and the United States, about the fact that they each spoke the same language, that so very many American citizens were of English stock. That there had been a great deal of intermarrying.

That the Americans, though they might not always admit it, had a very great feeling of veneration for the British Crown and the almost mystical concept of kingship. Or anyway, very many of them had.

The King said, 'H'm.'

'Your Majesty, if I may say so, there is in that great land of America a good deal of respect and affection for yourself and your family. I believe this can be put to good use in a very relevant way. The American Ambassador-to-be, Mr Grant, is known to be well disposed towards us. Mr Haggerty is in that respect a largely unknown quantity. I believe his heart has to be captured. Therefore I suggest an invitation to Buckingham Palace together with Mr Ambassador Grant would be a most significant and much appreciated gesture –'

'Enough to ensure the loan? I think you overrate my power of attraction for the Americans, Mr Churchill!'

'With respect, sir, I do not agree. The King of England, the King-Emperor . . . there is jealousy, there is opposition to the concept of the British Empire I don't deny, since it is undeniable. But the hearts of the American people are a different story.' Mr Churchill paused and puffed for a moment at his cigar. The King found it remarkable that Mr Churchill should have been able to silence the irascible and forthright Lord Fisher. Mr Churchill went on, 'If the loan should seem to be unforthcoming during what are certain to be lengthy discussions with the Prime Minister and the Treasury, then I would further suggest this: that you personally, as monarch, might make an appeal to the people of the United States, to be published in the American newspapers – a matter which I think I can promise would be achieved.'

'For the loan, Mr Churchill?'

'Perhaps not for the loan only, sir. For the United States to enter the war – and bring confusion and alarm to the Kaiser!'

'That is a very large suggestion, Mr Churchill.'

Mr Churchill inclined his head. 'Indeed it is, sir. But I believe very firmly that if we are to win this war, if we are to survive as a free nation, then the United States must be brought into the war. Soon we shall find ourselves quite unable to continue without their active participation against Germany and its mighty army.'

Soon after this His Majesty brought the audience to an end. Mr Churchill, he found, was a most remarkable man. For a politician, for a Cabinet Minister of the first rank, he was at forty young. His personality and his tongue had dominated the discussion; Mr Asquith had scarcely uttered. Even more extraordinary, Fisher had mostly held his tongue though it had been obvious the First Sea Lord had been consumed by some inner fire. As King George walked with the sailor and the two members of his government to their motor-car he made a comment.

'The *Laurentia*, Mr Churchill. I understand she is currently on passage from New York to Liverpool.'

'Yes, sir.'

'With Americans aboard in quite large numbers.'

'Yes, sir.'

The King spoke thoughtfully, almost in an aside so that the words were heard with difficulty. 'Suppose the Germans should sink the *Laurentia* . . . with American passengers aboard?'

'A rhetorical question, sir. We have, after all, a navy still in being.' Mr

Churchill caught Lord Fisher's eye. No more was said. The motor-car took the three men to the railway station at Wolferton, where the special train was waiting to take them back to London. Taking his leave of Mr Asquith in Downing Street, Lord Fisher announced his intention of walking across Horse Guards Parade to the Admiralty.

He put a friendly hand on Mr Churchill's shoulder. 'Come with me, Winston,' he said. 'We have things to talk about now.'

'Eustace!'

'Yes, mama?'

Lady Barlow rose to her feet. 'We shall leave the saloon. That dreadful man has come in. Fielding I believe his name is.'

'It's very comfortable here, mama. I –'

'Do as you're told, Eustace.'

'Yes, dearest mama.' The tone was a little peeved. 'Where shall we go? It's awf'lly cold and wet outside –'

'We shall go anywhere where that man is *not*,' Lady Barlow stated and went past Leon Fielding with her nose in the air. The singer stood just inside the after door, looking about himself with an air of bewilderment. Other passengers in the lounge turned their backs. All except one: the American, Elmer Houston Pousty, Quaker about to enlist as a medical corpsman.

He had heard the story, much embellished by the time it had reached him. He was no believer in the casting of stones and knew that boys could be fibbers.

He went across.

'Looking for someone, Mr Fielding?'

Fielding looked at first startled, then grateful 'Oh, how very kind of you, Mr – ?'

'Pousty.'

'Oh, yes. Yes, I am. It's Ming.'

'Ming?'

'Yes, my little dog.' Fielding hadn't got his perambulator with him. Pousty had heard all about that as well; no one who looked and acted like Leon Fielding could hope for any degree of anonymity aboard a ship, however large.

'I guess you didn't bring her with you, Mr Fielding. The little dog's safe enough, back in New York.'

'Oh no, I would never have left her. Never. I really don't know what can have happened. It's so easy to fall overboard, and I doubt if the Captain would stop the ship.' Fielding looked anxiously up at the American. 'Do you think he would?'

'Well, now, who's to say? I tell you what: let's walk around and look. How's that?'

'It's terribly good of you.'

Pousty took hold of Fielding's arm and together, slowly, they left the lounge. Fielding was somewhat unsteady on his feet, and not just because of the lurch of the deck. He was shaking, too, and muttering to himself, something Pousty couldn't catch. He was obviously in a pretty bad way, the young American thought, something had touched his mind. It was clear enough what that something was. As they meandered aft along the enclosed deck running alongside the lounge, Pousty tried to get the singer to talk coherently. It seemed that the ship's doctor had called upon him in his cabin, where the Staff Captain had advised him to remain for the time being. Dr Fellowes had had an aloof, cold manner and had been disdainful. He had prescribed a bromide and this had been brought by a nursing sister. It had done no good and then Fielding had remembered Ming, whom he insisted again was aboard the liner and had at all costs to be found.

So he had left his cabin to look.

Pousty recognized that Fielding's mind had become unhinged; more unhinged than before. He had no idea what was to be done about it. It hadn't sounded as though the doctor had been of much help. They continued to walk the deck, up and back again while the wind battered at the glass screens. Pousty was aware of people peering through from the first-class lounge, their expressions in some cases tarring him with Fielding's brush. Birds of a feather – so what? Elmer Pousty's aim in life was to do a little good when the opportunity came his way. After a while he managed to talk Fielding into going back to his cabin.

Once again the cabin was searched for Ming. Just in case. The perambulator, pushed into a corner, looked somehow pathetic. Pousty grinned at his own thoughts: if he wasn't careful he'd start believing the dog really was on board somewhere.

Walking, after his visitors had left, in the grounds of Sandringham Hall, His Majesty reflected gloomily on the war and what it was doing to everyone's lives and to his empire. What, though this had to be considered a minor matter, it was doing to Sandringham. There was a shortage of gardeners for one thing. So many had volunteered to fight and were now somewhere in France or on the high seas keeping the White Ensign flying over troubled waters. Weeds grew in the gravelled paths.

Sighing, the King bent and uprooted some tufts of spiky grass and some dandelions from a flower-bed.

He thought about Mr Churchill.

A good fellow, of course, but full of stupid notions. Far from always right as the man himself seemed to believe. There was this wretched Dardanelles campaign, with soldiers, largely from New Zealand and Australia, very stout fellows, dying in their hundreds. Ships, both naval and merchant, being lost – losses that could be ill afforded, each sinking weakening the sea links with the empire, weakening the homeland's ability to survive possible starvation. The Dardanelles had been Mr Churchill's idea from the start, forced through against a good deal of opposition in Cabinet and in the House. Often a foolish man; and nothing more foolish than to suggest that he, the King of England, Emperor of India, should go as it were cap in hand to beg salvation from the President of the United States.

'Bloody fool,' the King muttered to himself. He prodded with his walking-stick at yet another weed. If only politicians could be dealt with as easily as weeds. Take Asquith: the man was facing difficulties in the House both from the Conservative opposition and from his own Liberals. In the King's view, he was going to lose his party's support; and who was to succeed him? Not Lloyd George it was to be hoped.

King George disliked politicians: at heart he was what Fisher had said of himself: a simple sailor, brought up to the sea from the time he had joined the *Britannia* as a cadet with no privileges of royalty allowed. His father, at that time Prince of Wales, had seen to that. The future King had suffered all the hardships of his fellows, had been chased by the seamanship and gunnery instructors, horny-handed petty officers, with just as much ferocity. He had been taught to respect his term lieutenant as much as he respected his grandmother Queen Victoria; he had been equally afraid of them both in their different ways. The Navy had made him a man as well as a prince, later to be King.

Fisher, now. That man was in some ways an enigma and was not to be trusted. He had a quick mind, which King George admitted with honesty he had not. But it was not just a quick mind; it was a flashy one. And it was not consistent. Fisher could say one thing one minute, something else the next. He was hard to catch up with. And today there had been some further quality, hard to pinpoint, but the King believed Fisher was reaching the end of his tether, that the conduct of the war at sea as First Sea Lord was becoming too great a strain. The King believed this and feared it too. A man under too great a strain was not fitted to be at the head of the Navy either in peace or war. Already the best of the Navy's past heads had gone: Prince Louis of Battenberg, Admiral of the Fleet and First Sea Lord until popular opinion had linked him too close to his German origins and had forced him out of the office he had filled with so much distinction and had left Lord Fisher in control, to the King's dismay. King George was not, could not be, unaware of feelings in the country in regard to his own German relations: after all, the Kaiser was his first cousin. There was so much common blood, royal blood on both sides of the fence. But the King had overcome that; there could be no question of disloyalty on the part of the King of England and of the dominions beyond the seas. Also, the King, although his influence on the conduct of affairs was great and he was listened to with genuine respect, was a convinced and determined constitutional monarch. He had, and knew he had, no direct executive authority such as was possessed by the First Sea Lord.

Lord Fisher, in control at the Admiralty under Mr Churchill, in control of the fate of the *Laurentia*, now closing the sea distances towards England. All those passengers, all those seamen. The King was well aware of the German proclamation published in the United States. The sinking of the passenger liner didn't bear thinking of. He recalled what he had said when the visitors from London had left: a wonderment as to what would happen if the liner should be sunk.

He had been aware of a look passing between Mr Churchill and Lord Fisher. Intriguers both of them. The King's heart missed a beat when he thought that possibly a careless word might have started some plot going in those two minds.

But surely not! Surely not!

Yet similar things had happened in the past. The British Empire had not been won by wholly clean hands.

'His Majesty,' Fisher said as he and Mr Churchill walked in the May sunshine across the Horse Guards, swinging their walking-sticks and from time to time lifting their tall hats to a lady bowing from an open carriage proceeding between the Mall and Birdcage Walk, 'His Majesty didn't believe the half of it and *damned* if I did either! It was no more than *tomfoolery*! You'll never bring in America that way, Winston. Believe me, I know! We need positive action, damned if we don't! *Fast*, too.'

'Go on,' Churchill said.

'I think you know what I'm getting at, Winston. You heard what the King said as we were leaving.'

'A chance remark, no more than that.' Mr Churchill waved his cigar. 'The monarch's been under a good deal of strain, as have we all.' He said again, 'A chance remark, such as anyone might make. Indeed, we've all been wondering it: what *would* happen if the *Laurentia* was to be sunk? H'm?'

'America would come into the war, of course!'

'Not necessarily, Jacky. Not necessarily. I tell you one thing that

77

would certainly happen: the Kaiser would bring coals of fire down upon his own head. There would be utter revulsion . . . condemnation from the whole civilized world. And I can't bring myself to believe that the Germans would risk that, Jacky.'

'I don't believe they'll attack the *Laurentia*, certainly, but nevertheless, they're nothing but *barbarians*!'

'It would certainly take a barbarian to sink the *Laurentia* with so many women and children aboard.' Churchill, who had spoken gravely, looked sideways at the First Sea Lord. Fisher's face was alight with some fever, some almost devilish quality giving a half-mad blaze to his eyes. Often of late Mr Churchill had noted the way in which the old Admiral – Fisher was seventy-four years of age – had become so angry, so impatient with anyone who tried to baulk him that his whole body seemed to swell and blood rushed to his face as though he were about to have an apoplectic fit. The signs were not good. Mr Churchill, little more than half Fisher's age, put a hand on his shoulder and again spoke gravely. 'No mad schemes, Jackie. I don't believe for one moment you would consider seriously . . . leaving women and children to the *chance* that they might be sunk by those barbarians you spoke of. The Fleet must be in all respects and at all times ready with preventative measures. And if these should fail, then ready with succour. The country will expect no less.' He paused. 'I shall expect no less.'

'You're singing a different tune today, Winston! Your remark only a day or so ago! You referred to the hand of providence when speaking of the *Laurentia*!'

'Ah, yes. But if it should *happen* that the *Laurentia* was attacked – a very different kettle of fish, I think. We must be seen to ensure, however, that she is *not* attacked.'

Fisher didn't comment further. But through his mind was running a thought that Winston was a time-server and at times a back-tracker – and a man whose mind was extremely difficult to penetrate and follow. Also through Fisher's mind there was running a scenario. A scenario in which a great national catastrophe was put to use, was put to salvation, a scenario in which President Wilson's hand was forced, and at the same time the German Emperor's hands were seen by the world to be dripping with the blood of the innocent.

Two birds with one stone.

Fisher's mind was itself filled with blood. He saw the one thing through that mist of blood: salvation for the British Empire. He did not see in his mind's single-sight eye the horror, the escaping steam after the explosion, the great ship listing and helpless, the men and women and children sliding across the heeled decks, being cast into the cold sea,

78

drowning as the lifeboats, hastily lowered from the canted falls, tipped their human cargoes out.

Not seeing that, the scene made sense. Fisher believed Winston Churchill had in some measure divined his thoughts to have spoken so solemnly against them. That was a pity. He, Fisher, had supported Winston Churchill in the Dardanelles campaign. As a man of honour, Churchill could scarcely fail now to return support with support.

On the bridge of the *Laurentia*, now four days' steaming from her landfall off the southern coast of Ireland, Captain Pacey saw all too clearly what Lord Fisher had failed to see. Pacey had been seeing it all along. His imagination had brought it all before him constantly. It was almost as though he had had a premonition, not unlike that voice, years ago in that windjammer, that had finally convinced Testament Thomas that he should steer his ship in the required direction. Every turn of the *Laurentia*'s thundering screws brought the vision closer, the vision of his command becoming a holocaust.

The Admiralty, in Pacey's view, was being complacent. He had been given no orders in New York other than his destination and his expected time of arrival. No orders had reached him on passage; there had been that signal reporting ahead the possible presence of U-boats as he neared the Irish coast. No advice at all as to alternative routes, safe routes – or routes as safe as they could be in time of war. No word as to a heavier escort, which he had requested back in New York.

Just a cruiser to be waiting westwards of Cape Clear.

Not enough in Pacey's view. Did those at home in the seats of naval power not realize what was at stake? Were they prepared to risk women and children? To any seaman, be he Royal Navy or Merchant Service, women and children afloat raised a very special care. Always they came first. They were utterly dependent on the ship's company. Now, their safety should be the first consideration of those ashore who could do something to help those at sea.

Too much complacency: the Germans – so Pacey believed would be the view of the Admiralty – would never attack a passenger liner.

But what if the Germans had received information about the *Laurentia*'s cargo of war materials?

Pacey, walking the bridge deep in thought, came to a decision. He went into the wheelhouse, out for a while from the tear and roar of the wind and the damp of the flung spray, and used the telephone to call the Staff Captain.

'Morgan, those two Germans. They were not responsive before, I know. But I'd like another go at them.'

* * *

Frederick Jones had been very badly shaken. The ship's Purser had spoken of the New York Police. They wanted to know where Maggie was. She was, in fact, in several places, none of them mentionable. So Mr Jones said desperately, 'I assume she's at the apartment.'

'It appears she is not, Mr Jones.' Purser Matthews glanced at the clock on the bulkhead of his private office: he had an appointment – one he did not wish to miss.

'Ha . . . has anything happened to her?'

'The cable didn't say. But the fact is she seems to have disappeared. Have you no suggestions, Mr Jones, something that would help the police with their enquiries?' Matthews was finding the man evasive; he suspected more behind this than had been apparent in the bare wireless message from New York.

Mr Jones put out the tip of his tongue and licked at his lips. They had gone very dry. He had to be very, very careful. He had to put things off as long as possible, that was the first thing. He said cautiously, 'She does lead her own life, you know. I don't keep her on a leash.'

Matthews leaned back in his chair and said with studied indifference, 'Can you elaborate, Mr Jones?'

Mr Jones felt sudden anger. 'Look,' he said in a loud voice, 'you're not the police, are you? I don't have to be interrogated, you know.'

'No, no – I'm sorry if I gave that impression. I didn't mean to. It's just a case of trying to help the police. And you. And Mrs Jones. That's all.'

'Well, you needn't go on trying,' Mr Jones said ungraciously. 'I've told you all I know – and the news has been most upsetting,' he added a little late. He was a poor actor even when his neck was at stake. 'If I knew anything of her movements, of course I'd tell you.'

He didn't even mention Maggie's sister in Arlington, not knowing that she had already been in touch with the police. He wanted breathing space, wanted to string it out as long as he could, so that he could disembark in Liverpool and get lost before any nets closed in. After leaving the Purser's office, however, he had another attack of fright: later, it might look bad that he hadn't mentioned the sister. There were also Maggie's lovers, who might be brought out into the light of day, who could tell?

That would go against him, too. The jealous husband, who had kept quiet about a possibly incriminating factor.

Having rid himself of Mr Jones, Purser Matthews made his way to Livia Costello's cabin and knocked, after casting glances up and down the alleyway. All clear.

He was admitted and the door was shut behind him. The actress, he found, was a little tight and there was a strong aroma of gin. As usual.

* * *

In the second-class bar Elizabeth Kent and John Holmes, both from Annapolis, sat over more gin. Small ones: John Holmes was not flush with money. He and Elizabeth had kept contact since embarkation: strangers in a strange world, there was companionship in the fact of their Annapolis homes. They talked now like old friends: they even found they had an acquaintance or two in common, and there was the town itself to talk about. John had told Elizabeth he aimed to join the British Navy as a seaman if they would have him.

'You have any seamanship experience?' she asked.

'Some,' he said, but didn't sound too sure.

'That's one thing I guess they'll ask.'

'Yes,' he said. He added, 'I've messed about, you know the sort of thing. Boats. Out in the bay.'

'Your family have a yacht?'

He nodded. 'Sure, a yacht. My dad and I . . . we used to sail whenever he could spare the time.' Already he was thinking of Annapolis as being in the past.

'Should help, maybe.' Elizabeth took a sip of her gin. She didn't believe John Holmes was used to gin. He didn't seem to be enjoying it. She asked, 'Have you any family still in Britain?'

He spoke of his grandmother, who was looking forward to seeing him again. She was pretty old, he said.

She had already told him about the sick father she was crossing the Atlantic to see. Now she spoke of him again, hoped she would get there in time.

'That bad?'

'Yes, I'm afraid so.'

'I'm sorry. He'll be worrying, I suppose.'

'About me? Yes, I expect he will. That proclamation. It's bound to be known in Britain by this time.'

He said more or less what he'd said to her when they'd first met on the train up to New York. 'He needn't worry. We're going to be OK. The Captain spoke of an escort meeting us soon as we're close to the danger area. You can rely on the British Navy. You can –' He broke off, looking confused and embarrassed. He suggested another gin but she said no, she'd had enough. She had the idea he'd been going to say, she could rely on him too. His face was red and he'd edged a little closer to her on the sofa they were sitting on. Maybe it was the gin, maybe it wasn't, but she had a further idea and it was that he was beginning to think of himself as a possible beau if that was the word. If so, it was laughable, not that she would dream of hurting him by laughing. He wasn't much more than a kid, though a kid who would grow up fast if he got into the British Navy. She was twenty-five and in love with Jonas Gorman, trainee

81

attorney in Annapolis, Maryland. He would be worrying, too: he was very unsure of himself when it came to Elizabeth Kent and she was well aware of it.

They were all worrying, on both sides of the Atlantic. The word of the German proclamation had gone to Britain. So had word of the individual telegrams sent anonymously by way of dire warning. John Holmes's grandmother in Worthing had by no means lost her senses in old age and she had read and was reading the newspapers keenly through a magnifying glass, mouthing the words to herself as she did so.

Nothing must happen to John. But he would never be safe again if he joined the Navy. It wasn't just the dangers threatening the *Laurentia*. It would be a continuing anxiety. His parents should never have let him come. Time enough if America should join the war, which they wouldn't. Old Mrs Holmes had a split mind on that – or had, until she'd been told John was coming over. Had he remained, he would have been safe so long as the United States maintained their neutrality. On the other hand, Mrs Holmes thought President Wilson pusillanimous. It was his *duty* to stand by his own kind.

Mrs Holmes had made all sort of plans when at first she'd heard of John's voyage. He would of course come and see her; Milly her maid could cope with the extra work. Mrs Holmes had thought back to the old days, years ago when the family had been all together in England. Often little Johnny had stayed with her. She had taken charge of him when the other children were being born, having him to herself for two or three weeks, and they'd done so many happy things together, going for walks, buying him ice-cream wafers, taking him to the pantomime on two occasions and once to London to Madame Tussaud's and the zoological gardens, a very tiring day for granny, but she hadn't minded. He had always been a very good boy, no trouble at all, and thoughtful for others. Of course, she couldn't do all that now. But she had seen to it that his room was ready for him whenever he should turn up. They could sit and talk and he would give her first-hand news of the family. She would give him good, sustaining meals, not the sort of pap she understood they ate in America, clam chowder and blueberry pie, and Long Island prawns, no real goodness. He would need feeding up before presenting himself to the naval medical officers.

Then the letter had come, reaching her only the day after the *Laurentia* had sailed from New York: John would not be staying with her, anyway not at first. He wanted to be handy for the naval recruiting people. Of course he would come and see her just as soon as he could, when he got leave.

She had told Milly at once. Milly had been fond of the boy too and was disappointed.

'Oh'm, that's a shame, such a shame. But you know what boys are, they don't think.'

Mrs Holmes would have no criticism of her grandson. 'Nonsense, Milly. Master John's quite right. And he *will* come, I know he will.'

'Yes'm. Oh, I do hope he'll be safe in that there liner'm.' Milly had clasped her hands and was looking anguished.

'He'll be in good hands, Milly.'

'Oh, yes'm, but them Germans, they do get up to some dreadful things! It said in the papers, they've been crucifying little babies on barn doors, in Belgium, and –'

'Oh, nonsense, Milly –'

'And that Kaiser, he drinks a pint of blood every day for breakfast –'

Old Mrs Holmes snorted. 'Really, Milly! Can you imagine the cousin of our dear King drinking blood for breakfast? Do be your age! Or stop reading *those* kinds of newspapers.'

'Yes'm.'

Milly had left the room, cap and apron trailing clouds of doom. Mrs Holmes looked after her: Milly was getting no younger either. They were growing old together. It was a shame that they should have to voyage down their last years wrapped in personal anxieties, and shortages, and bad news every day in the newspapers. The army was making no progress at all on the Western Front and even the Commander-in-Chief, Sir John French, was alternating between confidence and a terrible depression, so the rumours went. And there was the most dreadful slaughter in the Dardanelles, thanks to Mr Churchill and Admiral Fisher.

Mrs Holmes sat at her window and worried about Johnny.

In Addenbrooke's Hospital in Cambridge Elizabeth Kent's father lay as weak as a kitten, scarcely able to lift a hand. He shook all over. The doctors had diagnosed what they called a slow decline, nothing specific.

After the specialist's rounds there was conferring.

'The man Kent,' the doctor said.

'Yes, sir?'

'Not long to go. Nothing we can do, I fear.' The medical specialist paused, tugging at the lapels of his black morning coat. 'There's a daughter, am I right?'

'Yes, sir,' the registrar said. 'Coming over on the *Laurentia* from New York.'

'When's she due in?'

'The eighth, sir. Saturday.'

'The girl had better hurry,' the specialist said, looking at his watch. He had a round of golf to play and was late already. 'Her arrival just might rally him.'

In New York Livia Costello's husband had lost no time: another woman's bed had beckoned. At breakfast he read the *New York Times*. There were suggestions that the Germans might be lying in wait for the *Laurentia*.

The woman asked, 'You worried? About Livia?'

Costello smiled. 'A sinking might work out a few problems. No bloody lousy alimony!'

'That's hard.'

Costello made a coarse remark and the woman smiled.

7

Captain Pacey had gone below to the cells to interview the two Germans. Their names were Gunther Prien and Rolf Freitag. They were still polite but uncooperative: they smiled and said nothing. They stuck to their story: they had stayed aboard too long and the ship had sailed.

Pacey probed as best he could. He did not intend to mention the arms cargo that he was carrying in his fore hold adjacent to the bulkhead of Number One boiler room and concealed on the lower orlop deck. But his questions were designed to discover what if anything the Germans knew about this lethal cargo.

Captain Pacey was no interrogator, no barrister aiming pointed questions in a court of law. His questions brought no answers; just the smiles and shrugs.

He left the cell and spoke to his Chief Officer. 'Harsher measures, Mr Arkwright. You'll have them removed to the orlop deck under guard. Go with them yourself. I want to know what their reactions are when you tell them they'll be left there until we dock in Liverpool.'

The order was carried out immediately. Later the Chief Officer reported that he had seen fear in the Germans' faces.

'Too close to an explosion if there's an attack,' Pacey said. 'You believe they knew?'

'I wouldn't say they knew just where the explosives were stowed, sir. But I think they know there's some aboard, and they'd guessed what was in your mind when you had them taken below –'

'And they put two and two together, realized I was putting them at first risk?'

'If there should be an attack, sir, yes.'

Pacey nodded. 'Where are they now, Mr Arkwright?'

'Still below, sir.'

'Very well. Have them brought up. Back to the cells.'

Pacey believed he had got something. Should he send a warning message to the Admiralty? If he did, it would have to go out either in plain language or in the international code which would be immediately readable in Berlin when the German monitoring services picked up the transmission from the *Laurentia*. Perhaps little would be gained. And much could be lost: any such signal would be likely to tell the Germans that the *Laurentia* was carrying what, in the current circumstances of America's neutrality, was strictly contraband. Pacey's name would not be popular in Washington thereafter, or with the Line's management. Or with Whitehall. On the other hand to send a warning that he suspected chicanery on the part of the Germans just might cause them to think again, to call off an attack if such was planned. Just might.

Or it might go the other way. It might give them the legitimate excuse. If only the *Laurentia* had been equipped with the naval codes and cyphers, readable only by those with the relevant decoding and decyphering tables.

But she had not. The Admiralty was to be blamed for that omission.

Pacey weighed it up, once again walking the bridge, trying to clear his mind.

In the end he made no signal. In all truth he had not enough to go on, though he was certain in his own mind that the Germans knew of the presence of the war cargo and could very well have alerted their High Command through the New York spy network before the ship had sailed. But why had they stayed aboard? There was no answer to that yet except that they may have been telling the truth originally when they'd said they hadn't made it down the last gangway in time. . . .

At dinner that night in the first-class saloon, attended by the Captain, General de Gard became forthright. He said, 'President Wilson is pro-German. That is the view of my country.'

It was something of a bombshell. Senator Melvin Manderton reacted strongly. 'That's a damnable thing to say, General. President Wilson is pro no one of the belligerents. He is very strictly neutral.'

De Gard was not to be deflected: he had a stubborn face, long and narrow, with a thin mouth beneath the moustache. 'Your President detests the French and British Empires. He is determined to see them crumble. One day he will be sorry, and by then it will be too late.'

'Now listen here,' Manderton said, leaning across the table and brandishing a fork. 'I –'

'It will be too late . . . when the German hordes, victorious in Europe, are clamouring at the doors of the White House. I say this, and I know it to be true.'

Pacey was about to do what he could to bring the talk to a stop when he felt the hand of Henry Sayers Grant touch the sleeve of his mess jacket. 'Your pardon, Captain,' Grant said in an aside. Then he addressed General de Gard. 'I understand your feelings, General. Your country is in the thick of it. You have Germans clamouring at your gates – I appreciate this, believe me. You have lost so many of your young men.

We in America grieve that such should be so. Also, there are many in America who would agree with you that matters should not be left until it's too late – we take that point, many of us.' He looked directly at Senator Manderton, who looked down at the tablecloth. 'I think you and Great Britain must be patient for a while longer. You should remember that we in America are to a very large extent isolated from Europe by virtue of the fact we are on the other side of a very wide ocean. We have never been involved in a war in Europe, as you have so many times, and Great Britain also. Time is needed, General, for President Wilson to acclimatize those in America who would not wish for war. In my view he is being wise, prudent. No more than that.'

De Gard, who had at first listened with obvious impatience, had simmered down. He nodded, and attacked his dinner, saying nothing further.

Tact, Pacey thought. Tact was a commodity not much needed at sea. You gave an order and that was that. It was different for an ambassador. Tact and charm oiled the wheels of diplomacy.

'Damned appalling manners,' Major-General Lord Rickards said to his wife. Word of the dinner-table dispute had spread, like most things aboard a liner. Lady Barlow, for one, had talked. 'Never could stand the French, never. Slimy lot, can't trust 'em an inch. Though mind you, I agree with much of what the feller said.'

The Allied reverses continued: the war over all was not going well. In the Balkans the German General Falkenhayn, reinforced with reserves from the west, had launched an attack on the Russian armies along the Dunajec in Galicia and had broken the line at Gorlice. The Russians, after enormous casualties, had retreated in disarray. On the Turkish front the landing at Gallipoli had been murderously met.

It was all quiet on the Western Front according to the press on both sides of the Atlantic, though the men suffering in the front line trenches might have been forgiven for not thinking it so, especially since the Germans had used mustard gas against a French division. And the bombardments continued; so did the sniping, so did the crump of the howitzers. So did the hunger, and the presence of rats, and the mud left behind by the winter rains. And soon there was to be another big push – the pushes were always big, urged on by the General Staff from the rear. There was to be another Anglo-British offensive against Ypres. It was doomed to failure, even though the French artillery was to throw 700,000 shells at the Germans, using 1200 field guns. The German machine-guns opposing the British advance, undemolished by the

British guns firing mainly shrapnel at the emplacements, would mow down the stumbling Allied soldiers like hay.

Then, once again, while the dead were being shovelled into the huge communal graves, it would be for a spell all quiet.

In Germany there was a quiet confidence in the eventual outcome of the war, for the British Army was known to be less professional than the splendid and dedicated army of the Fatherland with its long martial tradition. In Berlin, along the Unter den Linden and through the Brandenburg Gate, soldiers marched and were cheered to the echo. In bandstands military bands played and the crowds sang *Deutschland Uber Alles* and other patriotic songs. There were in the papers cartoons of the King of England, of Mr Asquith and Mr Churchill, of Field Marshal Lord Kitchener and Admiral of the Fleet Lord Fisher, the latter being shown as a wild boar with tusks dripping blood. Much play was being made of one of Lord Fisher's utterances, made in private but reported via the underground spy network to Berlin.

Lord Fisher had asked rhetorically: *'Can the Army win the war before the Navy loses it?'*

A fine sentiment for an admiral! And it showed beyond all doubt that already the British were losing heart. They might well surrender. That was the joyous feeling in the air, and Fisher's hasty words went down well in the naval port of Wilhelmshavn, home of the First Squadron of the High Seas Fleet. It was talked of with laughter in the wardroom of the naval barracks, a splendid building, or set of buildings, with accommodation for almost 2500 officers and men. In the wardroom, drinking *schnapps* with a group of U-boat commanders, men who knew her husband well, was Frau Eppler.

'The war will soon be over, Ilse,' one of the young officers said, 'and you will have Klaus home again.'

'Yes,' she said.

'But not before we have sunk many more British ships. And not before the High Seas Fleet has met the British Grand Fleet –'

'And destroyed it,' another put in.

There was a chorus of agreement. Already noisy toasts had been drunk to His Imperial Majesty, to the glorious memory of the great Prince von Bismarck, to von Hindenburg and to Admiral Graf von Spee. Now another was drunk: to the swift and final destruction of the British Grand Fleet. This was drunk with much enthusiasm. It was, out of deference to the female guest and her lineage, followed by another.

'To Admiral von Neuburg . . . and his daughter!'

Ilse smiled her pleasure at the honour. Finally a toast was drunk to *Kapitanleutnant* Klaus Eppler, at sea aboard U-120. Ilse raised her glass. It was noted that she had a glum look; and there had been rumours. The rumours were not pleasing to Eppler's fellow submariners; many of them were of the old school, some were Prussians with all a Prussian's idea of military honour. It would never have crossed their minds to seduce the wife of a fellow officer at sea on his country's service. It was not done; there were other women in plenty available for the young heroes of the German Empire.

That applied to most of them. Not to all. It was noted that when Frau Eppler left the wardroom, another officer followed at a distance behind her, discreetly but not discreetly enough. An assumption was made that the two intended coming together outside the barrack gate. The assumption was not wrong. The officer summoned a cab with a flick of his fingers and they went to Frau Eppler's hotel where she was awaiting the return from patrol of U-120. In the cab, in a low voice, the officer made a disclosure. He said, 'There is word that Klaus has certain orders, Ilse.'

'What are these orders?'

'To sink the *Laurentia*. If he is successful, he will be – much acclaimed.'

Her eyes lit up as she turned to him. 'A hero?'

The officer nodded. 'Yes, a hero.'

Ilse Eppler clasped her hands together and gave what sounded like a sigh. Her companion watched the expression grow on her face; there was a rapt look and she seemed not to be seeing himself, or the cab, or the streets thronged with seamen in their dark blue rig with the smart caps and the trailing ribbons gilded with the names of their ships. The officer read the signs well enough: if Klaus Eppler became an overnight hero, Ilse would bask happily in the reflected glory of his heroism. Any seduction must be swiftly achieved before the *Laurentia* was sent to the bottom; afterwards it would be too late. Poor Klaus, the officer thought, Ilse is a very shallow little bitch. . . .

In Ilse's hotel room the officer brought a bottle from the capacious pocket of his uniform greatcoat. It was a bottle of Coats' Plymouth gin, yellowish in colour. British. Ilse remarked on this.

'British, yes. When I was in Plymouth a little before the war . . . I was given it. I saw the distillery, which is close to a small harbour known as the Cattewater, rather dirty. Now I open it . . .' He did so, and Ilse produced glasses. 'To drink again to the sinking of the *Laurentia*. I find this appropriate, do you not agree?'

It was not only Captain Pacey who was worrying about the contraband cargo stowed below in the *Laurentia*'s lower orlop hold. In America there was anxiety as well, and this anxiety was in the mind of the Pan-

Atlantic Line's cargo superintendent in New York, who was of course aware of the nature of the special cargo that had passed through a loophole in the port regulations. For reasons simply of convenience it had long been the practice for liners to gain sailing clearance by means of an incomplete cargo manifest for deposition with the Collector of Customs for the port. The reason: when, as sometimes happened , the number of passengers sailing was not fully known in time for sufficient stores to be embarked, last minute purchases were made at the dockside just before sailing – too late for inclusion in the manifest. A truer manifest was rendered after sailing and landed with the pilot; and in the current circumstances certain items could then be omitted. And the Collector of Customs for the port of New York, who happened to be staunchly pro-British, was prepared to turn a blind eye to what, in fact, he knew was going on.

There were risks, if the *Laurentia* should happen to be torpedoed, if the arms cargo should blow up and reveal itself. Risks both for the Collector of Customs and the shoreside cargo superintendent.

The loading of the liner had been the usual scene of bustle and chaos on the surface, but chaos that was fully under control nevertheless. There was so much to be put aboard, both by way of actual cargo and ship's stores for the passage to Liverpool: potatoes measured in tons, green vegetables, fresh fish in thousands of pounds weight, dried fish in boxes, poultry, a mountain of eggs including quail eggs from Texas and many, many other items – gin, whisky, liqueurs, coffee, fresh fruit, cigarettes, beef, chocolate . . . geese, turkeys, flour for the Liner's bakery, thousands of tins of condensed milk.

All this and more had come to the PanAtlantic berth at about the time the *Laurentia* had been ready for sea. It had come in horse-drawn waggons, in motor lorries, in handcarts. It had been off-loaded by hundreds of dock workers and either hoisted aboard in the cargo slings or brought on men's backs, men with heavy sacks over their heads and dangling down over their shoulders, up the working gangway to come under the supervision of the chief and second stewards, the chef, chief barkeeper, the head waiters in the saloons.

It had been easy enough for other things to go aboard under concealing markings. As well as the ammunition the loading had been authorized of apparently harmless substances: copper ingot bars; many barrels of oil fuel; almost 4000 boxes of cheese and many tubs of butter and cases of lard plus sundries, the sundries being the only items to appear on the manifest. The foodstuffs were in fact destined for the Superintendent of the Naval Experimental Establishment, Shoeburyness.

Articles of foodstuff, for belligerents' consumption – things of the war?

According to US regulations as a neutral country – yes.

To Germany? Perhaps. If she knew. And there were, as ever in war, spies everywhere.

The third-class passengers, who had the use of the second-class lounge, were a mixed bunch; mostly they sat around in vests and braces, not mixing with the genuine second-class passengers who tended to look down their noses at those who did not dress for dinner. The great unwashed tended to bring with them the stale air of the lower accommodation decks, the stench of closely packed human bodies, to say nothing of the wailing of unhappy children, seasick children, bored children.

They were also a mix of nationalities; though mostly Scots, Irish and English, there were assorted continentals, the races that made up a large proportion of the United States of America – Poles, Scandinavians, Italians, Greeks. Senator Melvin Manderton began his fact-finding mission in the second-class bar. Of course it was the scene inside Britain that he wished to investigate but he could make a start amongst the returning British expatriots.

He offered a drink to a middle-aged man with braces, vest and moustache, a typical worker. Manderton was man-to-man, hand on shoulder. 'What's it to be?'

'Well – thanks, mister. Wouldn't say no to a Scotch.'

'Sure.' Manderton ordered a Scotch for himself as well. He paid. 'Keep the change, son,' he said to the barman, waving a generous hand. He led his victim to a table. They sat. Manderton kept a hand on his glass: the ship had quite a roll, and things could slide. 'Going home, right?'

'Yes.'

'Mind if I ask why?'

The man looked at him directly. 'Who asks, mister?'

Manderton revealed his status as a senator from Wyoming. 'Where do you come from?'

The man said, 'Dublin.'

Manderton's eyebrows went up. 'Irish? Don't sound it. But I meant, where in the States?'

'Portland, Oregon,' the man said.

'Couldn't find work, maybe?'

'I found work, all right, mister. I'm a skilled carpenter. Plenty of work going.'

'Then why – ?'

Again the man looked back at him squarely. 'I'm going back to join in the war, mister, that's why. Because the United States don't seem like they're going to.'

'To fight for Britain? An Irishman?'

'Sure thing, mister. All the Irish aren't rebels, not by a long chalk. So don't you go thinking that. My father fought for the Queen in the Boer War. Connaught Rangers. Killed at Spion Kop, he was. So I'm going back to join his regiment.' Suddenly he grinned. 'Maybe one day your boys'll be over too. Once we've done the fighting for them.' He drained his glass and stood up. 'Thanks for the drink,' he said. He made no offer to buy one himself.

Senator Manderton got to his feet, thoughtfully. He would tell Haggerty of his experience; Haggerty always seemed interested in the Irish – naturally enough, of course.

Each day a news-sheet was distributed throughout the ship, containing summaries of world news as picked up by the radio operators who maintained a constant listening watch, not only on the emergency frequencies but also on the routine transmissions to ships at sea. This news-sheet gave information on many important matters: stock exchange prices from London and New York, news of personalities, news of the war.

Rickards was interested only in the war news. It was not good as he read between the lines, sitting alone in the first-class writing room. The news was filtered out by the Staff Captain and the Purser: there was no wish to worry the passengers. But to Rickards, as an experienced soldier accustomed to high command and staff work, the signs were there. Too much lack of real movement, all too static. Each side mounted their attacks, each side repulsed, a few hundred yards were gained and lost, gained and lost again. All the time the casualties mounted. Rickards remembered the South African war. So many men thrown away. So many dead from the diseases that had spread like wildfire – dysentery, enteric and others, all killers. And very little the medical staff could do to stop it or to keep alive the men who succumbed.

But that was war. It was Rickards' regret that he was too long in the tooth for recall. Nobody wanted a dodderer, though privately he believed he could still teach the youngsters a thing or two. He'd tried, of course. He'd written many letters from Canada since the previous August, the August of 1914. None of them had even received the courtesy of an answer until he'd become angry and had written a stinker to the Secretary of State for War himself: Lord Kitchener, whom he had known in South Africa. Admittedly the reply had come in Lord Kitchener's own hand, but it merely stated that Rickards' request had been noted.

On arrival in London, he would try again. A forlorn hope, of course, but a man had to do his best and not give up.

As he was reading the news-sheet, someone approached: two people. Lady Barlow and the son. Rickards started, irritably, to get to his feet. Earlier in the voyage he and his wife had been approached by Lady Barlow, who had recognized a gentleman beneath the threadbare suit; Rickards had not recognized a lady, but never mind, gentlemen were polite and he'd talked to her. Now, she said, 'Please don't get up, Mr Rickards.'

'I'm not that old, dear lady.' He added perfunctorily, 'Do sit down.'

She did so, with a sigh and a flounce of her silk dress. Eustace hovered until he was sure his mother was comfortable, then sat himself. Lady Barlow, looking around, said, 'I trust Mrs Rickards is well.'

'She's not, as a matter of fact.'

'Oh, dear, I'm ever so sorry. What's wrong, if I may ask?'

'Headache,' he answered briefly.

'Has she seen Dr Fellowes?'

'That the feller's name? I sent for him and he came.'

'Yes, he's *so* good –'

'Whisky breath,' Rickards said. 'Useless. Won't have him again.'

Lady Barlow said, 'Oh, I *am* surprised. Eustace has found him *excellent*. Haven't you, Eustace?'

'Yes, mama.'

'Most attentive. A very understanding man, such a nice manner.' She gushed on and on about the excellence of Dr Fellowes. She appeared to have had a long experience of medical men. So had Eustace. Rickards grew intensely irritated, wanting nothing so much as to kick young Barlow up the backside and heft him out onto the deck. Exercise would do him a damn sight more good than Dr Fellowes' attentions, pandering to a titled mother. In the end Rickards could hold it in no longer. He turned to Eustace.

'Well, Barlow. How's the heart today, eh?'

'Still awf'lly dickey, sir. I have a lot of trouble . . . have to take things easily, you know. My mother insists.'

'Not in the right place, then?'

'I beg your pardon? Not –'

'Your heart,' Rickards said loudly and got to his feet, leaning on his walking-stick. 'Not in the right blasted place. If it was, sir, damme, you'd be going back to the United Kingdom to join up as a private soldier!'

This time it was Lady Barlow herself who had been in medical need. Dr Fellowes, attending in her stateroom, prescribed sal volatile. She was quite faint and also tearful.

'That *dreadful* man,' she said, her voice strong enough. 'He must be *very* common – and I thought he was a gentleman! Shows how wrong

93

you can be.' In her distress she had very nearly omitted the 'h' of 'how'. (Sir Albert Barlow had been knighted as a result of making money out of the supply of tinned beef to the soldiers in South Africa, which was a fact fortunately unknown to Major-General Lord Rickards.) 'I don't suppose that man has *any idea* what it's like to be in the army and – *fight*! Such a suggestion, to join up as a common soldier! *Of course* I would see to it that you were given a commission, Eustace.'

'Yes, mama.'

'If it wasn't for your heart.'

The *Laurentia*, as she proceeded on her way at eighteen knots across the windswept North Atlantic, carried the hopes and good wishes of some thousands of people on both sides of the ocean. It was not just the families of the passengers and crew, though theirs was the heartbreak to come and the nagging anxiety as, majestically, the liner came across the seas towards the lurking U-boats of the German Navy.

There were others, concerned for different but important reasons. Some of those reasons lay in the mail that the *Laurentia* was carrying in her mail room under the charge of the second officer. Much of that mail was of extreme urgency, if not to the war then to private individuals and firms. In particular a law firm in Paducah, Kentucky, in correspondence with a firm of solicitors in the city of London. It had been a long business and it concerned the claim of a United States citizen to the title of Chief of an ancient Scottish clan, the Clan MacKerrow. In 1764 one Angus MacKerrow, a cousin of the then Chief, had been despatched as a remittance man to the American colonies. He had not been wanted in Scotland on account of his drinking and womanizing and his having managed to get through a good deal of his inheritance on the death of his father. In America Angus MacKerrow had drifted. He had been a frequenter of the saloons and had eventually died with a bullet in his brain, a bullet fired by the British in the War of Independence. But not before he had fathered a son by the daughter of a saloon owner. By the time the American MacKerrows had reached the sixth generation, the Scottish family, the main line of the MacKerrows, had died out; they had not in any case been prolific. Years of legal wrangling between Edinburgh and Paducah, Kentucky, and the production of documents by the Lord Lyon King of Arms who had sought to establish an heir had resulted in a possible claim by the American MacKerrows to the Chief's estate. In short, it now appeared likely that a certain US citizen by name Fillmore MacKerrow could succeed to the chieftainship and also a baronetcy.

Fillmore, possibly Sir Fillmore MacKerrow, Bart., was currently situated in Death Row in the state penitentiary, awaiting the electric chair for the murder of a prostitute in Louisville, Kentucky. Sir Fillmore, who happened to be black, had nothing to leave his son, currently aged six, but the prospect of inheriting a British title. This he was determined to do; but he would be successful only if a heavily sealed communication from the law firm in Paducah reached the office of the Lord Lyon King of Arms in Edinburgh, Scotland. Of course, so far as could be told there was no reason why it should not. And even if what Sir Fillmore, with morguelike humour, called 'Fry-day' should cut short his life before the letter arrived, then his son would still inherit. Or so his attorney had said.

Another anxious party was the British Treasury.

In her third-class baggage room the *Laurentia* carried five million pounds' worth of gold bullion, big bars of the stuff in boxes of great weight, loaded in as much secrecy as possible at the pierhead berth. This gold was desperately needed for the British war effort, as desperately as was the loan that Patrick Haggerty was going across to negotiate – or block with impossible strings.

The gold was yet another of Captain Pacey's worries. Did the German High Command know about it? If they did, then the *Laurentia* became an even greater prize. Even, perhaps, when added to the arms in the lower orlop hold, a legitimate one. Which made it all the more surprising and worrying that the Admiralty had not seen fit to provide the strong escort that Pacey had pleaded for. One cruiser to meet the liner westward of Cape Clear . . . it simply was not enough.

The Flag Officer in Charge at Queenstown in County Cork was of much the same mind as Captain Pacey out at sea. One elderly cruiser, HMS *Bristol*, under the command of Captain Charles de Ferriman Lugard, RN, was not enough. FOIC had made the point to the officer in overall command – Vice Admiral Sir Henry Coke, who was responsible for Area 21 covering the south Irish coast. Coke had thereupon made representations to the Admiralty. Not once, but many times.

Finally, the First Sea Lord himself spoke on the telephone to the Flag Officer at Queenstown. 'Hood, this *unreasonable* request of yours –'

'Far from unreasonable, sir.'

'Don't damn well interrupt me when I'm speaking to you! I won't have it! You of all people . . . relieved from the damn Dover Patrol *by my own order* because you let U-boats past the Dover defences! You're virtually in *disgrace*, Hood!'

'Really, sir, I fail to see –'

'Fail, yes, fail, fail, fail!' There was the sound of a fist being thumped. 'An appropriate word to be sure! The *Laurentia* will be met by the *Bristol* and will be perfectly safe! The *Laurentia*'s Master knows the route and knows the risks. A *fool* would not be appointed by the PanAtlantic Company, my dear Hood!'

'Captain Pacey himself has urgently requested a stronger and earlier escort, sir –'

'Yes, yes! To be sure he has! In order to cover any errors of judgment he may himself make!' The voice on the telephone rose to a pitch of near hysteria. 'If Captain Pacey should lose the *Laurentia* then, since he cannot be a fool, he will be a rogue! A *rogue*, d'you hear me – and I shall personally hound him to the ends of the earth!'

The instrument clicked sharply in Hood's ear. He sat back at full arms' stretch from his desk, his face white with anger. He mopped at his forehead, shook his head in utter disbelief, although he had cause to know what Lord Fisher was like: sometimes charming, mostly quite impossibly rude and arrogant. Now the First Sea Lord had surpassed himself. It was in Hood's view almost as though Fisher wanted the *Laurentia* to be lost. Hood caught himself up quickly: never must he allow his own furious anger to lead him into disloyal and ridiculous thoughts.

8

THE Rickardses had turned in. Rickards reached out and switched off the light. 'Good-night, Emmy. Sleep tight.'

'Yes, I will. If you don't snore, Jeffrey.'

Rickards answered with a snort. It was by his lights a loving snort. The ship rolled and pitched beneath him, though not as badly as hitherto. There was the everlasting creak of woodwork and the sound of the ventilators, and the throb of the engines far below. Rickards was no man of fear; his record of service in the field was proof enough of that. But he often wondered how men could take the sea. It wasn't just the war; the sea was never safe. Look at the *Titanic*. Look at all the ships that had been lost on their peaceful voyages, especially the sailing ships with their dreaded rounding of Cape Horn and its virtually never-ending gales. Pacey, he knew, had served his time in sail – they all had, the deck officers of the liners. They would have yarns to tell. Rickards' thoughts drifted as he moved towards sleep. He would be relieved when the ship was safely into the berth at Liverpool; he was worried about Emmy. The headache had not gone; he might have to suffer Dr Fellowes again. He had been tormented these last few years by the dreadful thought that when he awoke in the morning he might find Emmy dead in her bed. That would finish him. Not a demonstrative man – he mistrusted emotion – he loved his wife dearly. She had been his tower of strength for almost fifty years now: their golden wedding would fall one week precisely after the *Laurentia*'s arrival in Liverpool. They had married when Jeffrey Rickards had been a captain of artillery serving in Peshawar on the North-West Frontier; he had been twenty-seven, Emily Mostyn-Johnston twenty-one. They had been married in Bombay Cathedral, a splendid social occasion: Colonel Mostyn-Johnson had been Military Secretary to the Viceroy; His Excellency and Lady Lawrence had attended the wedding.

So much glitter, so much pageantry, so many colourful uniforms of the British Army in India and of the Indian Army. The Viceregal Bodyguard, the Bengal Lancers, Probyn's Horse – scarlet and white, and the dark blue of the guns, the red of the infantry, the green of the rifle regiments. The great reception, and Jeffrey Rickards wishing only that he could escape with Emmy and find themselves on their own except for the retinue of native servants that accompanied any British officer in the sub-continent.

Rickards had served four more years in India, coming home by the P&O as a major, promoted early for valour in the field. He had dragged a subaltern to safety under a hail of fire from the Pathan tribesmen, and had subsequently led the reprisal party that had burned down the village whence the Pathans had come; since then he had worn the ribbon of the Victoria Cross. He had served since in Gibraltar, Malta, Bermuda and in various home stations, including the depot at Woolwich. At the start of the South African war he had been a brigadier-general commanding the artillery in South Wales, and had been sent to Cape Town on promotion to major-general. When Lord Roberts, himself a gunner, had taken over as Commander-in-Chief in South Africa from Sir Redvers Buller, Rickards had been asked for as his Chief of Staff. When the war ended, he had been rewarded with a peerage.

So many memories. . . .

They crowded in now, as Rickards listened to the creak of the *Laurentia*'s woodwork and the throb of the engines and the wash of the waves along the liner's plates. Personal memories of long ago when he'd been young and active, personal memories of the long-drawn, bitter fighting against the Boer farmers in South Africa who had proved themselves far better at war than the British had ever thought possible. Memories of the young Winston Churchill as a subaltern of hussars and as a war correspondent of the *Morning Post*. Memories of a much-loved nephew dead in his early twenties on active service.

The nephew had been Tom Davenport, son of Rickards' sister married to a surgeon colonel of the Army Medical Staff, retired before the name change to the Royal Army Medical Corps. The surgeon colonel had been a man of fiery temper, an Irishman from County Longford. He had also been the meanest man who, in Rickards' opinion, had ever walked the earth. He was far from poor, but Rickards' sister Susan had been forced to cut up her wedding dress to make clothes for her babies. Not one penny would the good doctor spend on his family. When young Tom had made it known he wished to follow an army career, there had been no suggestion of Sandhurst. If Tom wished to join the army, then he must do so as a private soldier and work hard for a commission.

Tom Davenport had been a mettlesome lad and had taken his father at his word. He had enlisted as a private in the Border Regiment at Carlisle Castle. A fine young soldier, he had been made a sergeant at the age of twenty – something of a record. As such he had gone with the foreign service battalion from Malta to the Cape in October 1899.

Major-General Rickards had contrived a meeting with his nephew when the latter's regiment had reached Pietermaritzburg in Natal.

Tom had given Rickards a first-hand account of the disembarkation at Durban. 'You should have seen the crowds, Uncle Jeffrey. It was as if the whole town had turned out . . . ringing cheers as we steamed in, women and children waving handkerchiefs. One girl got up on a gate by the railway line and waved a Union Flag as our special train went past. They were all shouting "Remember Majuba". '

Majuba: Majuba Hill, where in the first Boer War in 1881 the Boers had defeated the British. That would be avenged.

Rickards had asked, 'Are you getting many wounded down from Ladysmith, Tom?'

'Yes, quite a few already since we got here.' Pietermaritzburg was the advancing base for the army. The 1st Border Regiment was in garrison for the time being, while farther up the line the Northumberland Fusiliers formed the line of communication. 'Last night around ninety were sent down. I spoke to one fellow who'd been shot in the stomach . . . bullet went right through and came out the other side. Some with arms and legs shot away –'

'Yes. It's not going to be so easy. Have you seen any action yet yourself, Tom?'

'Just a little.' Tom grinned. 'Quite exciting. Outpost duty – Bissetts Hill. There were a hundred and twenty of us but we were pretty heavily outnumbered –'

'Facing fearful odds, eh?'

'You bet, Uncle Jeffrey. They sent some bullets across and we had some casualties, but we picked off some in return. The worst aspect, I find, is you can't wash much. Shortage of water except for drinking – in the outposts, that is.'

Later in the campaign they had met again. Tom Davenport had force-marched with his regiment from Aliwal North in Cape Colony to Wepener in the Orange Free State to relieve two thousand Colonial troops who were under siege by the Boers. It was a 100-mile march. The Border had started out on Easter Sunday in pouring rain; they had marched throughout the long days and rested at night, though 'rest' was scarcely the word, Tom had said.

'Enemy territory, of course,' Rickards said.

'Yes. So we all had to be pretty alert and ready for the word from the picquets. It wasn't too bad till we got to Ronsville with about eighty miles still to go. The Boers made a stand at Bushman's Kop . . . we advanced in fighting order and fought them to a standstill. Not a standstill really – they turned and ran after a few hours of artillery bombardment, plus our rifles.'

'Any casualties to your fellows, Tom?'

Tom shrugged. 'Six wounded, that's all. Quite mild after our experience in Natal, after I last saw you, Uncle Jeffrey.' The young sergeant had elaborated on those experiences; Rickards learned a lot of what it was really like for the soldiers in the field, from the other ranks' point of view. It had been useful. Rickards had not seen Tom Davenport again after that; soon after, he had been commissioned – commissioned in the field, with genuinely no direct avuncular influence – as a second lieutenant in the 2nd Wiltshires. Such were the casualties that in that rank Tom had acted as a company commander and adjutant of a half battalion; for this he received – he wrote in a letter – sixpence a day extra pay. He had seen more hard fighting in the bush north of Pretoria, the Wiltshires having suffered a large number of casualties before moving on to the 'gold reefed city' of Johannesburg in the Transvaal. One sentence in that letter had made Rickards laugh a little: 'I have just got a new horse, better than my last one.'

In the years to come, people might be saying that about the new-fangled motor-cars that were all the rage among the moneyed.

So young Tom had fought on, with seemingly a good career as a regular officer ahead of him. Then Major-General Rickards had seen his name in a casualty list: Second Lieutenant Thomas Jeffrey Davenport, died of disease contracted on active service. Rickards had cursed savagely: the damned diseases that were killing so many young men, more than the Boer bullets in fact! When would the doctors learn to cope? Then finally, when on home leave the next year he visited his sister, he saw the other letter, from the Wiltshire Regiment: 'Dear Mrs Davenport, I am sending you herewith two snapshots of groups of our officers, each of which contains a picture of your late son. . . .'

Finis.

A different young man from Eustace Barlow.

Sleep did not after all come that night to Rickards: there were too many ghosts.

There was anxiety over sickness elsewhere in the *Laurentia*'s passenger accommodation. Little Olof Lundkvist was finding breathing difficult still, and he still had a temperature more than twenty-four hours after Alva had first reported to Dr Fellowes.

In the middle of that night, Dr Fellowes was called out again. Again he took the child's temperature, again he made an examination.

'Have the bowels moved?'

'No. He's scarcely eaten –'

'Yes, I see.' Dr Fellowes recommended a purgative: he would send round a Gregory Powder. If that didn't work, then castor oil would be tried. Dr Fellowes didn't say so, but he was flummoxed. He had read the American specialist's report but he was himself years out of date.

However, patients – or their parents – could always be reassured by a confident manner and the application of purgatives. With the young, purgatives were usually all that was required. It was not for nothing that an official Board of Trade requirement was that shipmasters were to ensure that all members of their crews under the age of eighteen were dosed each Sunday morning with Black Draught, a liquorice-based purgative of great strength. This was administered whether or not the recipients were constipated.

Alva Lundkvist was not convinced. 'But little Olof, he has not eaten . . . there is no appetite.'

'H'm. Well, we shall see. There is no cause for anxiety, dear lady. Simply keep the boy in his bunk, and warm. That is important. He'll eat when he's ready . . . when he feels hungry. I shall call again in the morning.'

Dr Fellowes departed; the woman, like any foreigner, was fussing, but never mind. The guineas mounted up when there were cabin calls, and the charge was higher at night. Nevertheless, something nagged at the doctor's mind: the report from that medical specialist had been weighty and was of course to be taken seriously. Dr Fellowes wished he could understand the half of it. However, the Liverpool arrival was not all that far off and once in port and landed ashore the case would no longer be his responsibility.

In the Lundkvists' cabin, after the doctor's departure, there were prayers. The boy turned and twisted restlessly, his face scarlet, his small body damp with sweat. Alva had changed his pyjamas frequently; the small garments, waiting in a heap for the steward to take them to the ship's laundry, looked pathetic.

Torsten Lundkvist got to his feet, easing himself up from his knees beside the bunk. 'It is in God's hands, Alva,' he said gently.

'Do you think the doctor knows what he is doing?'

'Of course! We must trust him.' Ten minutes later the Gregory Powder was brought by a night steward wearing blue patrols. The powder was mixed with water in a glass. Olof was made to drink; he spluttered and cried. But doctor's orders must be obeyed to the letter. Torsten Lundkvist set his teeth and clamped the boy's nose between finger and thumb, and the lips opened, and the purgative was poured in, the mouth being then held shut until there was a swallow.

Dr Fellowes came again after breakfast. Olof was no better, although there had been a movement of the bowels that saved him from the castor oil.

During that night a further message reached the *Laurentia*'s radio room from the New York Police Department. This, once again, concerned the passenger Frederick Jones, architect. The message was brief and contained no detail. It simply stated that Mr Jones was not to be permitted to disembark in Liverpool until he had been interviewed by the British police. Contact had, it seemed, been made with the Home Office. The message indicated cooperation.

The message was brought to the attention of Staff Captain Morgan before breakfast. It was brought by the Purser himself. 'What do we do?' Matthews asked. His hands had trembled a little as he'd passed the message over. It was not to do with shock or anything like that: Livia Costello was an insatiable woman and two nights of her had left their mark.

'First, we don't say anything to Mr Jones,' Staff Captain Morgan said.

'I was wondering about that. You have possible suicide in mind, sir?'

'We have to. That's if he's guilty of wife murder.'

'Isn't that putting too heavy a construction on it?'

'I don't think so, Matthews. Look, we have a cable from New York Police making enquiries about a missing wife. We know Jones is touchy – there was the incident with that harmless boy, the Lundkvist boy, when Jones was throwing bread to the seagulls. You said yourself his manner was unhelpful after that first cable had come in. His bedroom steward reported there was something odd about the non-arrival of the wife – didn't he? The wife was booked and didn't turn up – you know that, of course.'

'Yes. . . .'

'It all smells fishy, Matthews. Very fishy. It's plain the man's likely to be arrested in Liverpool. In the interval therefore – if he's told – he might do something foolish. Apart from Jones himself, we don't want to upset the passengers. Not on this voyage. So keep mum.'

'The Captain –'

'I'll be having a word with the Captain shortly. Not only about this.' Morgan tapped the message form. 'There's something else you're going to have to know about and cope with.' Morgan paused, then added, 'Those Germans have come up with a bombshell.'

Ahead in Britain, in Walthamstow, Mr Jones's old mother was counting the hours until Frederick berthed in Liverpool, caught the boat train to Euston Station and arrived at the nursing home where she had been put by her sister Freda Bonfield. She was very ill but fully conscious and she knew she was going to die. Her thin, bluish fingers plucked at the sheet and her eyes were haunted. She feared death; she had not lived what the Lord would call a good life. She had been guilty of envy, greed and jealousy. She had attended church throughout her life but never with any real conviction; the mouthings of psalms and canticles and prayers had left her dreaming of other things: of a more romantic lover than Frederick's father, for one thing. Humphrey, her late husband, had been a good man but dull. Plumpish and with an owl-like expression of never-ending goodwill, he had behaved in bed like the accountant he was by profession, conscientiously, with a neat precision and muttering to himself, as though casting a column of figures and arriving, rather quickly, at the sum total.

Always when he had reached his climax he had said, 'Ah, there.' And after Frederick had been born, it was as though there had been a final audit. Almost, anyway – perhaps at that stage it had been more of a trial balance. He had not given up entirely; but within two or three years he had. Finally. And Ada Jones had not been all that sorry; Frederick's birth had been far from easy. But there were those dreams and often they had centred on the parson in the pulpit. That was not, could not be, God's idea of churchgoing.

And the jealousy: she been insanely jealous of Frederick's wife, whom she had never met. Why should a distant American woman take Frederick from her? It was unjust, to say the least, after all she had done for Frederick when he'd been a little boy and then a youth and then a man – he had lived at home until he had gone to America. She had been a loving mother; that would count with God, anyway.

In this, her terminal illness, she had a thought, obscure in its origins but strong in her mind, that she discussed with Freda her sister.

'If Frederick gets here in time. . . .'

'Of course he will.' Freda Bonfield, thick waisted and grey haired, leaned forward towards the bed. Her stays creaked, the whalebone protesting. "You're going to be all right, Ada. The doctor – '

'Oh yes, the doctor. He doesn't know what I'm going through. Anyway, as I was going to say – Frederick might intercede, don't you think, Freda?'

'Intercede?'

'With our Lord. Goodness knows, I did enough . . . he was always grateful. If I forgive, and if our Lord's told . . . He'll be forgiving too.'

'Forgiving?' Freda looked blank for a moment. 'Oh. You mean Maggie? Are you going to tell Frederick he's forgiven for marrying Maggie, Ada – that you're going to accept her?'

Ada Jones nodded. Tears formed in her eyes and rivuletted down the seamed cheeks, which were like parchment, yellowish and dry. 'I must. I've been unkind, I know that. I shall tell Frederick that, yes. I believe our Lord will be pleased. If only dear Frederick gets here in time. . . .'

She was very distressed; her sister saw that it meant a very great deal to her that Frederick should be with her at the last and for that very specific reason. Neither of the sisters, of course, had any idea that the daughter-in-law lay in so many segments in upstate New York.

Or that a meeting in the next world – if Frederick should hang – might be fraught with many conflicts of interest and some stern disapproval from God, with Frederick proving a poor intermediary.

In the Court of the Lord Lyon, the Lyon Office in Edinburgh, Unicorn Pursuivant was reporting to Rothesay Herald.

'The claim appears entirely genuine, Sir Graham, but we must await the further information from America. We can't proceed without that.'

'The final link – no.' Rothesay Herald, a long, thin man with aristocratic features, sighed. He had prayed that that final link, the proof positive of the MacKerrow succession, might be inadmissible; but from what he knew already that was unlikely. It was, he thought, grotesque. The Clan MacKerrow was an ancient one, with ancestry going back through a female line even to Robert the Bruce, King of Scotland, the victor of Bannockburn, the humbler of the English King Edward. And the inheritor of the chiefdom was an American, and black. And in prison awaiting execution.

It scarcely bore thinking of. Of course, should the letter from the Kentucky law firm not arrive, and there were always dangers at sea in time of war – and this voyage of the *Laurentia*, which ship he understood from a transatlantic cable to be carrying the mail, was especially fraught – if the letter should fail to arrive, then Sir Fillmore would not himself inherit. But there was the son. Sir Ingersoll MacKerrow!

Rothesay Herald shuddered.

Unterzeebooten 120 was well on course towards the southern tip of Ireland. Broadcasts from the naval command in Wilhelmshavn had kept Klaus Eppler informed of the progress across the Atlantic of the *Laurentia*. Signals from the British Admiralty to the Flag Officer at Queenstown, and vice versa, had been intercepted and the code broken. Eppler knew that there was concern in British naval circles. There might be a reaction to this concern.

Eppler consulted with his First Lieutenant.

'We must not go in too soon, Dirnecker. The British cruisers will be alert.'

Dirnecker said, 'The British have little strength in Queenstown, Herr *Kapitan.*'

'There is still a risk. I shall go farther west, and a little north. Until the *Laurentia* is much nearer. And perhaps the British more lulled.'

Eppler passed the order for an alteration of course. Throughout the boat there was a quiet elation; a big blow was about to be struck at the enemies of the Fatherland. Each one of the crew had his allotted task in the forthcoming sinking. Each one of the crew was indispensable and would be fêted as much as would their Captain on return to base. All would share the glory. Each man was determined to do his duty to his utmost. The crew was very efficient. And all was ready, the great torpedoes in their tubes awaiting *Kapitanleutnant* Eppler's word. The hoists stood ready to load more torpedoes into the tubes should they be required. As yet no one could tell how many torpedoes would be needed to sink so large a ship as the *Laurentia*, but the general view was that one, maybe two, would be enough. No liner, however large, was divided into so many watertight compartments as a warship. And her sides were unarmoured, comparatively thin steel plates whose rivets would burst asunder very quickly under the impact of high explosives sent against the hull at something like thirty-five knots. Also, there would be panic among the many hundreds of civilian passengers to whom both the war and the sea were so unfamiliar. There were women among the passengers; none of the U-120's company could be unaware of that. They were sorry – and sorrier for the children; but war was war, and their Kaiser's word was law. There would be no holding back when the firing order came.

Klaus Eppler had conquered his doubts and apprehensions; he had forced them by an effort of will below the surface, much as he forced his submarine down below the waves by flooding the ballast tanks. He had flooded his mind with the glory that was the Fatherland and the Kaiser and the German Empire. *Deutschland, Deutschland über alles . . .* Eppler had heard that the British were envious of so noble a tune and were accustomed to sing a hymn to the same tune: *Glorious things of thee are spoken, Zion city of our God.*

Doubtless on Sundays that would be sung aboard the British warships of the Grand Fleet, sung at the drum-head services in the field in Belgium and France, sung too by the British King in Windsor Castle, joined by Mr Churchill from the British Admiralty. Perhaps the British comforted themselves by making use of a German tune. Eppler, ordering the lowering of his periscope preparatory to diving stations, thought how very stupid the British were. A good thing, of course; they would be sure to bungle the escort of the *Laurentia*, once they had made up their minds to provide an escort at all.

'Is this on account of little Ming?' Leon Fielding stared from wide eyes, red-rimmed eyes at his bedroom steward, Hawley. Hawley, entering after a brief knock, was accompanied by a man whom Fielding had seen around the passenger accommodation, a tough-looking man with an air of authority.

Hawley answered his question. 'Not to do with the little dog, sir, no.'

'No, I did rather think not. I've come to terms with the fact that I left Ming in New York, you know. I'd forgotten that, I really can't think why. What is it you want?'

The other man answered. 'Staff Captain's orders. Cabin search.' The speaker was the second steward, Stanley Parker: knowing all about Fielding's trouble over the Craigson boy, a matter as yet unresolved, his manner was curt; he didn't like that sort of carry-on, didn't like it at all. Such a man deserved the lash – flogging, as once carried out aboard His Majesty's ships, with the miscreant tied down to a grating and lashed with the cat-o'-nine-tails until the blood ran red. When cut down half-alive, salt was rubbed into the stripes as a cleansing agent. '*All* cabins.'

'Oh. May I ask why this is?'

Second Steward Parker was already poking about behind the various steel pipes that ran through the cabin. It was Hawley who said, 'Routine, sir. Just routine.'

'Oh, I see.' Leon Fielding had not previously travelled by sea in wartime. It was quite extraordinary what changes the war had brought about.

9

BEFORE the Purser had come to him with the cable about Mr Jones, Staff Captain Morgan had already reported to the Captain on the bridge. Pacey had been standing by himself in the port wing.

'Good morning, Morgan.' Pacey, Morgan thought, looked just about all in.

'Good morning, sir. I'm sorry to have to bother you –'

'That's all right, Morgan. What is it?'

'The two Germans, sir.'

'Well?' Pacey's eyes had narrowed.

'They've just talked to the sentry, sir. Or one of them did, anyway.' Morgan paused, keeping his voice low although before long the whole ship would have to know. 'He said there was a device aboard. An explosive device, big enough to tear the guts out of the ship.'

'Good God! When was this?'

'Ten minutes ago, sir. I went down to speak to the Germans myself, at once. They're both insistent. And they don't know where it's situated.'

Pacey rubbed at tired eyes, stinging with salt and constant use of his binoculars. 'My first reaction: I don't believe them! It's just a ploy to get us all worried, nothing more. If there's anything in it, why give the game away, the *German* game?'

Morgan shrugged. 'Probably sheer funk. They know it's somewhere and they don't want to get blown up after all.'

'So if they did know where it was –'

'They'd lose no time in telling us.'

'Yes. I still see it as a means of rattling the whole ship, Morgan.'

Morgan said, 'It could be, I agree. They looked scared enough, but they could have been putting on an act.' He hesitated; he knew that Pacey was very tired, overtired really – he was no longer a young man. He went on, 'Whatever it is, we have to take it seriously. You'd agree, sir?'

Pacey nodded. 'Yes, of course. Full search of the ship, Morgan. Like a dose of salts – right through. Go round yourself and alert all heads of departments and the masters-at-arms. Have those Germans brought to my cabin – I'll see what I can dig out.'

'Aye, aye, sir. And the passengers?'

Pacey blew out his cheeks. 'We don't want a blasted panic, Morgan, that's the last thing. . . . They're to be told for now it's a matter of routine when approaching tricky waters. They won't believe it, I know. I'll speak to them all as soon as I've talked to those Germans, and give them the facts then.'

The two masters-at-arms took general charge below under Chief Officer Arkwright. The bosun and his leading hands made the search of the seamen's quarters for'ard; the engine-room storekeeper co-ordinated the search of the firemen's and trimmers' accommodation. In the engine room and boiler rooms Chief Engineer Hackett with his senior second engineer did the job himself, and a long time it was to take, though Hackett would have been very surprised indeed if anybody had managed to penetrate his kingdom with a bomb, much less have the time to conceal it anywhere. But orders were orders and the Old Man was dead to rights. Nowhere in the ship was left unsearched: the officers' cabins, even the Master's accommodation and the bridge and wheelhouse and chart room not escaping. The chief steward's stores, the galleys and pantries, bakeries, engine-room stores, paint store, bosun's store, linen rooms and laundry – the lot. And, of course, the whole of the passenger accommodation. On the whole the ship's company took it all in its stride, philosophically if with the usual seaman's grumbles and moans about what the officers expected of them.

The passengers reacted in their individual ways. Those in the third class were more or less as philosophical as the crew: they were used to being given orders. It was part of their lot in life.

But not Lady Barlow's.

The knock had been followed by an entry, no time for Lady Barlow to collect herself: she might, she thought angrily, have been undressed. Her bedroom steward came in with the assistant second steward.

She glared, drawing herself up. 'What on earth –'

'Very sorry, madam. Captain's orders.'

'To invade my cabin?'

'Not invade, madam. We have orders to carry out a search –'

'What for, may I ask?'

The assistant second steward temporized. 'Just a check, madam. On watertightness. Leaky rivets, see. Or could be.'

He guessed the old battleaxe wouldn't know the difference between a rivet and a poached egg, wouldn't tick over that leaky rivets didn't exactly occur on an inboard bulkhead. Leaky rivets had been the brilliant idea of the second steward, and they were being blamed right through the cabin accommodation.

Lady Barlow, however, stood her ground. She stood it like a rock. 'I do not propose to submit to this.'

'But the Captain –'

'Captain, fiddlesticks! I am a British subject in my own cabin and this intrusion might have been most objectionable. I shall not permit you to carry out this – this *search* until my son is present. I have never heard of such a thing as to burst into a lady's room!' Lady Barlow's chest heaved with anger. 'Go and find him. Tell him I wish him to come to my cabin *at once*.'

The assistant second steward met the eye of the bedroom steward. 'Off you go,' he said. 'You 'eard what the lady said.'

While Leon Fielding's cabin was being checked with a nil result, that of Mr Frederick Jones was visited. Mr Jones was not at first present but returned from a visit to the gentleman's lavatory to find his cabin in the occupation of his bedroom steward and another man.

He went quite pale and when he spoke he stuttered badly.

'What's this for?' he managed to ask at last.

'Just a search, sir. Captain's orders.'

'You won't find anything here. I didn't –' Jones broke off; whatever he did he must never commit himself. Panic smote; there could be a tooth. His count might not have been accurate after all. 'What are you looking for?'

Out came the yarn about leaky rivets and that made matters much worse since it was an obvious lie. Mr Jones was an architect, not, certainly, a naval architect or marine surveyor, but he did know that internal rivets didn't leak, not unless the ship was sinking and the alleyways were full of water.

He had gone paler now and was shaking all over his body. 'Wh-what did the Captain say?' he asked.

'Say, sir? Just ordered a search like, that's all, sir.'

'He was not . . . specific?'

'Just the rivets, sir.'

Mr Jones shook and gnawed at his nails. He watched like a hawk despite his nerves. No tooth emerged; but obviously something was in the air. There was suspicion – there must be, for his cabin to be searched. Mr Jones's mind went back to his motor trip down from Arlington to New York. The Wappinger River. The leg that had got away. He shook more than ever and mopped streaming sweat from his forehead and cheeks.

The search was completed.

'Thank you, sir. Sorry for the intrusion.'

The bedroom steward and the other man went out into the alleyway.

'Weird bloke,' the bedroom steward said. 'I dunno . . . takes all sorts, I s'pose, eh? You'd think he'd done a murder, way 'e was shaking. Bin funny all along, 'e 'as.'

In his cabin, Mr Jones began his own search, a desperate one. Just in case there was an undiscovered tooth: the Captain might order another search at any moment.

'If you don't mind, sir and madam.'

'No, no, of course not. You have to obey orders. You're acting very properly.' Major-General Lord Rickards had been very accustomed to orders, taking them in his younger days and giving them when he became more senior. 'Matter of ship safety, I take it?'

'Just the rivets, sir, that's all, like I said.'

'Oh, yes,' Rickards said. He'd been given the yarn and he didn't believe it for a moment but he didn't propose to question what had originated from the Captain. But he looked the steward straight in the eyes and gave a fractional wink. Then he took Emmy's arm. 'Come along, my dear. We mustn't be in the way of ship safety.'

They left the cabin, making for the lounge. The bedroom steward grinned behind the departing backs and said, 'More fly than he looks, eh? Decent old codger. So's the old lady.'

Making for the lounge, Rickards was wondering. A search at sea – most unusual in his experience. There had to be a very important reason. He remembered the Germans and began to put two and two together. He said nothing to his wife; if the Captain didn't want anything known, it wasn't up to a passenger to raise queries.

In the lounge the Rickards encountered Eustace Barlow. Rickards overheard what was being said to him by one of the stewards: 'Beg pardon, sir. 'Er Ladyship asks you to go to 'er cabin. Pronto, she said, sir.'

Once again Rickards put two and two together: Lady Barlow was now under search, or her cabin was. This was confirmed when Eustace asked what Her Ladyship wanted and the steward spoke of the search. Eustace went into a kind of tantrum. 'Well! I must say, you've no right to search *anybody's* cabin. No wonder Her Ladyship wants me.' He caught Rickards' sardonic eye and appealed to him. 'Mr Rickards, did you happen to hear that?'

'Yes, young man, I did.'

'Well, it's jolly rotten, isn't it?'

'A matter of necessity, Barlow. Ship safety. I, too, have submitted. Rivets, you know,' he added tongue-in-cheek as he met the steward's eye. 'Popping out all over the place. If I were you I'd obey your mother's summons very promptly. Field the rivets, don't you know. Stop one landing in Her Ladyship's bosom.' He paused, then spoke solemnly, in a whisper close to Barlow's ear. 'If it did . . . it would have to be retrieved.'

Eustace Barlow's face had gone scarlet. 'Oh, I say!' he said in a high voice, and left the lounge.

'I guess,' Senator Manderton said, 'my cabin is kind of United States territory, inviolable. Right?' He stood in the cabin doorway, solid and tough spoken.

'I'm afraid not, sir.' The bedroom steward gave a cough into his hand and thought fast. 'US territory it may be, sir. But it's surrounded by British territory, like. And British sea.'

That was a mistake. 'British sea my *bum*, stoo'ard. Heck! You British really do think you own the goddam world!'

'British sea by naturalization, sir. Seeing as we're on it. Occupying it, like.'

'Temporarily.'

'Yes, sir. Just as you say, sir.'

Manderton grinned. 'Okay, so you win. I know I'm only a passenger and the Captain's God. I guess our captains are the same.'

'A captain's privilege, sir.'

'Megalomaniacs. Ever hear the story of the cock-yolly bird, stoo'ard?'

The steward had; but passengers were there to be humoured so he said, 'No, sir?'

'Got itself big ideas, the cock-yolly bird did. Like captains, all that gold on their sleeves and hats. Sense of power – goes to the head. The cock-yolly bird, it told itself it could fly in circles for ever, see? Ended up going in ever-decreasing circles till it disappeared up its own fundamental orifice.'

The steward kept a straight face. 'Fundamental orifice, sir?'

'Asshole, stoo'ard.'

The British were not fast in the uptake, something to be remembered when Senator Manderton passed the results of his fact-finding mission to Congress.

While the search proceeded, Captain Pacey spoke to the two Germans, Rolf Freitag and Gunther Prien. They were evasive and slyly smiling. Pacey mistrusted their story. He put it to them straight. 'There is no device aboard my ship. Is there?'

Prien answered. 'You do not know, Captain. You cannot be sure. So you will continue to search the ship.'

Pacey stared at them as they stood between three seamen detailed as escort. He scanned the faces; they met his look with smiles. Pacey would have liked to have applied pressure, a little strong-arm work, but these

Germans ranked as prisoners-of-war and as such were entitled to proper treatment. He said, 'If there is such a device, then if it blows, you blow too. But you know this already.'

'Yes, Captain.'

'Which was why you spoke about it.'

'Yes, Captain.'

'But you do not know where it has been placed.'

'No, we do not know.'

'Nor who placed it, and when?'

They didn't know that either. Pacey asked more questions, repetitions of questions asked at his first interrogation, where in the USA they had come from, when they were last in Germany, and others. They appeared to answer honestly. But Pacey got no farther ahead.

He terminated the interview. 'The search will go on,' he said abruptly. 'You will be taken back below to the cells.'

'If the ship should blow up, Captain –'

'You will be brought on deck if possible. The rules of war, the Geneva Convention, will be kept to aboard my ship. But I cannot do the impossible. I think you know what I mean.'

Rolf Freitag narrowed his eyes. 'You mean you will leave us, saying that to bring us up was impossible.'

'Only if it proves to be just that – impossible. It will depend where the damage occurs. And I have my passengers to consider before yourselves.' Pacey watched for a reaction: was there sudden fear in the faces, or was there not? Hard to say. Pacey had them removed below, and climbed slowly to the bridge. He looked out into improving weather. The wind had fallen and the sky was blue, though the sea's surface was still broken into white horses. The bow-wave creamed back from the liner's stem, to mingle aft with the wash from the four screws. Pacey took a deep breath. The sea was clean. Or it had been until the outbreak of the war. Since then it had run red with the blood of seamen, and had acted as a shield for the German U-boats that had loosed off their torpedoes from beneath the surface and then sometimes come up to rake the sinking decks of British ships with gunfire. Then down again, to slink away to the Fatherland or to sink more ships.

The sea, of course, had always been an enemy; seamen knew that. Its smiling face, as now this morning, could change quickly into ugliness, the lash of a gale, the tearing, shrieking tempest that could overwhelm a ship, stop her in her tracks, catch her, perhaps, unawares and cause her to broach-to, to lie across wind and sea so that she couldn't steer back to her course but had to lie helpless in the sea's grip, battered at without mercy. In his days in sail Captain Pacey had often come close to disaster, sails torn from the bolt-ropes off the pitch of the Horn, masts ripped out as though by a giant's unfeeling hand . . . or lying on a lee shore with rocks close, rocks that could rip out a ship's bottom in minutes, with helples seamen flung into the water to perish by drowning or impact with the rocks.

Looking out across the water towards distant Britain, Pacey thought about Testament Thomas, his one-time captain so many years ago in what now seemed a different world – a world, Testament Thomas used to say, where ships were wood and men were made of iron. Some time after the young Pacey had left sail for steam, Testament Thomas had been lost at sea and with him his ship and most of her crew. The three-masted barque *Conington Hall* that the old man had commanded had been carrying a cargo of wool, home from Australian waters to 'Falmouth for orders' as had been the customary way of putting it for homeward-bounders. Coming up the South Atlantic, north of the Falkland Islands and a long way from both South America and South Africa with his self-combustible cargo, Testament Thomas had faced perhaps the worst thing any seaman could face: fire at sea. Smoke had been seen coming from Number One hold. Immediate steps had been taken to douse the flames; but the fire had spread, outrun the pumps' capacity, and in a very short time the *Conington Hall* had been ablaze from stem to stern.

Odd, Pacey had often thought, how a ship could burn with all that sea around her. But they could, and did. Once abandoned, the barque had burned to the waterline, and had continued burning inside the hull until it had become a shell ready to collapse inwards with the weight of water.

Testament Thomas had ordered the lifeboat to be launched as a precaution when the fire had started; the boat was secured by a grassline to the poop and trailed astern ready for use when the order came to abandon. When the order was inevitable, Testament Thomas had given it. His crew had jumped overboard and had swum for the lifeboat. Testament Thomas, himself pushing his first mate over behind the crew, had stayed aboard. Pacey knew why, knew why he would probably do the same himself: at sea, in the Merchant Service as in the King's ships, the ship was the Captain and the Captain was the ship, one entity, indivisible.

Pacey, years later in Liverpool, had met a very old man, one he remembered from his apprenticeship, a seaman who had been with Testament Thomas aboard the *Conington Hall* on her last voyage. He'd said he owed his life to Captain Thomas.

'A terrible sight it wor, sir. Lord love me, I can see it still! Cap'n, 'e took up his position right aft, sir, abaft the wheel, atop 'is own cabin that was burnin' like the bleedin' fires o' hell. I see 'im go, sir, lit up like a candle. Right to the last 'e were singing a hymn. I can 'ear that too.

"Nearer my God to Thee, nearer to Thee". ' The old seaman had lifted a shaking hand and rubbed tears from his eyes. 'I never did see the like afore or since, an' I 'ope to the good Lord I never do.'

It could happen again. It could happen aboard the *Laurentia*, and it could happen to a lot of people.

Captain Pacey turned on his heel and went into the wheelhouse. He used the voice-pipe to the Staff Captain's quarters: no reply. Pacey sent a messenger to find Morgan, ask him to come to the bridge.

Morgan came, doubling up the bridge ladder. He saluted the Captain. Pacey asked, 'All well, Morgan?'

'Yes, sir. Search proceeding – nothing found yet.'

'The passengers?'

'Restive, sir. Some of the women are pretty worried. As you said – the yarn about tricky waters isn't believed. Not by many of them at all events.'

'No. I understand that. Pass the word, Morgan – all passengers to assemble in the first-class lounge. I'll talk to them.'

'Give them the facts, sir?'

Pacey nodded. 'That's what I said I'd do. And the time's come.'

He was still worried about panic. Panic came mostly from a lack of knowledge of what was going on. That had to be put right.

It was a crush, like an overcrowded train. Lady Barlow complained about it; Eustace did his best to act as a buffer but could not be at all sides of his mother simultaneously. John Holmes and Elizabeth Kent attended together, John's arm around Elizabeth protectively though she didn't need it. Leon Fielding was a nuisance, attending with his empty perambulator. Senator Manderton became entangled with it and exploded.

'God damn! That *goddam* pram! Do you have to bring it with you?'

'Oh, I *am* sorry.' Fielding removed his straw hat apologetically, looking confused, and pulled the conveyance out of the way. It impacted against Mr Jones, who was too *distrait* to protest. 'It's Ming, you see. I don't –'

'Oh, heck!' Senator Manderton, jaw out-thrust, pushed away from Fielding, whom he considered as nutty as a fruit cake. He elbowed aside the Descartes children, all six of them present with their parents: the smaller ones were unreliable if left on their own in the cabin, and it was the eldest son's right to hear the Captain at first hand. The man Craigson was there, the one with the complaint about Leon Fielding. As he pushed by, he made loud comments about old men who should by rights be under lock and key, or anyway under arrest in their cabins. Leon Fielding, overhearing as he was meant to, looked on the verge of tears. It was so unjust; he'd meant only to be friendly.

Patrick Haggerty attended with Ambassador-to-be Grant.

'I reckon it's to be about the search,' Haggerty said. 'That's what I call a liberty, searching the cabins of US citizens. Maybe thought we were smuggling, I guess!'

'Let's hear what he has to say before we judge, Patrick. Captain Pacey . . . he's a level-headed sort of man, wouldn't you say?'

Grudgingly Haggerty nodded. 'I reckon so, yes. They're not all tarred with the same brush.'

Grant looked sideways at the banker. He had a shrewd idea what the brush referred to was: the English as against the Irish. Not that Pacey had indicated what his personal thoughts about Ireland might be: he very likely had no views either way. Grant believed that in fact there was more awareness of the Irish question in New York than there was in Britain. So many expatriates, and they were always the most vociferous, more nationalistic than the natives. Grant had formed the opinion, since embarkation, that Patrick Haggerty was a poor choice for negotiator of the loan so desperately wanted and needed by the British. Wilson had boobed, and maybe by intent. Wilson was certainly nobody's fool, but he was devious. Just like the British Winston Churchill in fact. All countries had them. But Mr Ambassador-to-be Grant hoped very much that the British would get their loan. He had a lot of time for the British, and more so since he'd been aboard the *Laurentia*. Not so much the passengers, who were a pretty mixed lot – that Lady Barlow, for example, and the dimwit son who was going to dodge the war, they were a God-awful pair. It was the crew, from Captain Pacey down. Solid and dependable, knew their jobs, emanated a feeling that the passengers were in good hands. Even the stewards, on the cabins and in the saloon and other public rooms. Excellent PanAtlantic service, willing and cheerful and often with a touch of humour, polite and attentive without being over-obsequious. It wasn't usually quite like that in America. Americans of that level could be awkward, sometimes downright rude and contemptuous, or they could go the other way and act oilily, and say all manner of things about you behind your back.

General de Gard was in the forefront of the passengers as the Captain came down from the bridge and stood before the muster, accompanied by the Staff Captain and the Purser. General de Gard was conscious of his own importance as the only ranking army officer aboard. He stared about superciliously; at his side was Adeline Scott-Mason, taking comfort, he knew, from the proximity of their two bodies. She'd had a premonition that Captain Pacey was going to say something unpalatable. She needed comfort; during the night, General de Gard had given it. That, he thought, should be sufficient;

he was a little irritated by her closeness now. There was in the General's view a time for love and a time for war. Madame Scott-Mason was becoming a clinging vine.

Livia Costello's eyes were fixed on Purser Matthews as he entered the lounge with the Captain. Matthews was another giver of comfort to passengers. He had proved very experienced in his seduction methods, not that he'd needed to bother much in her case. She had been more than ready, and part of her readiness was centred on revenge against Larry her husband, soon to be her ex.

While Captain Pacey conferred for a moment with his senior officers, Henry Sayers Grant watched the Rickards joining the fringe of the muster, down at the back end of the lounge. Arm-in-arm, like a couple of youngsters. The Rickards represented, in Grant's view, the best of the passengers, the best of the British. They had an air about them; an air of breeding and of having seen better days. Rickards' threadbare suit was basically a good one, well tailored, carefully brushed and cleaned. He was like Britain itself, Britain as it was now, threatened and bleeding financially to death under the strain of war and a long and honourable history – give or take a few episodes like the attempt way back to impose taxation on the American colonies without representation. Like old Rickards, Grant thought, though in fact he didn't know just how honourable, not being aware of the old man's rank and title.

Captain Pacey, man of few words, didn't waste time.

'Good morning, ladies and gentlemen. I've asked you to come together so that I can explain the search of the accommodation – I realize this has been an infernal nuisance and no one regrets the necessity more than I do. The fact is, our two German prisoners have made statements . . . saying there is an explosive device planted aboard the ship. . . .'

There had been a babble of voices and some of the women had burst into tears. Two had fainted; one, to the irritation of General de Gard, had been Adeline Scott-Mason. She sagged at his side, having first clutched at his arm so that he had taken a list like a torpedoed ship, a simile he thrust quickly from his mind. Captain Pacey had gone on to say that he had a fair idea the Germans had been lying, that it was no more than an attempt to harass everyone aboard. His ship's company, he said firmly, would not be rattled; he believed the passengers too would take it for what it was worth. In the meantime, naturally, the search would continue. Nothing would be left to chance. He asked the passengers themselves to help.

'If you all keep your eyes lifting – anything suspicious anywhere. A packet where it shouldn't be, anything that looks unusual anywhere in the ship – that's the best way I can put it. Leave it alone and inform the nearest member of the crew. . . .'

Going back to the bridge, Pacey was well aware that many items aboard a ship would look unusual to landlubbers. The ship's company would be in for a busy time with false alarms; but that was better than something being overlooked.

The search went on. The ventilator shafts were probed, the big bell-mouthed ventilators that caught the wind on deck were checked, no stone was left unturned. Nothing was found. A storm in a teacup? Pacey was convinced he'd been right about the Germans. But the Germans were succeeding if their aim had been to spread alarm. The atmosphere in the ship was changing dramatically. The dangers into which they were steaming had been brought home much more vividly by the Germans' subterfuge than via the daily news-sheet giving information about a distant war across the English Channel and beyond.

The one person whose spirits lightened was Mr Jones. At first he had believed the cabin search to be personal to himself. Even when he had found that the search was general, of the whole ship, he had still been desperately worried. There were those teeth. Not all had gone to the seagulls; some bread-embedded molars or incisors, he knew not which, had dropped down, spurned by the seagulls, to the next deck, the embarkation deck. He had made a furtive search but had found nothing. For all he knew, they could have turned up. No reason, of course, why they should ever be connected with himself, but the guilty mind plays tricks.

But now it was all right. It wasn't teeth, it wasn't any part of Maggie, it wasn't the New York Police Department. It was only the Germans.

There was a song in Mr Jones's heart now.

Livia had gone straight to the Purser's private office. Matthews had just left the Captain; he had work to do on the cash balance: the *Laurentia* carried a lot of money in US dollars and in sterling. He looked impatient when Livia came in. Like General de Gard, he preferred to keep love and duty in separate compartments. As it happened, Livia was set to combine the two.

'I'm scared,' she said, and looked it. She had a very pale face and her hands were shaking.

'Rubbish! You heard what the Captain said. Panic over, Livia.'

'Is it?' she asked derisively. 'He's asked us to keep a look-out. I don't call that finis if you do.'

'Sheer precaution. There's absolutely no need to worry, Livia. I assure you of that.' Matthews' eye strayed to his desk; his ears strayed to the general office beyond the bulkhead. Sometimes his juniors could have big ears, like antennae: his ways were fairly accurately guessed at by his own staff. But nothing must ever come out further, as could happen accidentally in indiscreet conversation that could be overheard. So they mustn't have their conjectures confirmed too far. The owners, the PanAtlantic Line directors, had high standards; if anyone fell below those standards, dismissal loomed.

Livia dabbed at her eyes with a handkerchief. 'I'm so damn worried, Ralph. It's all kind of getting on top of me, I guess.'

'Just don't let it.'

'Oh sure, it's all very well saying that, nice and easy! Look.' She went closer to him, took his face in her hands. He smelled the gin on her breath. 'I want you to promise me something, right?'

Alarm bells rang in Matthews' mind. 'Depends what,' he said.

'I want you to promise me . . . if anything happens, if we get blown up, if we get torpedoed, you'll look after me.'

'Look after you? Personally? I have my responsibilities, my boat station, Livia!'

'Sure, I know that. But you're saying no? After all we've been –'

'All right, darling,' he said quickly, not wanting a resumé – those big ears not so far away. 'You've been great, really great.' Matthews knew very well, knew it beyond all possible doubt, that he could never accede to any request for 'looking after' any one person at all, never mind who. It was established policy of the Line, for instance, that no relative of any of the crew travelled in the same ship. If any one of the crew knew of even, say, an aunt by marriage about to book, his duty was to dissuade her. If he could not, then he was duty bound to report the facts to PanAtlantic, whereupon he would be taken out of the ship for that voyage. There must never be any relationship ties if ever disaster should strike, in peace or war. A crew member's duty was to the passengers as a whole.

So it was definitely no go. But promises come easy to philanderers and Matthews didn't want Livia Costello shooting her mouth off around the ship. So he said, 'Of course I'll look after you, darling. Of course I will.'

Leon Fielding answered the tap at his cabin door, fearing the worst, fearing arrest and the police and disgrace when he reached England.

But it was the knock of a friend: Elmer Houston Pousty, Quaker of goodwill.

Such a relief! 'Oh, it's you, Mr Pousty!'

'Large as life,' Pousty said amiably. 'Mind if I come in?'

'No, do, do. I'm so glad to see you. So very glad. I'm so worried – about what the Captain said. Do you think he knows what he's doing?'

'Doing? In what respect, Mr Fielding? I reckon he knows, all right.

You don't get to be a master mariner if you don't know what you're doing.'

'No, no, of course not. In a – a seafaring sense. I meant, in regard to not believing those Germans, you see. Anything could happen at any moment, couldn't it?' Fielding blinked up at Pousty, his eyes beseeching, asking for reassurance.

'I guess not. Though the search is still going on, just in case. We're in good hands, Mr Fielding. Just forget it, right? Let's talk of something better. What we're going to do when we reach Great Britain?'

'Oh, yes.' Fielding dabbed at his face with his handkerchief. 'You said you were going to join in the war. I don't call that much better, really. So dangerous.'

'Just a medical corpsman, Mr Fielding. Not a man with a gun.'

'Well, no, but bearing stretchers is very dangerous too. The Germans make no distinctions, so I've heard. They don't always respect the Red Cross, even on ambulances. They're so very brutal, Mr Pousty. Do take care.'

Pousty laughed gently. 'I'll do that, all right. I promised my momma. I aim to carry out my promises. But don't let's talk about me. I never did ask you . . . what are you going over for, Mr Fielding?'

Leon Fielding's mouth sagged open and a look of utter bewilderment came into his eyes. He said, 'Do you know, I don't know. I – I've forgotten! It's really most extraordinary, *most* extraordinary.'

'Well, I guess it'll come back to you, Mr Fielding –'

'I don't know that it will. It's gone, quite, quite gone.' He paused, cogitating hard. 'It's been all the worry, don't you know. That wretched little boy, so mendacious, and the dreadful father, such a loud man and so coarse. And poor little Ming.'

His gaze went to the empty perambulator. He reached out for it and pulled it across, rocked it to and fro. 'I do remember now, saying goodbye to little Ming. And mummy. But that's all.' He looked at Pousty, still very bewildered. 'I wonder what I was going for? It's very worrying, not knowing.'

'Sure must be something important.' A singing commitment? No, the old guy was too old, didn't look capable any more. It would be cruel even to suggest a singing tour or whatever. Pousty said again, 'Must be something important that'll come back to you.'

'Yes. But it's most dreadfully worrying now you've brought it up. Dreadfully.'

'Yeah, I see that, Mr Fielding. Look out, you'll upset the little pram –'

Fielding had canted the perambulator. Now he did indeed upset it. It went over on its side. From its interior a waterproof cover, then a pink blanket of good quality, came out in a heap. With them came a sliding wooden cover over a sort of false bottom, a pit where a child – or in this case a doll – at the sitting-up stage would place its feet. Out as well from the pit came something else, a brown-paper-covered package. Pousty picked it up.

'What's this?' he asked.

Fielding looked, appearing puzzled. 'Well, really, I don't know. I think mummy must have put it there perhaps. For Ming. Tinned food most probably.'

Pousty gave it a shake. It was quite heavy. Then he heard a ticking. He thought about that search still going on; he realized that anything could have been hidden in that perambulator when Fielding had maybe left it unattended on embarking, showing his passage ticket, making some inquiries at the Purser's office. Crazy maybe – but crazier things happened and Pousty didn't hesitate. He said, 'Ming stayed behind, remember, and food cans don't tick.' Clutching the brown-paper package he moved fast for the door. Forgetting his Quaker upbringing for the moment he said, 'Jesus Christ Almighty, Mr Fielding, this here's a bloody bomb!'

'It went right overboard, sir,' Pousty reported to the Captain. 'I knew your orders about contacting a steward or someone, but I didn't reckon there was time, so –'

'You were quite right, Mr Pousty. You're a brave man and you may have saved the ship. At the very least there would have been casualties. If Mr Fielding had taken that perambulator close to the ship's side below decks, well, it could have blown out a plate, stripped the rivets. Not that we know how big the charge was.' Pacey paused. 'Any ideas as to how it could have been planted?'

Pousty expounded his theory. 'Easy done, sir, I reckon. And maybe those Heinies genuinely didn't know its location. There could have been another man, an accomplice.'

Pacey nodded. 'That's very possible. There's always any number of people milling around on sailing day. The Press and all that, the Godspeeders. I'm very grateful, Mr Pousty, and so will the Line be. And I'll be having something weighty to say to whoever should have searched that perambulator.'

'I'd better have a word with Fielding, Morgan,' Pacey said when Pousty had gone below. Pacey was in his day cabin with the Staff Captain and Matthews. 'Purser, I'll ask you to have Mr Fielding paged. It's unlikely, I suppose, but he might be of some help – he might have seen this hypothetical accomplice.'

Matthews went to the door and opened it. Then he turned round. 'Paging not necessary, sir. Mr Fielding's here.'

'Ask him to come in.'

Pacey got to his feet, hand outstretched in greeting. Leon Fielding entered. His perambulator was not with him. He said, 'I'm really very sorry. Most sorry – I hope you'll forgive me?'

'There's nothing to forgive, Mr Fielding. We all know it wasn't your fault.'

'Oh, well, that's really very kind of you, very kind, and very forgiving, Captain. I do appreciate it.' Fielding paused, looking puzzled again. 'But I wonder how you knew?'

'Knew, Mr Fielding? I don't –'

'I've only just realized it myself. I had put that parcel there for safety. I've remembered that, you see. Mummy knows how forgetful I am, and the alarm clock was to wake me in the morning. It's a very valuable one, made of alabaster. I'm so sorry if I've caused any bother.'

10

Pousty's dash for the open deck had been seen by a number of people, and more people had seen him cast the package overboard. Pousty had spoken to some of them, saying that he had, as he firmly believed, found the device planted by the Germans. He parried all questions as to where he had found it: he had no wish to add to Leon Fielding's troubles by promulgating any idea that the singer could have a link-up with the Germans, which would have been a conclusion many of the passengers would have leapt to. Fielding was facing enough opprobrium already.

The search went on; and the word spread that Mr Pousty's discovery had been a red herring. But the incident somehow had the effect of making matters worse; almost as though a real device had been found and now another was being looked for.

The unease aboard the *Laurentia* increased.

In the hotel in Wilhelmshavn Ilse Eppler had received a message. This had come from her father, Admiral von Neuburg. The Admiral wished to see his daughter immediately. Ilse, from long habit, obeyed the summons, taking the train to Berlin and her family home.

Admiral von Neuburg welcomed her with a kiss but there was something in his manner that disquieted his daughter. He took her to his study, a place filled with old furniture, old books and charts. There was the mahogany roll-top desk that had graced the Admiral's quarters when last he had been at sea, flying his flag in the battleship *Derfflinger*.

'Sit,' he said, and she sat in a large leather armchair. Her father paced the room, stopped by a big window and looked out on his garden. Then, abruptly, he swung round.

'There has been talk, Ilse.'

'Talk, father?'

'Talk, yes. I think you know what I mean.'

'I don't know that I do.' Ilse's face was pale, but two spots of red now appeared in her cheeks.

'Then I shall explain, Ilse. There has been talk . . . that you have been consorting with other officers in –'

'Consorting,' she broke in flatly. 'What is that supposed to mean, father?'

'That you have had affairs.' The Admiral held up his hand as she started to speak again. 'I shall not ask you to confirm or deny – I say only this: if there are or have been such affairs, then they will stop. I shall not have the name of von Neuburg sullied by . . . a wife who betrays her husband while he is on active service for the Fatherland and our Emperor. And remember this, Ilse: I have much time for your husband. He is a fine young officer, brave, resourceful, ready to die for his country. Do you understand?'

She nodded, not speaking. Her father's tone scared her; she had always been a little afraid of him. He was an officer of the old school, hard, domineering, steeped in tradition, the fighting tradition of Germany, ever jealous of his family's name and honour.

He spoke again. 'Klaus is at this moment charged with a particular mission. I have heard that there is talk in Wilhelmshavn of this mission. Is this so, Ilse?'

'Yes, father.'

He nodded. 'As I thought. I have taken steps to have this brought to the attention of the Naval High Command so that it can be contra-dicted.' Even in retirement, Admiral von Neuburg had many strings to pull. 'British spies are everywhere, Ilse. The operation must not be jeopardized. Obviously, you know what I'm talking about.'

'Yes, father. The *Laurentia*.' She looked at him closely. 'I think you do not approve, do you, father?'

His voice snapped. 'It is not for me to approve or to disapprove. What is ordered must be obeyed. It has fallen to your husband to have the honour of carrying out the orders. I know that he will not fail. And I expect you also not to fail – not to fail your husband. Is that clear, Ilse?'

It was clear. Ilse Eppler knew that she had been given unequivocal orders. She knew also, without it having been put into words, that for the sake of those whose careers could be put in jeopardy by a word in the right quarter from Admiral von Neuburg, she must break off her liaisons. Or make an attempt to do so.

She spent one night at home in Berlin. Next day she travelled back to Wilhelmshavn to await the return to base of U-120. When she reached the port she learned that the officer who had produced the bottle of Plymouth gin in her bedroom had been ordered at a pier-head jump to the Mediterranean theatre of the war, and specifically to the sea areas off the approaches to the Dardanelles.

'Frankly, Prime Minister, I'm more concerned at this moment with the Dardanelles. The *Laurentia* can be left to look after herself. The Dardanelles cannot. Out there is a running sore.'

Mr Asquith sighed; Winston Churchill was always a tiresome man to deal with. And the Dardanelles campaign had been sponsored by Churchill himself in league with Lord Fisher, another difficult man. They were responsible for terrible slaughter: the casualties to the British, Australian and New Zealand troops had been frightening to a politician, a Prime Minister leading a great nation at war. Mr Asquith was no militarist; back in 1907, before he had become Prime Minister, he had opposed the naval estimates, preferring to see money spent on public welfare rather than defence; although he had reversed himself in the following year, he knew he had antagonized Lord Fisher – not a difficult thing to do. And Fisher was running rings round him: four months earlier Fisher and Churchill had conceived a scheme to come to the aid of embattled Russia by striking through from the south – from the Mediterranean towards Turkey by way of the Dardanelles passage. Fisher had proposed a land and sea attack on the Turkish positions, using battleships to bombard the Dardanelles forts while troops were to be put ashore south of the entry to the strait. This plan he had put to Churchill, who had at once seen the Navy's chance: Churchill's fighting instincts had responded wholeheartedly to the idea of the battle squadrons, the heavy battleships, reducing the forts to rubble and forcing a passage through the Dardanelles, past Gallipoli where there would be Greek support and into the Sea of Marmara.

In theory it had sounded splendid: a new front to be opened up, something more profitable than the backwards and forwards surge of the entrenched armies on the Western Front.

Later, Lord Fisher had seen doom in the proposed operation. He saw that Churchill had let his boundless enthusiasms run away with him; that by oratory, dazzling arguments, he had swayed more experienced minds towards what was to become a tragedy of war. Fisher had made his disgreements strongly known. At a meeting of the War Council, Asquith had decided that the operation must go on; he had seen no alternative, once committed. Fisher, furious, had jumped to his feet and left the room, tendering his resignation from the office of First Sea Lord. Lord Kitchener had followed him, and persuaded him to go along with the collective decision rather than precipitate a crisis.

The landings, or the attempts at landings, had been bloody in the extreme. By 18 March the battle-cruiser *Inflexible*, much needed by Admiral Jellicoe in home waters, had been crippled. Many battleships had been sunk. More and more replacements were demanded from the home commands. The Army was complaining that the Navy was leaving the soldiers to die, deserting them in their hour of need.

It was replacements that were responsible for Mr Churchill's call upon the Prime Minister.

He said now, emphasizing each word by a thump on the table,

'Monitors. Aircraft. Repair ships. Cruisers and battleships, Prime Minister. Destroyers. They are vitally needed out there.' Mr Churchill was aware that a crisis was developing between himself and his First Sea Lord. Fisher was unwilling to deplete the Grand Fleet, wishing to maintain the uneasy balance between the British and German main battle fleets. Both Churchill and Fisher knew they were fighting for their own jobs as well, and in Churchill's case also for his political future.

Mr Churchill went on, 'I say again, Prime Minister, those ships are vital. We have already committed much. We must not lose that now through faint-heartedness, an unwillingness to follow through.'

Mr Asquith tried to press his point. 'My dear Winston, to send cruisers – cruisers especially – would be to reduce the availability of escorts in home waters. The U-boats are known to be very active off the south-western approaches. You should not lose sight of the facts. The *Laurentia* is by now almost half way across from New York. I have already made that point. We simply cannot afford to risk the *Laurentia* . . . for one thing, Haggerty's aboard, the New York banker. His arrival is urgent – we must have that loan. Also there is Ambassador Grant. And there's a French general aboard – General de Gard. . . .'

Churchill was dismissive of all French generals. He conceded the point about Patrick Haggerty – it had been raised before, of course. But in Churchill's view there were other and more important considerations. Recently he had had more talks with Fisher; Fisher also was of the opinion that a single cruiser escort would be quite sufficient to meet the incoming liner off Cape Clear. Fisher in fact had been quite off-hand about it, not seeming concerned about the liner's fate. But once again he had made an oblique reference to the fact that the entry of the United States into the war was of paramount inportance.

Churchill had asked quietly, 'Above the lives of hundreds of passengers, Jacky?'

Fisher's answer had been in character. 'Little people! People of no consequence, most of them! We have an *Empire* to guard, Winston, you and I! No one else is of much damn help! Kitchener, for instance, is nothing but a *stuffed shirt* filled with megalomania!'

Today, closeted with Mr Asquith, Mr Churchill continued to press the case for naval reinforcements to be sent post-haste to the Dardanelles. The *Laurentia*, he repeated, was in no very particular danger and it was very highly unlikely the Germans would risk her sinking in any case. With so many women and children embarked, she was perhaps the safest ship afloat. . . .

One among many who did not share Mr Churchill's complacency in regard to the *Laurentia* was Captain Pacey's wife, Mary. Mary Pacey, worrying about a son and a husband at sea, still mourning a soldier son killed in Flanders, went through the long days in an agony of mind. The Paceys rented a small house in Southsea, which suburb of Portsmouth had always been William Pacey's home. Mary Edwards, as she had been, was the only daughter of a parson, vicar of St Jude's Church, also in Southsea, now dead as was her mother. There had been opposition to the marriage: sailors were a roistering lot according to the vicar and his wife, given to drink and other vices which the vicar did not go into precisely. Nevertheless, the marriage had taken place in Mary's father's church: William Pacey had gained approval because he was honest and sober and had a strong belief in God. Also because he was manly and dedicated to his profession – the vicar had realized that he would get on in life.

When her husband was at sea Mary Pacey went daily to her father's old church of St Jude and knelt in prayer in a pew off a side aisle. The sea was always dangerous, even in peacetime. Mary had vivid memories of the tragedy of the *Titanic*, another great liner, of the White Star Line, friendly rivals of PanAtlantic. That had been only four years ago; the memories were fresh. The Paceys had known two of the ship's officers who had perished; they had known Captain Smith, who had gone down with his ship. The newspapers of the time, of course, had been full of the loss, the loss of a ship said to be unsinkable. The *Illustrated London News* had carried the most harrowing sketches of the great liner's end, the tilted decks, the clouds of smoke and steam, the crammed lifeboats, some of them upturned on lowering.

Mary Pacey, as the *Laurentia* ploughed on across the North Atlantic, prayed that nothing of that sort would happen. A torpedo would be worse than an iceberg: a great explosion, killing and maiming, ripping a great hole in the liner's steel plates to bring horror and confusion below decks. Her husband, she believed, would follow the example of Captain Smith of the *Titanic* and refuse to leave his shattered command.

'Oh God, save them all,' she said aloud. There were tears in her voice. She had read the reports from America in the newspapers: she knew about the German manifesto, the threat to sink the *Laurentia* thinly veiled, the telegrams sent to some of the passengers indicating a U-boat attack once the liner was within range of the German submarines.

In the aisle alongside her pew, a man moved slowly. He stopped when he saw Mary Pacey, waited until she rose from her knees and, turning, saw him.

'Oh!' she said in some confusion. 'I didn't realize –'

'Please don't apologize for praying, Mrs Pacey!'

She was even more confused; the man was the vicar, the Reverend

Andrew Horsman whom she knew well. She said, 'I'm so worried, Mr Horsman.'

'Of course you are.' He motioned her back into the pew, and sat beside her. He saw a rather dumpy little woman in her early fifties, not fashionably dressed, of a faded prettiness and with a kind face now creased with her anxieties. He tried to find words of comfort: he was not good at it, though in all conscience he had had plenty of recent experience as was to be expected in the premier naval port of the Empire. So many seamen had been lost, so many families had sought comfort from the church. But Horsman had always found it difficult even in times of peace when he felt obliged to offer comfort to widows and sons and daughters. To himself, his words tended to sound hollow, no more than the expected mouthings of a man of God. Yet his own faith was deep and genuine. He believed implicitly in the existence of God, in the virgin birth, in the whole Bible story. He knew there was going to be a life hereafter and that this present earthbound one was no more than a preparation. Earthbound was the right term: afterwards, the freed spirit would soar to the heavens, earthly concerns forgotten, crutches cast away. The halt and the maim would be whole, the blind would see, the deaf hear. The love of God would enfold all persons who on earth had dwelt. Mr Horsman was a very conventional clergyman and knew it. He disliked and distrusted those who were not, those who found it fashionable to cast doubt on what so many generations of God-fearing men and women had never thought of questioning. The doubters were the ones who had taken a personal bite at that apple, those seduced by the serpent in the Garden of Eden.

'You must have trust in God, Mrs Pacey,' he said now.

'I have,' she said simply. 'But He can't answer everyone's prayers, can He? So often, there's a conflict of interests. I don't know if you follow.'

He nodded. 'Oh, yes, I think I do. I believe you're referring to the Germans, Mrs Pacey. Am I right?'

'Yes,' she said. 'The Germans will want the *Laurentia* to go down. That's something I have to face.'

'You believe they'll be praying . . . to that end?'

'Yes, I do. It stands to reason, Mr Horsman.'

'Yes, perhaps.' He nodded: the conversation wasn't going quite the way he'd envisaged. 'But I'm quite certain God doesn't answer *bad* prayers. Not the sort that would bring sorrow to so many people. Sorrow and hardship.'

'Well, I don't know so much. *We* pray that way too, don't we? Or the naval chaplains do, I'm sure. They pray for the Germans to be sunk and drowned, don't they?'

Horsman pursed his lips. He tried to answer carefully. He said, 'I

127

don't really think so. Only in a very general way, for victory. Victory over evil – the Germans are evil, of course. I really do believe God can sort the – the wheat from the chaff, Mrs Pacey.'

'But don't the Germans consider us evil?'

'If they do,' the vicar said firmly, 'they're wrong. Quite wrong! *Our* cause is just. That, you see, is why I say, put your trust in God. God the arbiter, the just judge.' He was sweating a little, finding himself a little out of his ecclesiastical depth. He rose to his feet: there was a meeting shortly of the parochial church council. 'Your prayers for the *Laurentia* will be joined by many, Mrs Pacey, my own included of course. Now I really must dash.'

Mary Pacey left the church by the south door, into Kent Road. She didn't feel much helped, except that merely being in what had been her father's church brought its own help. She wondered, not for the first time, what her father's reaction to the war would have been. She believed he would have been stunned, grieved by man's folly. At the time, he had had much to say about the war in South Africa, which had started shortly before his death. But whatever his views he would have carried on the daily round, as now Mary had to. Doing so she went to the Mikado café in Palmerston Road for a cup of coffee and a plain biscuit. Then there was the shopping: Handley's store for some sheets to replace some worn ones; Pink's for groceries; MacCreary's for some fish for that night's supper – fish at least was quite plentiful, though there were shortages already in other foodstuffs. There was talk of rationing to come. If it wasn't for the merchant ships bringing in food, the country would starve in no time. The newspapers had said that. William had said it too; she had often felt that William would have preferred to command a ship carrying vital cargo to Britain, rather than passengers to consume more food after arrival.

Aboard the *Laurentia* there was another man of God, the Reverend Jesse Divine, minister of a smallish sect based in Nashville, Tennessee – the clergyman who had been disgruntled at not being asked to take matins on the Sunday. He often remarked that it was his surname that had led him into the ministry. He was a large man in his early sixties, florid faced, beetling eyebrows, built like a bison, a man who would have fitted well into the open air life rather than the pulpit. He was an outgoing man, an extrovert of enormous energy. His mission was to bring God to the people rather than the other way round. There were, he was accustomed to say, plenty of more orthodox ministers doing just that and they hadn't had a conspicuous success. Their congregations attended because it was expected of them. They showed off their Sunday-go-to-meeting clothes, and the young men made sheep's eyes at the girls across the aisle. They didn't really get to meet God. So God, in the Reverend Jesse Divine's view, had to be brought out of seclusion and into the lives of the people.

The morning Mary Pacey had encountered the vicar of St Jude's in distant Southsea, Mr Divine, who preferred to be called the Reverend Divine, had been pondering how best to bring God to the third-class passengers aboard the *Laurentia*. He had been walking the boat deck; and in so doing had fallen in with Elmer Houston Pousty, Quaker from Chicago.

'A very good morning to you, Mr Pousty.'

'And to you, Reverend. Weather's better.'

'Yes, indeed, and we should thank God for that. It will make conditions better below. I have the third class in mind particularly. There's little comfort down there, and much crowding.'

Pousty nodded. 'Yep. If anything happened. . . .'

'A torpedo – exactly. Poor souls! I fear they can't be very happy, with that in their minds, Mr Pousty.' They paced on, clutching their hats against what was still a strong breeze. 'I have it in mind to raise their spirits. But how?'

Pousty glanced sideways, a faint grin twisting his mouth; he had had a number of conversations with the Reverend Divine and knew the way his mind worked. 'Raise them towards God, Reverend?'

'Yes.' The Reverend Divine spread his arms wide and raised then towards the sky in a huge gesture. He wore a black cloak; that, with his great bulk, gave him the air of an enormous bat. 'God is with us, even though He is up there aloft. Given the chance, He will lift their spirits towards His heaven, Mr Pousty.'

'Sure. If He's given a bit of help?'

'Help? But surely –'

'Get them in the right kind of mood first. Soften 'em up for penetration. Kind of – of let God in by stages – get me?'

'Guess I don't, Mr Pousty –'

'A sing-song,' Pousty said with enthusiasm. 'A real, old-fashioned sing-song. Sentimental songs – you know? Make them dream of home. That'll get to them, Reverend. Then you bring in God. Right?'

The Reverend Divine nodded thoughtfully. Pousty went on, 'It's not only that. You know what a sing-song does. Makes people forget the hardships. Like the songs round the camp fires in the old days of the push west, the old-timers with their covered wagons. . . .'

So there was a sing-song that morning, before the bugles sounded for the stampede rush that was luncheon in the third class.

There was a number of Australians embarked, sailing to Britain to enlist in the armed forces. They felt that that way they would be in the firing line faster than if they went back to Australia and joined their own army. Already the ANZACs were fighting in the Dardanelles; the Australian sector might need replacements closer at hand than Sydney or Brisbane, Melbourne or Fremantle.

The Aussies had some beer inside them and they joined in the singing, loudly. Australia drowned out the United States and Britain both. 'The Star-Spangled Banner', 'Carry me back to Old Virginia', and 'Marchin' Through Georgia' succumbed, as did songs from the British music halls, to 'Waltzing Matilda' and songs about Ned Kelly. The Australians crashed their songs out, brooking no opposition. While they sang they swilled beer and the raucous voices grew louder. The singing became more uninhibited, and never mind the fact that there were women present. Many of the songs were anatomical. The Reverend Divine raised his own loud voice in protest, waving his arms like a windmill.

'Gentlemen, please! Think of the ladies –'

'That's just what we are doing, mate,' a voice roared back. 'Don't tell me you didn't hear the bloody words!'

The Reverend Divine certainly had. The last one had been about Old King Cole, who got up to the most extraordinary antics in the middle of the night. Raising his voice still louder, the Reverend Divine began to thunder out Tipperary. The British at all events took this up and the Reverend Divine mopped his brow in some relief. But when it ended the Australian contingent came back in with a coarse-looking man yelling out a limerick.

'There was an old man of Madras,' the man yelled. 'Whose balls were made of brass. In stormy weather they clanged together and sparks flew out of his arse. How's that one, Reverend?'

'I –' The Reverend Divine saw that it was hopeless. Another limerick was bawled out, something about an old man of Australia, who painted his private parts with a dahlia. Yet another cut in on this one, and a punch was thrown. That did it. A *mêlée* broke out. The fighting became general, British against Australians, US citizens against both, a real mix-up in which tables were wrenched from the deck and smashed and bottles of beer and glasses flew. Pousty took a blow on the head from a bottle and was rescued by the Reverend Divine just as Master-at-Arms Warner came in through the for'ard door of the third-class lounge to read the Riot Act. God hadn't had a look in.

The Reverend Divine was breathing hard and his collar and tie were awry.

'Gee whizz,' he said as with Pousty he beat it for more civilized parts of the ship, 'if that master-at-arms hadn't showed up, I guess I'd have half-murdered some of those foul-mouthed bastards! You know something, Mr Pousty?' He breathed harder than ever, his eyes flashing fire. 'I guess I'm going to represent to the Captain that alcoholic drinks shouldn't ought to be served in the third class. They're no better than animals down there.'

Pousty, as the originator of the sing-song, kept his mouth shut.

Back across the miles of ocean that streamed astern of the *Laurentia*'s propellers, President Woodrow Wilson looked out from the great windows of the White House on a very different scene, one of peace and tranquillity, of the green of well-kept lawns, of super-smart Marine Corps sentries guarding the great entry doors at the top of a flight of steps. From behind the President there came the sound of music, quiet and soothing: his daughter Eleanor, married to the Secretary of the Treasury, was playing the piano. . . .

Music hath charms.

President Wilson's breast was savage and made no response to the piano. He fingered his lanternlike jaw, adjusted his spectacles, glaring from the window. He was a man of peace, and his principal wish was to keep his great country peaceful in the midst of war. He saw no reason whatsoever for the United States to join in a war that was none of its own making. He would resist to the death any suggestion that America should pull the British chestnuts from the fire.

But those suggestions had been made, and made very firmly by certain persons in the US administration, and in Congress – and in the press too. Earlier in the year, when President Wilson had been doing his level best to preserve the neutrality of the United States, and agreement had been reached that a note of protest should be sent to Britain against the British misuse, on a number of occasions, of the American flag – this had been hoisted by British ships in areas liable to German attack – some sections of the press had spoken against the President's apparent bias against Great Britain.

But the British themselves were unhelpful to say the least. In mid-March an announcement had come from London that a total embargo was to be placed on trade with Germany. American ships would be prevented by British warships from entering German ports. This had resulted in an outburst of fury against Britain; lobbies for copper and cotton among other commodities were instituted. German propaganda agitated for an American embargo on war materials, and this aroused strong sympathy from the various Irish societies.

An anti-British wave was washing over the whole of the United States. Then it had begun to move the other way. Some US nationals were lost from time to time, when the German U-boats had attacked British vessels. These deaths had acted as a catalyst for the differing views in the administration, and Wilson had been caught in the middle of a boiling row. Secretary of State Lansing had spoken of atrocious acts, and of German lawlessness, and had demanded positive action. Others had declaimed the principle that US nationals travelled aboard the ships of belligerent nations at their own risk.

Wilson dithered: he was still for neutrality, but felt that events were building up against him. A surge of opinion, not yet too strong, was in the process of insisting that it was time that America showed the world that the eagle still had wings. And now the *Laurentia* and those pointed German warnings . . . if anything should happen, if the *Laurentia*'s passengers with so many United States citizens among them should turn out to be the innocent, helpless pawns of the war game, what then if the President of the United States of America had failed to act decisively and in time?

Bill Warner, senior master-at-arms of the *Laurentia*, had banged a few heads together, literally as well as metaphorically. For his pains he had been knocked to the ground, but had been hoisted to his feet by a sober Australian who had rounded on his mates and told them not to look for more trouble. Then Warner had got his hearing, and he read them all a lecture on proper behaviour at sea. There was danger around them all the while, he said, and riotous carryings-on didn't help. A loud voice told him it had been the Holy Joe's fault; this, Bill Warner disregarded. Holy Joes tended traditionally to be blamed for everything; they were unpopular at sea. Bill Warner, in his younger days, had sailed with men who believed that Holy Joes were Jonahs, bringing bad luck to a ship. Parsons and corpses were linked in the seafaring mind with ill-luck and foreboding.

He made a report to the Purser and the Staff Captain. Morgan said he would speak to two men whom Warner had isolated as likely trouble-makers, ringleaders in the outbreak of fighting. Morgan would guarantee it wouldn't happen again: he would use the threat of the cells. The Aussies wouldn't want to be placed in the same accommodation as the Germans. Apart from that, no action would be taken and the third-class bar could continue serving drinks. This question had already been raised by the Reverend Divine, who had been given his answer. To deprive the Australians of their beer would lead to worse trouble. Before Warner left he asked about the Fielding affair.

Morgan said, 'Have you any special reason for asking, Warner?'

'Just that there's hostility against the gentleman, sir.'

'Very overt?'

'At times, sir, yes. Passengers turn their backs, that sort of thing. Some of the kids have yelled after him.'

Morgan blew out his cheeks: this was a problem of a sort that no one liked being landed with. He said, 'All right, Master, thank you for reporting. I'll keep you informed.'

When Warner had gone Morgan turned to Purser Matthews. He asked, 'What's your view, Matthews?'

'Least said, soonest mended.'

'That's singularly unhelpful! You may well be right, but you're far from realistic. I certainly didn't get the impression that man Craigson was going to drop the charge. And it's not up to us aboard the ship to bring any pressure to bear – not that it would help Fielding vis-à-vis the other passengers. It has to take its course, that's all.'

'A course that ends – or begins – in Liverpool.'

'Yes. It's Fielding himself I'm worried about. In the interval, that is. He's pretty weird to begin with – God knows what all this may precipitate. I'm half-inclined to put a watch on him. A reliable steward, detailed as shadow!'

'No need, sir,' Matthews said. 'He's already got a shadow.' He told the Staff Captain about Elmer Houston Pousty. 'A brave man,' he added, 'and very conscientious in a self-imposed task. He'll see Fielding doesn't do anything drastic.'

He left the Staff Captain's accommodation, heading towards the first-class accommodation where he would meet Pacey at the start of Captain's Rounds. Reaching the state-room section, he took a critical look around together with the assistant second steward. The Old Man had a keen eye and used it. He also wore fresh white gloves for each Rounds, and was accustomed to running his hand along the back sides of steam pipes and so on in the alleyways and public rooms. If dust showed on the gloves, somebody was for it. And whoever got the first blast, where the passenger accommodation was concerned it all came the way of the Purser in the end.

Away back in Annapolis, Elizabeth Kent's fiancé, Jonas Gorman, trainee attorney, had made himself a list of dates, starting with the day he'd said goodbye to Elizabeth at the railroad station. He crossed off each day as night came. He had no real idea of how many days of waiting he had in store; it all depended on Elizabeth's dad and on the wartime sailings back across the Atlantic.

Each day was like a year; a year of hell. He, too, had read that well-advertised German warning. There was no doubt in his mind that the *Laurentia* was a marked ship. Not a man accustomed to prayer, Jonas Gorman now got down on his knees every night and every morning. He read the papers just as soon as he could get hold of one. Each time he was expectant of the worst. No news was said to be good news, of course.

But the bad news wouldn't come all that fast. Even as he read daily of no news, he knew that in that very moment of reading the *Laurentia* could be sinking. If Elizabeth went, so would all the meaning of his life. He tried to give himself courage by telling himself the British Navy would be in full control, that a great ship filled with passengers would be a first priority, that the warship escort would be strong enough to deter anything the Germans might send out.

It didn't help; the British were not all that hot, in actual fact. They hadn't done particularly well so far in the war.

In his state-room Patrick Haggerty, working yet on the complex draft of his polite refusal of the British request for a loan, read the *Laurentia*'s daily news-sheet.

He read of events in Ireland, of more attacks on the British garrison at the Curragh, of British soldiers shot dead in the Dublin streets. He read of the names of Irish patriots – of Eamon de Valera, of James Connolly, of Joseph Plunkett and of Sir Roger Casement. In Ireland there was a great deal of sacrifice going on. In the United States there were a great many Irishmen. No American administration could ever afford to disregard the Irish vote or the strength of Irish feeling that would manifest if ever Washington entered the war on England's side.

Haggerty recalled a remark made to him by Senator Melvin Manderton only the night before, over brandies after a rubber of bridge. 'Don't you, as an Irishman, regard it as a typical British cheek that they have the damn gall even to *ask* for a loan.?'

Haggerty's reply to that had been fairly non-committal; but yes, that was precisely what in fact he did think.

They were not going to get it anyway. The refusal was going to deflate a lot of people who thought they were of importance in the world. Prime Minister Asquith, Lord Fisher at the British Admiralty, even King George. And, overridingly perhaps, Mr Winston Churchill, who so dearly wished to bring his mother's country into the war and see her young men die.

Haggerty put his work aside, locking his papers into a briefcase which he then locked into the desk drawer. He went out on deck, into the fresh and still-boisterous air. He walked along the embarkation deck and then up the ladder to the boat deck. Two people, oldsters, were seated in deck-chairs and covered with rugs. One of them wore a bowler hat, the other, the woman, a hat tied down beneath her chin with a scarf. Her face was covered with a sort of net that also depended from the brim of the hat. Haggerty recognized that they were the Rickards. There was a gap between the rugs and Haggerty saw that the old fossils were holding hands, all lovey-dovey. He passed them by without a good morning:

there was something about old man Rickards that spoke of a military past, of an England that was surely going down the drain into history, of an England that saw no shame in its record of Irish oppression, of an England that once had had the infernal neck to treat Americans as colonists and now expected them to come to their salvation in the Flanders mud, the stink of death and cordite, and the thunder of the guns that were of no concern to the United States.

11

'WE'RE just not being kept informed,' the man Craigson said. 'Treat us like dummies, that's what they do. For all we know, we could be right where the Jerry U-boats are.' He lit a cigarette, sucked at it viciously, his face twisted. He was feeling bitter about the way his complaint had been treated: it hadn't, in his view, been taken seriously. If it had been, that Fielding would have been locked away where he couldn't get up to any further harm. Craigson referred to it now; he was speaking to one of the Australians, one who'd had his head thumped by the master-at-arms in the fighting.

'That Fielding,' he said bitterly. 'Case in point, that is. The bloody brass, it doesn't take any notice of third-class passengers. Eh?'

'Reckon you c'd be right, mate. That Pommie's a poofter if I ever see one. All that talk about mummy – my word! Wouldn't last five bloody minutes in Sydney. Wonder you don't take the law into your own hands, mate! I would.'

'You would?'

'Sure thing.'

Craigson looked thoughtful, his mean eyes screwing up, his mouth thinning to a hard line. Squelch Fielding to a pulp – there would be a lot of satisfaction in that! But the Aussie was going on. He was harking back to what Craigson had said before veering off onto the poofter: about them being treated as dummies. No one treated Australians like that, not if they wanted to go on living with a whole skin. Big Jake Ommaney came from the Australian bush originally, up by the Mitchell River in the York Peninsula, in Queensland, where men were men and women were glad of it. He'd mined copper for a living and he was as tough as a nut. He'd left Queensland after killing a man in a fight, as a result of which he'd been sent down for manslaughter.

On release he'd gone south to New South Wales and Sydney, where he'd drifted around the Cross – Kings Cross, the red light district where a living was to be picked up in all sorts of ways, few of them honest. After a year in the Cross, he'd been shanghaied aboard a British steamer and had woken up from the drunken stupor that normally preceded a shanghai-ing to find himself out in the Pacific beyond Sydney Heads, bound down for the Bight and Cape Leeuwin, and then Simonstown in

South Africa and finally Chesapeake Bay and Newport News, where he'd jumped ship and gone to New York. He had become a longshoreman, a docker. Then, after the war had broken out, he'd begun to feel the need to join in a real fight. So he was one of those going to Britain to join up. He would bellyache at the recruiting office for a draft to an Aussie outfit, probably fighting in Gallipoli. He wouldn't join a pommie outfit, where it was all yes sir and no sir, and salute a bunch of bloody snobs. . . .

Meanwhile, Big Jake sensed a fight of a sort closer at hand. He said, 'You're dead right, mate. They don't tell us anything. Cargo, that's what we are in the third class, the bloody steerage. Dirt, I reckon. I reckon something else, too.'

'What?'

'Call a meeting, why not? A protest meeting. Get all the blokes together, insist they want to be told what's what. Get that Captain down to the steerage, and face us, man to man. Eh? How about that, mate?'

Craigson nodded. 'It's an idea, Mr Ommaney. I'll think about it.'

'You do that. But don't take too bloody long, thinking. We're not all that far off bloody Britain now. Where the U-boats'll be for sure.'

In the first-class writing room Rickards was once again busy with a letter, this time addressed to the War Office, one more plea for a military appointment in any capacity that the Secretary of State for War might think appropriate. Anything: Railway Transport Officer, Remount Depot – and in any rank. He knew in his heart that it was hopeless but he still had to try, to leave no stone unturned in his efforts to help his country in war. In the letter he wrote that after disembarkation in Liverpool he intended taking the train to London and would attend in person as soon as possible; he might even reach the War Office before the letter, he reflected, depending upon how far the war had affected the postal delivery. But the overland distance was not great, the mail might be landed with the inward pilot, and in any case there would still, presumably, be the statutory four deliveries a day in London. . . .

He sealed the letter and placed it in an inside pocket for posting at the Purser's office. He left the writing room.

Across the compartment sat Lady Barlow with Eustace. Lady Barlow was also composing a letter. This was addressed to an acquaintance in the Foreign Office and it contained a request to do with her son. Eustace, she wrote, naturally wished to serve his country; but equally naturally could not do so in any military capacity on account of his heart. On the other hand, he was ideally suited for a position in the Foreign Office. Diplomacy would suit him very well; titled parentage would be an immense advantage, of course. He spoke a little French, too; and he had attended Westminster School. (She didn't say so, but Eton had not accepted him. It had been made politely plain that corned beef knights' offspring were not their cup of tea; at Eton they were all snobs.)

Suspending her own operation, Lady Barlow stared at the disappearing back of Mr Rickards. A desiccated old man, she thought, rude and rather common, and what clothes! Ten years at least out of date, and almost threadbare. She wondered what he had been in his younger day. Perhaps something like a bank manager – they were not extravagantly paid and no reason why they should be.

Expelling breath, she looked towards the table where the old man had been writing. Her eye was caught by a light brown envelope lying on the carpet, a somehow official-looking envelope.

She laid down her pen. 'Eustace.'

'Yes, mama?'

'There is something on the floor. There. Go and get it.'

'But it's –'

'Don't *argue*, Eustace. So bad for your condition.'

'Yes, mama.' Eustace went over to where Rickards had been sitting, bent and retrieved the envelope which he took to his mother.

She scanned it and felt her face flush. A hand went to her breast. The envelope bore the printed words ON HIS MAJESTY'S SERVICE and it was addressed to Major-General The Lord Rickards, VC, DSO. Lady Barlow felt quite faint. What had she said to him in the past? But perhaps he had a poor memory – the old usually had.

She gathered herself. 'Eustace!'

'Yes, mama?'

'Did you read that envelope?'

'No, mama –'

'Then do so now.' Lady Barlow thrust the envelope at her son.

'Good heavens, mama!'

'Exactly,' she said, her tone grim. 'You've not impressed him much, I think. You must make an effort, Eustace. A *Lord*, blimey!' In her excitement she was forgetting herself and her practised veneer. 'You go for it, boy! A lord's just the thing to get you into the diplomatic, just the bloody thing!'

John Holmes walked the boat deck with Elizabeth Kent. He was tongue-tied, at an awkward stage of his life when he was too conscious of his youth and inexperience. He'd had friendly relations with girls of his own age back home in Annapolis, but it had been just that – friendly, no more. He had never been in love. Not until now. He didn't know how to express it. He feared a rebuff. Elizabeth seemed unattainable in any case; older than himself and with a fiancé in Annapolis – she'd stressed that. John really had no chance unless a miracle occurred; but he wanted desperately for her to know his feelings. They might then have a few moments of a kind of intimacy before they parted in Liverpool. Not the final intimacy, of course – not with an engaged girl. But an intimacy of the mind, a state in which she understood and sympathized. Kisses could be exchanged, perhaps, no harm in that. No real harm. John Holmes didn't realize it but he was in love with the idea of being in love. Elizabeth Kent did realize it, and had began to realize something else: young men going off to war needed to feel they had a girl in the background, someone very positive to fight for, or at least an experience to look back on and cherish in memory.

She knew also how tongue-tied John was. So she drew him out. 'Something on your mind?' she said tentatively.

'Oh, no. Not really.'

'Get along with you! It stands out a mile and I don't believe it's the war. Or your folks back home in Annapolis. Why not come out with it, Johnnie?'

He was blushing and stammering. 'I – I –' They walked on; the deck was slippery in a few places, the wash-deck gangs who'd operated earlier, before the passengers went to breakfast, had failed to squeegee down properly. The *Laurentia*, lifting to a wave passing beneath her bottom, lurched a little and they slid. They ended up by the starboard guardrail, in the lee of a lifeboat. And they ended up with John's arms about her, quite by accident. He held her shoulders a little longer than he need have done. Then he bent his head and kissed her, rather awkwardly.

She didn't seem to mind. She said, 'Look, you've got grease on your coat.' He had; he squirmed his head around and looked. Heavy grease, from contact with the lowering gear for the lifeboat. He mumbled something about it not mattering.

'It'll collect dirt,' she said. 'Come down to my cabin. I've got some benzine cleaner.'

'Sure it's all right, Elizabeth?' He was diffident still.

'Yes,' she said firmly, 'quite all right.'

They went below to the second-class cabin accommodation. Elizabeth shared a cabin with another woman, and the other woman wasn't there. Elizabeth told him that the other woman was a nun, Sister Perpetua, of a nursing order and crossing the Atlantic to join the British house of her Order and, she hoped, get to France to nurse the sick and wounded from the trenches. Sister Perpetua spent almost the whole day reading her Bible and other religious literature in the second-class lounge. Looking back afterwards, John realized that she had made a particular point of stressing that Sister Perpetua was highly unlikely to put in an appearance.

He removed his coat and Elizabeth produced the benzine bottle. Then, with a curious look on her face, she put it away again. She said, 'Well, Johnnie, what are we waiting for?'

He didn't believe it. Stammering again he said, 'Do – do you – do you mean –'

'Yes,' she said.

He was totally inexpert; Elizabeth guided him gently. It was the most wonderful experience of his life. And Sister Perpetua, as predicted, stuck to her religious reading. Afterwards, John Holmes's head was in a whirl; Elizabeth must obviously be in love with him, there could be no doubt about that. But what about the fiancé in Annapolis? A bridge to be crossed later. First there was a war to be fought. But now he would go into it with a girl to wait for him, like all the other fellows would have, young men exchanging photographs in the crowded mess-decks of the battleships and cruisers and destroyers of the British Navy that awaited him. What he hadn't the knowledge to realize or understand was that Elizabeth had waited a long, long time for the same as she had been getting from the official in the State Department and, because of Jonas Gorman's strict principles, hadn't been having since. Neither did he know the curious effect being out on the broad ocean in a liner with all its trappings had on so many women travelling alone. The moment a liner had cast off the wires and ropes binding her to the quay, all home links were severed and a strange new world was entered upon, a world all on its own with no one ashore knowing what you were doing. You lived for a time on a different plane, and only returned to normality when once again the wires and ropes went out on the other side of the ocean. Elizabeth Kent – and this John didn't know either – would never see him again once the *Laurentia* had docked in Liverpool. The episode would be over, contained in the hothouse atmosphere of a liner at sea.

That night love on a different plane, but for similar sea reasons, took place in the first-class stateroom of General François de Gard. There was, however, a difference: Adeline Scott-Mason meant to stick to François de Gard like a leech. This was not a shipboard romance that ended with a clean cut. François de Gard was a lifeline and a meal ticket and French generals were romantic figures anyway, with their elegant uniforms and a fragrance of the Third Empire (wasn't it?), and Louis XVI, and Marie Antoinette, and the Napoleons. And of course Paris and its gay and wonderful life.

There was just one difficulty: for all that he was a romantic French general there was a stiffness about François de Gard, almost as though he were constantly on duty in the Tuileries or whatever, or the French Military Academy at St Cyr; he was almost English in his stiffness, his earnest conscientiousness to perform according to the book as he thrust and delved.

Adeline Scott-Mason was not, in fact, aroused, but she played her part, grunting and groaning or giving little ecstatic cries as appropriate, and it seemed to please the General.

'I am a good lover, *chérie?*' All Frenchman were of course good lovers.

'Yes,' she said. 'Very good . . . dearest François.'

Also in the first class, there was discord of a basic nature. Purser Matthews, thrusting an arm out of bed to look at his watch since he must not be caught by the bedroom steward, happened to make a remark about Livia Costello's husband.

'Larry? What the hell about *Larry* for God's sake?'

'Don't you think about him?'

'Like hell I do! Larry's a worm, crept out of a rotten apple. Right now, he'll be in some bitch's bed that's for sure.'

'H'm. . . .'

She sat up and looked at him, her breasts rubbing against the early-morning stubble of his chin. 'He's a louse, see? A dirty, rotten louse that's never taken any bloody interest in my career except for what he's gotten out of it by way of not having to spend his own bloody money on me and also by way of crumpet, girls who've dropped into his rotten, lecherous lap off of me, girls I've worked with, or just known, in the theatre. So just shut your gob when it comes to Larry. Larry the louse. Okay?'

'If you say so,' Matthews said, grinning. Then a thought struck him that should have struck him earlier and he asked, with a note of caution in his voice now, if in spite of all she intended going back to him when she returned to the States.

She gave a high laugh. 'Do yourself a favour,' she said, 'hang a piece of crêpe on the end of your nose in mourning for your brain, all right?'

'You mean . . . you're going for a divorce, Livia?'

'You bet your bottom dollar I am!' Livia thumped back into place beside him and the breasts were withdrawn. 'You and me, we've got something good going, I reckon.'

'Yes,' Matthews said, but didn't say it with conviction. He had no intention of becoming involved in a divorce case, since if Larry Costello chose to counter-investigate, which he might in order to tone down the alimony, the Line was going to learn interesting facts about one of their trusted senior officers and that was simply not on at all. Of course, the alimony might be enough to keep him in comfort, married to Livia, for the rest of his life. But then again it might not; Larry the louse didn't sound as though he'd part with money without a big fight and lawyers were slippery creatures when their palms were greased well enough.

It wasn't worth the risk. But it was going to be a difficult job of extrication. Very difficult. For instance, no snivelling letters of revenge must ever be written to the PanAtlantic Line. He would be out on his ear in less than half a dog watch.

When Chief Officer Arkwright had come off bridge watch a tap came at his cabin door. It was Bosun MacFarlane.

'Sorry to bother you, sir.'

'That's all right, Bosun. What is it?'

'Strange behaviour of a passenger, sir.'

'Mr Fielding, and Ming?'

The bosun allowed himself a grin, standing to attention in front of the Chief Officer, square and weatherbeaten, cap in hand. 'Not Mr Fielding, sir. I know Mr Fielding. It's a Mr Jones, sir. The one who upset the Swedish lady over –'

'Yes, I know the one. What about him, Bosun?'

'Walking up and down the boat deck, sir, and the embarkation deck –'

'Passengers do!'

'Yes, sir.' Passengers tended to get in the way of work, too, and Bosun MacFarlane's tone was somewhat weary of passengers and never mind that they formed the *raison d'être* of any liner. 'But Mr Jones . . . he keeps looking all about, as if he's lost something, sir. Messing about around the boats, too.'

'He'd better stand well clear of *them*,' Chief Officer Arkwright said. 'We don't want the gear interfered with.'

'No, sir. I told 'im to lay off, sir.'

Arkwright grinned. 'Politely, of course?'

'Of course, sir.' MacFarlane kept a straight face, very formal. In fact, he'd given Mr Jones a bit of an ear-bashing. The lifeboats were the ultimate salvation for the passengers and crew, or would be if anything nasty should happen. Anyone mucking about around the falls and the lowering mehanism was very unwelcome and MacFarlane had said so, plain and clear.

Arkwright said, 'Keep an eye lifting, Bosun. Don't hesitate to let me know anything further.'

'Aye, aye, sir.' MacFarlane went away about his many duties, supervising the men of the deck department, which included the deckmen who tended the passengers' open-air entertainment, quoits pitches and so on, and the swimming pool, and assisted in the running of the daily tote on the ship's run, the sea miles logged since the previous noon, a figure worked out on the bridge after the deck officers had taken their noon sights to fix the ship.

Going down to the boat deck, MacFarlane saw that Mr Jones was at it again, and muttering away to himself as he scurried about, eyes lowered in his curious search for God knew what.

It was in fact a question of Maggie's teeth.

With all his mounting anxieties about what the Purser had said, and the New York Police Department's interfering ways, Mr Jones had become more and more fearful that he could have miscounted in the first place and could have missed some teeth since as a result.

He was haunted by teeth now, as though each one, molars and incisors, had a life of its own. Or rather, now, a spirit, one that came and went in his disturbed mind. He had carried out a most meticulous search of his cabin, not once but a number of times after his bedroom steward had finished in the cabin and was unlikely to disturb him. Bunk and bedding, drawers, hanging cupboard, bunkside cupboard, wash-hand basin and even the concealed tank below the basin that collected the dirty water after Mr Jones had washed. He had examined the carpet closely on hands and knees: jagged teeth could become caught up on tufts and so on.

No teeth.

By this time Mr Jones had in fact convinced himself that he had made a false count initially. He searched the decks, poked about round all the lifeboats in case there had been a lodgement somewhere whilst he'd been casting the bread pellets, with teeth embedded, at the seagulls.

No luck. Before being approached and reprimanded by the ship's bosun, Mr Jones's antics had attracted some of the children, among them the six young Descartes. They were polite children and the elder boy had addressed him as 'sir' when asking what he was looking for and could they help; but behind the politeness had been suppressed giggles and Mr Jones had become annoyed.

'What's it do with you anyway?' he'd asked angrily.

'Oh – sorry! Nothing at all, of course –'

'Then leave me alone if you don't mind.'

'But we thought we might help,' one of the smaller children said, her eyes gleaming with mischief.

'Well, you can't.'

'But if you tell us –'

Real temper flared. 'Just bugger off for God's sake, can't you?'

That had caused a sensation. Some of them knew the word and knew that it was forbidden. Only the lowest of men used such a word. The Descartes children moved away, whispering between themselves and casting backward looks. Mr Jones regretted his outburst as soon as it was uttered. The story would spread, of course it would, and he would attract more attention and soon somebody, some busybody, would put two and two together and come up with teeth – there had been the Swedish boy he'd turned on whilst casting the bread pellets.

Mr Jones trembled and shook and began to sweat. He'd done it this time, been a real fool. Too late now to apologize and offer some sort of innocuous explanation. He looked down at the sea streaming past the side of the *Laurentia*, greenish with still some white horses, the closer water disturbed into foam as it rushed back from the liner's bows to mingle astern into the wake. He thought of other water, the Wappinger River in upstate New York where Maggie's leg had so unfortunately got away. He thought of Maggie in her various parts, buried but liable to digging up by animals or suspicious humans. As with the teeth, he seemed to have lost count of Maggie's parts. And it had been a very final act; like Humpty Dumpty whose adventures his old mother used to read to him in early childhood, Maggie would never be put together again. He thought of his mother, awaiting in Walthamstow news of the *Laurentia*'s docking. What would she say if ever she learned that Maggie was dead, killed by her own son?

Be pleased, most likely. About the fact of death, anyway. But not if he was to swing. That would be the end of her. Poor old mother. . . .

The broad Atlantic Ocean, clean and washing, seemed to beckon. It seemed to rise up to meet him as if in welcome, as if in a request for him to submerge himself in its bosom. This was, of course, simply because at that moment the liner rolled over to starboard. . . . Mr Jones pulled himself together, pulled himself up short. He mustn't give in. He was reading too much into the New York Police Department, not seeing things straight and as they were or might well be. Just a normal routine enquiry; he was, after all, the next-of-kin of the departed.

Sister Perpetua, descending in due course to her shared cabin, never knew what had taken place there during her absence. Her mind was pure and saw no evil anywhere; and Miss Kent was such a very nice girl. Miss Kent had spoken of her fiancé waiting for her in Annapolis, and the fact of the fiancé was quite enough never to allow carnal thoughts to enter Sister Perpetua's mind. Engaged girls were pure and wholesome and that was that.

Sister Perpetua had not in fact had a sheltered upbringing, not at least until she had entered the Convent of the Sacred Soul of the Blessed Virgin Mary, now grown larger and formed into an incorporated company with headquarters in Jackson, Mississippi. Her father had been what she was to learn was referred to as a 'poor white', a poverty-stricken man with a vast beard like Moses trying to scratch a living from poor soil, worked-out soil in a state that had in fact a very rich and productive soil. Granville O'Flanagan had come from Ireland with no knowledge whatsoever of cultivation and less interest; in Dublin he had studied law but spent more time drinking then studying. As a result he had failed to qualify and had emigrated to America, where he had drifted. Being a man of exceedingly bad temper, especially when drunk, and also being many miles from his nearest neighbour, he had no friends to help or advise him when he had drifted into a smallholding. So he had scratched in his two dilapidated acres, trying to grow and sell peanuts.

He had one abiding interest apart from drink; and the result had been fourteen children, all of them girls. Sister Perpetua, then plain Judy O'Flanagan, had been third from eldest. Thus she had witnessed some of the procreation: the family lived in a clapboard hut with the one bedroom.

Semi-starvation had been the order of the day. Sister Perpetua's washed-out, overworked mother had grown a few vegetables in a peanut-free patch, potatoes mainly. They had had to suffice. The joy was great when Judy had begun to show an interest in religion as the result of a visit by a priest of the Faith from Jackson, riding around the country on a horse that had been better nourished by far than the O'Flanagans. Father Driscoll, also an Irishman, was a good man who had taken a fancy to Judy. She had a bright face and an alert manner and treated him with great respect. His first visit had not been his last; and in due course, with rejoicing at one less mouth to be fed, the girl had departed with Father Driscoll for the Convent of the Sacred Soul of the Blessed Virgin Mary.

She had enjoyed her novitiate; the food was plain but was still luxurious compared with home and the nuns, though strict, were kind. Her bed was a plank with a blanket to cover it, but this was little enough hardship and quite similar to home. Emerging at length from her period as a novice, Sister Perpetua had been admitted to the Order and had started training as a nurse.

All that had been a long, long time ago: Sister Perpetua was now in her late fifties, her shaven head beneath the wimple would have been white had the hair remained in situ, and her face was seamed with lines and wrinkles. Time had made her an excellent and kindly nurse, and now, steaming for Britain aboard a great liner, she was approaching with joy and thanksgiving the most stupendous adventure of her life. She had no fear whatsoever; she was going to do good, to alleviate appalling suffering, and God would protect her. Whilst on passage, so would Captain Pacey.

* * *

Captain Pacey, unaware of his God-assisting role in the eyes of at least one of his passengers, did not go down to the saloon for dinner that night.

'I'll eat in my quarters, Mullins,' he told his steward.

'Very good, sir.' Mullins studied the Captain closely: he was showing strain, the strain of command in war and of long hours spent on the bridge. All those passengers ... some of them bigwigs – Senator Manderton, Ambassador Grant, banker Haggerty, General de Gard the froggie ... it wouldn't do for Captain Pacey to lose the *Laurentia* on this voyage. Mullins, whom Pacey knew to be absolutely trustworthy and who never once had fulfilled his function as expected by the crew of any Captain's tiger, i.e., the function of a big ear, had in fact overheard quite a few remarks that had passed between Pacey, Staff Captain Morgan and Chief Officer Arkwright. The wireless operators, it seemed, had intercepted general signals to all shipping from the Admiralty saying there were German submarines on station between the *Laurentia*'s position and St George's Channel that led up into Liverpool Bay.

Well, there would be U-boats, of course; nothing new in that. On each wartime voyage, you didn't feel safe until you'd made the turn to starboard past the Skerries off Anglesey and had entered the Bay; and even there, you could still catch a tin fish if the Germans were bold enough and you were unlucky. Whether or not all this was only to be expected, Mullins, who knew Captain Pacey's every mood, knew that he was dead worried, particularly in regard to what stage a warship escort would be provided.

Mullins went down many decks to the main galley where he had words with the chef about Captain Pacey's dinner. While he was engaged below, Chief Engineer Hackett rang through to the Captain and asked if he might come up: he sounded anxious himself.

'Of course, Chief. Right away.'

Hackett was with the Captain within five minutes. He had put on his uniform jacket, the purple stripes showing between the gold rings on his cuff, but he still wore his engine-room overalls beneath and the white trousers showed oil stains and grease. He refused Pacey's invitation to sit down.

'Won't take long, sir. But it's urgent and it's technical and I thought I'd better come up personally. It's the low pressure turbines. There's a fault in the valves. . . .'

Hackett went into his technical explanation. Pacey was not a technically minded man, had never been trained as such. He had been brought up to wind power and to the handling of sail to drive a ship through the water. The gist of the chief's explanation was that if the engines were to be put full astern, which meant high steam pressure, a steam feedback might occur: the steam, blocked in its attempt to escape via the drive of the turbine, would build up dangerously and could blow a main pipe.

Pacey said, 'There was no trouble when manoeuvring in New York, Chief.'

'No, that's true. The fault has only now developed. You see, I have it in mind that if you should need to go full astern in an emergency, say an attack –'

'Yes, I take the point. Can you do a repair job?'

'I'll be trying my best, sir. But really it's a job for the ship repairers ashore. We should shut down, by rights. But as I say, I'll do what I can.'

Pacey nodded. 'All right, Chief, fair enough. Keep me informed . . . and I'll try not to use full astern unless it's absolutely unavoidable.'

Hackett went below again. In his quarters he stripped off his jacket and made his way to the air-lock into the engine spaces where his senior second engineer with a number of juniors was making a further examination and assessment of the trouble. To shut down the turbines would be far too risky and Hackett had never even offered it as a suggestion; only as a statement of desirability. The ship was not yet into the U-boat attack zone but an adventurous U-boat commander might take a risk on his fuel capacity and go beyond the zone; and there was always the chance of falling in with German surface ships, cruisers or armed auxiliaries.

In his day cabin Pacey considered the new difficulty: it could be most serious. It was not the first item of trouble to occur since he had assumed command of the *Laurentia*: initially he'd had a lot of fault to find with the state of the ship – davits that had failed to work properly, defective trim tanks, lifesaving equipment not maintained to his satisfaction – and the general performance of the low pressure turbines. With the exception of the latter now having developed an actual fault, all this had been ironed out and Pacey was reasonably content with his ship.

But, on another front as it were, the overall picture of this current voyage, he had not liked those general signals from the naval authorities at home, hadn't liked the absence of any direct contact with the *Laurentia* apart from that signal of a day or two ago indicating the likely presence of U-boats in the vicinity of Cape Clear. The Admiralty, he believed, was being remarkably complacent, still, it seemed, unwilling to despatch a proper escort. Captain Pacey had little patience with the often rigid RN mind and outlook. There was a lot of constipated thinking around . . . and considering, as now he did, the word 'constipation', Pacey was reminded of an elderly admiral still on the active list of His Majesty's Fleet, one Admiral Sir Frederick Inglefield, who had personally dreamed up, earlier in the war, a scheme to frustrate the German Emperor's U-boats. Seagulls were to be trained to empty their bowels on German periscopes, thus obliterating the view of the German officers peering through from their control-rooms. It was not explained by the gallant Admiral how the seagulls were to be made to co-operate in this patriotic endeavour or how precisely they were to be expected to take their aim. Another of Inglefield's ideas was to provide motor-launches each with two swimmers embarked; when a periscope was observed, the swimmers would head for it and place a black bag overit and would then, with a hammer, break the glass of the lens. Incredibly, both these expedients had in fact been tried out; but not surprisingly neither had been a success. To Pacey, they just showed the degree of sheer daftness that sometimes occurred within the brass-bound minds of the Royal Navy.

In Walthamstow Mrs Bonfield was visiting her sick sister Mrs Jones, who had rallied a little in the nursing home.

She had with her a copy of the *Evening News*.

'Says here about the *Laurentia*, Ada.' Freda Bonfield rustled the newspaper. 'Been a wireless message. Trouble with the police, dear, that's what.' She simplified it for Ada. 'They're going aboard in Liverpool when the ship gets in. There's a man to be questioned. They don't give a name. Oooch, I wonder if it's a spy, Ada!'

'Well, I'm not worried about spies, Freda. Just Frederick, that's all I care about. I do hope he's all right and not seasick. And those Germans, such brutes by all accounts.' Ada's voice was weak and her attention began to wander again. Her fingers plucking at the sheet, she stared across the room, through the window that gave onto a brick wall: not a very nice view, but there were trees beyond, big ones whose tops she could see. Frederick had always liked trees as a child, climbing them and just looking at them as they either gained or lost their leaves according to the seasons. They had so often taken the omnibus, horsedrawn in those days, to the various big London parks, Clapham Common, Hampstead, Hyde Park and Kensington Gardens. Little Frederick had played around the trees, making up his own games for he was something of a loner, even digging holes with a seaside spade and pretending to be a squirrel, hiding a stock of nuts for the winter months. . . .

Ada drifted again, her eyes haunted. Freda Bonfield looked at her with concern. Only Frederick could do any good now, she was convinced of that. Just his presence, so she could die, if she was going to die, happy. She'd been devoted to Frederick, though Freda Bonfield had never had any great opinion of him, considering him shifty.

'Okay, MacKerrow, move your ass, all right?'

Even the occupants of Death Row had to have their statutory exercise. Fillmore MacKerrow moved as bid. Then he asked a question of the guard.

'Hey, lissen. That *Laurentia* got to Britain yet?'

'Not that I hear. You're not Sir Fillmore yet.' The whole penitentiary knew about that, knew about the vital letter sent from Paducah, Kentucky to the London solicitors and, ultimately, to a guy called the Lord Lyon King of Arms, a fairly typical limey mouthful that might mean anything from a sheriff's deputy to a bird's bum.

'Better hurry,' Fillmore MacKerrow said. It was not long now to Friday. He had made no request to see his son before that final day dawned; he had no interest in him whatever, no love. It wasn't quite correct to say no interest at all, however. Just so long as he handed something down. Sir Ingersoll MacKerrow would sound real good. That liner just had to reach Britain in safety. Fillmore MacKerrow muttered something about lousy Germans and carried on with the exercise period, shuffling round the scuffed sand of the pen yard.

12

In Queenstown the secretary to Vice-Admiral Hood lifted the receiver of his telephone and demanded connexion with Whitehall. The Irish voice in the telephone exchange said it would take time. The secretary, a Fleet Paymaster by rank, said that the Vice-Admiral wished to speak to the First Sea Lord in person and was asking for a speedy connexion.

Nothing ever moved fast in Ireland. It didn't on this occasion. The secretary tapped his fingers on his desk and looked out across Cork harbour, across Haulbowline Island with its ordnance depot and naval dockyard. Cork had a splendid harbour, big enough to accommodate the entire British Navy had there been depth of water enough in the channel or at the berths to take the mighty dreadnoughts . . . waiting for his connexion, the secretary allowed his mind to wander. He was pleased with his appointment; it meant a relaxation from the sea itself with all the sea's alarums and excursions and it meant two other welcome things: proximity to his wife, and an opportunity to indulge his hobby, which was the ancient history of the British Isles. County Cork had much to offer: numerous raths, cromlechs, barrows, caves and stone circles.

A series of clicks and disembodied voices sounded in the secretary's ear, some Irish, others English. He was about to be put through: he sent his petty officer writer to advise the Vice-Admiral: Vice-Admirals did not keep the First Sea Lord waiting on the telephone or anywhere else.

Vice-Admiral Hood took up the instrument. Fisher's voice rasped at him. 'You asked for me, Admiral. Here I am! What is it this time?'

'*Bristol* despatched, sir. With orders to steam on a squared search of the approaches and make back reports to me. Then to head for the rendezvous with the *Laurentia*.'

'All right, Admiral! Why the hell –'

'Your pardon, sir. I think it is very far from all right. I say once again, the escort is by no means sufficient –'

'I have already –'

Hood persisted. 'With respect, First Sea Lord. There are U-boats suspected in the area of the *Laurentia*'s approach course. I suggest that at the very least the Master should be advised to make a wide deviation and –'

'Absolute nonsense! I am quite certain the Germans will not attack the *Laurentia*! And in the meantime our cruisers and torpedo-boat destroyers are urgently needed in other and more important theatres of the war! Do I make myself plain, Admiral Hood?'

There was a final rattle and click. Vice-Admiral Hood hung the receiver back on its hook. 'It's the same old story,' he said bitterly to his secretary. 'He's utterly immovable. God knows what the record's going to show afterwards – if it does happen the *Laurentia*'s attacked.' He looked at his watch. 'Are you busy this afternoon, Turner?'

The secretary said, 'I can be spared, sir.'

'Good! Get your walking-stick . . . I feel like a good long tramp somewhere. Help to see things in perspective – at this moment my mind's too full of women and children at risk out there, and obstinate old men at the top – which is strictly *off* the record, Turner. Fresh air and exercise may help us to see the damned war as a whole, which I have to admit is probably what the First Sea Lord's doing himself.' Hood paused, looking out across the harbour as the secretary had done earlier. 'After all. . . .'

'Yes, sir?'

'The *Laurentia*. She's just one ship. One ship among many. Perhaps I need to remind myself of that.'

A report was brought to the Purser's office by the senior lounge steward on duty in the second-class lounge. Matthews reported to Staff Captain Morgan.

'Trouble, sir. The third-class passengers seem to be holding a protest meeting.'

'Protesting about what, Matthews?'

'That's unclear so far. But there's a lot of heat and steam being generated. I've been along for a look . . . without making it too obvious.'

'Quite. Who's behind it, do you know that?'

'The man Craigson, I believe, sir. The one who lodged the complaint about Fielding.'

'All right, Matthews. I'll alert the masters-at-arms. We won't go to panic stations, however. I've seen this sort of thing before, in the old *Lucretia*. It could end in a simple deputation, either to the Captain or to myself. If so, we'll handle it from there.'

'Very good, sir.'

'Keep me informed, Matthews. We won't let it get out of hand. That fellow Craigson's likely to be a trouble-maker . . . a mess-deck lawyer by the look of him.'

Craigson was a good talker when he had a audience. Back in England before the war, he'd been active in trade union affairs, branch secretary in fact. He knew very well how to rabble-rouse. He told the assembled passengers that it was all a matter of class. Class afloat, like class ashore. They were at the bottom of the heap; in the eyes of the Captain and the other nobs, they didn't count for a row of pins. The working class never did. It was up to them to show the nobs that they were not content with what was dished out to them, and he didn't mean the food. He meant information.

'We're all alone,' he said, 'in mid-Atlantic. Anything could happen at any moment. Apart from boat drill and a load of printed instructions in the cabins, no one's told us what to do nor what to expect. We're in their hands, which is where they want us to be. U-boat fodder, and what do they care. Eh?'

Big Jake Ommaney had been stationed among the passengers, in a strategic position in rear, where he could shout across the many heads. He was flexing his muscles as though he expected a fight. Now he came in on cue.

'They don't bloody fool us. They don't bloody fool Aussies – eh, mate?'

'They', whoever 'they' might be taken to be, did not; nobody fooled Aussies. The Australians among the crowd shouted their approval. Purser Matthews, standing outside the lounge, reckoned that none of them really had the slightest idea of what Big Jake Ommaney was going on about. They just liked the idea of a fight, liked the prospect of pitting themselves against anyone in authority.

Matthews decided that at this stage there was nothing to be usefully done about it. But he watched and listened. Big Jake Ommaney was going on, his face glistening with the sweat that ran down his face into the neck of the singlet that he customarily wore, even in the dining saloon.

'They just keep us in ignorance, see, in case we stir up a bloody fuss and make things difficult for 'em. No one what's in charge of anything likes anyone stirring up trouble, right?'

There was another chorus of aproval, this time sounding more hostile. Ommaney yelled out something about sending a deputation to the Captain. 'Go to the bloody top, why not? Go to the skipper, let him see how we feel about bloody poms.'

This was popular, at any rate among the Australian contingent. It was always a good idea to let the poms know that they were not held in high esteem by real men. A shouted discussion followed while a deputation was decided upon and its composition worked out. This proved easy enough; it was a foregone conclusion that one of the spokesmen in the deputation would be Big Jake Ommaney and the other would be Craigson. These two were considered to be sufficient for the purpose.

'And straight to the bloody skipper,' Big Jake said. 'No mucking about with the bloody minions, my oath! They just do what they're bloody told. Like we've agreed, it's all bloody class.'

Somebody asked what the next move was. Big Jake glared. 'Just told you, mate. Straight to the bloody skipper.'

'S'pose 'e's on the bridge, eh?'

''E can bloody come off it, can't 'e? We're fare-paying passengers. Right?'

There was no time like the present: Big Jake and Craigson left the lounge and made their way to the boat deck, with Purser Matthews, having warned the bridge by telephone, following at a distance.

Matthews was waylaid by Senator Manderton from Wyoming. 'You look worried, Purser. What goes on, may I ask?'

Matthews was in a hurry. He said brusquely, 'There's nothing going on, Senator.' He pushed on past. Behind him came a number of the protesting passengers, anxious to see what Big Jake was going to do when he bearded the Captain, anxious also to give him due backing and by weight of numbers increase the pressure on the Captain and his officers to be more forthcoming.

Senator Manderton sensed matters of interest. He had his fact-finding mission much in mind. It was, in his view, going to be important to Congress when he got back to the States and his future career might be at stake if he didn't get things dead to rights – by which he understood telling Congress what they wanted to hear. (The difficulty was, he wasn't entirely certain what they did want to hear. There was a distinct schism in Congress and this was centred mostly around whether or not the United States should enter the war. Manderton sensed that at this moment, or at any rate up to the time he'd last been in close touch with Congressional opinion, the feeling was that America should stand well clear – that in fact Congress supported President Wilson. He also knew that this could shift very suddenly indeed depending on the progress of the war in Europe. There were, in fact, plenty of Anglophiles in both Houses of Congress.) Currently he was sensing a strong degree of frustration on the part of the more rudimentary passengers. This was grist to his mill and he determined to make the most of it. He approached a skinny little man wearing a bush hat and a vest and smoking a pipe that produced a thick cloud of very strong, very foul smoke.

'A very good morning to you,' he said heartily.

'G'day, cobber.'

'Trouble, is there?'

'Could be, I reckon.'

'Ah. How's that, then?'

'We're bloody fed-up, that's what. Bloody ship, all them Germans waiting.'

'Yes, gee, I do understand that. And I sympathize. I'm surprised so many of you should be going to Britain at this particular time. There must be –'

'Bloody home, mate. Bloody home! The old country . . . got to help out.' The little man blew more smoke and looked through it, sardonically, at Senator Manderton. 'Know something, cobber?'

'What?' Senator Manderton metaphorically poised pencil over notebook – you didn't in fact, or he didn't, take actual notes, you used your God-given memory, which was better than putting interviewees off their stroke from the word go. Many people didn't like their words being taken down verbatim. 'Go on,' he said. 'Go on – cobber.'

The skinny man said, 'It's not up to the Yanks 'oo 'aven't come into the bloody war to badger Aussies 'oo 'ave.'

You couldn't win every time; Congress might not like that one. Senator Manderton apologized churlishly and moved away. One of the troubles with limeys, in which term he included Australians, was that they never had liked facts. They lived on fictions, one of the fictions being that they were still a great Empire fighting unsophisticated Boer farmers or primitive blacks on the North-West Frontier of India.

There was a surge of third-class passengers from the lounge now. Senator Manderton was thrust aside as they headed for the companion-way to the upper decks. On the boat deck Mrs Rickards, wrapped in a rug, was sitting in a deck-chair. There was a second chair close by and this was occupied by Lady Barlow.

Lady Barlow was talking. Like an oil gusher, he thought, in Texas. She was talking about her son, Eustace, whom Manderton considered a fairly typical useless Englishman of the privileged classes.

He heard Lady Barlow say, 'As you know, if it wasn't for his heart. . . . But *of course* he wishes to do something. Eustace is not the sort to, well, sit in London drawing-rooms while the boys are fighting in Germany.'

'France,' Mrs Rickards corrected.

'Well, yes, France I meant. So we were thinking of the Foreign Office, you see. Or have I told you before? The thing is, influence is always *such* a help. I'm sure you understand. As one woman to another. As one *mother* to another, I'm sure –'

'Yes. Oh, yes, I do understand that, Lady Barlow. But I'm not sure I understand farther than that.' Mrs Rickards was floundering, wishing Jeffrey would hurry up and join her. The Barlow woman was so vulgar, so brash, so much the sort of person Mrs Rickards would wish to avoid at all costs whenever possible. Aboard a ship it was not very possible.

And she was going on. 'Let's put it this way, shall we?' The woman leaned closer; she wore a heavy and pervasive scent – very expensive, but vulgar. 'As one *lady* to another – Lady Rickards.'

Mrs Rickards started and flushed.

'I think we should stick together,' Lady Barlow announced. 'Help where help's possible. If you see what I mean.'

Mrs Rickards asked the question direct. 'Why did you address me as Lady Rickards just now?'

'Well, you are, aren't you, dear. I mean, let's call a spade a spade, shall we?'

'I'm asking you how you knew.'

Lady Barlow smiled; then, appallingly, she winked. 'Let's say a little bird told me. No names, like, no pack-drill. The point is, Lord Rickards could put in a word for Eustace. Such a distinguished soldier, I'm sure. It would carry such weight, dear. After all, Eustace is my son.' She paused, and coughed. 'I'd be ever so grateful. I'd show you just how grateful,' she added meaningfully.

'Precisely what do you mean, Lady Barlow?'

Lady Barlow leaned even closer. 'Look, dear. I've got the shekels. You haven't, that's obvious. I'm a generous person. So what do you say? Just a letter, that's all. And a personal meeting with someone important. I'm sure your hubby wouldn't mind.'

Hubby. Mrs Rickards shrank from the woman's vulgarity. She said, 'I know my husband would do no such thing. And as for your offer . . . I consider it the most insulting and wounding thing I have ever heard.'

'Oh. Really.'

Mrs Rickards' heart was beating fast and she felt a curious faintness creeping over her. Then she saw, with immense relief, that Jeffrey was coming. She said, 'Lady Barlow, if you wouldn't mind. I was keeping this chair for my husband –'

'I see.' Lady Barlow heaved herself to her feet, her eyes furious. 'Stuck-up old bitch, aren't you?'

She flounced away, looking down her nose at Rickards as she passed him. Rickards took the vacated deck-chair. 'What was all that about, Emmy?' he asked.

In a shaking voice, she told him. Fury showed in the old face but then suddenly he seemed to crumple. 'So it's come to that, has it? We've come as low as it's possible.' He reached out for her hand. 'I'm sorry, Emmy. I've not been a very good provider.'

'Oh, Jeffrey.'

* * *

Later Rickards said, 'I think we ought to get that ship's doctor to look at you, Emmy.'

'Oh, no. I'm perfectly all right. Perfectly.'

'But you –'

'No, Jeffrey. Really, no. It was – only that awful woman. I'm quite all right now.' She didn't look it and she didn't feel it, but the doctor charged for cabin visits and she knew Jeffrey wouldn't hear of her attending the surgery. Rickards looked at her in concern; there was a curious stiffness about her face, as though the muscles had gone rigid. He'd been noticing it for some while, and her mouth was often open and there was copious spittle. Her walk, too, seemed to have been affected: short, hurrying steps.

He didn't like it but none of it really added up in his mind to anything very specific. Just a need for an overhaul and a tonic, perhaps.

Big Jake Ommaney had reached the foot of the bridge ladder, with Craigson and the back-up party. From the bridge the Staff Captain, alerted by the Purser, looked down. Behind him was the junior third officer, second Officer of the Watch.

As Big Jake put a foot on the ladder Staff Captain Morgan called down to him.

'No passengers allowed on the bridge.'

'Bollocks to that.' Big Jake looked round at his support. ''Ear that, did yer? Typical. Take bloody refuge in their rules and regulations. Not with us they don't, eh, mates?'

There was vocal support. Big Jake turned back to the Staff Captain. 'You the skipper, mate?'

Morgan's voice was even, unflurried. 'I am not the Captain – no. I am the Staff Captain. I take it you have something to say. I suggest you say it from where you are.'

'Not to you, mate! Skipper. No bugger else.'

From behind Ommaney, the two ship's masters-at-arms pushed through the crowd. They reached the foot of the ladder. Master-at-Arms Warner said, 'Cut out the language, mister.'

Ommaney turned. 'What if I don't, eh?'

'That'll be up to the Staff Captain.' Warner was a big man, as big as Ommaney, and much fitter; no bulging stomach for one thing, no beer gut. He looked ready to put into operation any order that might come from the bridge. Ommaney hesitated for a moment: the sea was the sea and in spite of his loud mouth he knew a lot of power was vested in authority aboard ship. While he was hesitating, the junior third officer had moved away. A moment later Captain Pacey took his place alongside Morgan. Pacey spoke quietly. 'What is it you wish to say?'

'You the skipper?'

Titles were not worth arguing about at this stage. 'Yes,' Pacey said.

'Right! You was the one we wanted. I don't talk to the monkey. On'y the organ-grinder. And I'm saying this: we're not bloody satisfied with what we've been told. There's been no bloody information given. There's two Germans aboard. There's been a bloody panic about a bomb.' Big Jake's voice had risen to a shout; he was working himself up into a lather and was becoming dangerous. He had realized that his earlier hesitation might have looked like second thoughts, like a desire not to go to town on the brass after all. If that was thought, he would quickly lose the advantage, and lose his support amongst his mates as well. He became therefore more truculent.

'We don't like the way things is going, mate. Me, I've got no bloody confidence that the officers know what they're bloody doing. You all stick together. We're just bloody cattle. U-boat fodder. What if the bloody ship sinks and all you lousy buggers –'

'That'll do!' Pacey's tone was sharp: he was back to the days in sail, when Testament Thomas's word had been law and all hands had jumped to it. 'You'll remember you're aboard a ship in wartime. You will not spread alarm amongst the other passengers. To that end, you'll keep your voice down now, and when you disperse you'll take what I've said as a warning. The same goes for all of you down there. In the meantime you may be assured that the ship is in good hands and so are your lives – as much as is humanly possible against sudden U-boat attack which will probably never come –'

'Don't give us that crap!' Big Jake shouted. 'Look, cobber, if you show your mug down below where you can be got at, why, I reckon you'll get a bloody pasting that'll –'

'Now you listen to me.' Pacey's voice had risen and it was unmistakably the voice of total authority. 'I shall quote the wording of the ship's Articles of Agreement. Under the terms of that Agreement, common to all ships once Articles have been signed, I am appointed Master under God and the ship is delivered into my hands lock, stock and barrel. I have complete authority to act in any way I see fit. I am empowered to place below in cells any person who in my view constitutes a danger to the ship. That applies to passengers as well as crew. Now – what's your name?'

'Bugger all to do with you,' Big Jake shouted back. He had lost all control of himself by this time; he took two or three paces up the ladder, his face murderous. Behind him Master-at-Arms Warner went up; the second master-at-arms moved between Warner and the back-up party. Warner got his arms around Big Jake's ample waist and heaved the Australian backwards. Big Jake lost his balance and both he and Warner landed flat on their backs on the deck at the foot of the ladder.

That started a general *mêlée*. Staff Captain Morgan swiftly locked the guardrail across the top of the bridge ladder and sent his messenger for extra hands to act as guards. Pacey went below to his quarters at the rush via his private staircase and unlocked his safe. When he returned to the bridge he had in his hand his revolver, the use of which in certain circumstances was authorized by the law. With it, he took up his position behind the guardrail at the head of the ladder.

The crowd, or mob as it was now becoming, had surged aft away from the bridge after Pacey had produced his revolver. They appeared to have no purpose other than destruction. The second-class bar had already been shut on orders from the Purser; but the Australians broke in and looted it. Spilt beer was everywhere, as were broken bottles. Individual fights had started and the jagged ends of the broken bottles had been used. Dr Fellowes was going to be busy as was his nursing sister, Betty Unwin. Maddened with rhetoric and beer, plus a quantity of gin and whisky, the mob stormed up the companionways, along the alleyways, spilled out onto the embarkation deck and the boat deck, yelling like lunatics.

There were more casualties in the rush, casualties among those passengers who hadn't left the decks to lock themselves into their cabins and staterooms in time. Sister Perpetua, once again at her religious reading, was upset from a chair in the reading room and left winded on the deck, her wimple crushed and dirty. She uttered prayers as she staggered to her feet with the assistance of Elmer Pousty, the Quaker from Chicago.

'Ups-a-daisy,' he said, trying to sound cheerful. 'Don't let that trash worry you, Sister, they don't know what they're doing. The crew'll have them under control soon, you bet your bottom dollar.'

'Poor souls,' Sister Perpetua said breathlessly, trying to straighten her attire. 'I shall continue praying –'

'Not now, you won't.' Firmly, Elmer Pousty took charge of the old nun, put an arm around her, and took her to the nearest place of safety, which was the Purser's office, where the bars were in place across the windows, over which the shutters had been pulled down. Pousty thundered on the locked door of the outer office, shouted that he was seeking sanctuary for a passenger, a nun. The door opened, cautiously, and a clerk looked out, summed up the situation, and admitted Sister Perpetua. Pousty left her there; he might be able to help restore order. A Quaker he might be, but he was young and strong and had no qualms about using his strength to put down mindless violence.

He made his way up through the decks. Reaching the boat deck he saw Fielding, looking lost and bewildered. The perambulator had shed a wheel as the mob had run past him, and he himself had been knocked to the ground and was now picking himself up.

'But get down to your cabin,' Pousty said.

'Best the perambulator – and Ming –'

'Don't worry about Ming now, bud. Get where you'll be safe.'

Pousty, before reaching the boat deck, had seen the ship's bosun, Andrew MacFarlane, with a deck gang. They were running out the fire hoses along the embarkation deck. A good dousing cooled hot heads, and the fire hoses could produce a heavy stream that, well directed, could knock men off their feet. They were much used, as MacFarlane knew, by the liners going through the Suez Canal: in Port Said Roads, the local traders were accustomed to come off in boats and often became over importunate, even trying to hook onto the liners' sides as they moved through for the canal entry. Hoses worked wonders on them, upsetting their boats, scattering their tawdry wares.

Soon after Pousty had gained the boat deck, he heard screaming, the terrified scream of a woman, and he ran full pelt towards the source.

He saw the Swedish woman, Alva Lundkvist. She was holding her head in her hands, and screaming still. The little boy, Olof, was clasping her around her legs, and crying. The husband was lying on the deck, his body twitching in agony. Then, as Elmer Pousty ran up, the twitchng stopped. The head lolled sideways.

Pousty, going to the Western Front in due course to succour the wounded, had not seen death before. But now, instinctively, he recognized it.

He knelt beside Torsten Lundkvist. There was nothing he could do other than get Dr Fellowes along to confirm the fact of death. He looked towards the tail end of the mob, at the after end of the boat deck.

He raised his voice, a shout of fury.

'You bastards! You lousy rotten bastards! You've killed a man!'

Killing had never been on the agenda. But any sane man must have recognized that if matters went too far, death would become a possibility. The word spread throughout the ship in no time, and it cooled heads better than fire hoses. There was now shock; and a strong degree of self-loathing. Dr Fellowes came up, made an examination, confirmed death and diagnosed a broken back. Torsten Lundkvist's body was taken below through a silent crowd of suddenly subdued passengers. Big Jake Ommaney and the man Craigson were taken under guard to the bridge where Captain Pacey read the Riot Act to them. They were the ringleaders, he said. All passengers and crew would be questioned as to what they had seen, but in the meantime Ommaney and Craigson would be held in custody, partly for their own protection.

Pacey asked if either of them had anything to say. Except to deny any personal involvement in the death, they said nothing. While Pacey was conducting the interview, there was an interruption. This came from Staff Captain Morgan, who drew Pacey aside. They walked to the opposite wing of the bridge: Morgan reported that two passengers, John Holmes and Fielding, had reported seeing Big Jake Ommaney, backed up by Craigson, attacking Torsten Lundkvist with a length of heavy timber.

Pacey went back to where the two men stood. He said, 'There is evidence of your involvement, both of you. Do you wish to say anything now?'

'It's bloody lies,' Ommaney said, his face suffusing. Craigson, shaking like a leaf with all obstreperousness gone out of him, echoed Ommaney's words.

Pacey said evenly, 'You will both be handed over to the civil authority when we berth in Liverpool. The matter will be entered in the ship's log as a case of murder on the high seas.' The charge, Pacey supposed, might be reduced to manslaughter; but so far as it lay within his power to do so, he would try to see that the murder charge stuck.

He turned to Master-at-Arms Warner. 'Take them below to the cells, Warner. Alongside the Germans . . . but see to it there's no communication between them or with anyone else.'

Bill Warner saluted. As the men were taken away, Pacey spoke to Staff Captain Morgan. 'There'll be a need to keep the body, Morgan. The police . . . we can't have a committal service.'

'No, sir. I'll have the body placed in refrigeration.'

'Yes, please.' Pacey stared across the restless sea, empty of all shipping but for themselves. His face looked haunted. He said, 'That poor woman – the widow. I'll have a word with her when she's ready. Sound her out, Morgan.'

Morgan went below. Pacey strode up and down his bridge, thinking about death, death of the sort that had just occurred. Thinking, too, about the on-carrying of corpses. Seamen were remarkably superstitious about death, about having the dead aboard. Testament Thomas in those days in sail had never kept a corpse aboard and to hell with the shore authorities. A man dead fallen from aloft was a man dead fallen from aloft, and the word of the Master was quite enough to satisfy the landlubbers.

Was he doing the right thing? Pacey wondered.

Right, to keep a corpse aboard on a war passage? He had any number of old-timers in his crew, the really superstitious ones. Would not the testimony of young Pousty, of Dr Fellowes, of Holmes and Fielding, be enough for the police in Liverpool, and the courts? The mob situation was well enough known by all on board and there would be more than enough corroboration of the facts – surely? – even in the absence of the body.

It was just one of the decisions to be made that plagued any master mariner . . . plagued him, did problems of all sorts, throughout every voyage. A shipmaster combined so many roles: commander, navigator, ship-handler, policeman, magistrate, diplomat, squire . . . on occasions parson, in some ships doctor and surgeon; adviser and mentor to officers and crew with personal problems, businessman, owners' agent . . . there was no end to it all. And in all things large and small the Master was the final arbiter, the one man aboard a ship who could make a final decision. Even in regard to the engine room: the Chief Engineer was just that – chief of the engineers – and naturally he knew his job. But the actual decisions were the Master's: did you, or did you not, order the engines stopped in wartime for one reason or another – as in the recent valve troubles, not yet sorted out by Hackett – did you go to Full Ahead or Full Astern in an emergency when there was the chance the engines might not take it? Whatever the Master might decide, the Chief would carry the order out. But if the result was broken engines, then it was the responsibility of the Master.

But now, of course, overridingly, was the possible threat from the Kaiser's *unterzeebooten* fleet. That report of U-boats, some days ago. And that inadequate escort: when in a few days' time the rendezvous was made, it would still be with just one old cruiser.

So now, as his ship neared the British Isles, there was the biggest decision of all to make, one that was plaguing Pacey with uncertainties. Did he abandon his set inward course, and not head for St George's Channel and ultimately Liverpool – a route that must be known to the German Naval Command? Did he make the decision of his own accord to deviate in a wide circle to the south, and then take the *Laurentia* into Queenstown, thus also shortening the period in the danger zone? Pacey did not possess the naval codes; and he could scarcely make a plain-language alteration signal that would be picked up immediately in Berlin or Wilhelmshavn. So if he decided to deviate he would miss the escorting cruiser. In so doing he might put in jeopardy nearly two thousand lives . . . as so he could by making the decision to adhere to his set course. . . .

13

THE First Lord's room in the Admiralty was thick with cigar smoke. The atmosphere was thick in another way as well: there was continuing disagreement between Mr Churchill and his First Sea Lord, a former friendship turning to a mutual mistrust that was coming out into the open. There was the continuing shortage of ships; the campaign on and around Gallipoli was using up too many ships, too many men. The steamer *River Clyde*, due to go down in history, had made a gallant attempt to put troops ashore on Gallipoli, at V Beach between Cape Helles and Sedd el Bahr. When the landing boats under tow, and the *River Clyde* herself, had closed towards the shore, the Turks had held their fire until after the landings had taken place and the boats were disembarking their human loads. In the terrible barrage that had then started, the Royal Dublin Fusiliers had virtually ceased to exist. As had the Munster Regiment when the next wave had streamed out along a line of barges set in place by naval ratings under close fire from the Turkish positions.

Churchill waved his cigar when Lord Fisher spoke of the Dardanelles operation. 'Don't blame me for it all, Jacky. You're as much part of it as I. This was a joint venture – that was agreed, you'll remember – '

'It's no longer a *venture*, First Lord!' Fisher brought a clenched fist down on the arm of his chair. 'It's a damn *mis*adventure! It's nothing but a drain! Battleships, cruisers, torpedo-boat destroyers – '

'Nevertheless, the Army's in good heart out there. The ANZACs at least can still laugh.' Suddenly Mr Churchill, his face cherubic, gave a deep chuckle that rumbled like low thunder. 'There's a story I was told yesterday, by a colonel back from Gallipoli, about Birdwood.' General Sir William Birdwood was the British commander of the Australian and New Zealand Army Corps on Gallipoli. 'He was on the prowl one night, actually wearing his ostrich feathers and cocked hat, with a cloak covering the rest of his – '

'Nonsense, First Lord! Birdwood – '

'That's the story, Jacky. It may well be apocryphal, I agree. Anyway, there Birdwood was – and he was halted by an Australian sentry. "Who goes there" and so on. Birdwood said, "Great Scott, my man, it's your duty to recognize your Corps Commander. Don't you know who I am? I'm *Birdwood*." ' Churchill paused. 'Have you heard it?'

Fisher shook his head impatiently. Often he had fancied there was too much misplaced levity about the First Lord.

'The sentry hadn't liked being addressed as "my man", apparently. He said, "Why don't you shove your feathers up your backside, mate, and fly away like any other bloody bird would." ' Churchill's chuckle came again. 'I'd like to tell Kitchener that one. These pompous generals!' There was no love lost between the First Lord of the Admiralty and the Secretary of State for War.

Fisher had not laughed. Churchill waved his cigar at him. 'A sense of humour, I've always thought, is a saving grace. Thank God the troops can laugh. I regard that story as typically Australian. They're a good bunch and we're fortunate to have them.'

'It's the Americans we want,' Fisher said savagely.

'Oh, I agree. But we also want their money, Jacky.'

'You're still pinning your hopes on Haggerty?'

'Yes, very much so.'

'And the Prime Minister?'

'Yes, him also. It's a lot we're asking, but we have at stake the future of the civilized world. We can only hope the Americans realize that as we do.' Churchill paused. 'When the loan's been agreed and implemented, then you shall have those cruisers you want, Jacky. You may rely upon me to press the Admiralty's case in Cabinet, and in the House. It is to the Navy that I shall see that that money goes.' He blew more cigar smoke. 'The *Laurentia*'s due into Liverpool in three days' time. The financial talks should begin early next week. If Haggerty arrives safely.'

Fisher's eyebrows went up. 'You mean – '

'I mean this.' Mr Churchill leaned forward, his expression suddenly aggressive. 'I referred just now to having pinned my hopes on Haggerty. That is not entirely so. I pin my hopes on getting the loan agreed. I do not pin them on Haggerty himself. Between you and me, Jacky, certain information has come to hand via Dublin. Haggerty's sympathies do not lie with Britain – there is too much of the Irish in him. He's apparently had links with disaffected sections of the Irish in America. I believe he is likely to wreck the negotiations. And if he failed to reach Britain, then another negotiator would be sent over, and I happen to know who it would be. For now, no names. But this person is very pro-English and the chances would be very much better.'

Fisher asked the question directly: 'What are you suggesting, First Lord?'

Churchill smiled. 'I'm suggesting nothing, Jacky. My prayers are with the *Laurentia* and all aboard her. But it would be . . . shall I say . . . very fortuitous if the man Haggerty did not arrive in London. The Germans . . . but I'll say no more. Except this: you are satisfied with the escort to be provided for the *Laurentia* as she comes within the danger zone?'

Fisher didn't hesitate. 'I'm providing the best escort possible – in the absence of enough ships to fight the sea war as it *should* be fought!'

'Just the one light cruiser, the *Bristol*?'

'Yes. *Bristol*'s had her orders. I've been in *constant* touch with Hood at Queenstown!'

'Ah, yes. Yes, that should I think be adequate.'

It had not been hard to read between the lines. And it was not just Haggerty, of course; Fisher knew that. It was the *Laurentia* herself. Churchill was beginning to see things the way Fisher himself saw them. And First Lord and First Sea Lord could do virtually what they wished in conjunction, cold feeling between them laid aside. And any leader in any war had to weigh one thing against another. However many deaths there might be aboard the *Laurentia* if the Germans struck, they could never be enough to set seriously against the likelihood that America would enter the war and save, over the next months or even years of fighting, millions of Allied lives.

Of course, nothing would be done actively to put the liner in danger; but passivity was a different kettle of fish. So, when a last representation came by urgent telephone call from Vice-Admiral Hood in Queenstown, Fisher's response was still the same: HMS *Bristol* was adequate protection.

Aboard U-120 *Kapitanleutnant* Klaus Eppler, watching through his periscope as he moved at slow speed at periscope depth, was lining up his instruments on a British freighter well down to her marks with cargo. The freighter, he assessed, was of some 3500 tons, a nice prize. The fact that some half an hour earlier she had taken down her Red Ensign and hoisted the American Stars and Stripes in its place was of no consequence to Eppler: the British were full of tricks and subterfuges and this was not the first time a British ship had sailed under false colours, sometimes American, sometimes the flags of other neutrals. It so happened that this time Eppler had seen for himself the transference of the ensigns so his conscience was totally clear and, of course, the facts would be entered in the log for the satisfaction of the naval authorities and the government of the Fatherland. . . .

All was now lined up. *Kapitanleutnant* Eppler passed his orders in a voice the calmness of which hid his increasing excitement, the excitement that always came when the kill was imminent. He thought about the honours awaiting him in the Fatherland when he brought his boat home from a successful patrol. He would stand higher in Ilse's eyes and that would be good.

'Fire one.'

There was a hiss of air and a plop; the boat rose a little as the torpedo was expelled from its tube. At the hydroplanes a rating adjusted the trim.

'Fire two.'

The hiss, the plop, the rise and the adjustment were repeated. No more torpedoes were fired. No more were necessary. Still looking through the periscope lens, Eppler saw both his torpedoes hit. One for'ard in the bows, the other amidships. There was flame and a billow of thick smoke. The freighter seemed to sag like a drunken man, and then very suddenly her back broke. The stern rose high in the air and her still-spinning propeller, and her rudder, could be seen. The fore end had already disappeared, shattered by the first torpedo and the damage compounded as the back broke.

Eppler saw men jumping over into the water and an attempt, a useless one, to launch a lifeboat. He ordered tanks to be blown, housed his periscope, brought U-120 to the surface and waited for the water to drain away through the washports in the conning tower. Some residual water came down as the clips of the hatch were thrown off. Eppler, with his First Lieutenant, climbed into the conning tower and took a deep breath. It was good to breathe fresh air after the close confinement of the submerged boat. He looked all around; already his watch through the periscope had assured him there were no enemy warships in the vicinity. There were still none. Just the two vessels, U-120 and the remains of the freighter showing above the surface. Soon she would be gone, another blow to England's ability to keep her people fed by means of imports. There were still the survivors, perhaps twenty men, swimming in the water. The lifeboat had upended at the falls, and Eppler believed her sides had been stove in. Soon the boat would be gone with the ship. There was wreckage around and some of the men might cling to it for a while in the hope of being picked up.

Picked up, perhaps – but not by U-120.

Eppler prepared to submerge, to steal back into the deeps and await his next kill. The orders had been made clear recently: survivors were no longer to be picked up. It was the fault of the English themselves: almost at the start of the war, the English had determined to treat the U-boats and their crews as pariahs, unclean things sullying the wide oceans of the world. Any captured German submariner was to be shot, no mercy shown. This had happened on a number of occasions. The Fatherland would retaliate; and did so.

Eppler's First Lieutenant, Dirnecker, clattered down the steel ladder from the conning tower behind his captain. As he clipped down the hatch above his head he asked, 'What next, Herr *Kapitan*?'

'Next,' Klaus Eppler said, 'as you know, Dirnecker, is the *Laurentia*.'

As the boat steadied, reaching the ordered depth, there was much activity. More torpedoes were placed on the hoists and moved along to be fed into the emptied tubes. With his target well in mind, and all aboard now knowing for sure what that target was to be, Klaus Eppler proceeded on course to cross the *Laurentia*'s track.

Alva Lundkvist sat in her cabin, staring at the white-painted bulkhead. She was dry eyed; she had not yet reached the stage of tears. It had all been so sudden, so cruelly unexpected. Just a walk on the deck, and then the mob, and Torsten falling. She could not say who had been responsible. There had been so many of them, all acting crazily. Captain Pacey had come down to talk to her, to offer his sympathy. Even then she had not cried. He had asked questions and she had been unable to answer them. She knew that more would come before the liner reached Liverpool, and then more again when the British police came aboard. Meantime Captain Pacey had not pressed. She sensed that he was a good and kindly man. He had made arrangements so that meals would be brought to her and little Olof in her cabin: she could not face the other passengers. They had left Sweden with such high hopes that America would make Olof well again, that once again they would be a small, close-knit, happy family with no more worries. Now Torsten was gone: she could still not fully realize it. When, some while after the visit from the Captain, there was a knock at her door – which she didn't hear – and then the door came open, she fancied it must be Torsten, that there had been some terrible mistake and he was all right after all.

But of course it wasn't Torsten. It was two persons: the Reverend Jesse Divine and Sister Perpetua.

She stared at them, holding tightly to Olof, who was red eyed and sniffling, not really understanding any more than Alva herself. It would be a long while before he took it in that he wouldn't ever see his father again.

It was the Reverend Jesse Divine, immensely looming in his black cloak, who spoke first.

'My dear lady, we come to assure you of our prayers, and of the certainty of God's help. A terrible thing indeed.'

Alva stared at him. She had her own strong religious feeling, as Torsten had had. It was not helping now. She didn't make any response.

'I am the Reverend Divine. This is Sister Perpetua.'

She nodded, slowly.

'Perhaps a prayer, dear lady, a supplication . . . and for forgiveness of the sins of the departed.'

Still she stared at him, then a sudden high spot of red showed in her cheeks. She was angry now. She said, 'Torsten was a good man, a man who feared God. He was not a sinner.'

'Ah, but we are all sinners, dear lady. All of us, in the sight of God. Myself included. No, none of us is without sin, and to offer prayers for –'

'It is not yet the time,' Alva said. In her clasp, Olof stirred restlessly. He had a high colour; he was far from well. 'When I wish to pray – ' She stopped. She was in a turmoil. The Reverend Divine as he called himself was so large, so filling of the cabin; she felt a constriction. She didn't know what to say. Then she caught a look passing between the clergyman and the elderly nun, a sharp look from the latter. The clergyman seemed disconcerted and as the nun slightly inclined her head towards the door, he seemed to take the hint and, with it, his leave.

When he had gone Sister Perpetua sat beside Alva on the bunk and took her in her arms.

'Oh, my dear,' she said, her voice breaking a little. She was very gentle. At last Alva gave way to tears and the two of them sat there, clasping each other.

Chief Engineer Hackett and his staff had worked on the valve defect without cease all that day and a good deal of the following night. Shortly after the next day's dawn Hackett reported to the bridge. Captain Pacey was not there; he was taking the chance of catching up on much needed sleep.

'Don't disturb him,' Hackett said to the first officer. 'It'll keep.'

'Good news, or bad, Chief?'

'Both really. I've not been able to improve matters, since I'm not a ruddy dockyard, but it's no worse. We should be able to manoeuvre in Liverpool, at least with the tugs' assistance.'

'And emergency alterations – ahead to astern?'

Hackett shrugged. 'Not so good. We don't want any undue strain. We don't want a blow-out.' He added, 'It's an ill wind, as they say . . . we're going to need the shipyard repairers. That means a decent spell in Liverpool for once. Get some time with the missus. I could do with that.'

So could First Officer Main, married only two years before and, thanks to the war, separated for long periods from his wife. The turn-round each time in Liverpool was shorter now; the married men felt the strain. So did their wives. Main happened to know that the Chief was much needed at home. His wife was an invalid and finding the war an added strain to cope with. None of the doctors, Hackett had said some while ago, seemed to know what was the matter with her. They thought it might be some sort of blood problem, anaemia, but they weren't very definite. They had told him, however, that ideally he ought to be at home with her, a daft thing to say, Hackett thought, to a ship's chief engineer with his job to do and his living to earn. However, he wasn't all that far off retirement now, provided they let him go while the war was on. If they did, by the end of the year he would be ashore for good and able to see to Agnes. He was well aware how much she would welcome that. Forty years, almost, of marriage, and he'd spent most of that time away at sea. Rotten for all wives, was the sea life.

But in his retirement years he was going to make it up to her. For one thing she wouldn't have any need to worry about his safety any more. She'd always been a worrier in regard to himself and naturally since the war had started it was worse than ever. She always felt he was never coming back, that her Frank was written down in some German book of the dead and that they wouldn't rest until his name had been crossed off.

Daft, of course. But women were like that, full of weird notions. Any road – Agnes was.

Hackett lifted a palm and smote the teakwood guardrail of the bridge. 'Well,' he said, 'that's enough talk. This won't bath the baby. I'll be getting back below.'

He went down the ladder. Main thought he was looking just about all in, as bad as the Captain. Working through the night left its mark.

Main, who throughout the brief conversation with the Chief Engineer had kept an eye lifting all round the horizons, took a longer look through his binoculars. Nothing in sight. All very peaceful, not like wartime at all. But then the greater part of every voyage was just that – peaceful. The enemy came suddenly, without warning, and then you were immediately at war, with chaos all around you. In the meantime the ship's routine held. Below on deck, the hands were turning out to start hosing down the decks under one of the bosun's mates, making everything clean and shipshape before the first of the passengers emerged from slumber. And so the day would go on. Watch would succeed watch; at noon all deck officers would take sun sights with their sextants to fix the ship's position, which would be marked on the chart with a small cross. Before that, depending on the general state, Captain's Rounds would have been held. Beef tea with diced toast would have been served in the lounges to those who wanted it; the bars would open up. The passengers would go to lunch; afterwards they might sleep, or read, or play deck games, or swim in the enclosed pool. Later, afternoon tea, drinks, and dinner. All very ordered, Main thought, except for all the personal problems and anxieties that might afflict individual passengers in their different ways.

Leon Fielding was drinking his beef tea in the first-class lounge when a steward approached. The singer had found that the horror of a passenger's death the day before had taken the spotlight away from his own alleged crime and he had begun to emerge from his seclusion – up to now he had merely left his cabin to take a little exercise on deck, which was how he'd seen what had happened to the Swede. He had been expecting a summons from the Captain ever since the mob violence, so was not surprised when the steward said the Captain wished to see him in his quarters.

'I'll go at once,' he said, getting to his feet and grasping the handle of Ming's conveyance.

'The pram, sir.'

'What? Oh, yes, the stairs. I wonder – if you wouldn't mind – '

'No trouble at all, sir. Just leave it to me.' The steward wheeled the perambulator away and pushed it behind the bar. Leon Fielding, still wearing his straw hat, climbed the companionways and ladders to the Captain's day cabin, where he knocked.

Captain Pacey rose to his feet from behind his desk. 'Good morning, Mr Fielding. I'm grateful to you for coming along.'

'It's to do with that terrible business, Captain?'

Pacey nodded. 'Yes. I would have asked you to come up sooner, but I've had many other matters to attend to.' Though he didn't say so, he had been planning that possible alteration of course, weighing up the alternatives and the dangers; also he had felt a personal repugnance at being forced to investigate a mindless killing aboard his ship when there were so many outside perils looming. The whole business of the Australians' behaviour had left a bitter taste.

He motioned Fielding to a chair. 'It's terribly upsetting,' the singer said. 'Ming – ' He stopped. This was not the occasion to speak of Ming.

'Ming?'

'It's of no importance, Captain. Just my little dog . . . who in fact is not aboard, so. . . .' Fielding's voice trailed away and he wondered why he had mentioned Ming. There had been so many worries, that must be it.

The Captain was going on. 'I'm going to ask you to tell me exactly what you saw yesterday, Mr Fielding.'

'Yes, of course.' For the first time Fielding became aware that there was another person in the day cabin, a young officer with a gold stripe backed by a white cloth one, a purser's clerk, sitting in a corner with a small table in front of him and some sheets of paper on it. Notes were going to be taken, evidently. So he really must get it right the first time.

'Well, Mr Fielding?' Pacey paused, hand hovering over a box of cigarettes. 'Do you smoke?'

'I – er – no, no, I don't. I'm dreadfully sorry.'

Pacey smiled. 'It's no matter. Please don't apologize.'

'I meant about – what happened.'

'Ah yes – I see.' There was a suppressed sound from the purser's clerk, like a smothered laugh. Fielding shifted uncomfortably, imagining he was an object of scorn to the seafarers. It was rather off-putting, he found.

The Captain pressed again. 'In your own words, Fielding. I understand you saw the incident.'

'Oh yes, yes, I did indeed. Such a dreadful business.' Mr Fielding removed his straw hat and dabbed at his forehead with a handkerchief. 'A great rush of men, yelling. I was struck by the Australian accent. So uneuphonious, you know. Ugly, really. Those curious As. They talk about Austrylia. I expect you've heard that.'

'Yes. So – '

'They knocked me over. And my perambulator. I was saved by young Mr Pousty. He's a Quaker, you know. From Chicago. Such a curious background – meat canning. I believe he has a very great deal of money.'

'Probably, Mr Fielding. Now – this rush of men that you saw. Can you positively identify any of them? Individually?'

'Yes, actually I can,' Fielding said. 'A very big man, fat – a large stomach. And a vest, with braces. So common. I really don't know how anybody can appear in a vest with braces, Captain – '

'Quite. Did you pick up a name, Mr Fielding?'

'Yes, I think I did. A Christian name, if any of those Australians are Christians. Let me think now.' Fielding put his head in his hands for a moment. Pacey and the purser's clerk exchanged looks. Then Fielding said, 'Yes, I've got it now. Jake.'

'Jake? You're certain?'

'Oh yes, quite certain. Only his friends pronounced it Jyke.'

'And this man – '

'It was he who struck the blow, Captain. Frankly, I was not surprised that it should be he. He looked like a great bully, a very undesirable character I would say.' Once again the singer wiped his forehead. 'How I detest bullies. I was myself much bullied at school, you know. I used to be laughed at, and taunted. I sang in my church choir before my voice broke. The other boys considered me sissy.'

'I'm very sorry. I – '

'Were you bullied at school, Captain?'

There was another suppressed snort from the note-taker. Pacey said, 'My own school days were short. Aboard a windjammer, there was no time for bullying. The sea itself did all the bullying that was necessary. I – '

'I don't consider bullying is ever necessary, Captain. Persons who indulge in it are fiends.'

'I agree,' Pacey said shortly. 'Now, Mr Fielding. The blow, which I

170

gather you saw being struck . . . will you please give me the full details of that blow, and also tell me if anyone else was involved in the attack.'

'On the Swede?'

'On Mr Lundkvist, yes.'

'Yes. There was a heavy blow. A large piece of wood was used to strike the Swede about the head, Captain. Then he slipped and fell down. I believe he struck his back on some kind of projection in the deck, I'm uncertain as to what. While he was on the ground, deck that is, another man kicked him.'

'Kicked him?'

'Yes, very viciously. In the back, you know. In the back.'

'This other man – I understand you can identify him, Mr Fielding?'

Fielding frowned in concentration. 'I don't know. I rather doubt it after all, Captain. I don't believe I would be sure. I was so – so horrified, you see. I was *so* upset. It was really quite unbelievable that such things should happen aboard a liner. I was indeed quite flabbergasted. I – '

'You didn't get a good look at the man, you mean?'

'Yes. Yes, that is so, Captain.'

'I see. Supposing there was to be an identity parade. Do you think you might be able to pick him out?'

'I really don't know. Of course, I would do my best.' The singer was looking worried. 'Yes, I would do my best, I really would. I am not, I hope, a coward and I do know my duty and the whole thing was so horrible. But I do think that if I were to pick a man out publicly, he might afterwards become vindictive. I'm sure you understand, Captain.'

'I do, and you have my word on it that there would be no opportunity for reprisals.

'You're sure?'

'I can absolutely guarantee it, Mr Fielding.'

'Yes. Well, that does put one's mind at rest, of course. There is another point,' Fielding added. 'Mummy . . . my wife, that is.'

'Your wife? Er . . . is there some connection, Mr Fielding?'

'Indirectly so, yes.'

'But she's not aboard as I understand.'

'No. She's in New York and will be most worried about me. If she hears that I am involved however innocently and peripherally in – in anything to do with murder – '

'She'll not hear, I assure you. How can she? Nothing will emerge, say to the press, until after we reach Liverpool, and by that time you'll have been able to send a cable if you feel it necessary.'

Fielding was shaking his head. 'You don't understand, Captain, if you'll not think me rude for saying so. My dear wife . . . she has extrasensory perception – second sight you would perhaps call it. She will *know* what is happening, you see. She will feel it. I'm so worried on her account, you – '

'I think I understand, Mr Fielding.' Once again Pacey was reminded of Testament Thomas and the way in which the old windjammer had been guided towards the lifeboat filled with dead and dying men. Not that there was the slightest resemblance between the singer and Testament Thomas . . . Pacey went on, 'If your wife has this – this ability to feel what is happening here, then she'll know beyond a doubt that you're perfectly all right – and will remain so vis-à-vis those reprisals you spoke of.'

Fielding looked up. 'You think so, Captain?'

'I am quite sure.'

'Yes, it is a point, certainly. Yes. I think perhaps you're right.' Fielding paused, looking once again distraught. 'The – the other business, Captain. I am so worried. It is nagging at me. I do so wish it were settled once and for all.'

Pacey gave him a searching look. Morgan had said earlier that Fielding had reported seeing Craigson attacking Lundkvist along with Ommaney. There was no doubt that Fielding would have recognized Craigson very positively, whatever the confusion of the moment. But if the man had been Craigson, as Fielding had apparently told Morgan, then if Fielding should pick him out at any identity parade, Craigson could say that he had done so only because of the 'other business' hanging over Fielding's head.

However, Pacey had another eye-witness: the passenger John Holmes, whom he had yet to see.

Referring back to Fielding's plea Pacey said, 'Mr Craigson has other worries himself currently, Mr Fielding. I think they may well take precedence in his mind. You should stop worrying.' When Fielding had gone below, Pacey sent for Holmes.

John Holmes went later to Elizabeth Kent, in her cabin. He asked, 'Sister Perpetua at her reading, is she?'

'I think so. Then she'll be doing her daily exercise around the deck. Once reading's done, she kind of becomes Sister Perpetual Motion.'

He laughed. 'Well put!'

'Oh, it's not my invention. She told me, back in her convent she was always on the go and that was what they named her.' Elizabeth paused. 'Well? How was it, with the Captain?'

'I told him what I saw. That big Australian and the guy who accused Fielding of – '

'Yes. Craigson.'

'Right.'

'So?'

'The skipper's going to get me and Fielding to make a positive identification. Or maybe just me.'

'And then?'

John spread his hands. 'Why, then, I guess he can make out a charge against one or the other.'

'You mean either Craigson or Ommaney could have been the one who killed Lundkvist?'

'Yeah. Sure, it'll depend on the medical evidence as to which . . . a medic's opinion on just what did kill Lundkvist: the blow on the head, or the kick that could have resulted in breaking his back.' John sat down on the bunk. He was sweating a little. He asked, 'You sure the old girl won't be back?'

'Pretty sure. She's got herself a job, apart from reading and walking. She's taken Lundkvist's wife under her wing.' Elizabeth gave a giggle. 'You suggesting something, or what?'

'Something,' he said. His hands were shaking a little; she read the signs.

'OK,' she said.

Pacey had decided to make no public appeal for witnesses, at least not yet. He might be forced into it but for the time being was content to rely on the testimony of John Holmes and perhaps Fielding. He hoped to be able to leave the rest to the police in Liverpool, who would make their own investigation before the passengers were allowed to disembark.

He did, however, send for the ship's surgeon, whose initial report had merely confirmed the fact of death and its cause: the broken back.

'If I asked you, doctor, to make a full postmortem examination, what would be your reaction?'

Fellowes shrugged. 'I could do it, of course. But I think it would be inadvisable.'

'Why so?'

'Because I doubt if the shore authorities – police, forensic, even the coroner – would thank me for perhaps disturbing evidence which they might prefer to elucidate for themselves, Captain Pacey.'

Pacey nodded slowly. 'Yes, I see.'

'What is it you wish to discover?' Fellowes asked. 'I've already established the actual cause of death. I see no necessity to go further.'

Pacey said, 'I want to know which came first. I mean – was Lundkvist dead from the head injury *before* being kicked? Or the other way round?'

'I think I've already answered that, Captain. The cause of death was the broken back, and that came as a result of the kick. In my opinion, that is.'

173

'In your opinion? Then there could be other opinions?'

'Yes. Yes, there could be.' Fellowes sounded cautious now. 'Head injuries . . . they're funny things. But the back. There would have been an injury to one of the vertebrae, with damage to the spinal cord and nerves. The – '

'Such damage could cause death?'

'Yes. My opinion was and is that the spinal column was fractured by the kick, a kick from a heavy boot heavily applied. There could have been previous damage, I suppose, a weakening as a result of the previous fall . . . only a full postmortem will establish that. And I say again, Captain, the shore people will see to that and they are the proper persons to do so.'

Pacey left it at that. He had done all that was required of him. He had so many other matters to attend to; more vital matters. The ship, obviously, came first. And the sea miles towards Britain were decreasing fast. That morning, as usual on this voyage as ordered by himself, full boat drill was held. Pacey, via Staff Captain Morgan, ordered fire drill to include closing of the watertight doors and hatches as well as the running out of the fire hoses.

During the afternoon all male passengers in the third class were mustered in the second-class lounge, which had been cleared of all other persons. The assistant second steward made the rounds of the third-class cabins and washrooms, ensuring that they had been vacated. Among the passengers were Big Jake Ommaney and Craigson, currently under no overt restraint. But all exits from the lounge had been locked; outside the square windows that gave onto the after decks, Bosun MacFarlane patrolled with a party of seamen. In the lounge itself, both masters-at-arms mingled with the passengers, watchfully, keeping not too far away from Ommaney and Craigson. Inside the main door were the Staff Captain, the Chief Officer, Purser Matthews and Chief Steward Kemmis. With them were Leon Fielding and John Holmes. The atmosphere was tense, and loud complaints came from the Australian contingent. Big Jake Ommaney was the centre of attention, and knew it. He was boastful, determined not to let himself down in front of his mates. But there was a brittleness in his boasting; it was, and this he knew too, sheer bravado. At the very least, once ashore in Britain, he faced a long term of imprisonment. In fact, he had shot his bolt. He knew very well what the presence of Fielding and Holmes meant.

Once the assembly had been reported correct, Staff Captain Morgan had told them what was required of them: when the Captain came down from the bridge, the passengers would file past the ship's officers and past Messrs Fielding and Holmes. They would not speak; they would pause for a count of five and then move on. That was all.

When the main door was opened to admit Captain Pacey, there was a stir and then a hush. Captain Pacey was a formidable figure who added at once to the gravity of the occasion.

He said, 'Good afternoon, gentlemen. I much regret the necessity for this.' That was all; Pacey nodded at the Staff Captain. Shepherded by the attendant stewards, the third-class passengers shuffled into a line of sorts and began to pass the scrutiny at the for'ard end of the lounge.

14

'THE goddam English,' the man in the Brooklyn bar said to Larry Costello, husband for the time being of Livia Costello, aboard the *Laurentia*, 'are not behaving any too good, buddy. Sure, I don't go for the Heinies either.' He took a swig at his Scotch. 'But the English, they've been sailing under the Stars and Stripes whenever it suits them. Even that *Laurentia*'s done it when it suits. Right?'

'I guess so,' Larry Costello said. He sounded uninterested: the war wasn't affecting him. He had no interest in the *Laurentia*, no interest in Livia either except, as he'd thought earlier, that the Germans might well rid him of an encumbrance. Currently he was waiting for a woman, an actress who knew Livia and was more than willing to fulfil her wifely functions for her. The man, who was verging on being drunk, was going on. Going on about President Wilson who might yet drag the US into the war. Secretary of the Interior Lane, it was well known, had been born under the British flag and even had two cousins serving in the British Army. Lane and Wilson were close colleagues . . . the voice went on: the speaker didn't like the English, didn't trust them. And he had, he said, a hunch that a whole lot of Americans were going to suffer in the *Laurentia* about which there had been so much goddam hoo-ha when she'd sailed from New York recently. His hunch told him the *Laurentia* was going to be torpedoed by the Germans.

'And then what?' he asked rhetorically, waving his glass of Scotch so that the contents swilled over. Just then a woman entered the bar in an aura of expensive perfume. She wore a mink coat and looked sexy.

Costello said, 'Welcome, honey. You got a cab out there?'

She said she had.

Costello said, 'Let's get out of here.'

'And then what?' the President prompted.

This was no semidrunk; this was Counsellor Robert Lansing of the State Department and he was speaking to President Wilson. Lansing, like the man in the Brooklyn bar, believed that the *Laurentia* was on her final voyage. He had taken to heart the warning, so much publicized in the press, from the German Embassy. He had his contacts in the German Embassy and he believed that the warning had been no mere threat, no propaganda exercise. The *Laurentia*, he said, might well be sunk.

That was when Wilson had uttered.

Lansing said, 'A swing of sentiment, Mr President, right across the land. You'll remember Thrasher, of course.'

'Yes.' A few weeks previously, a German torpedo had sunk a British liner, the *Falaba*, en route to South Africa. One casualty had been a US citizen named Thrasher, a mining engineer. There had been an outcry in the press, a swing of sentiment away from the Germans. That American death had acted as a catalyst on a small scale, bringing the different factions in the government to a state of ferment. Strong action had been called for, by Counsellor Lansing among others. But still Wilson had vacillated. In every public speech he had plugged the line of strict neutrality – 'in thought as in deed', as he was accustomed to put it. Wilson was a procrastinator, and preferred to spend time writing down his thoughts on paper so as to sort them out, rather than expose himself to the cut and thrust of cabinet meetings where he might inadvertently commit himself. Now he said, 'I do not believe the worst will happen – '

'But if it does, Mr President?'

'I said I don't believe . . . I refuse to believe that the Germans will take the risk – '

'Just so long as *they* believe, and very firmly believe, that the loss of so many American lives would lead inevitably to war. That, to my mind, Mr President, is the best safeguard for the *Laurentia*. But it needs to be stressed unmistakably. It needs that right now.'

Wilson sighed and got to his feet to look out across the lawn of the White House. He said over his shoulder, 'I myself am not committed . . . whatever happens to the *Laurentia*. To lose more American lives in a war would scarcely be a recompense for those that might be lost if the ship is torpedoed. I would, I think, say this: we Americans . . . there is such a thing as being too proud to fight.'

Lansing stared at the thick, morning-coated back. Neither of the men could realize how those words, once spoken in public, were due to echo around the world in the days ahead. Wilson turned then and said, 'In any case, there will be no sinking. My assurance of that lies in the fact that Grant's aboard. The Germans would never take the risk of perhaps drowning the United States Ambassador Elect. I feel quite sure of that. It is Grant who is the salvation of the *Laurentia*.'

When Counsellor Lansing had gone, Wilson returned to the window. Broodingly he looked out over Washington and the course of the Potomac River. Washington, he thought, was a beautiful city, the flower of America. Set at the head of the tide waters and navigation of the Potomac it had been mostly built on the bottom lands, in a virtual amphitheatre surrounded by great bluffs. Above the bluffs the residential part of the city had begun to spread some years ago. The street plan of the main part of the city was regular, symmetrically radiating from Capitol Hill. The streets and avenues were wide – ninety to a hundred and sixty feet. There were no less than 3600 acres of public parks. The city's buildings were splendid – many libraries testifying, in the President's view, to the broad scope of the American people, their education in a free society . . . the Library of Congress contained almost two million books, while the municipal library, housed in a magnificent building of white marble, had been given by Mr Andrew Carnegie. Washington was the home of a number of universities – the George Washington University, the Georgetown University, the Catholic University of America and the Howard University, together with the Carnegie Institute.

There was a rush of blood to President Wilson's head: he was a patriot first and foremost, and patriotism didn't have to mean war. Washington had seen its wars – the War of Independence when the English had been soundly beaten and thrown out, and the terrible trauma of the Civil War between north and south, brother's hand turned against brother, whole families split between the two factions.

War was uncivilized, was the very antithesis of all that Washington now stood for. Of what all America stood for. The sight of the splendid city renewed the President's spirit and resolve each time he stood where he was now standing and looked out over the establishments of learning and thereby, in his mind, of peace and progress.

There could be no progress in a war. War by its very nature was a retrogression. No man could do better for his country than to keep it out of war, than to maintain a strict neutrality.

But both the British and the Germans were making it very difficult. Wilson felt an enormous sense of unfairness that events outside America's control seemed at times likely to overwhelm the land. The land of freedom. While he remained at the window sounds came to him, sounds that seemed to echo his own thoughts. The sounds came closer, military though they were impressing themselves deeply on the President's mental awareness. The music came from the brass band of the US Marine Corps.

Wilson mouthed the words to himself.

> Oh, say, shall that star-spangled banner still wave
> O'er the birthplace of freedom, the home of the brave.

Brave. You didn't meet bravery only in war. One day, perhaps, the people of the United States of America might have cause to thank a president who had stood out against the jarring demands of the warriors, who had stood out firmly for what he believed in, for the vision of a peaceful, neutral America.

But, in spite of all he'd thought, and all he'd been saying to Counsellor Lansing, it was going to be extremely difficult to hold the line if the *Laurentia* should be attacked and sunk. If that should happen, one thing was absolutely dead certain sure, and that was that the British would make the most of it. And the one that would make the most noise would be Mr Winston Churchill.

Not a happy thought.

In the British Admiralty, the First Lord took up an internal telephone and spoke into the mouthpiece, gruffly and briefly. Within half a minute a uniformed Captain RN entered the room.

'The *Laurentia*,' Mr Churchill said.

'Yes, sir?'

'Show me where she is, Captain.'

'Aye, aye, sir.' The naval officer moved across to the large map pinned to one wall of the First Lord's room, a war map for Mr Churchill to follow and supervise the whole of the war at sea, a wall that faced the big windows looking out over Horse Guards Parade, a place that might be considered the home territory of the war on land, presided over by Lord Kitchener, Field Marshal and Secretary of State for War.

On the map, the naval captain moved a small red flag.

'That's her position, sir – '

'Estimated?'

'Dead reckoning from her last reported position by noon sight – '

'When was that?'

'Yesterday. Her position now is latitude – '

'Yes, yes, I don't want your naval jargon, Captain. How far off – let's say the Old Head of Kinsale – is she?'

The naval officer said, 'A little over 1000 miles, sir.'

'And in terms of time?'

'Two and a half days at eighteen knots.'

'Approximate, I suppose?'

'We can only be approximate, First Lord.'

Mr Churchill grunted. He sounded irritable; he had risen very early that morning, as was in fact his usual custom. Also in accordance with his custom he had drunk a brandy whilst still in bed, and had lit a cigar. Thinking his own thoughts, rehearsing a speech he was to make later that day, he had been careless: he had waved his arms, which meant he had waved his cigar, and he had burned Clementine sleeping beside him, and she had been unusually angry. That had upset the First Lord;

then his breakfast had not been to his liking. The liver and bacon had not been sufficiently hot and had had to be sent back to the kitchens. The kedgeree, on the other hand, had burned his tongue and he had given a roar of anger that had caused Clemmy to spill her coffee on the otherwise spotless tablecloth. . . .

Not a good start to the day.

'Is there anything else, First Lord?'

'What? No. Back to your desk, Captain, while others sail the seas.'

The naval officer was stung into a retort. 'We don't choose our appointments, First Lord. We're given them.'

'I know all that!' Mr Churchill snapped. 'Kindly do not argue with me, Captain.'

The officer, not a young man, turned abruptly and went out of the room without a word. In his opinion Winston Churchill was a whippersnapper, a young upstart, who had lost no time in upsetting many of the more senior officers at the Admiralty with his demanding, dictatorial ways and his assumption that he was always right, an assumption that was being proved baseless with every day that the Dardanelles campaign continued on its bloody, casualty-filled way. Currently there were rumours inside the Admiralty, and outside its walls too, that Mr Churchill would not be averse to hearing news that the *Laurentia* had gone down. God knew, the country was in the most desperate need of American help – war materials, guns and ammunition, food, ships, men.

Alone again Mr Churchill, who knew very well what a number of people, serving officers and civilians accustomed to their own way in the Admiralty's administration, thought about him, was unmoved. He grinned to himself and made a gesture, with two raised fingers, towards the door through which the naval captain had left. Then for a moment he sat wreathed in cigar smoke, his eyes, heavy lidded, half-closed in thought. The room in which he sat was old and redolent of history, the history of Great Britain's glorious past. Into this very room would have come news of Lord Howe's great sea victory, the Glorious First of June, back in 1794 when he had inflicted a crushing defeat on the wretched French – Mr Churchill still considered the French a bunch of scoundrels, even though the two countries were now allies, and always most resolutely refused to pronounce French words as the French did. Here also would have come the news from Trafalgar and the sad tidings of the death of Vice-Admiral Viscount Nelson of the Nile. In this room would have been discussed the vile horrors of the French Revolution and the scenes at the guillotine when King Louis XVI and his aristocrats were delivered in the tumbrils to the descending knives and the flashing knitting-needles of the haglike harridans whose gruesome pleasure it was to watch the fall of noble heads. Then in this room there would have been talk of the long desired final fall of Napoleon Bonaparte after his escape from Elba and his raising of the French Standard, and the hundred days that had led to his defeat at the hands of the British under the great Duke of Wellington, assisted by the Prussians under Blucher. The Germans, Britain's old allies against the scheming French. Mr Churchill knew that there were still generals in the field who had to be tactfully restrained from speaking of the French as the enemy. *Plus ça change, plus est la même chose.* Churchill smirked; the French had a way with telling phrases, to be sure. Allies and alignments shifted, and you were still at war with somebody or other.

War, Mr Churchill often felt, was ennobling. To fight for one's country brought out the best in a man. He himself not infrequently wished he was back with his regiment of years ago, the 4th Hussars, fighting in Flanders even if it meant mingling with the French. He had seen a good deal of fighting in his younger days: with the Spanish forces in Cuba in 1895, with the Malakand Field Force two years later, and later still, whilst correspondent for the *Daily Telegraph* in India, he had seen service with the 31st Punjab Light Infantry under General Sir Bindon Blood. After that he had served with the Tirah Expeditionary Force where he had been orderly officer to Sir William Lockhart; and thereafter he had proceeded to Egypt, where Lord Kitchener had been entering upon the final stage of the reconquest of the Sudan.

Churchill believed that his finest military hour had come when, attached to the 21st Lancers, the Death or Glory Boys as they were known from their cap badge, he had taken part in the cavalry charge at Omdurman.

Churchill knew himself to be a warrior at heart. His whole instinct was to hit the enemy hard and keep on hitting him.

But Great Britain had never before faced a war quite like this one. An almost motionless war, with the troops dug like slugs and worms into muddy trenches, trenches that were steadily and rapidly draining away the very lifeblood of the Empire in an attempt to hold the line against the Kaiser's well-disciplined armies.

An attempt that was beginning to appear likely to fail. No one country – no one Empire, for the response had been most heartening from the Empire – could survive unaided. The French had already proved useless. . . .

Churchill, staring out still over Horse Guards Parade, remembered that there was a French general aboard the incoming *Laurentia*. General François de Gard, a desk-bound general, all light blue and tawdry gold with tassels, and a moustache. He would be no damn loss, Mr Churchill reflected. As the First Lord stood at the big window, like President

Woodrow Wilson in Washington across the North Atlantic, something happened that was also similar to what had occurred outside the White House.

A company of His Majesty's Scots Guards, marching in from the Mall with a swarm of cheering Londoners marching with them, turned on to the Horse Guards to the thunder of the drums and brass. They marched past the Admiralty building to the music of 'The British Grenadiers'.

A lump came into Mr Churchill's throat. He felt tears prick at his eyeballs. Then, a moment later, the brass fell silent and the pipes took over. It was a haunting moment as, in the thin spring sunshine dappling the trees in Green Park, the first weird wails of inblown air swelled out triumphantly. Triumphantly, yet with the usual sense of sadness. If this was a recruiting drive, Churchill thought, it would be highly successful.

He listened.

> Should auld acquaintance be forgot
> And never brought to mind. . . .

Auld acquaintance! Yes, there would be a rush to the recruiting offices after the Scots Guards had marched back to barracks – but it still wouldn't be enough.

And there was plenty of 'auld acquaintance' between Britain and America. So huge a proportion of Americans came of British stock, English, Irish, Scots, Welsh. They simply could not hold back.

'What, dear God,' Mr Churchill said aloud in an agony of mind for his mother's great country, 'what is holding them back now?'

Later that day some of the possible answer emerged, or at any rate the answer as propounded by the Prime Minister, Mr Henry Herbert Asquith, starchy in his wing collar, with stiff cuffs showing below the sleeves of the morning coat. Certain ministers had been summoned to a meeting at Number Ten Downing Street; the subject under discussion was the arrival aboard the *Laurentia* of banker Patrick Haggerty from New York and the much-hoped-for loan. Present were the Chancellor of the Exchequer, the Foreign Secretary, Lord Kitchener from the War Office, and the First Lord. Kitchener, Churchill knew, would be anxious to grab all military allocations from the loan for his own aggrandizement: the fleet would come nowhere in Kitchener's reckoning. Kitchener was too self-centred, too arrogant, by half.

The Prime Minister remarked, 'We're perhaps a trifle premature. On the other hand, it's as well to decide on priorities as soon as possible. We all, I think, know the urgency – '

'The armies in the field,' Kitchener said, 'are the – '

'I have a more urgent need for the fleet,' Churchill interrupted, sitting forward in his chair, his chin jutting and his face formidable. 'This country of ours ... it was built upon sea power, by the weight of our broadsides, by the seamanship of great – '

'Damn battleships have never, or scarcely, been to sea since the war started,' Lord Kitchener announced. 'Swinging at buoys or at anchor in Scapa Flow, or in the Forth, or in the Cromarty Firth, off Invergordon! Settling on their own garbage by now I shouldn't wonder. What use are they, may I ask – eh?'

Churchill said, his face flushed, 'It was not of the battleships I was speaking. I want destroyers, cruisers, minelayers, minesweepers. Principally I want destroyers and light cruisers so that I may institute a proper system of convoying ships to these islands. On land, the war may go one way, it may go the other. The front line shifts its position a half mile or so almost daily! But one thing is certain, gentlemen, and it is this: if food fails to reach this country, our people will starve – no matter what happens on the land in France and Belgium. Starvation is never far away. And it is upon our merchant ships that we depend for food – and supplies of oil fuel from the Middle East, from the Persian Gulf. And it is upon the warships of the Royal Navy that we depend for the safe passage into Britain of the merchant ships. I insist that I have priority in this matter.'

Kitchener glared angrily. He was about to speak when he was stopped by the Prime Minister's raised hand. 'One moment, my dear Kitchener, one moment. I've already said we may be premature. I repeat that. I believe we may never get the loan we've asked for.'

'But – '

'Listen to me, please, Winston. I have had words with Colonel House.' All present knew of Colonel House, the personal representative in London of President Wilson, knew of his closeness to Wilson, knew too of his own opinion, which was that America should enter the war on Britain's side – and soon at that. House, like Ambassador Page – soon to be replaced by Henry Sayers Grant, currently aboard the *Laurentia* – was a good friend to Britain. 'House has put forward a theory – no more than a theory, but it is one worth heeding, I fancy.' Asquith paused.

'Well, Prime Minister?' Kitchener said in an impatient tone.

'House believes the loan will not be granted. He believes Haggerty will impose terms so unacceptable to us that we shall be obliged to turn them down.'

'You mean, Prime Minister,' Churchill said, 'that the loan will in fact be offered, but – '

'Yes, it will be offered. President Wilson wishes to be seen as helpful to us, short of going to war. He wishes his generosity to be seen, and he wishes – according to House – for it to be seen that *we* are ourselves our worst enemies, that we are the ones to make difficulties and in effect throw back the American generosity in their faces.'

'I see. Or I think I do, Prime Minister.' This was Winston Churchill again. 'But did Colonel House prognosticate what in fact Haggerty's, or Wilson's, terms might be? I think it is important that we should know that.'

Mr Asquith said, 'If House knew – and I don't know whether or not he did – he wasn't saying. His was simply a warning to us not to count our chickens.' He paused, ran a tired hand over his eyes. 'But if I were asked to make a guess, I would say this: America is jealous of this country, of our Empire, of the sway we, a small and physically insignificant island, hold in the wider world, especially perhaps of our Indian Empire and its riches, the enormous prestige that that Empire of the East confers on the British monarch, the King-Emperor. America has nothing to equal that, and I believe it rankles.'

'You think that pure damn jealousy,' Lord Kitchener began roughly, 'is at the bottom of their whole refusal to go to war with Germany? Is that it, Prime Minister?'

'I didn't go so far as to say that,' Asquith answered, 'but yes, I believe that is certainly an element.'

'Damn small minded,' Kitchener barked.

Mr Churchill entered a defence for the United States: he was himself too close to America to allow that charge to pass. There was, he said, nothing small minded about either America or President Wilson himself. He believed it would be merely a question of time, that in due course the American people would see for themselves where their best interests lay, and when that time came the pressure would come upon Congress and the White House itself. Lord Kitchener was heard to remark, more or less beneath his breath, that the American people needed a kick up the backside to propel their awareness somewhat faster and that the fastest way of doing that might well be for the *Laurentia* to be sunk. That, Kitchener said, would shake Wilson's complacency more than anything else would.

15

'THEY'RE OK in some ways,' Senator Manderton said in Haggerty's state-room, 'but they're so goddam *bombastic*. It makes me hate them sometimes, though I guess it shouldn't. They just can't help it most of the time. It's second nature.' Senator Manderton was feeling sore, his feathers badly ruffled. He had conscientiously pursued his brief, his fact-finding mission designed to find out what really made the limeys tick. This time, he had concentrated his attack on the crew and had started on a deckhand, an elderly man with a black patch over one eye and a stiff leg that made life difficult on the heaving, wet decks of a liner. That patch, and that leg: the British Empire hadn't done him all that much good. And he'd looked as though he knew it: he had a disgruntled look and Senator Manderton had observed him muttering away to himself as, on the boat deck, the old fellow had manoeuvred himself around the passengers in their deck-chairs or playing deck quoits on a marked-out court. The mutterings and the cast looks had not seemed polite, somehow.

The old seaman's name was Albert Bromhead. From the corner of his eye he had seen Senator Manderton bearing down upon him like a windjammer under full sail. He'd heard yarns about Manderton, who had become known as a busybody who asked many questions. Albert Bromhead didn't like being questioned, but Senator Manderton was a passenger and Bromhead's livelihood depended on passengers, so he stopped when hailed.

'Excuse me,' Senator Manderton said, and gave a big smile. 'I was wondering if I might have a word.'

'Yessir?'

'I aim to find out, in a general sort of way, what you British tars think about the war that's going on in Yurrup, all right?'

Albert Bromhead moved to the ship's rail, cleared his throat and spat over the side. He didn't like being called a tar. Senator Manderton wondered if the expectoration might be taken as an unspoken answer, representing what the old guy thought about the war. But there was, as it turned out, no connection. 'Beg pardon, sir,' Bromhead said, 'About this 'ere war, now. I reckon it 'ad to 'appen. That Kaiser, 'e got too big for 'is boots. Now it's 'appened, well, we got to win it, see?'

'So you're happy enough?' Manderton paused. 'That eye patch. That a result of the war?'

Bromhead had in fact lost the eye during a nasty fight over a woman in the Liverpool dock area many years earlier. But why confess that? 'Yes,' he said. 'Attack by a U-boat, right at the start. Not this ship. I was sailing with Blue Funnel, sir. Got shot in the eye, I did, when the bugger opened fire. Beggin' your pardon for the language, sir.'

'Right in the eye?' Senator Manderton asked incredulously. 'Where did it come out? The bullet. Or was it, er, shrapnel?'

'Bullet, sir. Come out the back 'o me 'ead, missin' me brains on the way. Hair's grown over the 'ole now, sir. The quack, 'e said I was dead lucky to be alive, sir.'

'I'll bet,' Senator Manderton said. 'And the leg? Was that the war too?'

Bromhead nodded; in a way it was. Returning drunk aboard one night in Cape Town back in the days of the South African war against the Boers, when he'd signed on a government-requisitioned cargo vessel, he had fallen from the gangway and cannoned off the dock wall before dropping into the water. Rescued, he had been left with a gammy leg, permanently stiff. He'd been landed ashore and spent many months in hospital, but, on coming out, had managed to get back to sea, the only trade he knew. 'Bleedin' Boers, sir. Joined the naval brigade I did . . . went up with the guns to Ladysmith. Caught a packet from a Boer rifle, tore something, I dunno, muscle I think the quack said.'

'You've had a raw deal,' Senator Manderton said with a show of sympathy. 'Should have been pensioned off, I guess, not exploited.'

'Exploited, sir? Not me, sir!' Albert Bromhead chuckled. 'I do the exploiting. I get tips a-plenty, sir, for seeing to the quoits and putting up the figures for the daily run. And other things. I save me pay, sir, and me tips. I'm not married like some, sending it all 'ome to the missus and kids. I'm on me tod, like. Got a nice little 'ouse in the Pool, terraced, but worth money. Most times I let it out. I'm one o' the exploiters, I am, one o' them crool, unscrupulous landlords.'

'You don't say!' There were many sides to the British, not all of them obvious. Senator Manderton was baffled. Pick a man you thought was one of the world's least fortunate citizens, and what do you get? It was making a nonsense of his yet-to-be written summary and report to Congress. But he persisted. He said, 'You've never felt that the – the system was grinding you down, that you've been dragged into service for the upper classes, that this war is being fought for them and not for you at all?'

The old seaman scratched his head, tilting back his uniform cap.

'Why, no sir, I don't reckon I 'ave. And it's my war, too. Don't want them Germans coming ashore in the Pool, taking over me 'ouse.'

'Well – no, I guess not at that. But the Empire? What do you think about the Empire, may I ask that?'

'I never do think much about the Empire, sir. All them bleeding blacks an' such. It's their fault, not mine – and they're safe under 'is Majesty's dominion.' Bromhead puckered up his face; he looked like a small brown monkey, Senator Manderton thought. Bromhead was cudgelling his brains for something he'd heard someone reading out from the *News of the World*, a poem it was, he'd been told, and he'd liked the sound of the words, very magnificent they were. 'You 'eard o' Rudyard Kipling, sir? A poet, the gennelman is.'

'Yes, yes, I – '

'What 'e wrote. "God of our fathers, known of old . . . Lord o' our far flung battle line . . . beneath 'ose awful 'and we 'old dominion over palm and pine." That's what the Empire means, like. Without it, where would we be, eh? An island in the North Sea. Poor as church mice, sir, like all them blacks.'

Senator Manderton had been shaken. He had broken off his interrogation rather huffily. Moving along the deck, he had looked back to see his erstwhile interviewee taking cash from that Lady Barlow, accompanied as ever by her witless son. The old man was being obsequious, almost bowing and scraping. Well, the limeys were welcome to that sort of life. But it wasn't up to US citizens to help perpetuate it. He could at least report that to Congress. In the meantime, he was reporting it to Patrick Haggerty; and Haggerty was nodding sagely and seeming to agree with his views.

'Had it too good for too long,' he said. 'It gets into the system – ruling, what, a quarter of the world's surface. I guess they need a correction now and again. Maybe that's what the Kaiser thinks too.'

Manderton cocked an eyebrow. 'And the President?'

Haggerty said, 'Well, I can't speak for the President. I'm not that close.'

'You must have formed an opinion, Patrick.'

'Yes, I've formed an opinion. It's no more than that, just an opinion.' He had no intention of discussing his views with Melvin Manderton, who might well repeat it, to his embarrassment, in places where it should not be repeated. Patrick Haggerty did not like Senator Manderton, considering him brash and not a good advertisement for the United States; but one did not fall out with US Senators. There were always times when their support might be invaluable and the more friends a man had at court as it were the better. Banker Haggerty's view was that it was high time the British Empire was disbanded, in the interest not only

187

of the United States but of the world as a whole. Too much power concentrated into too few hands was an evil that led automatically to grandiose thoughts and behaviour and to ideas of further conquests. The British Empire should be brought up short; Haggerty believed that President Wilson held more or less similar views. And, whether or not he realized it fully, Wilson had handed Haggerty the means of possibly bringing it about; or anyway of starting the process. Haggerty could play power politics with that loan, so desperately desired by the British. It would be granted on those conditions that he had been working on, drafting his proposals while the *Laurentia* came ever closer to the British shores. The most important condition would be to do with the Empire.

If the British caved in to the US demands, well and good. If they didn't? No loan. To save their face, it would all be done with full discretion, utter secrecy, no leaks to the press. And Senator Manderton must not know. Haggerty knew very well that the great majority of US citizens wouldn't like it, seeing it as sheer dirt. He knew that mass sentiment was slowly but surely turning towards Britain. Blood was thicker than water; the ties with Britain were immense and strong. So, in his own case, were the ties with Ireland. And he knew that that, too, would be known across America if anything came out while the war was still going on.

At the muster of the third-class passengers both Big Jake Ommaney and Craigson had been picked out by John Holmes.

'That one,' he said to the Captain after each of them had passed by.

'You're certain?'

'I'm dead certain, sir.'

'Very well. Mr Fielding?'

'I – I think so, Captain. I'm sure about the big man. I'm not so sure about the other – oh, I know him, of course.' The singer was shaking, obviously scared out of his wits. Pacey assessed what was going through his mind: of course Fielding had recognized Craigson. He was scared now of any involvement at a future trial, when Craigson's complaint against him was bound to be uttered in open court. The defence lawyers would see to that. Fielding would be held to scorn, possibly face a charge of perjury, the man who had interfered, allegedly, with Craigson's boy and was now offering false evidence to ensure Craigson's being put out of circulation.

Fielding was going on. 'I couldn't possibly make a statement, Captain. I couldn't swear, you see. It's a very big thing – a charge of that sort. A man's life perhaps . . . no, I really couldn't possibly. You must see that, Captain.'

Pacey nodded. The singer would be little use anyway as an eventual court witness; he would be shot to pieces. Abruptly Pacey said, 'Very well, Mr Fielding. We have one positive identification and that will have to do.' He turned to Staff Captain Morgan. 'Thank you, Staff Captain. The passengers may disperse. The two accused to be returned to the cells.'

He swung round and left the lounge. Fielding went straight to his cabin. He sat miserably on the bunk, knowing that he had failed in a duty. He was a coward, a poor master for little Ming. Even the empty perambulator in a corner of the cabin seemed to rebuke him. But it was no good; he simply could not face what he knew must follow if ever he pointed the finger at Craigson. After a while there was a tap at his door and Elmer Pousty came in. He saw the state Fielding was in, but he said nothing about the muster. He knew the score. And he sympathized with the distraught singer. He would not press until Fielding himself came out with it.

Rickards had prevailed upon his wife to allow Dr Fellowes to be sent for. Prevailed was perhaps not the word: he had issued an order. She was unwell and must be seen to. He brushed aside the question of the fees. Emmy came first. Apart from anything else, his sons would expect that.

Dr Fellowes came. With him on this occasion was his nursing sister, Betty Unwin.

Dr Fellowes carried out an examination. Stethoscope, ophthalmoscope, auriscope, pulse. A number of questions. He took her hands in his own and gave a non-committal nod, which could have been either assurance to the husband or confirmation of a theory.

The examination finished, he stood up. '*Anno domini*,' he said. 'It comes to us all, you know.'

'Yes, I do know. But is there no treatment, Dr Fellowes?'

'I'll send a tonic,' he said.

And your inflated bill, Rickards thought, no more impressed by the ship's surgeon than he had been on the earlier visit. Fellowes left the cabin, walking along the alleyway with Sister Unwin.

'What do you think?' he asked.

'That shake, Doctor. The pill-rolling motion, thumb and fingers. Parkinson's?'

'I think so, yes. The facial tautness, lack of expression . . . Odd it hasn't been remarked earlier. She's no chicken.' Fellowes knew he should have recognized the signs on his first visit to Mrs Rickards. He was failing too often to recognize things.

Sister Unwin asked directly, 'What do you propose to do, Doctor?'

Fellowes gave a short laugh. 'What can I do? Nothing. It's not an immediately fatal condition. A deterioration, perhaps slow, perhaps fast,

I can't say.' He sighed. 'We know so little about nervous conditions . . . I shall not tell the husband, Sister. When they're ashore is time enough for them to consult their own medical man. I'll advise that but I'll go no further.'

They had reached the surgery. This was adjoined by the doctor's stateroom. 'A glass of sherry, Sister?'

'Thank you, Doctor,' she said.

For himself, Dr Fellowes poured a stiff whisky. Drinking it, he stared somewhat glumly at Sister Unwin. It was many years since he, a bachelor like virtually all ships' doctors, had had a woman. Whisky was the compensation; or had been at first. Now it had become a steady habit that had largely atrophied performance, and to a less extent desire. Now and again over the years between something had stirred; but not with Sister Unwin. She was large and bony, not unlike a horse, and very virginal. It was a pity. But there was always the whisky. A doctor's professional life at sea was not a busy one, so it didn't really matter.

Sister Unwin saw to the tonic a little later; and it went along to the Rickards' cabin together with a note of the doctor's fee. The *Laurentia* was not far off journey's end now and soon the Purser would be collecting the medical fees for handing over to the surgeon.

The previous night had been a bad one for Frederick Jones. He had had a particularly vivid dream, a real nightmare of weird proportions.

He could have sworn he was in fact wide awake when Maggie had appeared in his cabin, coming out from the wardrobe, not entering through the door, which was odd in itself though at the time he had accepted it as normal, he didn't know why.

Maggie had been looking disjointed – well, that was to be expected, of course, considering. Limbs loose, with gaps between them and the torso. And only one leg.

'What do you want?' he'd whispered in a blue funk, holding the sheets tight to his chin like a fearful virgin.

She had, she said clearly, come for her teeth. She didn't mention the leg. It wasn't fair, she'd said, to take away her teeth, whatever would she do when she arrived at Heaven's gate, looking a fright? What would they think? (Afterwards, Mr Jones was to find it strange that she hadn't arrived either there or the other place before now; she had been dead for some while. Possibly it was on account of the dismemberment . . . but he didn't think about that while Maggie was still there before his eyes in his cabin.)

She was accusing him of her murder, upbraiding him for a wicked act, and, subsidiarily, for putting his wretched old mother before herself, not a husbandly thing to do.

'You can talk,' he'd quavered. 'What about Irwin Ford?' Irwin Ford had been the lover in Arlington. 'And the others. That wasn't, well, wifely, was it?'

She'd started to cry at that and her body, or aura, had gone all funny, kind of dissolving; then it had formed again, and had turned its back on him and said it was going to the Captain to tell him the facts and then Frederick would be made to walk the plank, or be keel-hauled. Maggie had floated out of the door and Mr Jones had gone after her in his weird dream. Also in stone-cold sober fact: he had been pleading with Maggie not to say a word to the Captain when suddenly he had found himself in a man's grip. The man was Master-at-Arms Warner, making his night rounds of the accommodation.

Mr Jones's heart seemed to stop and he stared wildly. 'What – '

'All right, sir. It's all right.' Warner's tone was soft, placatory. He'd heard that it could be dangerous to wake a sleep-walker; at first he hadn't realized Mr Jones was sleep-walking. A gentleman muttering funny things to himself and wandering around the cabin alleyways in his nightshirt could be drunk and needed to be stopped in case a lady saw him; and the gentleman hadn't responded when spoken to. 'I'll see you to your cabin, sir.'

'But I – what – '

'No trouble, sir.' A firm clasp was put upon Mr Jones's arm and he was propelled towards his cabin, the number of which he gave Warner on request. Mr Jones was in a bad way now, wondering what he might have said, what his apprehender might have heard. Mr Jones himself had not the slightest idea, although he could still see the terrible apparition of Maggie with her dismembered limbs, one leg, and no teeth. Of course, she had come about the teeth.

But – again of course – she hadn't really come at all. It had all been due to his own mental state. She had been so much on his mind, or rather the manner of her death had. It had been very foolish, very risky. He had acted much too hastily over that but it was too late now. He just had to stand from under, that was all, as best he could, if ever the weight of the law loomed over him. Which now it might.

Bill Warner saw him into his cabin and then left. He summoned up the night steward on Mr Jones's section and told him to watch the cabin. If the passenger came out, the night steward was to persuade him back in again and if he failed in his persuasion, then he, Warner, was to be informed immediately.

That done, Warner climbed to the bridge and made a report to the Officer of the Watch.

Elsewhere in the ship another person had left her cabin and migrated.

This was Adeline Scott-Mason; and her destination, which had been safely reached, was the stateroom of General François de Gard. During the night she confessed her anxieties as to the ship's safety.

'You will be all right,' the General assured her.

'But there've been so many rumours about U-boats, François.'

He made a contemptuous sound. 'Rumours, rumours . . . what do these people know, *ma chérie*? Only the Germans know. Do not, I beg of you, pay any attention to rumours.'

She persisted, snuggled now against his back. 'Those proclamations weren't rumours. The Germans . . . they more or less said they'd sink the *Laurentia*.' She remembered some earlier, similar, German utterances that had subsequently been borne out by the fact of sinkings. 'It would be so horrible. . . .' She shuddered and held him tight, her salvation if the worst should come. 'An explosion, and fire probably, and all the people rushing about madly, panicking.'

'There are many lifeboats,' he reminded her. 'And you shall come with me in mine.'

'We're not at the same boat station, François.'

'Pay no attention to that, *chérie, ma petite*.' General de Gard heaved himself over in the bed. It was not a mere bunk, but it was not large. Adeline felt squashed until the General had sorted out his bony limbs and torso. His arms went round her. He whispered into her ear, 'At times of emergency, one acts with instinct for the loved ones. And there will certainly be confusion, yes. You will come with me.'

She frowned; she was aware of the traditions of the sea. 'Don't they say women and children first?'

'Yes, yes. . . .'

'We could so easily become separated, François.'

'No, we shall not, that I promise you, *chérie*. Now please stop worrying, I implore you.' The General's hand roved and she gave a shiver of delight. Perhaps all would be well even if the attack did come; it was possible the French hadn't the same firm view as the British in regard to the sea's principles, and after all François was a general who might one day become a Marshal of France. It might be his duty to save himself, for his country's sake. Yes, that was quite possible. She remembered, and remembered with a small pang because the memory was disloyal to a passionate lover, that her British father-in-law had once remarked that the Frogs were a gutless lot.

There was particular anxiety, as the *Laurentia* neared British waters, in two homes in Annapolis, Maryland. Jonas Gorman, Elizabeth Kent's fiancé, bit his finger nails and, whilst at his work in the attorney's office, was unable to concentrate on vital matters of law. The apartment, when the day's work was done, offered no solace. It was bare, barren without Elizabeth. Gorman couldn't remain in it. He went out and drank bourbon, which helped. He visited friends, mutual friends with whom he could talk about Elizabeth; he sought all the reassurances he could get. It wasn't, in his case, just the dangers of the ocean crossing: he was still haunted by the thought that Elizabeth might not return to America.

Of course, if the old man died it would be different.

And across the city were the Holmeses, whom Jonas Gorman did not know (though he had unknowingly seen them at the railroad station on that agonizing night of departure). When John Holmes had taken the train that night for New York, his mother, like Gorman but for different reasons, had believed she was never going to see her son again. Back home after he'd gone off she had broken down in tears. John's father had been unable to comfort her. She had clung to him that night, crying without cease. In the morning she had been white and haggard. For the next day or two she had moved like a wraith, going about her household tasks as if in a dream.

Now, with the *Laurentia* within two or three days' steaming of the danger zone, she was haunted by the recent German proclamation.

'They mean to sink the ship,' she said. Her voice shook. 'How can they be so truly wicked?'

Her husband took her in his arms and gave her a squeeze. 'Don't dwell on it – it isn't going to happen. They can't be that bad. John wouldn't want you to be worrying, dear.' He paused. 'Next thing we'll hear is a cable to say he's OK, and a letter from mother to say we've not been feeding him properly over here, you know what she is. Now, look on the bright side, honey! The *Laurentia*'s a great, big ship with a fine captain and the British Navy's waiting for her at the other end.'

So was Klaus Eppler aboard U-120. The British Navy, he knew from wireless reports received from the U-boat command, was almost totally absent from the area. True, armed merchant cruisers, converted liners, of the Northern Patrol were steaming up and down the Denmark Strait between Greenland and Iceland, a long way from the *Laurentia*'s track, and torpedo-boat destroyers of the Dover Patrol were fully occupied in the Channel. But German intelligence sources knew that the British naval base at Queenstown had few ships, and such as there were consisted of a handful of elderly light cruisers, one of which had already left port and was steaming to cross the track of the inward-bound *Laurentia*. It had been easy enough for the German Naval Command to intercept the British signal traffic and to make their assessment accordingly.

And duly to inform *Kapitanleutnant* Eppler.

U-120, on the surface as dusk fell, was charging batteries and giving her crew a little exercise on the fore casing; and some welcome fresh air. Klaus Eppler, with his First Lieutenant, relaxed in his conning tower and smoked a cigarette.

'The weather conditions are excellent, Dirnecker.'

'Yes, *Herr Kapitan.*' Dirnecker scanned the seas through his binoculars; not all the day's light had gone yet. The sea was empty. But, as Eppler had said, the conditions were good for attack: not much sea running, but enough wind to bring a kerfuffle of small breaking waves to the surface, enough to disguise the feather of spray that would be caused by U-120's periscope as, submerged, she sought out the target and lined up her sights, with the torpedoes loaded into their tubes. Dirnecker's prayer was that the weather would hold. He was not worried about the British escort, known now to be HMS *Bristol.* The British Navy List, of which U-120 had a copy, showed the *Bristol* as being under the command of Captain Charles de Ferriman Lugard, RN. Because the German Naval Command was in all things thorough, it had been checked and reported that Captain Lugard's last appointment had been command of the depôt ship at Freetown in Sierra Leone, a former liner that never went to sea but remained firmly moored in the Rokel River surrounded by dug-out canoes propelled by the native Kroo race. Dirnecker smiled to himself, thinking of this: there was a simile of a sort. Captain Lugard, a man no longer young, sounded as though he might himself well be what the British called a dug-out. In which case his mental faculties would not, perhaps, be of the most alert. What was more important was that the *Bristol*'s maximum gun range was around six miles and, although her laid-down speed was given as twenty-five knots, it was understood that she was currently unable to approach this more closely than around eighteen knots. And, of course, a submerged submarine was a submerged submarine . . . U-120 would show only the tip of her periscope and then, when she had loosed off her torpedoes, she would blow tanks and go down deep, then make her way, perhaps to another target if such should offer, or straight back to the Fatherland and the welcome to those who had struck such a decisive blow.

Struck.

Other things were scheduled to be struck, this time inside Germany itself. Admiral von Neuburg had travelled already from Berlin to Wilhelmshavn so as to be among the first to congratulate his son-in-law when he came victoriously back to base.

He brought news for his daughter Ilse.

'I have spoken to the Kaiser,' he said. 'His Imperial Majesty was kind enough to receive me in person. He has no doubt of the success that

Klaus is to achieve. He believes the sinking will have an immense effect upon the neutrals who trade with the British Empire, that it will be very salutary in helping to bring about Britain's collapse ... through an inability to maintain supplies.'

Ilse asked, 'He is not worried about the Americans, father?'

Von Neuburg shook his head impatiently. 'Decidedly not, Ilse. He is certain it will never bring the Americans into the war against us. They have been fully warned and those Americans who embarked aboard a liner carrying contraband war materials did so entirely knowingly and at their own risk. No country could do more than we have done. Now there is something else.' His tone was full of portent; his eyes shone with family pride.

'Yes, father?'

'His Imperial Majesty talks of striking a medal, a commemorative medal in celebration of the sinking. A medal to commemorate for ever the valour of your husband, Ilse!' He went heavily across the room to where Ilse was standing in front of the fireplace, and took her in his arms. 'Is this not a most splendid honour, my dear child, that shortly there will be a medal struck in honour of Klaus Eppler, U-boat ace ... with possibly an Iron Cross as well?' If von Neuburg had had reservations about the killing of women and children, they seemed to have been overcome by his Emperor's enthusiasm. ...

There would be honour for the officer who gave the order that would sink the *Laurentia*, and lesser honours for his crew. Across a large part of the world there would be no honour but there would be tears. There would be families to mourn from all parts of the United States of America, from Portland, Oregon to New York State, and in Canada. There would be fatherless and perhaps motherless children widely spread in Britain, from Cromer in Norfolk across Wales to Galway Bay in Ireland, from Land's End to Thurso in the far north of Scotland. Many would mourn those of the Australian contingent that were to die; and a number in New Zealand also. In the third-class section of the *Laurentia* there were other nationalities, former immigrants to the United States who were crossing the seas in war to bring comfort to old people, parents and grandparents left behind in Italy, Greece, Austria-Hungary, Serbia, Roumania, Bulgaria. There would be sadness in the idyllic islands of Greece, in the villages of Tuscany, in the crowded back streets of Naples where in so many cases the emigrating son was still the breadwinner who sent money home.

One of those from Italy, though by birth Maltese, was Guido Pascopo; Maria his wife, a genuine Italian girl, had not sailed in the *Laurentia*. She had remained behind with her nine children in Little

Italy in lower Brooklyn, while Guido made the dangerous voyage to Liverpool whence he would transship to Naples and then to Valletta where his old mother and father lived and whom he had not seen for more than twenty years, which was when he had left for Italy and then the New World. He had met Maria in New York, and had married her, within four weeks of disembarking. Maria's parents were now dead, but she understood the pull that Guido's parents exerted upon him. And she would be all right in his absence. She had not only their children, but also sixteen aunts and uncles and, at the last count, seventy-one cousins.

When Guido sailed back again to her side, which would be in some six months' time, a total of ninety-seven family members, plus perhaps some in-laws, would be waiting at the PanAtlantic pier to welcome him back.

If he came back.

Maria had wept many tears when Guido had sailed. He was going into colossal danger; and at the very least he would be seasick, for he was no sailor. Maria was a good Catholic, a regular attender at Mass, a regular attender at the confessional although it was hard each time to think of any sins she had committed, other than the almost inescapable ones of treading inadvertently upon an insect, or of having fleeting thoughts of jealousy of persons who had made more money than Guido although not working half so hard for their families as he, or of occasional bitter thoughts about the waywardness of one or two of her older sons, for the emergent youth of today was not as their fathers had been before them. They tended to disregard the acquired wisdom of their parents, and to wish to go their own ways.

Since the departure of the *Laurentia* Maria Pascopo had spent every moment she could spare from household duties on her knees in church. New York City contained 2100 churches, not all of them, of course, Catholic; Maria attended St Patrick's Cathedral on Fifth Avenue, for the bigger the church the closer she felt to the Virgin after whom she had been named. Prayers from such a source must surely be accorded a closer hearing than those from lesser churches. . . .

She prayed for Guido's safety on the high seas, both this side of Britain and beyond. She besought mercy for a man going himself upon an errand of mercy – to bring joy to his old parents who loved him. She prayed also for his physical well-being upon great waters. 'Holy Mother of God, calm Guido's stomach I beseech you, when the ship rolls about in the big waves. Assure him of my great love for him, that I think always of him. Holy Mother of God, all this I pray for, that his way may be easy in the distant parts to which he is going. . . .'

When not at prayer, when not cooking and dusting and making so many beds and washing so many clothes in her own apartment, Maria, who was a good woman, walked along two blocks to visit a cousin who was sick in bed and to do what she could to help with the chores. This cousin was also able to read the newspapers to Maria, who had never bothered to learn English properly, living as she did in an Italian immigrant community, and had only a few of the more necessary words.

What was written in the newspaper was not good hearing. There was a lot of noise from the Germans, and some condemnation of the British from the White House. President Wilson, Maria was told by her cousin, had been scathing about the British use on occasions of the American flag.

'Will the *Laurentia* use the American flag?' she asked.

The cousin had no idea. He worked in a delicatessen; that bounded his life, his imagination stuck fast in tins of biscuits and barrels of fresh farm butter and suchlike. But he expressed an opinion.

'The *Laurentia* is big, she will not sink even if torpedoed, Maria.'

'You think this, Emilio?'

'Yes. Her sides are of iron, and strong. In any case, she will not be torpedoed, Maria. The Germans will not do this, and take the risk of bringing America into the war. That is what everyone is saying.'

'At the delicatessen?'

'At the delicatessen, yes.' And it was true, by and large. Few New Yorkers believed the Germans would be so stupid. But now Emilio advanced a theory. He said, 'Do you know, Maria, if the *Laurentia* is attacked and sunk – but I do not believe she will be, so do not worry – if she is, then it is more likely to be from the British themselves rather than from the Germans.'

Maria shook her head in bewilderment. Why should the British do that? Emilio went on to say that the British wished to find a way to force America into the war. But whether an attack came from the Germans or from the British, it didn't matter to her; she thought only of Guido and his kindly ways, and his always smiling, moustached face, and his curly black hair, and of bed – she cut that thought off from her mind. To follow that, even with her own husband in mind, would be a sin to confess and the Holy Mother of God would doubtless be displeased whether the priest forgave her or not.

16

Master-at-Arms Warner's report to the bridge during the night hours had been brief but alarming. First Officer Main was the senior Officer of the Watch; deciding against waking Captain Pacey, who was in urgent need of rest before bringing his ship into the war zone, he called Staff Captain Morgan.

'Will you come to the bridge, sir, please?'

'Urgent?' Morgan could be heard up the voice-pipe, stifling a yawn.

'It is, sir. Not navigationally, but – yes, it's urgent.'

Morgan was on the bridge within three minutes, dressed in his uniform jacket over pyjamas and a grey woollen muffler around his neck.

'Well, Mr Main?' Morgan saw that the master-at-arms was in attendance. Frowning, he followed Main into the chart room abaft the bridge.

Main said, 'A report from the master-at-arms, sir. He apprehended Mr Jones – you'll remember?'

'The wife, yes. Well?'

'Mr Jones was sleep-walking.' Main paused. 'Sleep-*talking* as well.'

'Talking? I believe that's quite a usual phenomenom with sleep-walkers.' Morgan swung round on Master-at-Arms Warner. 'What did he say, Warner?'

Warner said, 'It was a bit of a mumble at first, sir. But I did hear something about teeth – '

'Teeth?'

'Yes, sir. I heard him say he'd fed them to the seagulls.'

'A curious thing to do. A curious meal! Whose teeth?'

'Someone called Maggie, sir. A woman, like. The gentleman was apologizing to her. Well, I thought it all very odd, sir, but decided the gentleman was, well, wandering in the head. Or just that he was sleep-walking and was a bit on the hazy side. Then he said something else, sir.'

'Well, go on, Warner.'

'Yes, sir. He said, quite clearly this was, sir . . . "I'm sorry about the leg, too, Maggie. I'm sorry I had to cut you up. I do know that wasn't right." That was all, sir. Then he woke up, sir.'

'I see. Where is he now? In his cabin?'

'Yes, sir. I warned the night steward, sir.'

Morgan said, 'We'll have to do better than that. Station yourself on the cabin door and don't let Mr Jones out. I don't think you'll need to be there for long.' Morgan knew that the New York Police Department had been interested in a Mrs Jones. Now it might be that Jones would have to be removed to the cells. Morgan turned to First Officer Main. 'Mr Main, rouse out the Purser if you please. He's to bring up the cables from New York, and confirm the Christian name of the wife. After that – we'll see.'

Master-at-Arms Warner went below to take up his post. First Officer Main sent the bridge messenger to wake the Purser, who was not connected by voice-pipe from his cabin to the navigating bridge. Matthews was not in his cabin. After some delay, the assistant purser, Harry Anneston, was woken from sleep and went along to the office and found the wanted cables from the New York Police. He took them at once to the bridge, where the Staff Captain was waiting, smoking a cigarette in the chart room. Morgan read: Jones's wife's name was Margaret. Margaret, Maggie.

Cells? Morgan thought for a moment. He mustn't be premature; to imprison a passenger wrongly would lead to a good deal of trouble for the Line. He said abruptly, 'I'll go down and talk to Jones. Where's the Purser?'

'I'm afraid I don't know, sir.'

'Not in his cabin, I understand.'

The assistant purser kept silent, full of discretion.

'All right,' Morgan said, knowing Matthews, making a guess. 'You'll have to do. I want a witness. We'll go down right away.'

When they reached Mr Jones's cabin they found the door open, the curtain blowing in a draught coming along the alleyway. Inside was the night steward, bending over Bill Warner who was slumped down by the empty bunk.

Mr Jones had known at once what had happened when the ship's master-at-arms had reappeared in his cabin doorway. He knew that Warner acted as a kind of policeman, responsible to the Captain for law and order aboard. Panic had struck.

Jones had reacted very fast, responding to an urgent need to escape. He had turned slightly in the confines of the small cabin and had taken up a heavy china chamber-pot from beside the wash-hand-basin cabinet and had in a flash brought it down on the master-at-arms' head. Warner, taken by surprise, had gone down flat, bleeding profusely from the skull. Mr Jones, eyes staring madly, had then left the cabin in his night attire and had scuttled like a rabbit along the alleyway and up the companion ladders to the open deck, making aft though he scarcely knew which direction he was taking. After he'd gone, the night steward had come along and had found Warner in a pool of blood. Before contacting the bridge, he had doubled away to fetch Dr Fellowes, who had not arrived by the time Staff Captain Morgan had gone down with the assistant purser.

In the meantime Mr Jones had arrived at the after end of the ship and had climbed the guardrail. With the intention of throwing himself over, he had looked down. The sight penetrated, made him pause.

The *Laurentia*'s enormous screws were thundering below; here, the vibration could be very strongly felt, juddering the deck.

The sea was being churned to foam, visible in the light from the moon that silvered it almost like day. Those great blades, whirling round at Mr Jones knew not how many revolutions . . . he would be churned to fragments.

A worse mess than Maggie.

He hesitated, trying to make up his mind. He knew, now, that he was going to hang. The knot beneath his ear, the jerk breaking his neck. Well – better to get it over and done with quickly.

He climbed to the teakwood top of the guardrail, teetering backwards and forwards. The wind tugged at his nightshirt. The garment billowed out over the stern, over the waves, over the rearing cauldron of foam from the screws.

Then something else tugged at the nightshirt. Mr Jones was pulled at, and fell backwards in a heap into human arms, those of Able Seaman Bromhead, on night watch and alerted by Staff Captain Morgan via the bridge.

'Ups-a-daisy, sir. It's all right now, sir.'

Passengers had to be treated with respect, even if they were murderers; word had reached Bromhead that the master-at-arms was a goner. Mr Jones was set upon his feet and then a number of other men came along at the double and he was manhandled below.

'What did you tell Morgan?' Purser Matthews asked.

His assistant shrugged. 'Nothing. I said I didn't know where you were, that's all.'

'Yes, I see. Well – that's all right, then. As a matter of fact . . . I was in my lavatory. I wasn't well. Something I must have eaten. I never heard anyone knock or come into my cabin.'

The assistant purser grinned. 'You wouldn't, would you?'

'So what's that supposed to mean, Harry?'

'Nothing. Nothing at all. Only – pull the other one next time, eh?'

It was an extra worry for Captain Pacey and had come just when he was going to need all his concentration for the safety of the ship and all aboard her. When the passenger Jones had been taken below to his cabin and confronted with the physical evidence of what he had done, he had broken. As Morgan reported to Pacey, he had confessed the lot: the attack with the axe, the dismemberment and dispersal, the escape of a leg that had gone into the Wappinger River. And then the teeth, and the feeding of the seagulls from the *Laurentia*'s boat deck. Pacey had what in the circumstances was an irrational thought: anyone who could do that to seagulls was the lowest of the low.

'Another damn inquiry when we reach Liverpool, Morgan.'

'I'm afraid so, sir.'

Pacey sighed. 'The cells'll be full. Those Germans, and Ommaney and Craigson. Now Jones.' He went off at a tangent. 'We have to think about poor Warner.'

Morgan said gently, 'Same as Lundkvist, sir. Needed as – evidence, I suppose you'd call it. No sea burial.'

'Well, I don't know.' Pacey sat back from his desk at full arms' stretch. 'It's a very clear-cut case – '

'No witness at the time of the murder, sir.'

'No, but the bloody man's confessed!'

'I still think we need the body for production in Liverpool.' Morgan added, 'The surgeon agrees.'

'Maybe,' Pacey said drily. 'But I'm not having that. I'm not carrying poor Warner on . . . to be messed about by pathologists and policemen and so on.' Warner had spent his life at sea; Pacey believed he would rather have a sea burial, that he should go over the ship's side into clean water. He said, 'There was no family, was there?' The question was rhetorical, as Morgan was aware: Captain Pacey had an encylopaedic mind where details of long-serving crew members were concerned, and he and Warner had been shipmates many times in the past. Pacey knew that Warner had been married and had lost his wife some years earlier, a victim of consumption. And there were no children. No one to want a corpse for burial ashore. Pacey knew more: Warner used to spend his leaves with a widowed sister, now dead herself. After that, Warner had preferred to spend his leaves standing by the ship in port. The sea had been his life, the ship his home.

Pacey gave the order crisply. 'Prepare for the committal, Staff Captain. I'll let you know the time shortly.' He got up abruptly from his desk, took up his heavy bridge coat with the four gold stripes on either shoulder, took up his binoculars and slung the leather strap and codline preventer around his neck. 'Leave his cabin as it is, Morgan. All personal effects . . . they're not for the shoreside vultures. Better – if anything happens – that they go down with him.'

Morgan said, 'I'll see to it personally, sir.' He forbore to ask, what if nothing happens and we reach Liverpool intact? What Pacey had said had been odd, really. It had been almost as though he believed they were not going to make it.

Pacey nodded and left the day cabin, making for the bridge. Morgan followed, but broke off at the foot of the ladder. He intended having words with Matthews. The ship's Purser had no business not being in his cabin at night when wanted.

Matthews had changed his story. His assistant purser had seen through it too quickly; others might do the same.

'Insomnia,' he said to the Staff Captain. 'I needed some fresh air.'

'Really. Your scuttles are fitted with windscoops, I fancy?'

'Well, yes, sir, they are. But there's the question of spray, you see. There's a bit of wind around – '

'On the windward side, Matthews. Not on yours. So you were on deck – but you weren't aware of Jones's antics aft?'

'I'd gone for'ard. Fore end of the boat deck.' Matthews spoke in an injured tone. 'I don't see – '

'All right, Purser. You'll stick to your story I don't doubt. But just bear in mind that nothing's secret aboard a ship – you should know that, you're not a fool. If you're poodle-faking around the passengers' cabins again, the Line will be informed and you'll be out on your ear. Just tell your lady friend that. This time I'll say nothing to the Captain – he's got enough on his plate.' Morgan reached out and tapped the three gold stripes interspersed with white cloth that adorned Matthews' cuff. 'You've earned those, I suppose. Make an effort to live up to them. You're no longer a spotty-faced purser's clerk.'

Morgan was furiously angry. With the ship virtually at war stations, Purser Matthews might have been required for even more vital matters than murder.

Leon Fielding mopped at his face: the cabin was stuffy but his reluctance to face the other passengers had returned with renewed vigour. His one support was Elmer Pousty, who had just looked into his cabin.

'How *dreadful* to have another murderer aboard! Really, I – I feel quite faint, Mr Pousty. It's quite knocked me over.'

'Reckon you could do with a drink. Brandy.'

'Yes. Yes, do you know, I think that would help. But to go to the lounge – '

'You don't have to,' Pousty said. 'Ring for the bedroom steward. It's all part of the PanAtlantic service. Why not use it?'

'Yes. Yes, I will. Would you mind – ?'

'Sure.' Pousty pressed the bell-push. The ship rolled to a sea and Ming's perambulator moved out from its stowage by the wardrobe. Pousty wheeled it back and fumbled around, putting the brake hard on. He studied the singer. Fielding was staring into space, not seeming to register, his mind far away. In New York maybe; with his wife, or with Ming. Maybe a communion of minds: Fielding had told him, as he had told the Captain, that his wife had some odd ability to know what was going on when he was not with her. Fielding didn't say a word while they waited for the bedroom steward to answer the ring, which he did after about ten minutes.

There was a knock and a head came round the door. 'You rang, sir?'

Pousty answered. 'Yes, I did. Would you be so kind as to bring a brandy for Mr Fielding?'

'Right away, sir. Horse's neck, sir?'

Fielding seemed uncertain. Pousty said, 'Better make it straight. And a double.'

'Yes sir. For you, sir?'

'Not for me, thanks.'

Steward Hawley went away. When he had gone, there was a curious sound from Fielding. A sob: Pousty saw that he was crying, his hands to his face now, tears streaming, shoulders heaving. Between sobs Fielding blurted out, 'The way people stare . . . all those *wicked* thoughts . . . that *dreadful* man . . . it's almost as though I'm being accused of murder myself. Murder . . . of a boy's innocence! I didn't do a thing, you know. Not a thing. It's all lies.'

'I know that,' Pousty said gently. 'So, I'm darn sure, does the Captain.'

Fielding said indistinctly, 'Most of them don't. I know that. I can't possibly face them, Mr Pousty – '

'But look – '

'The voyage is – is tainted. The omens are bad. That man's lies . . . the murder of a member of the crew . . . that bomb scare. The German warnings before the ship sailed. It's all coming to a point. I feel it, you see. I see doom. I believe we are going to be torpedoed and that we shall all drown. I'm so glad – so very glad – that poor little Ming is not with us. She at least will be saved.'

Pousty didn't know what to say. This was way beyond his experience. Fielding was shaking badly, staring into space again, face uncovered. Elmer Pousty, expectant soon to be driving ambulances in war-torn Europe, had heard stories of strong men who had been reduced to wrecks by the constant bombardment of the guns along the Western Front. Reduced to gibbering wrecks as their ears rang to the explosions, wrecks that in some cases had run from the trenches, fighting crazily to the rear, anywhere away from the never-ending din of a long bombardment, to end up in custody of the military police on a charge of cowardice and then, one grey dawn, lined up before a firing squad. Shot in cold blood, some mother's son who had broken.

Fielding gave the appearance of going the same way. Maybe the doc ... but Pousty doubted the efficacy of the ship's surgeon. Reverend Divine? No, not Reverend Divine: the cleric seemed to strike the wrong note somehow.

Maybe that nun, Sister Perpetua.

Mrs Rickards sat with her husband in the lounge; she had found their cabin too confining, and anyway she was feeling better, which may have been due to Dr Fellowes' tonic or might not. It tasted nasty enough to be effective, certainly. Also it was quite expensive so it must be good. As a result of both these considerations, Mrs Rickards had faith in it, which had probably made it work notwithstanding.

Rickards himself had no such faith. 'Gnat's water,' he'd said after a sniff at the neatly wrapped bottle, good quality paper sealed at the top with red sealing-wax, just like a medical man's wares ashore, now opened to show a liquid faintly tinged with pink colouring.

'I'm sure it's good, Jeffrey.'

'Take it, then.'

She had, two teaspoons as instructed. Now, faith-healed for the time being, she sat in the lounge and looked out through the big windows at the North Atlantic. Some way off, another ship was passing, going the other way, a liner like their own, but with the house colours of the White Star Line. She drew her husband's attention to it.

He got up and went out on deck. He heard someone say that the ship was the *Olympic*, sister ship of the *Titanic* . . . He went back into the lounge and told his wife. She nodded; she had picked up the ship's daily news-sheet that had come from the radio room. 'Oh dear,' she said.

'What is it, Emmy?'

'Renewed activity on the Western Front, Jeffrey. A heavy attack on our trenches – '

'Repulsed, I imagine.'

'Oh yes, it says that. With heavy losses to the Germans.'

Rickards took the sheet from her and read. Read, with his military knowledge, between the lines, which were brief enough. Heavy German losses: well, perhaps – but they always said that and no doubt the Germans did too, in the opposite sense. The German attack had come in the vicinity of Ypres, which was where Rickards knew both his sons were engaged with their gun batteries. They would not, of course, be in the trenches, and the report spoke only of the trenches as having come under attack, presumably by the German infantry, but there would also have been field guns engaged, and almost certainly the British gun positions would have been shelled.

Well – a soldier expected that. Soldiers were trained for it.

Emmy was speaking.

'What was that, Emmy?'

'I said I hope the boys are all right.'

'They will be,' Rickards said gruffly. 'They know how to take care of themselves, Emmy.' But did they? No, they didn't; they were both too forthcoming, both too keen, not to show off, certainly not that, but to be in on the action; more, Rickards suspected, than was really required of officers of their rank. There had been so many pranks in the childhood days, so many adventures that could have ended in tragedy. Ice cracking up beneath skates on deep rivers; bicycle races along country roads where already the odd motor car was beginning to be seen; dangerous trees climbed to the top; cliff edges approached too closely in crumbly parts when on holiday in Cornwall; a tumble down one once, and the necessity for a sea rescue of one son with a broken leg – but he'd been back there on the next holiday, no more cautious than before. A time on Dartmoor when one of them had vanished completely, in a sudden mist not far from Dartmoor Prison where a convict had escaped the day before. The boy had turned up safe and sound next day, cold and hungry but no harm done except to a mother's (and also, but hidden, a father's) peace of mind.

So many things like that, recalled now in a golden glow of the past. Happy days mostly, before he and Emmy had emigrated to Canada and found disillusion in a financial sense. So much had changed since then.

A large figure approached: the American, Reverend Divine.

'Good morning, Mr Rickards, Mrs Rickards.'

Rickards never addressed a parson as 'Reverend'. 'Good morning, Mr Divine.'

'The *Olympic*'s just gone past, did you see?'

'Yes.'

'A terrible thing that was – the *Titanic*. Sure shocked America. It was a while back . . . but the memories remain, I guess.' The Reverend Divine pulled up a chair and dropped into it heavily. He had an audience and he made the most of it. He talked about the *Titanic*. He talked in great detail, almost as though he had been one of the survivors, which he was not. He'd been in Texas at the time but he knew all about it, the horrors and the band playing to the last, or nearly, as the great ship went down. The lifeboats that had turned turtle, the separation of families, a degree of panic with men in some cases fighting for a place in a lifeboat. He spoke of God who, in a number of instances, had been right there beside the suffering and in other cases had apparently not. The Reverend Divine reckoned that God would have had little time for those who had thought only of saving themselves.

After a while Rickards cut it short: it was all too relevant to what might lie ahead for the *Laurentia*. He got to his feet, stiffly, and gave an arm to assist his wife. He had, he said, some letters to write.

Fielding had arrived on the bridge, where no passenger was supposed to go other than by invitation of the Captain. Pacey who, with his first and second officers, had been finalizing his plans for his approach to the British Isles, emerged from the chart room and saw the singer engaged in an argument with the Officer of the Watch.

'What's this, Mr Fielding?'

'Oh, Captain.' Fielding lifted his ridiculous straw hat and came across the deck. 'I'm told I shouldn't come up here – but it's so important. I do hope you don't mind. I simply had – '

'You're here now,' Pacey said, his tone grim. 'You'd better tell me why, I think.'

'Yes. Yes, of course. It's because I'm convinced we are going to be sunk, you see. By the Germans. I have no doubt about that at all. I – '

'Damned nonsense, Mr Fielding! And I'll be obliged if you'd not repeat what you've said to anyone else. To any of my passengers. I will not have alarm spread – '

'Oh, but I don't think you fully understand, Captain.' Fielding's voice was urgent and in some degree compelling because he so obviously believed what he was saying; it came from the heart, Pacey could see that. The singer went on, 'The *Olympic* . . . I understand she has just passed us. She crystallized it finally. A warning, don't you see? Remembering the *Titanic*, you know.'

'Nonsense,' Pacey said again. 'The *Olympic* simply passed us on her normal track for the Ambrose Channel lightship, if a little to the south of it. I assure you there was nothing sinister about a normal passing of ships at sea.'

Fielding was paying no attention. His eyes stared now, as they had stared in his cabin, and again he was sweating. He said, 'I suggest you turn the ship round. I suggest you take us all back to New York. If you do not, you will have so many deaths on your conscience. So many hundreds. I'm sure you must see that.'

Pacey stared back at the singer. He said formally, 'Thank you for the warning, Mr Fielding. I'm obliged . . . what you say will be noted.'

'I – '

'That is all, Mr Fielding. Remember what I said about not spreading

206

alarm. That can be considered a serious offence in time of war. Remember that as well. Now kindly leave my bridge.'

The voice of authority, harshly used now, penetrated. Fielding flushed, seemed about to speak again, thought better of it, raised his straw hat, and went towards the ladder. Pacey turned to the Officer of the Watch. He said, 'Staff Captain on the bridge – with my compliments.'

He walked to the starboard wing of the bridge, his face set hard. Fielding was, of course, not to be taken in any way seriously. But he could do much damage if he chose. And Pacey, whose passengers and ship's company were always on his mind as regards safety, had not liked the reference to his conscience. He knew only too well that, Fielding or no Fielding, if anything should happen to cause loss of life, it would remain with him until his own death.

Morgan reached the bridge. Pacey told him what had taken place. 'I understand he has been befriended by Mr Pousty.'

'Yes, sir.'

'Talk to Pousty then, Morgan. Tell him I'd be grateful – more than grateful – if he'd keep Fielding's mouth shut in front of the passengers. I don't mind how he does it. But if he fails, then I shall have to put Fielding in restraint until we reach the United Kingdom.'

Early the next morning, close to dawn after the watch of seamen had scrubbed and hosed down the liner's decks, the body of Master-at-Arms Warner was committed to the deep. In the engine room the telegraph bells rang the engines to stop. Chief Engineer Hackett, on the starting platform, repeated the order, and bells rang in acknowledgement on the bridge.

The Officer of the Watch reported, 'Engines stopped, sir.'

'Thank you.' Pacey caught the eye of Staff Captain Morgan and they both descended the ladder, down by the Captain's deck and aft to the boat deck, and down again to where Warner's body lay on a plank in a gap where the guardrail had been shifted away. Body and plank were covered with the Red Ensign, the Red Duster under which Warner had spent so many years of his life. The ship lay very silent, still with a residue of way upon her, rolling gently to the waves passing beneath her keel. Everyone present – all the ship's officers off watch, Bosun MacFarlane and his bosun's mates, the second master-at-arms, a party of seamen to tend to the plank – was conscious not only of the solemnity of the occasion but also of increased danger from beneath the sea when a ship lay with engines stopped. Pacey, however, was not worried. They were not yet into the danger zone; had they been, the committal would not have taken place. The *Laurentia*, by Pacey's reckoning, was still outside the range of the biggest of the German underwater fleet.

Before beginning the short, simple service Pacey glanced up at the after decks, the after ends of the boat deck, the embarkation deck and the promenade deck. A handful of early-rising, exercise-taking passengers was there, looking down. Among them he saw the elderly nun, Sister Perpetua, kneeling by the rail in an attitude of prayer.

Pacey, removing his uniform cap and placing it beneath his left arm, opened his prayer book. In a strong, carrying voice he read: 'I am the resurrection and the life, saith the Lord: he that believeth in me, though he were dead, yet shall he live; and whosoever liveth and believeth in me shall never die.'

Then Psalm 90 was read: 'Lord thou hast been our refuge. . . .' After this the seaman's hymn was sung by all present. Pacey could hear Sister Perpetua's voice clear from the after end of the promenade deck. 'Eternal Father, strong to save. . . .'

As the hymn came to its end, Pacey nodded at Andrew MacFarlane at the head of the plank. MacFarlane began very slowly to lift it, tilting it towards the water. Pacey read, 'Forasmuch as it has pleased Almighty God of His great mercy to take unto himself the soul of our dear brother here departed: we therefore commit his body to the deep. . . .'

The plank tilted further; the Red Ensign rucked up a little and was pulled straight over the bulky body beneath. Then, gathering momentum, the corpse slid from under the ensign's folds, twisted in its canvas shroud fitted and sewn by Able Seaman Bromhead who in his days in the windjammers had been a sailmaker, twisted formlessly down into the North Atlantic, bending in the middle, to take the water with a splash and, lead-weighted at the feet, to vanish into the immensity of the sea.

Pacey, at the salute as the body had started its journey, remained motionless for a half-minute longer. There was still the heavy silence, broken only by two sounds: harsh noises from the circling seagulls, and a sob from Sister Perpetua.

Pacey brought his hand down. He could incur the displeasure of the police on arrival, even thereby of the Line; but he had no regrets. Warner had gone as a seaman should, his body undisturbed by the medical men who might have probed further the cause of death however obvious it had been to Pacey and Dr Fellowes.

'Staff Captain?'

'Sir?'

'Inform the bridge, if you please – telegraphs to full ahead.'

Below, Chief Engineer Hackett gave a deep sign of relief as the telegraph bells rang in his engine room and he passed the order to start the great shafts turning once again.

17

THAT sea committal had affected the ship deeply. No one aboard had been unaware of it: the sudden stopping of the engines, the changed motion of the liner as she had rolled in the shallow troughs of the sea, the silence broken by the strong voices of the seamen as they had sung the hymn. Men more accustomed to songs of a different sort had sung with sadness and reverence; the occasion had been fraught with melancholy and a vision of the future, the future not far away when so many more could be about to die. Pacey, alone in his cabin after the committal service was over, had got down on his knees and uttered a private prayer, firstly for the dead Warner, then for Mary his wife in Southsea, not far from the naval dockyard. He prayed that no harm should come to her if the Germans should attack the naval port with their aeroplanes which, if the war went on for long enough for the flying machines to extend their range, they might.

Pacey had a firm belief in God. That, he sometimes thought, could have been the early example of old Captain Testament Thomas in sail. Testament Thomas had once said that no man who went to sea could fail to believe in God. He had instanced the changing weather, the rolling patterns of huge cloud formations, the violent storms succeeded by days of calm and splendour when danger was past. He'd seen God in the fact of survival. He'd spoken of the great beauty of sunrise and sunset in many parts of the world, in the Indian Ocean and the Bay of Bengal, in the China Seas and the great Pacific Ocean, as well as around Australia, in the Mediterranean and the Atlantic. Testament Thomas had seen God in the low-slung stars of tropic nights, so close that they seemed like lanterns within the grasp of a man. These wonders could derive only from a superior being whom men called God.

Pacey felt much the same way.

But now there was the unease among the crew; not only Warner's death from murder and his committal. There was also Lundkvist, still aboard. A corpse aboard a ship at sea.

Captain Pacey felt it as he made rounds that forenoon. It was an emanation, and it had spread to the passengers. It was also almost physically in the air. There was a total absence of any gaiety. Pacey remarked on it when rounds were over. The senior officers had gathered in his day cabin, a routine discussion of the progress of the voyage. Present were Morgan, Purser Matthews, Dr Fellowes, and Chief Engineer Hackett, plus, somewhat on the fringe as a kind of NCO, Chief Steward Kemmis.

'Tension,' Pacey said. 'Did anyone else notice it?'

They all had, in varying degrees.

Pacey said, 'It has to be dissipated. It's not good. We're now three days' steaming off the Fastnet. Three days . . . we have time in hand yet, I fancy.'

Morgan cocked an eye at the Captain. 'Have you something in mind, sir?'

Pacey nodded. 'Yes. The fancy-dress ball.'

Morgan was surprised. 'The decision was taken not to hold it – '

'I'm aware of that, Morgan,' Pacey said irritably. 'Because of that German proclamation, and the general war situation. But at this moment, and for a while longer, we're not *in* a war situation. So why the hell not? A fancy-dress parade . . . it's always been a success! It would break the spell if that's the word. Relieve the tension. Give them something else to think about for a while at least. I've an idea that man Fielding's been spreading his stupid notions in spite of my warning.' He turned to the Purser. 'Matthews?'

'Yes, sir?'

'See to it, if you please. The usual thing, all departments coordinating. And instead of waiting for the night before arrival, which I agree would scarcely do – we'll hold it tonight.' Pacey saw the expression on Matthews' face and said, 'Yes, I know it's damn short notice and it won't give either the staff or the passengers much time to prepare. But we're used to improvising at sea, and we all know the ingenuity of passengers, the younger ones anyway. Let's make it a splendid effort . . . the best fancy-dress ball ever put on in the North Atlantic!'

Hackett said, 'Well, sir, there's one thing about it: it'll be one in the eye for Kaiser Bill!'

Guido Pascopo, third-class passenger and husband of Maria praying in New York's St Patrick's Cathedral for his safety and his stomach, had been a much bewildered man ever since embarkation. He was a small man, and he tended to become obscured by crowds. On sailing day, the liner's lobby outside the Purser's office had been a very, very crowded place with everyone bumping into everyone else and all of them besieging the Purser's staff with questions. They were in a strange and unpredictable world, not all of them for the first time of course, but for Guido Pascopo it was for the very first time since the voyage out so many years ago and now liners were very much bigger and busier than they had been then.

First there had been the Notices. As an immigrant, Guido had had to read many notices, but his English was very poor, despite his early years in semi-English-speaking Malta, and he had difficulty in reading the very important notices that seemed strewn throughout the ship. They concerned the times of meals, the care of valuables, the making of complaints to the Purser, the use of washrooms and lavatories in the depleted third-class accommodation and so many, many other things, some of vital importance he understood. Many of the notices were showing diagrams of lifejackets and so on.

Guido Pascopo had bumped into an old man with much white hair beneath a very curious floppy-brimmed straw hat.

'Oh dear . . . I'm so sorry.'

'It was my fault, *signor*,' Guido said humbly in his weird English.

'Tell me: are you having difficulty?'

'*Si, signor*,' Guido said, side-stepping round a perambulator that the elderly man was holding on to.

'Allow me to help,' Fielding had said; and he had done so. He had explained about the lifejackets and about boat stations, which were indicated by red or green arrows around the accommodation, directing you to either port or starboard depending on where your particular station was. He had explained a notice about the alteration of clocks: all the ship's clocks would be advanced daily, or rather nightly, so that you would be more or less unaware of it, until the liner reached home waters and came into the meridian of Greenwich. Fielding, going back to the more important business of boat stations, explained to Guido that the emergency signal would be four long blasts on the steam whistle, which would be heard loudly below as well as on deck.

'If that happens,' he'd said, 'dress yourself in warm garments and put on your lifejacket – you'll find it in your cabin, I believe.' He read again. 'Yes, in your cabin. Then go to your boat station. That's all.'

'*Si, signor*. It is simple?'

'Oh, yes, very simple.' Just then the kind *signor* had been swept away from him by the pressing crowd. After that he had fetched up against a big, loud man with an Australian accent who was haranguing a uniformed person who looked important.

'Table seating,' the big man was saying in a hectoring tone. He pronounced it 'tyble' seating. 'Bloody class distinction, I reckon. One saloon for the nobs, another for the common herd, eh, is that right?'

'Not quite that, sir.' The important-looking man was Chief Steward Kemmis. 'The passage money is – '

'That's what I bloody meant. But that's not what I was talking about as it so happens, mate. I was speaking of the sittings. First and second, right? Second lot gets the first lot's leftovers – eh?'

'No, sir. It's merely a question of space available, and there's no distinction made between the two sittings.'

'Like hell there's not.' The Australian turned his attention elsewhere, looking belligerent; the chief steward shrugged philosophically and went about his business. He'd seen the lot in his day. Even in the first class the stewards had much to put up with from time to time. Autocracy, sheer rudeness . . . the real nobs were all right, treated their inferiors decently and with politeness even if they did expect orders to be obeyed at once if not sooner as the saying went. The ones with too much money were the worst on the whole. The business tycoons from both sides of the Atlantic, more especially the self-made ones. And a lot of money had travelled by PanAtlantic over the years: Vanderbilts, Oppenheimers, Astors, Morgans . . . and they were still there, the very rich, the socialites, lavishing their money on this trip to Britain, elegantly dressed in the lounges, furs and blazers and sparkling linen; not a care in the world, never mind the war. Perhaps that uncouth Australian had had a point of a sort.

Kemmis moved briskly towards the first-class saloon. There was always much to do, much to supervise, on sailing day. The head waiters, the bar staff, the pantrymen who kept the table waiters supplied with the orders, were as busy as bees with their preparations. The tips depended on good, fast service. The head waiters and table waiters were accustomed to arrive in Liverpool and New York with their pockets stuffed with five-pound notes or ten-dollar bills, some of which largesse customarily found its way to the pantries behind the scenes, for the pantry staff contributed their share of labour to keep things moving. And helped to earn the tips.

During the morning of the day Master-at-Arms Warner was committed to the sea, another death took place ashore in England. A cable from Cambridge, England, was received in the liner's wireless room and was taken to a second-class cabin. Addressed to Elizabeth Kent, it was brief: REGRET TO INFORM YOU YOUR FATHER KENNETH KENT DIED THIS EARLY MORNING. It came from the Medical Superintendent at Addenbrooke's Hospital.

Sister Perpetua happened to be with Elizabeth in the shared cabin; that helped. But Elizabeth found the cabin claustrophobic, and went up the companionways to the boat deck and the blustery wind. The death had not been unexpected but when the blow came it was not eased by expectation. It would take time to sink in. Currently all Elizabeth could think about was the likely reaction of Jonas Gorman when he heard the news. It would set his mind at rest that she would be coming back to Annapolis fairly quickly. And that, she supposed, was on the credit side.

The announcement was made about the fancy-dress ball. There was an immediate whirl of activity on the part of the passengers and ship's company. There would be a special menu in the saloons; that kept the chef and his galley staff – assistant chefs, butchers, bakers, cooks, vegetable cooks, sweet cooks, galley hands, scullions and porters – fully occupied. The Purser's staff conferred with the ship's printer to arrange for programmes and numbered cards to be rushed out. The public room stewards began to prepare the lounges for the dancing that would take place before and after the fancy-dress parade. The bedroom stewards produced as if by magic all sorts of gear for the participants to wear or make into curious costumes. The stewardesses assisted the ladies with reshaping and fitting. It was to be, by order of the Captain, a splendid occasion.

The reactions of the passengers varied a great deal.

'Ridiculous,' Rickards said to his wife.

'Why, Jeffrey?'

'Why?' Rickards snorted. 'We're close to dangerous waters now, that's why! It's not fitting. It's – it's a ridiculous distraction.'

'But it won't distract the crew, Jeffrey.'

'Perhaps not. But it'll distract me, I can tell you that! Having to put up with some people's idea of what's dramatic, or attractive, or funny! I've no doubt that Barlow woman will attend as Boadicea. One thing – we're having no part in any of it.'

'Very well, Jeffrey.' Mrs Rickards had no wish to attend as it happened. She considered herself far too old for such activities; and she was not feeling at all well. She was very worried about the shake in her hands, the way she seemed suddenly quite unable to hold a glass or a cup without spilling the contents.

Alva Lundkvist was appalled by the announcement. Her husband's body was aboard, deep down in the liner's refrigerated section. The whole thing was very unseemly and said little for British sensitivity. She said as much to Sister Perpetua.

'And that poor man who was killed also. Such a ship!'

Sister Perpetua understood. But she said, 'The Captain has so many things to think about. So many responsibilities. He must please so many different persons. He must think of his ship as a whole.' She had penetrated the Captain's mind, believed she had seen his purpose. 'We must not think too much on death, my dear. It isn't good. What has happened has happened. I believe the Captain thinks we should be shaken out of sad thoughts.'

Alva Lundkvist didn't answer; she was eaten up with her grief, with the worries that were still with her over little Olof, who had scarcely ceased crying for his dead father, asking continually where he had gone. The grief was not helping his condition. Dr Fellowes had come at her request, and had said with gruff impatience that the boy must pull himself together. Which seemed now to be much the same as Sister Perpetua was telling her in regard to herself.

She would not, of course, attend the fancy-dress ball. She would continue to have her meals in her cabin and shut her eyes and ears to the cavortings in the public rooms.

Another who would not be attending was Leon Fielding. He was more than ever sensitive about his fellow passengers' opinions and had it not been for Elmer Pousty he would never have appeared in public at all. Wild horses would not have dragged him into the public eye, done up as some sort of exhibition.

Elmer Pousty didn't disagree; he couldn't see Fielding taking part in such festivities at the best of times. But he did say, 'You've been well used to appearing in public, Mr Fielding.'

'Yes. Oh, yes. But never again. That's over. I shall never sing again, of course.'

'Plenty older than you still do.'

'Yes, perhaps. But not now. Everyone will know, you see.'

'I don't think that's true at all, you – '

'Oh yes, it is, Mr Pousty. Once we reach Liverpool, and the police . . . all the scandal, what the newspapers will make out of it. It's so much worse for someone who's been a public figure. I dread arriving in Liverpool, really dread it.' He sat in his cabin chair, a pathetic, crumpled figure with the straw hat on his head and a hand reaching out to Ming's perambulator, pushing it back and forth as though it contained a baby.

'I,' General François de Gard said, looking at himself sideways in the mirror in his state-room, 'shall go as . . . whom would you suggest, *ma chérie?*'

Adeline Scott-Mason looked him up and down and giggled. 'Napoleon?' she said.

He looked surprised. 'Very clever, *ma chérie*. That is what I have for myself planned.'

'Planned for myself,' she corrected automatically. 'I think that's old hat, François.'

'Old – hat?'

She explained. The General was displeased: he took himself and his country with extreme seriousness. 'There is nothing of – what you say – about Napoleon Bonaparte. He was a great man, a great soldier, and he is La France, and I shall go as him.'

'And I shall be Josephine.'

'No, no. That would be . . . indiscreet, *ma chérie*.' His tone was stiff, very disapproving. She understood what he had not put into words: it would be much too pointed. She supposed he was right.

'Marie Antoinette, then,' she said. 'We might just as well be old hat together.' She stifled a yawn, wondering what sort of Napoleonic gear François would manage to find aboard a ship. His own general's uniform could form the basis, no doubt, but he would need a Napoleon-type hat, cocked variety and worn sideways to distinguish him from the Duke of Wellington. And somewhere to tuck his hand, in the Napoleonic gesture or stance. Also boots. Poor François! He didn't look in the least like Napoleon, with his long face, large nose, and small moustache. Perhaps he would sacrifice the moustache in the interest of historical accuracy; she hoped he would. She found it prickly, like a brand new toothbrush.

Meanwhile General de Gard was preening, seeing himself in his role of splendour. He would probably, looks apart, carry it off well. He was something of an actor, and keen on the theatre as it happened. Adeline believed he was seeing himself, now, on the stage with the acclaim of the New York audience ringing in his ears like the cheering of the Paris crowds more than a hundred years before, as the genuine Bonaparte had ridden his charger along the Champs Elysées or wherever. With François, mostly in a party of prominent American military brass and senators, she had seen a number of shows in New York in the weeks before embarking aboard the *Laurentia*. They had seen Ruth Chatterton in *Daddy Long-Legs* at the Gaiety on Broadway, Hall Caine's *The Eternal City* at the Astor, Marie Dressler at the Bronx Opera House, and Arnold Daly in George Bernard Shaw's *You Never Can Tell* at the Garrick. They had attended *Twin Beds* at the Fulton; the *New York Times* had carried an advert in the form of a verse:

> If you think you know all that can happen
> To madden a man when he weds,
> There's a lot you can learn at the FULTON
> At the festive rip-roaring TWIN BEDS.

That, thinking of François and the gleam in his eye when he had looked at her as she read it out loud, had tickled her sense of humour.

On Friday, 30 April – last Friday would you believe it, she thought now, the night before embarking – they had been virtually shanghaied by an American ex-President, Theodore Roosevelt no less, into attending a lecture on temperance given by Secretary of State William J. Bryan at the Carnegie Hall, starting at 8pm. Theodore Roosevelt, diametrically opposed to Secretary Bryan's stance against any suggestion of the US entering the war (Bryan was a pacifist and according to Roosevelt something of a loony) had said it should be a laugh. Bryan, he'd said, spent more time lecturing on temperance than on his business at the State Department. In the event, although there were some jeers and barracking from the audience, from Americans who didn't like Bryan's views on the war, it wasn't exactly a laugh: Bryan was by nature a sermonizer. Adeline had never been so bored in her life; and François had been very irritable afterwards and had drunk more brandy than was good for him. Or for her, for that matter. The French might be good lovers but not when drunk, and François, Madame de Gard having retired to bed with a headache, not surprisingly, had made boozy overtures – the first time he had tried it on – which she had rejected knowing the result would be a fiasco.

Tonight, she reflected, François was going to be in his element. And she had better consult with the stewardess and see what could be done about Marie Antoinette.

'I think we must attend, Eustace,' Lady Barlow said when the word reached her in the first-class lounge. 'It will be expected of people like us, of course. We should give a lead.' She added, 'And I'm not having that Rickards woman taking the limelight either, snobbish bitch.'

'Rightyo, mama.' Eustace was all for it. 'What will you go as?'

'I don't know yet.' Lady Barlow frowned in concentration. Several roles went through her head, and one in fact was Queen Boadicea as predicted by Rickards. But Boadicea was rejected: she would need a chariot. Britannia, Queen Elizabeth, Mrs Pankhurst who was so much in the news being a suffragette and going to prison to be force-fed, no thank you very much . . . Lilly Langtry, Lady Godiva.

Lady Godiva . . . wife of Leofric, Earl of Mercia who was a snob like the Rickards woman, and cruel to his serfs with it. Lady Godiva, for reasons of philanthropy, had ridden naked through the streets of Coventry, oh, a long time ago, several centuries.

That would shake the Rickards woman. Not that she need be actually naked, of course.

She put it to Eustace.

He was flabbergasted; mama was too fat, but this he could never say. But he expostulated about propriety; she cut him short.

'Not really naked, Eustace. Just something flimsy.'

'But you'll need a horse, mama. And what shall I go as?'

She looked him up and down. He was skinny, but tall. 'You shall go as the horse,' she said.

The third-class passengers were to be allowed to join in. Pacey's idea was to lift the tension throughout the whole ship, so the whole ship should join in the fun while fun was still to be had. A number of the female Australian contingent opted, not unexpectedly, for 'Waltzing Matilda'. Amongst the men the bushranger Ned Kelly was a popular choice. So was Kaiser Bill; so to a lesser extent was Little Willy, Crown Prince of Germany. Others would go as simple men from the outback, rustics with loud, rude songs to sing and beer bottles to carry. Amongst the other nationalities, and in the other classes, other choices were made: Garibaldi the Italian patriot, Attila the Hun, the Scarlet Pimpernel, Citizen Robespierre known to his French Revolutionary comrades as the Sea-Green Incorruptible on account of his stern concept of duty and the colour of the coat he always wore. Alexander the Great, Julius Caesar, a pope of unspecified date, a member of the Spanish Inquisition, Christopher Columbus, a number of Founding Fathers who had sailed in the *Mayflower* so many centuries ago from Plymouth in the Old World to set about establishing the New, Eskimo Nell, Old King Cole, and General Custer.

Elizabeth Kent didn't want to be one of the merry-makers, with her father so recently dead in Addenbrooke's Hospital in Cambridge. John Holmes said he believed it would be a good thing for her. There was nothing to be done about the fact of her father's death and life, he said, had to go on.

'That's what they all say. It's a cliché. It doesn't go on. Not like before,' she said. 'You can say what you like.'

'It'll take you out of yourself.'

'You sound like Sister Perpetua, John.'

'Well, she's right. It can't do any harm.'

'Look,' she said passionately, 'I'm not going. I'm just not going! All right?'

'All right,' he said huffily.

'You go if you want. I don't care.'

It was the first disagreement, the nearest they had come to a row. In the end neither of them went. John found he hadn't the heart. Elizabeth had changed and he felt within himself that the change would be permanent so far as he was concerned, that there would be no more intimacy from then on out. Her father's death had thrown her back to

Annapolis and the waiting fiancé. He was her rock now and back to him she would go, mentally.

Senator Manderton, Ambassador-to-be Henry Sayers Grant and banker Haggerty conferred over bourbon in Haggerty's state-room. They would all attend: Grant had persuaded them. It was their duty to support the Captain, he said: Staff Captain Morgan had told him, privately, of Pacey's ideas and he approved them wholeheartedly. The ship needed a tonic, he'd said to the other two.

Grant himself would go as George Washington. Manderton opted for John Paul Jones, the Scot from Kirkbean in Kirkcudbrightshire who had obtained a commission in the American Navy and had got as far as threatening the safety of Edinburgh after capturing the English King's ship *Serapis*.

'Tactless,' Grant said, but grinned. 'Patrick?'

'Give me time,' Haggerty said. He, too, grinned. 'Maybe I'll go as Charles Stewart Parnell. Or Napper Tandy?'

'Even more goddam tactless.' This time Henry Sayers Grant frowned. You didn't insult a host nation. Napper Tandy was anathema to the British. Born in Dublin in 1740, he had become secretary to the Dublin United Irishmen. Then, on account of the distribution in 1793 of a pamphlet inveighing against the Beresfords, sons of the Marquis of Waterford, one of the leading English families domiciled in Ireland, he was forced to flee to America, thence to France, from where he took part in an invasion of Ireland. Later he was captured by the Germans and handed over to the British Government, tried and sentenced to death. He was, however, freed and lived on to become a legend both in America and in Ireland.

'Never do,' Grant said.

'Only joking,' Haggerty said. But it was obvious to the others that Napper Tandy was a part he would very much have liked to play.

Grant spoke again. 'Nothing Irish, Patrick. This isn't the time or the place. Especially, if I may say so, for you.'

Haggerty understood that the reference was to his forthcoming part in the loan negotiations.

'I can't possibly do that, mama.'

'Do what, Eustace?'

'Go as – as that.'

'What?'

'The horse. Think of my heart. You're rather heavy.'

'Don't be silly. I shall take my own weight on my feet. I won't actually *sit*.'

'But it would look so bad, mama, if the home authorities get to hear – and then I say that with my heart I can't – '

'Go as the Peeping Tom, then!'

'What did he do?'

'What it says, looked.'

'Oh, you mean a real Peeping Tom.'

'Of course I do, silly.'

'Oh, I really don't think – '

'But then if you was to do that, Eustace, what would I do for a 'orse?'

'I don't know, mama. Perhaps . . . perhaps something will turn up.'

Like a horse, Lady Barlow snorted. 'Not much help, are you, Eustace! It's high time you pulled yourself together and *did* something for your mother. Won't be the 'orse – sound sour about being the Peeping Tom – I don't know, what your father would have said I *don't* know.'

Mama was steaming up for a tantrum. Eustace left her to it and took no notice when she yelled after him across the first-class lounge.

The children were to have their own fancy-dress party the following afternoon. The six young Descartes would attend in the role of the offspring of Old Mother Hubbard, the eldest boy agreeing to be dressed up as Old Mother Hubbard herself, and the boot being left to the imagination. The stewards and stewardesses, always pleased to do what they could for any children aboard, surpassed themselves in the collecting together of clothing, even to the making of a realistic bonnet for Old Mother Hubbard. Other favourites were Snow White and the Seven Dwarfs, President Wilson, the King of England and An Intrepid Aviator. There were no goggles to be had but Staff Captain Morgan, who with Purser Matthews was coordinating the whole show, offered to provide a pair of binoculars. This the children's hostess, Miss Greatorex, accepted with effusive thanks. At the drop of a hat Miss Greatorex, aged forty-one, would have granted Staff Captain Morgan anything he might have wished.

Morgan was aware of this and stood well clear. 'About the tea-party,' he said, cutting her short with a superfluous question since he knew the drill backwards. 'It'll take place after the judging as usual?'

'Yes, Captain Morgan – '

'Right.' Morgan went away; fancy dress or no fancy dress, he had much to do. Matters of greater urgency: there had been a report from the second master-at-arms, who had replaced Warner, of discontent in the cells. The Australian, Ommaney, had made loud complaints about being in the proximity of German nationals. He had been backed up by his friend Craigson.

* * *

Still many sea miles to the eastward of the *Laurentia*'s current position, U-120 lurked submerged, safe as houses from the British Navy. She was currently lying stopped, lifting and falling a little to the deep sea movements, the surge and swell of the North Atlantic's undersurface currents, the electric motors moving only now and again as *Kapitanleutnant* Eppler used his hydroplanes to keep his command at a safe depth. He was in position now, close enough to the *Laurentia*'s expected track.

Expected.

There could be alterations. The Master of the *Laurentia* might perhaps anticipate events and change his course accordingly. But there would not be very much scope for avoiding Eppler. All transatlantic liners approaching the British shores expected to make their landfalls within a comparatively short scope, a restricted area. The Fastnet, the Old Head of Kinsale – and that was about it. Bound for Liverpool, a ship could of course alter to make, say, the Bishop Rock her landfall, altering again for St George's Channel; but the English were predictable and seldom reacted swiftly to changing events; and the *Laurentia* would still need to steam pretty close to where Eppler lay.

For perhaps the hundredth time Eppler conferred with his First Lieutenant, scanning the chart laid out on the chart table aft of the periscope housing. That, and a scale drawing obtained years ago from the liner's builders of the *Laurentia*, showing her system of watertight bulkheads and the layout of the ship above and below decks – the cargo spaces, the engine and boiler rooms, the fresh water tanks, the trimming tanks, the bunkers, the mail room and the baggage room and the rest.

'We must go for the war material stowage, Dirnecker.'

'And we don't know where that is, *Herr Kapitan* – fore or aft. It is a chance either way – for the first torpedo. Myself, I suggest there.' He placed a finger on the liner's fore hold, on the starboard side between the for'ard boiler room and trimming tank. 'I would aim for the boiler room, close to the hold, *Herr Kapitan*, for the most damage. If we are lucky, it will be just the one torpedo. A second aft if necessary. That, I think, will ensure the total destruction . . . the total destruction that will satisfy the High Command.'

'And His Imperial Majesty.' Eppler turned his attention once again to the chart. He spoke of his reflections on a possible alteration of course by the *Laurentia*. 'If she has not reached the position *here*,' he indicated a small cross on the chart, 'by 0400 hours on Friday, then I shall alter closer to St George's Channel, where she will be impossible to miss.'

'*Ja, Herr Kapitan*. But I think that because such a miss *is* impossible, her Master will *not* alter. He will be aware of the impossibility.'

'Yes. It is a death trap, Dirnecker, that ship. And still I am convinced that no one in Britain or in America believes that she will be sunk! They do not believe that Germany would attack civilians. And more especially children, Dirnecker.'

Dirnecker shrugged, his face hard beneath the peak of his cap. 'A hazard of the war, *Herr Kapitan*. There have been the warnings. Neither the British nor the Americans can say that there have not been the warnings. And remember our Naval Command believes that the liner is fitted with a battery of 6-inch guns.'

'Yes, you're right, I know.' Eppler said no more; but he was in fact deeply disturbed, though not about the supposed six-inch guns, since he did not propose to surface. He had his duty; but to kill children coldbloodedly was monstrous. He had overheard conversations throughout the boat and he knew that his ship's company, or some of them, were equally disturbed. It would be something that would remain in their memories for the rest of their lives. So many of his seamen and engineers were fathers, as he would have liked himself to have been. Dirnecker was not married; and Dirnecker was a hard man, ambitious for the command that he would no doubt get after U-120's triumphant return to Germany. Children meant nothing to him, so much had revealed itself over the last few days. And Eppler believed that if he were to show weakness, the slightest reluctance to fire his torpedoes at the *Laurentia* and her children, then Dirnecker would not hesitate to put his Captain under arrest and take over the command and the firing himself, justifying his actions to the Naval Command in the Fatherland by pointing to victory and success and the failure of Eppler to carry out his duty.

But of course there would be no failure on Eppler's part. Too much was at stake. Not his reputation alone, but his marriage also. No, there would be no failure.

Steaming towards the waiting jaws of U-120, the *Laurentia* completed the arrangements for the two fancy-dress parties. At the appointed time on the Wednesday night the passengers made their way in their disguises towards the first-class lounge where the ship's orchestra was playing lively or romantic tunes.

Much imagination had been used. The Black Prince appeared, in armour of black cardboard, shinily painted. Spurs, fashioned from tin cans, adorned his heels. Charlemagne was present, flourishing the sword (wooden) with which he had forced Christianity on the Franks. The man who wore this disguise was short; he had no knowledge of how tall Charlemagne might have been in life, but was aware that he had been the son of Pepin the Short, so shortness seemed appropriate. Close behind Charlemagne came the notorious Colonel Blood, who in 1671 had stolen the Crown Jewels. The sea was represented by Lord Nelson, Sir Francis Drake in ballooning breeches and long socks – there was a gap which somewhat destroyed the effect, but no one minded – and Sir Henry Morgan with pirate's hat and a bottle of rum which was being steadily depleted.

Lady Barlow caused shock when she appeared: though no flesh was visible except for face, neck and arms, she was quite clearly, if only from the cardboard notice attached to her bosom, Lady Godiva. A number of passengers were amused, more were scandalized: Lady Godiva was not a suitable subject for the first class. At a distance lurked the Peeping Tom: Eustace had won his battle about not being the horse.

Mr Ambassador Grant made a convincing George Washington; Senator Manderton appeared not to have quite the dash of John Paul Jones. Banker Haggerty had not after all joined in the fun. He was aware of his dignity as a prominent New York man of finance and in any case had wanted to go as an Irishman; nothing else appealed.

The biggest sensations after Lady Barlow were General de Gard and Adeline Scott-Mason. Napoleon Bonaparte strode into the lounge in a uniform that, if not too close to Napoleon, was at least authentically French. The cocked hat, set sideways with the *tricolore* of France attached to the crown, was realistic and showed little sign of its origins, which were a pair of black knickers (Adeline's) stretched over a frame made from strong wire obtained by the General's steward from the bosun's store. For footwear the General had borrowed a pair of seaboots from Staff Captain Morgan. As with Sir Francis Drake, there was a gap, in this case between the seaboots and the greatcoat. But it was the General's physical appearance that was so striking: his figure was good, he was tall, he carried it off well, aided by his own innate arrogance and fine opinion of himself. Marie Antionette at his side was very regal in an evening dress that had cost the earth in a New York salon before sailing. To deck this Adeline Scott-Mason, who had deposited her valuables in the Purser's safe soon after embarking, had brought from safe custody genuine jewellery that had set her English husband's New York bank balance back, some years earlier, by something in the region of a quarter of a million dollars.

Purser Matthews attended with his assistant Harry Anneston and the four clerks from his office. These juniors had the task of pinning the prepared numbers to the various costumes, ready for the judging which would take place after the parade.

Eskimo Nell caused some difficulty.

Eskimo Nell looked tough, a dinkum Aussie. The clerk who approached with his label and pin entered fully into the spirit of the evening. Grinning, he laid hold of a breast that had the appearance of a concealed orange. Pin and label poised, he thrust into the orange. At the first hint of pressure there was a yell in a harsh Sydney accent.

'Do you bloody mind, mate? You touch me again and I'll have the Captain on yer!'

The clerk, much embarrassed, apologized. But he failed to use tact. Stammering in his confusion, he said, 'I'm awfully sorry. I thought you were a man, dressed – '

'All you bloody poms are the bloody same, don't know a man from a woman. *Poofters!*' Eskimo Nell flounced away, seeking comfort from a real man, Ned Kelly, bushranger.

Miss Greatorex, children's hostess, had been buttonholed by an actual man dressed as a woman. This man had gone as DORA – the Defence of the Realm Act had recently become law in Britain to ensure the closure of public houses during certain hours in order to reduce drunkenness among the workers in the all-important munitions factories. News of its unpopularity had reached New York. The man looked as lugubrious as might be expected of DORA and carried a pamphlet on temperance that he had picked up outside Carnegie Hall on the night of Secretary Bryan's lecture. The donor had been a spotty girl with an earnest expression, wearing a Salvation Army type bonnet, and the man had pocketed the pamphlet good-naturedly and forgotten about it until the announcement of the fancy-dress ball. Not by nature a teetotaller, he was currently well on the way to being intoxicated.

'On your ownsome?' he'd asked Miss Greatorex, who had a lonely and available look; all was grist to a toper's mill.

'Yes,' she said, colouring a little.

'Why, I guess that's too bad.'

'I'm used to it,' she said with simple honesty.

'I guess we'll rec – rectify that. Might I ask your name?'

'Miss Greatorex,' she said.

'That's great. Sorry! Earl MacRea,' he added, introducing himself.

'Oh, a Scot?'

'Once, I guess. Not now. Yankee through and through and proud of it.'

'Of course,' Miss Greatorex said politely.

Earl MacRea seemed pleased. 'For a limey, you're not too bad. How's about a drink, miss?'

'Oh – thank you. Yes.'

'So what's it to be?'

'I think a little brandy perhaps.'

'Whatever you wish, lady.' Earl MacRea signalled for a steward. Brandies were brought, large ones after a whisper between the steward and Mr MacRea. It didn't stop at that; Miss Greatorex liked the attention, liked the brandy too, and became giggly and coy. The dancing went on, ended temporarily with the grand parade and the judging by Staff Captain Morgan, Dr Fellowes, Purser Matthews and a representative non-participating passenger from each class. Miss Greatorex had lost interest, didn't even register that the first prize had gone to Napoleon Bonaparte and Marie Antoinette, didn't hear Lady Barlow's loud, angry comment that it was a case of snobs again, keeping in with each other and that probably the Rickards woman was behind it. Miss Greatorex was enjoying herself, really letting her hair down, something she had not done since she was in her twenties, much too long ago.

She continued drinking brandy later on in Earl MacRae's state-room, which was in the most flagrant disregard of Company's Regulations but by now she didn't give a hoot. She did not, however, agree with the later suggestion of Earl MacRae, a suggestion that caused her to flush a deep red.

'Oh, *no*! Most certainly not! How *dare* you! I'm not that sort of girl.'

Mr MacRae was angry. 'Girl,' he said in a nasty sort of voice. 'Huh! Didn't lead me on by any chance, did you?'

'I certainly did not.' By now Miss Greatorex felt that she was losing some control over her diction. She got to her feet a little unsteadily. 'If you'll excuse me . . . thank you for the – the evening. I feel a little unwell.'

She tottered from the cabin. Mr MacRae made no attempt to follow. He cursed to himself and ripped up the temperance pamphlet violently. From the cabin doorway Miss Greatorex hurried along a short alleyway to the open air of the embarkation deck, taking the leeward side, since she had some knowledge of the sea, and vomited. It was not until she reached her own cabin that she realized she had lost her false teeth, a full set top and bottom. Her first panicky thought was a report to the bridge, teeth overboard or something . . . then she realized that short of trawling the bottom of the North Atlantic her teeth were gone forever.

God's punishment, she was sure. And the very next day she was due to supervise the children's fancy-dress party. They were all so much looking forward to it. For them, it would be the great day of the voyage, and for the proud parents too. There was always a lovely feast, a buffet beautifully prepared by the galley staff and stewards, jellies and cream, plenty of cakes, jam, milk and so on. And the party always ended with a sing-song, nursery rhymes chiefly, with appropriate movements, led by Miss Greatorex. Here we go round the mulberry bush, with no teeth.

On the day of the adult passengers' fancy-dress ball, Staff Captain

Morgan had gone below to the cells to have a word with Big Jake Ommaney and to listen to his complaint.

The complaint had been stated, baldly. 'I'm not going to be right next to no bloody Germans . . . not when the ship gets closer in, my oath! It's not bloody right.'

'It's bloody inevitable,' Morgan said crisply. Ommaney looked a little rocked at having his Australian adjective thrown back at him. 'There's no accommodation available elsewhere in the ship and you're here by your own fault in any case.'

'Look, I – '

'I repeat, no alternative. But I assure you, you'll not be left down here, any of you, if there's trouble.'

'By which you bloody mean – '

'By which I mean if a U-boat or anything else hostile is sighted, you'll all be brought up on deck. Meanwhile, you stay where you are.'

Morgan stepped back from the cell door, which was once again locked by the master-at-arms. Big Jake Ommaney peered through bars set across the small window, lips drawn back in an animal-like snarl. Morgan registered the yellowed teeth, big enough to be fangs. Next to Ommaney, Craigson whined that he was being persecuted; Morgan took no notice. Across the small cell space Morgan saw the Germans playing a game of cards. Next to them was Frederick Jones, double murderer. Jones was lying on his plank bed, flat on his back, staring up at the white-painted deckhead, eyes open and seemingly fixed on a line of rivets.

With her mixed bag of passengers and her concealed war material, the *Laurentia* pushed on through the uncaring, age-old highway of the North Atlantic, closing the gap between safety and the lurking peril.

18

LIKE Haggerty, the Rickardses, Alva Lundkvist, John Holmes and Elizabeth Kent, a number of the other passengers had not attended the fancy-dress frivolities. Some were too old, some, like Elizabeth Kent, were just not interested having, like her, their own worries and sorrows. Livia Costello had been too drunk, drowning her own sorrows and uncertainties as to her future. She had been deserted by Purser Matthews; no more cabin visits now. She felt she had been deserted by everybody. She had in fact surfaced towards the end of the fancy-dress parade, just after the judging, and believed, in her fuddled state next day, that she had created a scene of some kind. She was just about aware of having had her arms grabbed by two people and then of being lifted and carried, presumably to her own cabin where, that next day, she awoke with a splitting head.

Elmer Pousty had not attended because he was keeping Leon Fielding company and listening patiently to the old singer's maunderings about Ming and his wife and New York, and the dreadful crime he was suspected of, and about past glories when he had been the centre of attention in his profession, the man that crowds had flocked to hear. It was sad, Pousty thought, to see him now. If in the next two or so days a torpedo was to strike, then it might well be a blessing if Fielding didn't survive.

The Reverend Divine had attended, though not in fancy dress; like Haggerty, he had his personal dignity to consider, and that of his church as well. But he had entered into the spirit of the evening and had laughed and clapped with the others, had even clapped, if half-heartedly, the appalling sight of Lady Godiva. He had quietened his conscience by recalling that Lady Godiva had been a good Christian woman with the very best of intentions, i.e., to do good for the unfortunate poor whom her husband would have oppressed. The Reverend Divine was not so sure about Lady Godiva's portrayer: Lady Barlow was a bit much for anyone, and the bane of the stewards in lounge and saloon and no doubt in her state-room too.

The Reverend Divine had done a good deed himself after the party: he had provided one of the pairs of arms that had prevented Livia Costello throwing a glass of Scotch at the Staff Captain and had thereafter helped to carry her to her cabin, but not, himself, to take any part in her undressing and being put to bed. This task had been carried out by Sister Perpetua, who had happened to be passing Livia's cabin at the time and had said that the poor woman should not be seen in such a state by any of the stewardesses.

The third-class passengers, or anyway a large number of them, had carried on the party after it was supposed to be over and had once again broken into the bar after it had been closed by order of the Staff Captain. They had created a certain amount of chaos and the decks were dangerous with broken glass.

Guido Pascopo had been appalled, even though he had witnessed drunken scenes in the sleazier quarters of New York from time to time. This was worse because it was taking place upon the sea in time of war, and because a ship was a very self-contained world, comparatively small upon the vastness of the ocean, and it was much more difficult than on the land to get away from noise, and drunken men with their raucous laughter, and the hurtling bottles and glasses that seemed always to accompany drunken Americans and British, and even more so drunken Australians it appeared. It was not like that in Italy, though certainly it had been in Malta when the British fleet was in port. In Italy, in the sunshine of the day or beneath the moon at night, drinking was a serious business and a pleasure at the same time, and there was seldom fighting, anyway only when a woman was involved. There might be the vendettas, and occasionally a knife would be slid into a man and his body would vanish, but it was all done with decorum and without unpleasantness. In Italy men did not become drunk to the point of vomit and they did not throw bottles about. Give them a woman and they were happy; the *vino* was of less importance. Italians were civilized persons.

And a woman was what Guido Pascopo would have liked to have been given now: he was a man of strong desires, which was perhaps a sin . . . but in any case there would be no woman. Just absent Maria his beloved wife, and certain photographs of Maria doubtless praying for him in New York. They were splendid photographs, taken of her some years earlier, and taken in the nude against a backdrop of a crimson velvet curtain, taken by himself of course, and quite expertly. Guido needed a sight of them now; seeing them he would be satisfied, mentally he would be with Maria again, and the torment of wanting a woman at this moment would cease. Or might cease. Anyway, it was the best he could do and remain spotless in the sight of the Holy Virgin.

His five cabin-mates were attending the drunken orgy and attending it wholeheartedly – he had seen them, staggering about. His cabin would be empty, the photographs could be brought out in total privacy – there had been very little privacy total or otherwise since the *Laurentia* had left

New York – and his eyes would run over the splendid contours of Maria, the swelling breasts, the full and rounded stomach, the thighs and buttocks of a real woman who had no patience with the stick-insect-like young girls of America and Britain with their preoccupation with whaleboned stays to make them appear thin. Maria Pascopo was a genuine Italian mother and proud of it, and Guido was proud of her as well.

He drew the photographs from his suitcase which he had stowed beneath his bunk, the bottom one on the left of the door, port or starboard he knew not which. It was a crowded and stuffy cabin, with no access to the fresh air – no porthole. Guido's hands were clammy as he brought out the photographs from their stiff cardboard folder and laid them with reverence on the bunk. He knelt by the bunkside, and offered up a prayer for Maria's safety and for the safety of the ship.

Then he opened his eyes and spread the photographs out on the blanket that covered the bunk.

He relished them. He kissed Maria's photographic breasts, he ran a finger down the thighs. It was a splendid moment and he was at first unaware of the racket down along the alleyway outside the cabin.

Then, too late, he registered.

The door was flung violently open before Guido had had a chance to conceal the photographs. His five cabin companions stormed in. They were, he noted, very drunk indeed. He was thrust into a corner of the cabin, where he fell to the floor. Maria's body was displayed to the five men. They reacted.

'Dirty little ponce.'

'Feelthy photographs . . . look, mate, it's bloody Port Said in the middle of the bloody Atlantic!'

Coarse reference was made to Maria's physical attributes; her buttocks were likened to the back of a Sydney tramcar.

Guido screamed at them, a stream of invective that they didn't understand. Then he implored them in his not too good English not to harm the photographs. They were, he said, of Maria, his wife. He loved her. But the photographs were passed from hand to hand for closer inspection. The comments continued and Guido grew more and more frantic with concern for Maria, whom now he seemed inadvertently to have dishonoured. Filthy drunken beasts . . . and now a woman had become involved. *His* woman, his own Maria! Beside himself with rage and a growing fear, Guido slid a hand down the inside of his trouser waistband. When the hand came out, it held a thin, very sharp knife with a long blade, bought a long time ago in Valletta where often the drunken sailors from the British fleet could become dangerous.

The knife flashed in the cabin's electric light, shining down from the deckhead above.

'Little sod's got a bloody knife!'

And that did it. There was a concerted rush; Guido was seized, his arms held tightly behind his back. There was a hasty conference. Then Guido was given a bum's rush, out of the cabin, along the alleyway, up the companionways to a higher deck level, and out on the open deck on the starboard side.

'Teach you a bloody lesson,' one of the drunken men shouted. Guido was hoisted willy-nilly to the guardrail and held, teetering in the men's grip over the waters, the night-dark waters, of the North Atlantic.

'No more bloody exhibitions, eh?' one of the men said. 'Next time, you – '

There was an interruption, a man shouting from a little farther aft. Running footsteps pounded along the deck. Guido was let go. Teetering, now without support, for the drunken men were trying to vanish, he went over the guardrail, dropping into the sea as the *Laurentia* steamed on at her eighteen knots.

Able Seaman Bromhead lifted his voice in a carrying shout to the bridge.

'*Man overboard starboard!*'

Some fifteen seconds later a lifebuoy smacked into the water a few yards clear of Guido Pascopo. Soon after this the Officer of the Watch passed the order to send away the seaboat's crew. Telegraphs had rung on the bridge, were repeated in the engine room. The liner's engines were put to stop, and as the way came off she drifted. Woken from sleep, Chief Engineer Hackett ran to the engine room and the starting platform in his pyjamas and dressing-gown, believing that already the ship was under German attack.

Captain Pacey had been called to the bridge, where he took a number of reports. He was much relieved when word came up from the after decks that the man who had gone overboard had been retrieved: it seemed to be a miracle that he had escaped the suck-in to the lashing propellers before the engines, by prompt action of First Officer Main, had been stopped.

'I'll want the full report as soon as possible,' Pacey said to the Staff Captain.

'You shall have it, sir. The Australians again, as I understand.'

Pacey nodded. 'Engines to full ahead,' he said to the First Officer, 'as soon as the seaboat's hooked onto the falls.' He turned back to Morgan. 'That was well carried out, Staff Captain. No delay – very commendable on the part of the boat's crew. I'd be obliged if you'd tell them that.'

'Yes, sir.' Morgan paused. 'One good thing that's come out of it – good exercise for the boat's crew and lowerers! Let's hope it's the same when . . . if . . .' He didn't finish.

'Amen to that,' Pacey said with feeling.

In the morning more reports reached Captain Pacey, back again on the bridge. These reports concerned the fresh break-in to the bar by the third-class passengers; they concerned the behaviour of Livia Costello and her removal to her cabin by Mr Divine and the help given by Sister Perpetua. They also concerned the reactions of some of the passengers who had not attended the fancy-dress ball.

'A few complaints,' Morgan said, 'relayed by Matthews.'

'Well, let's have 'em.'

'Mr and Mrs Rickards. Noise, chiefly. Kept going too long and they couldn't sleep. It did tend to spill over from the lounge, sir.'

'I see. I sympathize with the Rickardses. Not easy, at their ages. Anything else?'

'Mrs Lundkvist, sir. Unseemly, she said, when her husband's still below. She was very upset. So was the boy, she said.' Morgan blew out his cheeks. 'It's a rotten business, that. The boy keeps asking where his father is, where he went so suddenly. You can't tell him his father's in refrigeration below.'

'Yes, I know. I'm extremely sorry she's been further upset. Extremely sorry. And that poor child. But one had to think of the majority, Morgan.' Pacey sighed, looked away across the broad ocean, with journey's end now filling his thoughts. So much sadness already . . . two deaths that should never have happened, passengers in his cells, a highly unusual occurrence in his experience. It would not be a happy landfall for some. For Fielding, to name one. 'Anything else?'

'Minor stuff, sir. A few objections to Lady Godiva . . . Damage to dresses by cigar and cigarette ends – all their own fault, I'd say. A couple of broken limbs to keep Dr Fellowes busy – in the circumstances, I see no liability on the Company. Both were pretty drunk, and skidded down ladders.'

'I'd better have full reports, just the same. What about Pascopo?'

Morgan who had carried out an investigation, gave a summary of what had taken place. He said, 'All the men involved had managed to disappear before Bromhead could do anything about them – he knew his first responsibility was to the man overboard – '

'Of course. He acted very promptly. I shall see that the Marine Superintendent in Liverpool is informed of that – Bromhead will have my strong commendation. One of the old sort – Bromhead.'

'Yes, sir. I – '

'And the culprits. From what you tell me, it's fairly obvious they were Pascopo's cabin companions?'

Morgan nodded. 'Oh, we all know who was involved . . . but they all deny it – obviously! They all clammed up. No one knew a thing about it. All very, very innocent. Pascopo's word against five. And he refused to produce the photographs to me.'

'It's not likely to happen again, I take it?'

'Highly unlikely, sir. They're dead scared, I think – they never intended the man should actually go over the side.'

'Well, unless something concrete emerges, someone's conscience say, we'll drop it. No harm's been done in the upshot. There's not going to be time to worry about that sort of thing from now on.' Pacey gave a short, humourless laugh. 'It didn't work out after all, Morgan – did it? The fancy-dress idea.'

Morgan disagreed. 'On the contrary, sir, it worked splendidly. In the main, anyhow. They're all a lot less tense, I believe – happier, some sore heads apart. It did the trick all right.'

'Well, I'm glad to hear it! Just prepare a report about the Pascopo business and let me have it in good time for sending ashore on arrival.'

Morgan saluted; the Captain certainly would not have time in the last stages of the voyage to carry out investigations into misbehaviour himself. Going below, Morgan went about his business. In the lounges last night's mess had been tidied up and things were shipshape again. The broken glass had been cleared away, much of it from the open decks, by the hands washing down in the so-called silent hours. Bosun MacFarlane had supervised personally, and had had a lot to say about the behaviour of passengers. There had been vomit mixed in with the broken glass, and traces of blood. MacFarlane had never seen anything quite so bad before. They seemed, some of them, to have gone mad. Maybe it was the war, and thoughts of what might lie ahead, so soon now.

Captain Pacey walked the bridge from side to side, passing through the wheelhouse where the quartermaster was keeping the ship on a straight course, no wiggles in the wake. The lookouts, Pacey saw, were watchful, scanning their arcs on either side through their heavy binoculars, searching for the feather of spray that would indicate a periscope. The day was fine, with a light wind to ruffle the surface enough to make identification of any feather difficult.

Ideal conditions for a U-boat captain. Though his ship was not yet within range – not yet but almost – Captain Pacey had told his steward that from now on he would not be leaving the bridge.

'Very good, sir. Meals too, sir?'

'Meals too, Mullins. A tray in the wheelhouse. And plenty of hot cocoa at night.'

'Aye, aye, sir.' Mullins would provide; Mullins had always kept a watchful eye on the Captain, who was not as young as he used to be. For anyone in command, war was a strain, the responsibility was tremendous, so many potentially panicky passengers, with the husbands looking out for their own families and bugger anyone else if the worst happened. Perfectly natural, of course, but it didn't help when the officers were trying to get boats away. Mullins, who had never himself been shipwrecked in peace or war, had the *Titanic* much on his mind as had so many other people aboard, and he knew the *Titanic* had been no picnic for anyone. And a torpedo could presumably be much worse than an iceberg. Not that there would be much for Mullins to do about it except do all he could for the Captain. Mullins worried about the Captain; he hoped he would get his head down in the chart room, where there was a long leather settee, as often as possible.

Pacey himself was thinking of something that had been raised by Staff Captain Morgan: that little Lundkvist boy, asking for a father who would never return. Sudden death was always a horrible experience for the bereaved, was so much the worse when it should never have happened, when it was the result of sheer brutality and callousness, and worse again for a child.

Pacey was remembering his own father's death. It had not been the result of brutality or callousness; and Pacey had not been a child when it happened, but it had been a time of total horror. The young Pacey had been at home on leave in Southsea, awaiting the taking of his examination for his Master's certificate, having completed his statutory sea time – four years for second mate, two more for mate, another year for Master. The Channel Squadron, as it had then been known, had been awaiting entry to Portsmouth Harbour from Spithead; there was a gale of wind blowing and the conditions as advised by the Queen's Harbour Master had been adverse for entry of the heavy ships. But the Admiral commanding the Squadron had urgent business in Whitehall and had decided to enter, transferring his flag to a cruiser, HMS *Marathon*. On account of the weather conditions and because, so it had been said, he was a man of some indecision, *Marathon*'s captain had asked for a pilot.

Pacey senior was on the shift, and was to be taken out in the pilot boat to embark aboard the cruiser. The young Pacey had been spending the day at the pilot station with his father, and had accepted an invitation to go out in the pilot boat and watch his father bring the cruiser in. The pilot boat had been lying alongside a big tug, and brows had been rigged across from the dockyard wall to the tug, and again to the pilot boat.

There had been quite a sea running, and the two vessels were lifting and straining. Pacey, with youth on his side, had jumped across, scorning the plank that formed the brow. His father, older, less nimble, had been caught by a heavy gust of wind that had billowed his oilskin out like a sail and he had slipped from the brow into the strip of water between the wall and the tug. He had not quite reached the water. His body had been crushed between the stone of the wall and the iron bulwarks of the tug as the vessel lifted on the surge against the jetty. Pacey had seen the agonized face in the moment before death had come as a mercy.

It was a sight he would never forget. Nor would he forget the bringing ashore of the shattered body, and the sense of sudden terrible loss, a father who moments before had walked and talked, ready to do his duty.

That Lundkvist boy. . . .

Something to occupy his mind, if only for a short while, something for him perhaps to think about afterwards?

It might help.

Pacey beckoned up the bridge messenger. 'My compliments to the Staff Captain. I'd like to see him when he can spare a moment. There's no urgency.'

The boy seaman went below at the double. Within twenty minutes Morgan had reached the bridge. 'You wish to see me, sir?'

'Yes, Morgan. That boy – Lundkvist. Do you know if he has much English?'

'Very little, sir.'

'His mother? She speaks good English.'

'Yes, sir.'

'Right! My compliments to Mrs Lundkvist . . . I'd be obliged if you'd do this yourself, Morgan . . . if she and the boy would care to come to the bridge, I'd be glad to show them around. The boy might find it interesting, don't you think?'

Morgan nodded. 'I do indeed, sir. If he's fit – he hasn't been well – that'll be up to Dr Fellowes – I'm quite sure he'd enjoy it.' Morgan paused. 'If he was allowed to take the wheel for a minute or so – ?'

'Good idea,' Pacey said.

'The boy's quite fit,' Dr Fellowes said. 'Malingering, that's all. Trading on the fact he's been to the States for treatment – that's my view. He needs to pull himself together.'

'But the fact of the father's death – '

'Oh yes, there's that of course. It doesn't help, I know. But even there . . . he has to come to grips with it sooner or later, hasn't he? No one's father lasts for ever.'

'So in your opinion it's all right to take him to the bridge?' Morgan asked.

'Certainly! Fresh air's the best thing for any growing lad.' Fellowes added, '*If* you can prise him loose from the mother.'

'She'll be coming too.'

'Oh, I see. I might have known.'

Alva Lundkvist had been at first doubtful; she hated the idea of talking to anyone, wished only to reach Liverpool, have the inquest and the police proceedings over and done with as soon as possible – though she suspected a whole series of delays while the law ground slowly through its formalities – and then go home to her parents in Sweden with Olof and her memories of Torsten. But, somewhat to her surprise, Olof had been excited by the Captain's invitation, so she had decided to accept.

Olof, she could see when they reached the bridge shepherded by Staff Captain Morgan, was impressed with the majesty of a ship's captain on his home ground. Pacey's tall figure, with the gold oak-leaved cap and the four gold stripes on the shoulders of his bridge coat, seemed to a small boy like the manifestation of God. The scrubbed and holystoned wood of the deck, the gleaming brass fittings, the two Officers of the Watch, the grey-haired quartermaster behind the great wheel that steered the ship, the polished brass handles of the engine room telegraphs, the very height above the waterline when Pacey took him to look over the side, the four great funnels streaming away aft – they looked different when viewed from the bridge – and trailing smoke from the furnaces where the firemen and trimmers worked away in tremendous heat and red light . . . it was quite an experience for a boy. Olof asked many questions through his mother, who was diffident with the Captain but managed to act as a reasonable link.

Olof was allowed to stand behind the wheel and take the place of the quartermaster, who nevertheless stood ready to grip the spokes if needs be.

'A nice straight course,' Pacey told Olof. 'Hold the wheel steady – you see? Like the quartermaster.'

Alva Lundkvist translated. Olof nodded, his eyes shining with excitement. The wheel dwarfed the small body. Quartermaster Hendry fetched a box and put it on the platform abaft the wheel, and lifted Olof to it so that he could see the binnacle and watch the movement of the compass needle as now and again a sea passing beneath the liner's bottom caused a small shift, which Hendry reached out to correct.

The boy was allowed the wheel for five minutes and managed to hold a fairly steady course for most of the time, his small arms assisted by the telemotor steering engine. Pacey smiled. 'What do you think, Hendry? Make a quartermaster of him one of these days?'

'Aye, sir, I reckon 'e could if he's a mind to it.'

'Praise indeed,' Pacey said to Alva Lundkvist, 'coming from the quartermaster.' Addressing Hendry he asked, 'Would you recommend the life, Hendry?'

The elderly seaman wiped the back of a hand across his nose. 'Aye, sir, though I preferred the windjammers, sir, with all their hard living. All gone now, sir – or nearly.'

Pacey nodded. He, too, had preferred being under square sail. There had been a freedom about the seas that had gone now like the windjammers themselves; days when a master's own skill sailed a ship, and found the best winds because of his long experience. Saved the ship, too, when the weather or fire below or shifting cargo brought extreme danger. Or, of course, lost it when the ship herself could fight no more, dismasted perhaps, the decks a shambles of smashed spars and the stumps where the masts had been, broken deckhouses and hatches, injured men with no doctor to attend them. The attempts to rig a jury mast and try to sail the ship to the nearest port . . . or, often enough, with nowhere left to rig a jury mast, it had been a case of floating around the world until another ship was met with, or if no ship appeared then a slow death from starvation as the food stocks ran out. So many ships in those days had been reported lost at sea, no details available, presumed sunk and the Lutine Bell rung at Lloyds of London to announce an insurance loss that to the interminably waiting wives and families meant so much more than an insurance claim. And no recompense for them.

That was the other side of the picture. Pacey gestured to Hendry to lift the boy down again. There was really quite a lot to be said for the present day and its comforts, even for the engines that drove the ships in place of rope and canvas. But the basic skills were going, machines were beginning to take the place of men's brains and brawn, and the engines brought stinking smoke to the skies and the ships, and clouds of coal dust when the ships were taking bunkers.

'Olof,' Pacey said when he had shown the boy the chart room and the wireless room just aft of it, and explained the use of the engine room telegraphs and the tell-tales that repeated back to the bridge, informing the Captain that his orders were being followed and obeyed below, and many other things, 'Olof, what else would you like to see?'

Alva Lundkvist put the question. Then she said, 'He wishes to see the engines, Captain.'

Pacey laughed. 'I rather suspected he might, Mrs Lundkvist! I'll have a word with my Chief Engineer.' Exceptionally, Hackett might stretch the regulations as Pacey had. Pacey himself went to the engine room voicepipe. Hackett was agreeable to having the boy down below, but not the mother. Pacey had expected that. Ladies' skirts could catch in machinery. Not only that: skirts were skirts, and the engine-room ladders were very steep with flat, open treads, and those below could see much that was otherwise hidden . . . and Hackett wouldn't want his ratings distracted.

'The boy can go down with pleasure, Mrs Lundkvist,' Pacey said. 'I'll get one of my officers to take him, but of course there'll be the language difficulty – '

'I cannot go too?'

Pacey shook his head. 'I'm sorry – no.'

'Then I am sorry too, Captain. He does not go without me.'

The boy's disappointment was all too obvious; the small face crumpled, but his mother was adamant. Staff Captain Morgan, standing by, began to see what Dr Fellowes had been getting at.

Henry Sayers Grant was standing at the for'ard end of the boat deck, by the door, now open, that led to the narrow deck running before the first-class lounge. There was a clear view over the liner's fo'c'sle with its heavy anchor cables held by the Blake slips and bottlescrew slips, the inboard ends of the cables vanishing down the navel pipe into the cable lockers where they were held by the cable clenches to port and starboard.

Grant was not thinking of anchors and cables, however: he was thinking back to New York harbour where at this moment a great assembly of the United States Atlantic Fleet would be taking up its positions ready for the Presidential review to be held on Monday, 17 May, some eleven days ahead yet. Aboard his yacht *Mayflower* President Woodrow Wilson would steam through the lines, getting under way at 3.30 pm. Followed by USS *Dolphin* and *Yankton*, the President would pass between the shore and the battleships *Louisiana*, *New Hampshire*, *Georgia*, *Nebraska*, *Rhode Island*, *Virginia*, *Utah*, *Florida* and *Kansas*. Thence he would steam around the end of the fleet lying in the Hudson River, returning between the battleships and the destroyer flotillas and arriving at his anchorage preparatory to dining aboard the super-dreadnought *Wyoming*, flagship of Admiral Frank F. Fletcher, Commander-in-Chief, US Atlantic Fleet. After dinner there would be boat races by the crews of the fleet; and from 8 to 11 pm the whole massive fleet would be illuminated.

On the following day at 9 am the President would again be waterborne, *Mayflower*, *Dolphin* and *Yankton* proceeding to an anchorage near the Statue of Liberty; at 9.30 the fleet would get under way and, at ten knots, would steam past the President in review order, and then the great ships would steam away to sea. The super-dreadnoughts, among them the *New York*, the *Texas*, the *Delaware* and the *North Dakota* along with *Wyoming* and the others, made a mighty fleet.

Ambassador-to-be Grant wondered what would be the feelings of the President as he watched those great warships with their massive armament – *Wyoming* carried six turrets, each mounting two twelve-inch guns to form her main battery with twenty-one five-inch guns in her secondary armament, all capable of being taken into action at 21.65 knots – Grant wondered what would be going through Wilson's mind when that moment of departure came.

Grant knew well what his own thoughts would have been: guns for embattled Britain, standing up for decency and a world free from German aggrandizement and aggression. Battleships and cruisers, destroyers and submarines that would swing the balance of war against overweening pride and ambition, swing it towards a small country fighting for its existence.

Bastion and outpost of the United States of America – that was what it came to. Grant was convinced of that. Beat Britain and France, the Kaiser would then turn the seaborne German guns and infantry formations against the USA, turn the U-boats against all American shipping.

During the period the fleet would be in New York Harbour prior to the review, the officers and men were to be royally entertained. There would be baseball parties, theatre parties, a reception for the officers at the New York Yacht Club, informal dancing on the USS *Granite State* sponsored by the 1st Battalion of the Naval Militia, New York Division. There would be athletic and vaudeville performances for the enlisted men, and another reception for the officers, this time at the Union League Club. There would be a dinner for the officers at the Waldorf Hotel, there would be fireworks from floats on the Hudson River, there would be band concerts on Riverside Drive. Many churches would hold special services on the two Sundays spanned by the fleet's visit. Finally, on the morning of 17 May, the day of the review, the men of the fleet would parade, marching from the assembly and landing point at Twenty-Third Street to Twenty-Fifth Street, Fifth Avenue . . . Central Park West to Seventy-Seventh Street and to North River where at 10.30 am the head of the parade would pass the reviewing stand.

Honour and glory – and high jinks. *Have fun, boys*, Grant said to himself on the *Laurentia*'s deck. *Have fun – but I'll bet I know what you're thinking, most of you young Americans. Same as me: let's cut the official ballyhoo and steam out for a grand purpose.*

Would Wilson see it that way?

19

From the *Laurentia*'s crow's-nest, just after dawn, a report was made by the seaman on lookout:

'Ship ahead, sir, one point on the port bow!'

'Can you identify?' the Officer of the Watch called back.

'Not positively, sir. Could be a warship, sir.'

The Officer of the Watch – Senior Second Officer Callander – went immediately to the chart room, where Pacey was stretched out on the leather settee that ran below a line of portholes in the after bulkhead.

He woke the Captain. 'Lookout reports a ship ahead, sir. She's not yet visible from the bridge, but she could be a warship.'

Pacey, fully dressed except for his bridge coat, reached out his legs and stood up, awake and ready on the instant. 'Perhaps our naval escort, Callander.'

'Or a German, sir.'

'Yes, perhaps, and we won't take chances. Sound boat stations, Callander. Master-at-Arms to bring up the men in the cells.'

'Aye, aye, sir.' The senior second officer ran for the bridge and yanked at the lanyard that brought the steam siren to life. A series of deep-throated blasts broke the serenity of the early morning, seemed to shake the ship. The sounds reached below, tumbled passengers and crew from their bunks, sent Chief Engineer Hackett doubling for the air-lock and the many ladders leading below to the starting platform. Staff Captain Morgan ran from his state-room, all but bumped into Chief Officer Arkwright who was running for the boat deck at full pelt. Below decks, Chief Steward Kemmis with the second steward and assistant second stewards was supervising the turning-out and shepherding upwards of the passengers together with the night stewards not yet relieved by the day staff. Men and women emerged in various stages of dress or undress: pyjamas, nightdresses and dressing-gowns were mostly the order of the day. Deck officers and leading hands went to the different boat assembly points on the embarkation deck, and began mustering their charges against the handwritten lists of those allocated to their groups, and seeing to the set of the lifejackets. On the boat deck, Chief Officer Arkwright took overall charge of the lowerers, seeing the griping-bands cast off and the falls started for launching if and when the order came from the bridge. Within minutes most of the lifeboats had been lowered to the embarkation deck where, held on the falls, they waited for orders.

The passengers straggled up, looking scared, all glamour gone from the women. Sleep was in the corners of their eyes. Livia Costello, almost dragged from her cabin by a stewardess who had much else to do, looked like death, her face pale, her hands shaking, bringing with her the sour stench of last night's gin and cigarettes.

The Chief Steward reported to Staff Captain Morgan: 'All below-deck sections cleared, sir.'

'Thank you, Mr Kemmis.' Morgan reported to the bridge.

Pacey, now on monkey's island above the bridge from where he had a longer view, called down. 'Run out fire hoses, Staff Captain. Close all watertight doors.'

'Aye, aye, sir.'

Pacey continued looking through his binoculars, searching the seas ahead for the intruder, who might be friend and might be foe. Below decks, in the cleared sections, the watertight doors began closing by automatic response to the pressing of a button in the wheel-house.

The *Laurentia* moved on; for now the engines had been left on full ahead. It would be Pacey's assessment of the developing situation if the oncoming ship should prove to be an enemy that would or would not send the word to Hackett to stop his engines and bring his engine-room staff up the ladders to the air-lock.

Four more minutes and the approaching vessel was within sight from monkey's island. Pacey called down, 'She's a warship right enough.'

One of two things could happen now: there would be a flashing light, a signal when the *Laurentia* was seen and identified to say that the vessel was her escort. Or there would be a ripple of flame and smoke from the newcomer's fo'c'sle as her main battery opened, sending her high explosive shells across the water.

A tense moment. Pacey felt his nails digging into his palms. He had not previously come under attack; he was facing a new experience even if one he had mentally prepared for from the moment war had been declared in the previous August, prepared for and determined what his actions were to be. But now, when the moment had arrived, there were many imponderables. How good would the German gunnery be? The Germans had a good reputation as naval gunners, were said to outclass the British ships every time. How long before they could lay and train with accuracy? There would first of all be ranging shots, shots that with luck would fall over or short, but shots that would tell Pacey the time had come for him to clear the engine room, get all remaining hands to their boat stations.

And then wait.

With no guns of his own, Pacey had no alternative. He could not hit back. He must stand and take it – they all must, crew and passengers together. All he as Master of the ship could do would be to act for the saving of the largest possible number of lives. In that moment, as he waited for the oncoming warship to show her hand, Pacey was more than ever conscious of one fact: the fact that the *Laurentia* did carry war materials in her cargo, contraband that could give the Germans their excuse if it happened that they knew about it. If. Pacey went back to the bridge where once again he turned his binoculars on the warship, soon fully in view, a light cruiser with two funnels and a lot of smoke. Then he saw the flashing of a signalling projector, short–long, short–long, short–long, a series of As, the general call, the preliminary signal for establishing contact between ships.

'Answer,' Pacey said. 'International code . . . ask for identification.'

The senior second officer took up an Aldis lamp and made a succession of Ts. A signal followed and was read off. The warship was HMS *Bristol*.

'Secure boat stations,' Pacey said with relief. 'Open all watertight doors. Re-stow all lifeboats.'

The reactions of the passengers were more or less what might have been expected. Leon Fielding, frozen with fear when the steam whistle had blasted off so very suddenly, had been taken charge of by Elmer Pousty and manoeuvred up the companionways to his boat station. He had been prevailed upon to leave the perambulator behind but whilst making ready had kept on talking about Ming and whether or not she would feel abandoned.

'She isn't here,' Pousty pointed out impatiently.

'Oh, she is! In my heart, don't you see – '

'Then she won't need the pram.'

'Oh – well, perhaps not. Perhaps not. But it's her home. I don't know that I can – '

'Just leave it,' Pousty said. 'You'll be holding up the whole ship, putting lives at risk – '

'Oh, I most certainly wouldn't want that.' Fielding took up a woolly scarf which he wound round his neck beneath his dressing-gown. Over the dressing-gown he pulled on a greatcoat, a full-skirted affair with a heavy cape hanging from the shoulders. Then the straw hat went on and he was ready. Afterwards, when the good news came that he was saved, he all but collapsed with relief and a late-coming feeling of shock. What might have happened didn't bear thinking about.

Lady Barlow was angry: she disliked appearing in public without due preparation. Eustace made it worse. 'You did appear as Lady Godiva, mama – '

'That was *quite* different, Eustace. Do try to talk sensibly. We might have been in the greatest danger and we were *not*. I consider the Captain acted irresponsibly and without any consideration for us passengers and our nerves. He should have made sure first. I think it's disgraceful and I shall say so to the PanAtlantic Line, just see if I don't!'

She turned sharply and all but bumped into a tall man, one of her companions at the Captain's table in the saloon. 'Pardon,' she said ungraciously.

Henry Sayers Grant removed his hat: not having slept well, he had been up and about when the alarm had sounded. 'My fault, ma'am, and I apologize. But I couldn't help overhearing what you were saying to your son about the Captain's actions. I have to say that I found his prompt response most admirable. He carries a very great responsibility, Lady Barlow, and we should all thank him for his instant reaction. That, I know, will be the opinion of the PanAtlantic Line too. Good day to you, ma'am.' Grant turned away; his tone had been cold, polite though his words were.

Lady Barlow had flushed scarlet: it had been a public rebuke. But she rallied quickly. 'I don't see what business it is of an American,' she snapped.

Mrs Rickards had been in a great state. Her hands were shaking badly and her face was stiff, with a look of seamed parchment. Her husband had had to force her out of the cabin and up the companionways to the embarkation deck and the milling throng of other passengers. She had stood there with her cork lifejacket on, cold and shivering in the wind, not speaking. Her relief was immense when the order came to stand down from boat stations and the word spread that the *Laurentia* now had her naval escort. Afterwards, in their cabin, she broke down, something she had never done before, the tears streaming down her face.

'Don't, Emmy.' Rickards fidgeted; he was no use with crying women, never found the proper words to say. He'd had a sister prone to weepiness. 'It's all right now. The Navy'll see off the U-boats. Nothing to worry about.'

'But if anything should happen . . . we're still a long way from port, Jeffrey. We've always been together.'

'So we shall continue to be, Emmy.'

'If there's an attack, if we're sunk?'

'Yes, Emmy,' he said stoutly, but was aware that he might be telling a lie. Women and children first at sea – he knew that. He wouldn't go against it. He would stand back until the women and children had been got into the lifeboats. After that – well, he would have to see. If there was no room left, then Emmy might have to face it on her own. But he wasn't going to say that now. He repeated that the escort had arrived and would not leave them until they had entered Liverpool Bay, all clear for the Mersey and the PanAtlantic berth. Still standing, like the soldier he had been, he bowed his head and uttered a prayer to God that nothing might happen to the *Laurentia* and most of all to his wife. Or, for her sake solely, to himself.

Relief was obvious throughout the liner now.

The passengers crowded the open decks to watch the *Bristol* passing down the port side, her signal lamp busy as her Captain exchanged messages with the liner's Master, then turning and steaming fast to take up her position ahead of the *Laurentia*. Lean and grey, with her many guns trained now to the fore-and-aft line, the White Ensign fluttering from the gaff, the commissioning pennant of Captain de Ferriman Lugard just visible at the foremasthead, she seemed, despite her comparative smallness, to epitomize British sea power, to carry in herself an echo of all the long line of naval victories: Sir Francis Drake and the defeat of the Great Armada; Lord Howe and the Glorious First of June; Lord Rodney and the rout of the Spanish fleet at Cape St Vincent; the crushing defeat in the following year of the French at the Battle of the Saintes; Vice-Admiral Viscount Nelson of the Nile, victor of almost countless actions, most notably at Aboukir Bay, at Copenhagen, and at Trafalgar. *Admirals all, they have said their say, the echoes are ringing still. Admirals all, they have made their way to the haven under the hill. But they left us a kingdom none can take, the realm of the circling sea, to be ruled by the rightful sons of Blake, and the Rodneys yet to be.*

It was very heartening.

But as the shades of evening came down that day more signal lamps stabbed through the half-light and ahead of the *Laurentia* HMS *Bristol* increased her speed and within half an hour had vanished into the gathering night.

Captain Pacey called for a muster of passengers in the first-class lounge. Attended by Staff Captain Morgan and Purser Matthews, he gave them news. Although under control, Pacey was furiously angry. He spoke briefly and to the point.

'HMS *Bristol*, as you know, of course, made contact early this morning. I had not been informed of the time of the rendezvous . . . her Captain made signals indicating that he was under orders from the Senior Naval Officer at Queenstown to contact *Laurentia* by dead reckoning from our last reported position, and to stand by us to the

Skerries. At 1900 this evening the *Bristol* made a further signal indicating that she had had orders from SNO Queenstown to detach and return.'

There was a buzz of disturbed comment, which Pacey silenced by a lift of his hand.

'I have asked both Queenstown and the Admiralty for clarification. And I have demanded a replacement escort. For now, that is all I know. Be sure that I shall keep you all informed as events develop. And be assured, too, that I and my officers and ship's company will be fully alert, and will do all in our power to ensure a safe arrival in Liverpool.' Pacey paused. 'And now, just a necessary word of warning: you should all keep your lifejackets handy by you at all times, day and night. When absent from your cabins – take them with you.'

Then, with Morgan, he strode rapidly from the lounge. Matthews remained behind, coping with a siege of anxious questioners, but there was nothing more he could tell them.

Two days previously, Admiral Lord Fisher, First Sea Lord, had reached his room at the Admiralty in a bad temper. Each day he had read the wirelessed reports from the inward-bound *Laurentia*, indicating her position as she closed towards the danger zone around the British Isles. Each day he had snapped at his staff; each day his own thoughts had crystallized a little more. These thoughts he did not reveal to his junior staff; but each day he had had discussions with Mr Churchill, First Lord, and with certain other personages: Vice-Admiral Sir Henry Oliver, Chief of the War Staff, and Captain Reginald Hall, Director of Naval Intelligence. There was discussion of the war materials aboard the *Laurentia*, the guns, the small-arms ammunition, the cased shells.

Did the Germans know of this?

'No,' Fisher said flatly.

Mr Churchill looked at Captain Hall. Hall shrugged; the loading had been carried out in the utmost secrecy in New York and the matter of the cargo manifests had been dealt with. The arms consignment had not been shown as such. Hall said, 'The American authorities were aware of this . . . they were very cooperative.' But he added, 'Nevertheless, I have had indications that Berlin *suspects* a contraband cargo – '

'Not so much suspects,' Fisher interrupted. 'More a case of propaganda before the event!'

This was discussed; Mr Churchill stated firmly that in no way could the *Laurentia* be regarded as a legitimate target of war; she was not armed. The Germans, it would be assumed, did not know, at any rate for certain, about the war cargo the ship carried. In the meantime an escorting cruiser, the *Bristol*, was on the way, closing the *Laurentia* still well out to sea beyond the Fastnet. A sensible precaution, and all that could be done. The matter was largely in the hands of God now.

With the liner due to make a landfall in forty-eight hours, Fisher received the word that the *Bristol* had made contact. This he reported at that day's meeting. When the meeting had broken up, Fisher and Churchill left the room together, Churchill drawing deeply on a fine Havana cigar, his chubby face disturbed, the expression not in its cherubic mood but wearing a scowl. Churchill was facing difficulties, in the House and within his party, and was feeling his position as First Lord to be somewhat uncertain. And Fisher had been exhibiting even stranger moods, his behaviour becoming erratic and, Churchill believed, unreliable. Also there had been that acrimony between them.

However, this was a time to be friendly.

He put an arm around Fisher's shoulder. 'In the past, Jacky, you and I have been good friends.'

'What are you cooking up now, Winston?' Fisher's tone was aggressive.

'I? Nothing.' Nevertheless, there was something Machiavellian in Mr Churchill's smile. 'We have the war at sea to conduct between us. We are the ones who count. We must have a united front. Times are hard – you know that as well as I do. We both need a victory, Jacky. Or perhaps just some good news. Something of inestimable benefit to Great Britain. Something to take the minds of the people away from shortages and rising prices and queues at the food shops, and the casualty lists from the Western Front – '

'And from the Dardanelles?'

From Gallipoli the news continued to be very bad. The possibility of a withdrawal of the troops and ships was much on the minds of both Fisher and Churchill; the effect of this on morale could be devastating. So many hopes had been pinned upon a swift blow at Turkey and a push through to the Kaiser's southern flank, the overwhelming of Austria already under Russian attack, the end of neutrality for Greece, Rumania and Bulgaria and their entry into the Entente . . . so many thousands of men had died, so many valuable ships lost. For the moment public opinion remained largely uninformed of the scale of what was approaching a disaster for British and Commonwealth arms, but the truth could not be held forever.

Something, as Winston had said, was needed. Currently, it was not hard to make a guess at what.

Fisher pondered; but did not put the question. He believed that a hint had been dropped. He excused himself from the First Lord, going back to his own room, where he sat at his desk with his head in his hands, still pondering.

During the afternoon, Lord Fisher received a report. There was U-boat activity north-west of the Fastnet; and the sailing of a cruiser from Devonport had been delayed and another cruiser, on patrol in the North Atlantic, had been steaming into danger on her then current course, which would have taken her across the tracks of other U-boats. Thus she had been diverted. Fisher was aware of the reasons for this: neither of those old cruisers was safe against U-boat attack without a destroyer escort. It would be possible, prudent perhaps, to order out a flotilla to steam to their assistance.

But there was a shortage of destroyers.

And the *Laurentia*?

The *Bristol* was as liable to be attacked as the other cruisers. She, too, was old. Coming in with her charge under escort, she too would cross at least one of the U-boat tracks. And attacked she would be – a legitimate target of the war, which the *Laurentia* was not. Fisher had never really believed the *Laurentia* would be attacked – all those women and children, so many Americans. An act of lunacy. The German High Command was not composed of lunatics. And the *Laurentia* carried the forthcoming Ambassador of the United States of America to the Court of St James.

On that point Fisher's thoughts ran parallel with those of President Wilson.

Ten minutes later the First Sea Lord had reached a decision: it was absolutely proper to recall the *Bristol*, with fresh orders to steam to the south until she was well clear of the U-boat areas and then alter for Portsmouth dockyard.

Fisher took up his telephone.

At 2050 a wireless message was received aboard the *Laurentia* from the naval base in Queenstown. This message baldly indicated a sighting of a U-boat proceeding westerly from the south Irish coast. Pacey, about to eat the dinner brought up by Steward Mullins, went from the chart room to the open bridge. He spoke to the First Officer.

'Submarine off the Fastnet, Mr Main. I shall reduce speed to fifteen knots, so as to approach the coast during the night.'

'Aye, aye, sir – '

'And alter course. . . .' Pacey went to the binnacle and studied the compass for a moment. 'To south-east by east, Mr Main. That should keep us around twenty-five miles clear of danger.'

'Alter now, sir?'

Pacey nodded. Main passed the new course to the quartermaster then went into the wheelhouse to pass the reduced revolutions to the engine room. Pacey sent for the Chief Officer and Staff Captain: there were extra precautions to be taken now.

'Beg pardon, madam.' Lady Barlow's bedroom steward had knocked and been bidden to enter.

'What is it, Cardew?'

'Black out your ports, madam.'

'Whatever for? I like them *open*. I am not accustomed to stuffiness!'

'Chief Officer's orders, madam – '

'Really. And 'oo does he think he is may I ask?' Lady Barlow's face had reddened.

'Couldn't say, madam.'

'I've told you before how I should be addressed.'

'Sorry, Your Ladyship.'

'That's better.' Lady Barlow watched the steward closing the ports and screwing down the deadlights. 'Leave those portholes open – I *told* you!'

'Sorry, Your Ladyship. Like I said, orders.'

'I shall report this to the Captain!'

'Very good, Your Ladyship. But if I was you, I wouldn't open the ports again. Do that, and you'll be charged with endangering the safety of the ship, soon as we get to Liverpool.'

'What blasted impertinence!' Lady Barlow hooted. Cardew left the cabin, shrugging. Outside he met the assistant second steward, and made a reference to a bleeding old cow. The assistant second steward grinned understandingly. Liners carried a lot of bleeding old cows from time to time but they always got their come-uppance in the end. They had to obey essential orders the same as anyone else aboard. This time, another unwelcome order was to be passed: no smoking on the open decks after dark. Other orders concerned the crew only: on the bridge and elsewhere, the lookouts had been doubled; the watertight bulkheads and doors had been shut where closure did not interfere with the essential work of the various departments; the lifeboats had been stripped of their griping bands and canvas covers; and the equipment and provisions – oars, stretchers, bottom-boards, boat's compasses, flares, axes, survival rations, water barricoes – had been checked once again. Then the boats had been swung out from their stowages on the boat deck and were hanging on the falls from the davit-heads.

The passengers could scarcely fail to see these preparations.

The tension was back with the liner now; there was a feeling of foreboding. There was now so little sea yet to cover. The Germans' chance was coming up fast, every turn of the great screws carrying them all right into the danger zone, the unavoidable danger zone around the British Isles.

On the starting platform below in the engine room Chief Engineer Hackett took the reports as they came in. There was still a problem with the low pressure turbines, still a potential fault in the valves. As Hackett had told Pacey earlier in the voyage, a sudden call for full astern could lead to a steam feedback. And as they neared the U-boat zone, full astern – emergency full astern from full ahead – might very well be called for.

If the valve should pack up then . . . but it just hadn't got to! Hackett gritted his teeth and went along for another personal inspection. He was feeling the weight of responsibility as much as was Pacey. Pacey might – would, of course – do his best on the bridge, but the ship could still fail on its engines . . . just like in the sailing days that the deck officers talked so much about, any ship could fail on its motive power, and a broken-down or shaky engine would have the same effect as a dismasting: *kaput*, as the Jerries would say. Often Hackett thought of himself and his black gang as a set of sails: when the bridge pulled, they were hauled round as if at the busy end of a rope . . .

Sister Perpetua, on one of her walks around the deck before dinner, saw the preparation of the lifeboats. The seamen seemed very busy; she wanted to ask questions, to ask for reassurance, but she didn't like to. As it happened, reassurance was at hand: a great batlike figure came along the deck, oozing goodwill.

The Reverend Jesse Divine.

'Good evening, Sister, hullo there.'

'Good evening, Father.'

He allowed the solecism to pass; after all, they all worshipped the same God and the nun, no doubt, spoke from force of habit, an unuttered joke that tickled the Reverend Divine and he chuckled to himself, and then apologized because he might have seemed rude.

'It's quite all right,' Sister Perpetua said. Then she plunged. 'I wonder what's going on? The lifeboats, you know?'

'Just an exercise, I guess. Nothing to get scared about.'

'You don't think so?' She was obviously very anxious.

'I'm sure so, Sister. We're in good hands anyway.'

'But that warship! The fact that it's gone – '

'A good sign, a sign that we're going to be OK or it would have stayed.'

'Well, there is that, yes, Father – '

'And it's not just that. And it's not just the Captain, who I reckon to be a very dependable guy. We're *always* in safe hands, as you know as well as I do, and I reckon God's on the British side.' The Reverend Divine laid a hand gently on Sister Perpetua's black-clad shoulder. 'But it'd do no harm to ask Him to keep a special eye open, just tonight and tomorrow – you and I, Sister, on behalf of all on board?'

She nodded. The Reverend Divine made a courteous gesture as much as to say 'After you'; she got down on her knees on the deck, resting her elbows on a lifebelt stowage, and was joined by the cleric. Church of Rome and Protestant Church of Nashville, Tennessee prayed together devoutly, united in a time of possible trouble.

From a nearby set of davits, Bosun MacFarlane watched them. He spoke *sotto voce* to the leading hand in charge of the lifeboat. 'Gives you the creeps . . . at a time like this. Just as if they believe we're going to be sunk. Like an omen.'

Parsons and corpses – always bad luck for a ship at sea. Now they had a nun as well. Two big blackbirds. *Four-and-twenty blackbirds, baked in a pie.* A torpedoed ship could be quite like a pie, baking in the searing heat of an internal explosion.

The prisoners – the two Germans with Big Jake Ommaney, Craigson and Frederick Jones – had been returned to the cell accommodation after the *Bristol* had been identified as friendly. Mr Jones had not particularly enjoyed his brief period of being out of his cell's constriction and in the fresh air of the open deck. He had felt very conspicuous, an object of fear and loathing, a man who had killed twice, a wife followed by a master-at-arms. Though he felt this, he had felt little else for some while now; his senses were dulled and he was largely apathetic. He was facing death by hanging after the due processes of the law; that was now quite certain, beyond all doubt. It would be better to die from a German torpedo. That would be faster than waiting for the law to move and pronounce, to wear the black cap and utter the doomful words about being hanged by the neck until he was dead, in some place of execution to which he would be taken.

Better for his old mother, too, now waiting for him to arrive and comfort her for what remained of her life. The shock would be immense, of course, whatever way he was to die, but it would obviously be preferable for her to know that he had died a manly death from enemy attack rather than have had his neck broken by a hangman's knot and his body cast in ignominy into a pit of quicklime as he believed happened to murderers.

Mr Jones was by now desperately sorry for what he had done, for what he had brought upon his old mother in the home in Walthamstow. Back now in his cell, he put his head in his hands and wept. He wept for his old mother, he wept for happy childhood days long past, he wept for what he had done though he still did not weep for Maggie. Maggie had brought him to all this by being murdered. But of course he ought to have charitable thoughts towards even Maggie. An uphill task; he needed help. It was not too late to try to make amends – or anyway, if not amends, then he could confess and obtain forgiveness perhaps. God's mercy was infinite – he'd heard that somewhere, probably in church.

He got up from the plank bunk and banged on the door of the cell. No one came and he banged and banged again, and called out loudly.

'For Christ's sake shut up!' Big Jake Ommaney yelled from behind his bars. 'Bloody pommie bastard.'

Someone came: the seaman on sentry duty, who had been outside in the flat taking final orders from the Chief Officer in regard to the safety of his charges in the event of an emergency. 'What is it?'

'I want a priest.'

'Priest?'

'Clergyman. Any religion'll do. You can't refuse me that. It's my right.' Mr Jones added, 'I've seen clergymen on board. There's one . . . a big man, with a black cloak. I want to talk to him . . . before it's too late.'

Leon Fielding, like Sister Perpetua, had been very worried about the preparing of the lifeboats, the rattle and clank of which activities he had heard banging through to his cabin. Also about the closing of the deadlights, big, round steel plates that had thudded into place when activated by his steward and had been clamped down hard with very big butterfly bolts. It gave the cabin the feel of prison, a foretaste perhaps of what lay in store for him when he was mendaciously charged with his alleged offence in a court of law. But first there were the U-boats, standing between him and whatever lay ahead.

He questioned Elmer Pousty, who told him what the bangs and crashes were due to.

'Oh, for our safety?'

'Why, yes, I guess – '

'Oh, that's good. What a relief!'

'What did you think they were, Mr Fielding?'

'I don't know. I think I thought it might be the Germans. But I really don't know. Everything's been such a worry, you've no idea.'

Elmer Pousty sat forward and said earnestly, 'Yes, I have, Mr Fielding. I really have. I understand very well. And I'm wondering if it might help you to talk.'

'We've talked quite a lot, Mr Pousty.'

'Yes, sure we have, but not – ' Pousty broke off, then laid a hand on Fielding's shoulder. 'Look. I'm a Quaker, as you know.'

'Yes – '

'Well, now, I mean *talk* – like we talk, from the inside, freely. You know what I'm getting at?'

'Er – no, I'm afraid I – '

'Then I'll tell you. When we meet, which might be in a meeting house or might be in a private house, a friend's house, we sit and wait for God to talk to us. Or rather – put it this way – we wait till God moves *us* to talk. Him through us. Until that happens, we sit in silence – '

'Just waiting?'

'That's right. Then one of our number gets to his or her feet and starts talking.'

Fielding looked blank. 'What about? I confess I've heard that Quakers – I've often wondered – '

'There's no mystery about it, Mr Fielding, none at all. We utter what God has put into our minds to utter, that's all. I have to admit, it isn't always sense – not God's fault, the fault of the human psyche that hasn't quite latched onto God's purpose at that particular moment. No one ever casts blame. But the fact of speech acts like, well, like a catharsis maybe.' Elmer Pousty paused. 'I reckon it might kind of do you good. Clear your mind, Mr Fielding. If you get me.'

'You mean *us*, now at this moment? That we should seek for God to talk through us? To me?'

'Sure, why not?' Pousty seemed very sincere.

'Yes . . . yes, perhaps.' Fielding's lips trembled; he looked to be on the verge of tears. 'But suppose . . . suppose God moves *you* to speak, rather than me? What then?'

'No problem. He would be sure to move me to say something that would help *you*, Mr Fielding.'

'You're sure?'

'Dead certain. That's if He does move us. It doesn't always happen.'

'I see. And Ming?'

'Ming?'

'Suppose God moved Ming . . . oh, no. Of course He wouldn't, would he?'

'Not very likely. Anyway – Ming's not here. Ming's safe in New York.'

'Yes. Oh, very well, then. What do I do?'

'Just sit, that's all. Compose your mind. Preferably, think blank. Give God His opening.'

U-120 was once again submerged, lying with her motors stopped. Whilst on the surface at the start of the dark hours, charging her batteries, a wireless signal had been received from the submarine command in Wilhelmshavn. This signal, transmitted in the German naval cypher, had when broken down into plain language indicated the last known position of the *Laurentia* and her current course. This position and course had been entered on Eppler's chart and he found he was very nicely placed for the carrying out of an attack. A small adjustment was all that was necessary; and this having by now been made, U-120 was lying almost motionless, almost in her ultimate firing position, some twenty miles to the south of the Old Head of Kinsale, around forty miles from Queenstown, with the Fastnet Rock bearing a little north of west. The *Laurentia* would not come within range until early the next afternoon assuming she maintained her reported course and speed; but already the torpedoes had been loaded into the tubes and the U-boat's crew were in all respects ready.

20

On the bridge, Captain Pacey had ordered the ship to steer a zig-zag pattern as his only possible defence against a torpedo attack. This course he took on his own initiative; no orders one way or the other had ever been received from the Admiralty. He would have expected, after that German warning in the New York press, some directives from the naval authorities as his command came closer – if not before. But there had been nothing.

The zig-zag was not maintained for long. As the light faded the Officer of the Watch reported a heavy fog bank ahead. The wind had dropped for some while past, but what little was left was warm. In the circumstances fog was not entirely unexpected.

'Cease zig-zag,' Pacey said. 'Resume course as before.'

'Resume course, sir,' First Officer Main repeated. 'Speed, sir?'

'Reduce to ten knots, Mr Main, and warn the engine room.'

Main spoke on the voice-pipe to Chief Engineer Hackett, now, like the Captain, continuously at his action station on the starting platform. Sudden alterations to the engines might be necessary. Hackett understood only too well, and thought again about his low pressure turbine. If a ship was sighted close, the bridge might want full astern very suddenly. Fog was one of the hazards of the sea; the Germans were not the only enemy.

Away above Hackett's head, the steam siren was now in action, blasting out its fog warning of a vessel having way upon her: every two minutes, a prolonged blast lasting six seconds. It was a mournful sound, doom-laden in present circumstances.

The fog signal had had its effect on the passengers; or some of them, those who had not bothered to read the notices in their cabins and elsewhere around the ship. These notices gave a clear indication of what constituted the alarm signal for boat stations and what constituted the fog signal as laid down by the Board of Trade. There was a difference between the two.

Alva Lundkvist had run from her cabin in fright, clutching little Olof along with both their lifejackets. Many passengers were doing the same, some of them already in their night attire. At the foot of one of the companionways stood a woman member of the ship's crew, a woman with apparently no teeth and, as a result, very sunken cheeks for her age.

Now, Miss Greatorex was doing excellent work. She called out, 'Ladies and gentlemen, please! This is no alarm. The ship is in fog, that's all. The steam whistle has to be sounded in fog.'

'We might have been told,' someone said. Alva Lundkvist, peering, recognized the actress, Livia Costello. 'Doesn't anyone get told a darn thing aboard this bloody ship?'

'I'm very sorry, Mrs Costello,' Miss Greatorex enunciated, but not very clearly. 'If you read the notice – '

'To hell with the notice. There's too goddam many notices. When's the damn thing going to stop, can you tell me that?'

'When the fog clears,' Miss Greatorex said, a little saliva drooling down her chin. Inwardly, she was still cursing Earl MacRae and his attempt upon her virtue, more especially the underhand methods he had used in trying to weaken her resistance. Meanwhile the passengers were moving away, their fears calmed. All except Livia Costello. With her recent experiences in mind, and knowing how ill she had felt and was still feeling, Miss Greatorex did her best with an obviously inebriated woman passenger.

'Oh, Mrs Costello . . . you don't seem very well – '

'I'm fine. What's it to do with you anyway?'

'I just thought . . . why not let me take you back to your cabin?'

'You go to hell. I'm okay.' Livia was swaying all over the place, cannoning off bulkheads as she moved along the alleyway with Miss Greatorex in rear like a sheepdog. Miss Greatorex uttered little disapproving clicks of her tongue: this was disgraceful, though not entirely unique among transatlantic voyagers.

The actress stopped and swung round groggily. 'For Jeez' sake,' she said, 'stop that bloody clicking. Like a goddam old mother hen. Go and get yourself a man, why not? Do you a world of good, you know that?'

Miss Greatorex flushed scarlet, drawing herself up. Then she said something she immediately regretted for its retailing would get her her dismissal from the PanAtlantic Line. She said before she could bite back the words, 'Really! Well, you should know, I imagine. What you've been up to with Mr Matthews – '

She stopped very suddenly. Livia Costello, her face like vinegar, lashed out with the back of a hand and took Miss Greatorex hard across her mouth where her teeth were not. The gums hurt most horribly and there was a little blood. Miss Greatorex turned and fled along the corridor.

Leon Fielding had not heard the steam whistle's roar; he seemed to be

255

in some sort of trance. Elmer Pousty interpreted the steam whistle's message to himself; no need to disturb Mr Fielding's concentration, if that was what it was, on the word, yet to come, of God.

Thus far the two had sat in total silence, waiting. One had often to wait a long time, but usually someone broke the silence before too long. Not this time. Elmer Pousty, growing cramped, had glanced many times at his watch. One hour passed, then two. Maybe God had nothing to say.

Then, suddenly and rather horrifyingly, Fielding stirred and uttered. With an astonishingly youthful movement, he almost leapt to his feet and began uttering sounds. The sounds were not, as might have been expected considering his personal worries, to do with the charge hanging over his head. The sounds were of – *barking*. Short, sharp yaps, like a Pekinese dog.

Ming had come through. Like a seance.

It was now a case for Dr Fellowes.

Not liking to leave the singer in his current state, Pousty pressed the bell-push for the bedroom steward, or maybe at this hour the night steward would answer.

'Mr Divine, a moment, if you please.'

The Reverend Divine turned and faced Staff Captain Morgan, who until now had had no opportunity of following up Jones's request for a priest. 'Why, yes, sir, at your service. What can I do for you?'

'Not for me. For the man Jones, in cells – '

'The man who killed . . . or is said to have killed?'

'Yes,' Morgan said, and explained. The Reverend Divine acceded immediately: he would be only too pleased to help a soul in distress. With Morgan he went below to the cells, and was admitted to that of Frederick Jones. Vulgar comments came from the cell occupied by Big Jake Ommaney. The two Germans got to their feet and looked through their bars, interestedly.

'Now, Mr Jones, how may I help you?'

'Pardon?' Jones seemed distrait, listless, not really paying attention. The Reverend Divine repeated what he had said. He would, he said, do anything he could to help.

'Even after what I've done?'

'The more so,' the Reverend Divine said promptly, 'because of what you've . . . what you're said to have done, Mr Jones. God's mercy – '

'Oh, I did it all right. Both times. What's the point in denying it now?'

'Well . . .'

'I want to confess, don't you see? I want to ask God for forgiveness.'

The Reverend Divine inclined his head and pulled his black garment

256

closer around his body. The cell was cold and dank, very close no doubt to the sea. He said gravely, 'God's mercy is infinite.'

'Pardon?'

'He listens to everyone and – '

'Sinners?' Mr Jones enquired anxiously.

'Sinners, yes. More especially sinners, so long as they're repentant. There is greater joy in Heaven over one sinner who – '

'Yes, I have heard that. That's really why I make so bold as to ask. Does He forgive murder?'

The Reverend Divine gave a cough into a large hand. 'I believe so, yes. So long as there is genuine repentance.'

'That's the trouble,' Mr Jones said hollowly. 'I'm not too sure . . . oh, I do honestly repent – what I did to that sailor. The master-at-arms, I think. I really am very sorry indeed. It was – inexcusable.'

'But not necessarily unforgiveable,' the Reverend Divine said gently.

'Well, I'm glad to hear that, but then, you see, there's Maggie. My wife.'

'Yes, I see.' The Reverend Divine had been given the outline of that by the Staff Captain, and had indeed picked up talk earlier, though he didn't know all the details any more than anyone else aboard.

'I want to talk about that.'

'Ah yes. To me?'

'Yes.' For a while Jones said no more; just sat there on his plank bed while the Reverend Divine waited patiently and listened to the mournful sound of the steam whistle, which seemed to make the ship reverberate even as far down below as this. He found it a horrible sound, somewhat akin to the tolling of a funeral bell. As the steam whistle continued, Mr Jones began. Still using that hollow tone, he told the Reverend Divine the full details. What Maggie had been like, lovers and all, and her cruel remark about his old mother in Walthamstow that had been the final straw that had driven Mr Jones to wife murder, an appalling crime. 'I admit it's appalling,' he said, 'but I was beside myself. Desperate.' He went on to describe the trip upstate in the hired car belonging to a friend, and he described the visit to his sister-in-law and then what followed on the way home to New York. The axe, the blow to the back of the head, the dismemberment, the hasty interment, the leg that had got away, the general destruction of other evidence. He spoke also of the teeth that had been concealed in bread pellets cast to the seagulls.

'I've been in a very bad state,' he said. 'Scared out of my wits, to tell you the truth.'

'And now you're sorry?'

'No.'

The Reverend Divine raised his beetling eyebrows. 'Not repentant? I thought – '

'Not about Maggie. I'm sorry I'm going to hang, of course, you'll understand that, I know, but I'm not sorry about Maggie and it's no use pretending I am. I've said I'm sorry about the man and I meant that. Very sorry.'

'Yes.' The Reverend Divine brought a big coloured handkerchief from a pocket beneath the cloak and mopped at his forehead, which had begun to sweat in spite of the cold dankness of the cell. This was a poser. Carefully he said, 'Well now, Mr Jones, the Almighty isn't likely to accept a half-repentance. Not so far as I know.' He corrected this since it hadn't sounded quite right. 'Indeed I am quite certain not. Also, the repentance must be genuine. Nothing is ever hidden from God. You cannot pretend.'

'No, I see that.'

'Well, then!'

Mr Jones shook his head dolefully. 'I thought perhaps some kind of compromise.'

'There is no compromising with God, Mr Jones. It is all or nothing.'

'I didn't mean that. I do see what you're driving at. But I thought I might ask God for forgiveness about that sailor, and then we'd see. If you follow?'

'No, not really. . . .'

'Well, can I put it this way.' Mr Jones sat forward earnestly, his gaze fixed firmly on the clergyman's face, which it had not been until now. 'If you were, say, to – to shrive me on the other murder, the one I'm truly sorry about . . . and then ask God to intercede on the other. On Maggie.' He stopped.

'You mean – '

'What I mean is, you and I could ask God to put repentance into my mind. Then with His help I would repent. Would that suit?'

'Having thus repented, you would then go further and ask forgiveness, am I right?'

'Dead right,' Mr Jones said, looking relieved at being fully understood at last. 'How about that?'

'It's an interesting point of theology,' the Reverend Divine said, 'and yes, it might work. It might work. We shall make the attempt.' Inside himself the Reverend Divine was sceptical; God might see this for what it was, a ploy and in a sense a subterfuge, but Mr Jones's need was all too obvious and one had to consider the sinners whilst still upon earth which this one might not be for all that much longer.

By this time the families both sides of the Atlantic were preparing for the

258

longed-for news that their voyagers aboard the *Laurentia* had landed safely in Liverpool. There had been increasing anxiety as the days went by and the liner came closer to home. The newspapers had had a lot to say. The *New York Times* had been full of gossip about the important and/or rich personages such as Henry Sayers Grant and Senator Manderton and Lady Barlow and others. There had been minor mention of Livia Costello. In Nashville, Tennessee there had been a couple of columns about the pastor and his travels, his stoutheartedness in venturing out upon war-torn waters in the name of the Lord. There had been much continuing speculation about whether or not the Germans would carry out in actual practice that veiled threat. The general opinion in the bars and in the streets and in Washington was still that they would not. So, the families apart, there was little real, pressing concern.

A cable had reached Annapolis from the *Laurentia*: Elizabeth Kent to Jonas Gorman, passing on the news that her father had died. A surge of mixed feelings passed through Jonas Gorman on receipt of the cable: he was sorry and he was glad. It was sad news sure enough but it did, or should, mean that Elizabeth's return to the United States could be relied upon, and fairly quickly too, once her father's affairs had been settled. Jonas Gorman, before going to work in the attorney's office, dropped by at his local church, knelt in a pew and prayed. He prayed that all would go well with the remaining stages of the *Laurentia*'s voyage. Elizabeth Kent, soon surely to become Elizabeth Gorman, meant all the world to him. He told God this.

In London *The Times* and the *Morning Post* had also made mention of the German threat and in Britain there was more anxiety, in fact, than in America. The British had by this time lived with the war for around ten weary months and everyone was aware that a number of merchant ships had been sunk off the British coasts. There was no escaping that, any more than one could escape the terrible casualty lists from the Western Front and the Dardanelles. So many families had lost their men: husbands, sons, brothers who had gone off to war singing 'Tipperary' and so on, full of fight and enthusiasm, unable to wait to strike a resounding blow at the Boche. Back on leave, much of the first flush of gaiety had gone. The menfolk were showing strain, they had lost their peacetime weight in many cases, they were bitter about the generals and their bombastic ineptitude, scathing about the news reports that kept on saying everything in the garden was fine when they had seen the slaughter for themselves and heard the continuing thunder of the guns in the artillery bombardments from both sides, seen the water-filled shell-holes in the Flanders mud, watched their comrades hanging dead or screaming wounded on the barbed wire.

The war was very much with the thinking part of the civilian population and there was much less confidence than in America about the *Laurentia*'s safety. Nevertheless, hope in most cases overrode fear. As always, it would never happen to them.

One of the hopefuls was John Holmes's grandmother, waiting in the comfort of her home in Worthing in Sussex; once again, scanning the newspapers through her magnifying glass, Mrs Holmes read about some of the passengers who would be disembarking on the Saturday. There was a lot about Henry Sayers Grant, about to take over as the US Ambassador; there was a certain amount about a man named Patrick Haggerty, coming to Britain for financial discussions with Mr Asquith and the Chancellor of the Exchequer. There was speculation that he might be invited to Buckingham Palace to meet Their Majesties the King and Queen, and perhaps the Prince of Wales if he were not with his regiment, the Welsh Guards, at the Front. Such a dear boy, His Royal Highness . . . always with a smile and a joke, so it was said, and so keen to do his duty and fight when really as heir to the throne he had no need to – was probably, in fact, old Mrs Holmes thought, rather a nuisance to the generals responsible for his safety. But he would go, and of course all honour to him, as to his brother Prince Albert, serving as a young naval officer with the British Grand Fleet.

The country was so fortunate in its royal family, even if they were related by blood to the monstrous Kaiser. Old Mrs Holmes was old enough to remember that dear Queen Victoria had never liked the Kaiser even though he was her grandson, and neither of course had dear King Edward the Seventh . . .

Mrs Holmes read on. There was a Lady Barlow aboard with her son Mr Eustace Barlow. Lady Barlow, the *Morning Post* said, was the widow of a certain Sir Albert Barlow who had been of great service to the British troops fighting in the Boer War, making certain that food supplies were maintained . . . Mrs Holmes, who had a certain shrewdness, made a guess that Sir Albert's efforts had not been unprofitable to himself. She had had a nephew who had served in the Boer War, in the Duke of Wellington's Regiment, and he had spoken very sharply about the profiteers, of whom there would be plenty more in this war no doubt.

The papers read, Mrs Holmes rang for Milly, who entered with wispy hair escaping from beneath her cap.

'You rang'm?'

'Oh, Milly. Is everything ready for Master John?'

'Yes'm. Nearly at any rate.'

'Good.' It was a nice fine day and Mrs Holmes felt like some fresh air, to be taken along the sea front. But not until the afternoon, when a band would be playing in the bandstand near the pier. 'The chair after luncheon, Milly. We shall listen to the band . . . then perhaps afternoon tea at Hubbard's.'

'Yes'm.' Milly sounded tired, and looked it. Her life was all work, up at six in the morning, to bed around ten pm, one half day off a week, when she visited her sister in Broadwater. And Hubbard's store in South Street, via the bandstand, was a long way from St Botolph's Road. But Milly was used to it; she had a stout heart and stout feet and old Mrs Holmes was a good mistress on the whole. She would cope; she knew Mrs Holmes was worried about Master John, and so indeed was she. The outing, the military band and the afternoon tea would be good for them both and Milly would push, heave the heavy bath chair up and down the kerbs of the pavements and across the roads to the prom as she, but never Mrs Holmes, called the sea front.

General de Gard was on deck as that evening the fog came down. With Adeline Scott-Mason he stood on the boat deck, looking for'ard, one hand thrust into the front of his heavy greatcoat, rather like – Adeline thought with amusement – Napoleon Bonaparte must have looked so long ago when gazing out across the English Channel from the coast of France towards England. The White Cliffs, probably. François seemed not to have cast off his fancy-dress role; there was a new set to his chin. But Adeline had observed a number of non-military aspects about François over the past few days: he was much concerned with his appearance and he liked his creature comforts and he liked his wine. And his women, of course. She wondered how he was going to like facing the German Army. Paris, and perhaps the front line, was going to be a very different proposition from New York and Washington and receptions at the White House. She was about to needle him a little on this when he turned from his Napoleonic stance and took her hands in his. 'It is cold, *chérie*. The fog, it gets into the throat. And the sound of the siren, it is so depressing. We shall go below, yes?'

'All right,' she agreed. They went below, though not directly to de Gard's state-room. Some discretion had yet to be maintained. Descending from the cold of the boat deck, François de Gard thought to himself that it would be very much colder in an open lifeboat if the worst should unfortunately happen. He had provided against this; his greatcoat, which he would be wearing beneath his cork lifejacket, had capacious pockets with flaps. In these pockets would be flasks of brandy to keep the cold out. His chief worry was that he might be forced to share these with others. It was unlikely, he knew, that the British would provide even a French general with his own boat in an emergency. The British, he sometimes thought, were too democratic by half . . . it should have been axiomatic that a general was of inestimably more use to the war than so many of the *Laurentia*'s other passengers. The Barlow woman for one, and her son, and that seedy actress, and the dangerous lunatic with the perambulator who had interfered with the young boy. With General de Gard's brandy would go also his copious reports on affairs of state in Washington. President Poincaré would be regarding these as of the utmost importance. Really, the British ought to recognize that.

Dr Fellowes had attended in answer to Elmer Pousty's call. Now he was impatient: there was nothing wrong with Mr Fielding so far as he could see.

'What was the trouble?' he asked.

'Oh, nothing,' the singer said. 'I was perhaps a little upset, don't you know. Nothing more. I'm terribly sorry you've been bothered, Dr Fellowes.'

Dr Fellowes clicked his tongue, and addressed Pousty. 'There was talk of him – '

'Yes, sure,' Pousty broke in quickly. He didn't wish to upset Fielding further. 'It's – it's stopped. Just after I sent the message to you.'

'I see. Well – ' Dr Fellowes went through his routines, a mere precaution: thermometer, pulse, eyelids pulled down, mouth open and throat peered down. Dr Fellowes pursed his lips, frowned, shook his head. 'What brought it on, Mr Pousty?' He was now disregarding Fielding except as a kind of tiresome specimen, something mindless.

Pousty did his best to explain. He spoke of an inward light.

'A light?' Dr Fellowes looked puzzled. 'Shining – from where precisely? A look in the eyes, d'you mean?'

'No.' Pousty explained that he was a Quaker and had been trying to help as was his duty. He referred to George Fox, as a result of whose preaching the Society of Friends had been formed. Fox had taught that there was a direct divine revelation given to every man and that, therefore, religion was primarily a matter of individual conviction and experience and that –

'Yes, yes,' Dr Fellowes interrupted after a while. 'And the *light*?'

Pousty said, 'George Fox called the divine revelation an inward light, Doctor. I – '

'Yes, I see. And there was a light, was there?'

'No. It didn't seem to come through.'

'Just the barking?'

'Yes, that's right.'

'I wonder why.'

Pousty gestured towards the empty perambulator in the corner of the cabin.

'H'm? Oh – yes, I see. Of course! That damn dog.' Fellowes emitted a breath of impatience. 'Just a brief mental aberration and it's gone now. All gone. I doubt if you'll have any further trouble, Mr Pousty, and I'll say goodnight.'

Fellowes departed, his stethoscope dangling round his neck. From his seated position on his bunk Leon Fielding said, 'Oh dear. It was so kind of you to bother, Mr Pousty. I do appreciate that.'

'It was nothing. Tell me, Mr Fielding: do you feel any better?'

'Oh, I was never ill really.'

'I mean in your mind? Any easier?'

Fielding thought for a moment, than said, with a look of some astonishment on his face, 'Yes, I really do think I do. It's quite surprising.'

It was more than surprising, Elmer Pousty thought, it's a real, honest-to-God, genuine miracle considering that Fielding's sole apparent reaction had been to bark.

That night, the lights burned late in the White House. Reports were brought at intervals to President Wilson, sitting in his study with its law-book-lined walls and his massive desk. These reports concerned the hour by hour position at sea of the *Laurentia*.

So very little farther now to go. Wilson prayed for word of a safe arrival. The moment that came through, he would be a happy man. His stand would have been vindicated, his belief that the German Emperor was a man of principle who would not stoop to the murder of civilians would be justified before the American people.

And one day they would thank him for keeping their great country out of the war, for preserving the breadwinners, the fathers, brothers and sons who wished nothing more than to carry on with their lives in the peace that was every American citizen's birthright since the English had been thrown out in the War of Independence. And afterwards, America would pick up the pieces of both the shattered sides, and continue in prosperity to lead the councils of the world.

In place of Britain? Wilson tended to shy away from that thought. It smacked of opportunism, of self-interest, of envy almost. Also, he did have those friendly feelings towards the British. It was just that he could not with a clear conscience go farther than that, could never commit America to anything more than the provision of goods of various kinds. He had turned a blind eye to certain arms shipments from time to time; he would stop at that.

The *Laurentia* carried arms. He knew that.

There were other reports coming through that night: the hardening opinions within Congress, the comments in the press, much of it far from pleasant reading to the President. There were, it was true, warmongers in the United States who would work against him. . . .

Wilson looked up at the clock: 2 am. He was very tired; bed beckoned. Just thirty-six hours left, by which time the *Laurentia* should have entered the Mersey River, safe from all German attack.

President Wilson went up the great curved staircase, slowly, his brow furrowed. Beside his bed he got down on his knees and spoke to God, prayers from a soul in agony, asking for a safe arrival for a great ship. There was nothing more any person could do now. Apart from the Germans.

21

THE fog spread eastwards of the *Laurentia*'s position, covering the waters between the inward-bound liner and the Fastnet. Lying submerged off the Old Head of Kinsale, totally undetected by the British, U-120 was also covered by the fog but this *Kapitanleutnant* Eppler did not as yet know. The presence of the fog was worrying to Admiral Hood in Queenstown. It would not be possible to send out escort vessels even if the order came at the last moment from Lord Fisher so to do.

On the other hand, the fog would impede the German submarines. Surfacing only to find the area blanketed in fog, they would doubtless submerge again to below periscope depth.

But after dark the following day the fog began to thin in the vicinity of the *Laurentia*'s homeward track.

That night, destined to be the last, there was an impromptu sing-song in the first-class smoking room. It was brought about by Henry Sayers Grant, a very human man who knew that spirits needed raising again. The passengers had by this time mostly done their packing in preparation for Saturday's disembarkation and they had nothing to do but sit about and think, and worry. Grant was assisted enthusiastically by the Reverend Divine and, oddly perhaps, by Sister Perpetua.

'A funny feeling in the ship, Sister,' the Reverend Divine had said.

'Yes. I've noticed it. It's hard to describe, but – '

'A holding of the breath, Sister.'

'Yes,' she said. 'That's it, I guess. Waiting for – something to happen.'

'We'll shake them out of it. Get them to let their hair down.'

They did, more or less. It was not like the third class: nothing crude, and no broken glass. The smoking room was well attended, and overflowed the doors. Senator Manderton was there with Patrick Haggerty; John Holmes went along with Elizabeth Kent. Mr and Mrs Rickards were present. The Descartes children had been put to bed but their parents attended. Alva Lundkvist was not there; little Olof was sickly again and needed her. Leon Fielding was still too embarrassed to show his face in public more than he had to and Elmer Pousty stayed with him in his cabin, where Fielding occupied much of his time pushing Ming's perambulator backwards and forwards, but did not bark again. Pousty had not suggested another session of waiting for the divine light. Purser Matthews in his mess dress went along with his assistant Harry Anneston and Staff Captain Morgan hovered, keeping an eye open. Although the nightwatchmen had been given orders to watch the gate that barred off the third class, and the master-at-arms was constantly patrolling, there could be trouble from the more boisterous spirits below when the sounds of song penetrated. Any fracas tonight would be nipped in the bud before it had a chance to get properly under way.

Henry Sayers Grant started the ball rolling. He had a good, tuneful voice. The Reverend Divine joined in. They started off with some catchy melodies from 'The Belle of New York', then went on to some of the songs that had come from Broadway in the weeks before the *Laurentia* had sailed. After that the nostalgic favourites from both sides of the Atlantic. Old songs mainly: 'Carry Me Back To Old Virginia', 'Marching Through Georgia', 'Yankee Doodle Dandy' . . . 'Nut Brown Maiden', 'The Bluebells of Scotland', 'The Rose of Tralee' and a number of other Scots and Irish songs that were as germaine to America as to Britain. 'When Irish Eyes Are Smiling', 'Loch Lomond', some of Harry Lauder's songs. And the ones from the war: 'Tipperary' of course, and back to the South African War – 'Soldiers of the Queen' for one, and 'Goodbye Dolly Gray'.

On the fringe of the crowd, the Rickardses sang quietly. When it came to 'Soldiers of the Queen' Mrs Rickards was aware of the way her husband's shoulders straightened and his voice grew louder as he joined in with a good deal of emotion. His war, and a grand bunch of men from all over the Empire. So many memories. Then someone started a song from a little farther back: 'We Don't Want To Fight'.

Rickards sang the loudest of all, a fire in his eyes.

We don't want to fight but by jingo if we do
We've got the ships, we've got the men, we've got the money too. . . .

There was a glint of tears in his eyes. Gently his wife put her hand in his. He squeezed it hard and held her close and never mind who saw. His younger days were coming back: when he had first been commissioned from the Royal Military Academy at Woolwich they had still been singing 'The Girl I Left Behind Me' and 'My Old Shako'. Now, those tunes had been forgotten . . . as Rickards, holding his wife's hand, sang on there was a voice behind him.

'Jingoism's a bit passé, Mr Rickards. If I were you, I'd play it in a lower key.'

Rickards turned: Haggerty. He didn't like Haggerty. He said sharply, 'There's nothing wrong with patriotism, Mr Haggerty. Just what we need now – need *again*.'

Haggerty's face held a lowering look, like a bull about to charge. 'All that about you've got the money. Why, your government's coming cap in hand to us for the cash to carry on. It's nothing but an empty boast.'

Rickards coloured, felt anger rising, would have liked to strike the man down, or try to. He still had a little muscle left, he had never run to fat. But of course he didn't: the man was a boor and he himself was an English gentleman. And another point: that letter of his, the one to the Secretary of State for War that would be posted as soon as they berthed in Liverpool, asking to be given some sort of job: Rickards knew that Haggerty's trip to London was to do with finance for the government. If it was ever mentioned that he, Rickards, had upset the negotiator, then he could say goodbye to any preference from the War Office. There was, unfortunately, truth in what Haggerty had just said. So Rickards swallowed his pride and apologized.

He said, 'We're all very much aware of American help. We're all grateful, Mr Haggerty.'

'Right,' Haggerty said, and moved away. The singing continued. There was no trouble from the third class. The sing-song came to an end just after midnight, after the singing of 'Auld Lang Syne', 'The Star-Spangled Banner' and 'God Save The King'.

As the National Anthem was bellowed out with much strong feeling, the doors were opened to the promenade deck to clear the air of cigar smoke and for the passengers to come out and take a last look at the night sea and the bow wave creaming back to join in with the wake astern. On the bridge Captain Pacey heard it.

He stood to attention, joining in beneath his breath.

> God save our gracious King,
> God bless our noble King,
> God save our King.

Pacey heard it to the end. Then he said, 'Amen.' King George was an emblem as well as a monarch, the steady hand on the tiller of State, a man who had himself gone to sea the hard way as a naval cadet and had eventually won command of a battleship before the throne had claimed him for a larger duty. His Majesty knew what it was all about, he thought as a seaman and he reacted as such. Pacey had heard stories in the course of his many Atlantic voyages, told by men close to the Palace, men who had exchanged gossip at his table in the saloon, or over a drink in the Captain's quarters. King George had quite often startled Queen

Mary with some very nautical turns of expression and not a few oaths too.

The singing ended. There was some cheering, and then quiet. Thursday night, the last night at sea before the Fastnet: the voyage drawing towards its end, towards Saturday's arrival in Liverpool. As ever, there was a kind of nostalgia.

'Fog's thinning, sir.'

The Officer of the Watch. Pacey said, 'Yes, you're right. Increase revolutions for fifteen knots, Mr Callander.'

'Aye, aye, sir.'

The message passed to the engine room, there was more vibration throughout the ship. Pacey watched as the bow wave increased; he felt the ship's response. Earlier he had decided to delay, to prevent his ship's arrival in the submarine zone until after daylight. By now, however, the delay had been greater than he had intended, because of the wreathing fog. After another twenty minutes the fog had cleared sufficiently for the steam whistle to be silenced and Pacey brought his speed up to eighteen knots.

The *Laurentia* went ahead, fast now for home. But as a precaution Captain Pacey ordered the zig-zag to be set once again.

'Miss Greatorex.'

She turned, recognizing the Purser's voice. 'Yes, Mr Matthews?'

'A good sing-song, a happy evening, Miss Greatorex.'

'Yes, Mr Matthews.' There was something odd in the Purser's tone, in his manner. She was tired and wanted to get to bed. Tomorrow morning she would be in demand, looking after a host of excited children while their parents went through all the paraphernalia of forms for Customs and Immigration prior to arrival.

'You enjoyed it? You enjoy your work, Miss Greatorex?'

'Oh yes, Mr Matthews, I do indeed.' She knew now what was coming and it did. She began to shake a little.

'A little bird has been telling tales, Miss Greatorex. To me. That particular bird won't tell them again, I can assure you. But that leaves you, doesn't it, Miss Greatorex?'

She didn't, couldn't, answer. Matthews went on in his hard voice, 'I advise you to be very, very careful. If what that bird said ever reaches the Line, I shall see to it that you are dismissed along with me. You'll never get another job afloat. You're a little too long in the tooth for that. On the other hand, you'll probably live a long while yet. You don't want to live it in poverty. Do you?'

Matthews didn't wait for any response. He turned on his heel and left her to stare after him, her face a picture of dismay. She had no life ashore; the ship and the Line were all to her – income, home, friendship of a sort. No man had ever been interested in her, except so recently Earl MacRae and that had been pure lust, nothing more – and it was possible Matthews knew about that and would use it in a lying way. Her life on leave was spent mostly in cheap lodgings in Birkenhead. She had no living relatives and she had never made friends ashore. If she was dismissed from the Line's service, she would be finished.

She turned and hurried away, tears streaming down her haggard, toothless face, making for the safety of her cabin. Then she halted, and stood rigid and white faced. Mr Matthews had said, or implied, that he had silenced Livia Costello. But had he, really and truly? Miss Greatorex had without difficulty summed up the actress as a self-centred bitch and a dangerous one. Mr Matthews must surely have seen that too, he was no fool, no first-voyage clerk. Livia Costello might well keep her silence about what had been between them, but only at a price. And if Mr Matthews failed to meet that price, then she, Olga Greatorex, would also be for the high jump and the lonely years ahead.

Acting on her sudden impulse, without thought, she changed direction towards Livia Costello's cabin.

In the Queenstown base and in the Admiralty there was as much tension in these closing stages as there was aboard the *Laurentia*. But Lord Fisher himself had gone to bed; it was as though he had washed his hands of the ship after giving the order to withdraw the escort. Or was hiding his head in the sand against some premonition of events to come.

Mr Churchill went in the early hours to the Admiralty's War Room, smoking one of his interminable cigars. There had been an aroma of brandy on his arrival from a good dinner; but the excellence of the dinner notwithstanding he was in a disagreeable mood as he studied the immense wall chart showing the dispositions of merchant shipping and naval vessels in and around the British coasts.

'*Laurentia*,' he growled.

A pointer was lifted. 'There, First Lord.'

Churchill grunted. 'Weather?'

'Fog, sir. Between her current position and the Irish coast, but clearing.'

'U-boats?'

'No positions known, sir.'

'But there are some, as I understand it?'

'Yes, sir – '

'Then why aren't their damn positions known?'

The duty captain shrugged. 'We have no means of detecting submerged submarines, sir.'

'Then it's time someone invented something – is it not, Captain?'

'It would be a very handy invention, sir.'

Churchill grunted again, turned away, prowled heavily around, head lowered, cigar smoke wreathing. Where was Jacky Fisher? Skulking, probably – Churchill made a good guess. Jacky had been behaving oddly; the doctors were worried, Churchill knew that. If anything should happen to the *Laurentia* . . . but if anything did happen, then it wouldn't be only Fisher who would find himself affected and his actions called into question. The whole civilized world would react, and not necessarily only against the German nation. The Palace would be much concerned; Mr Churchill had heard privily that His Majesty was suffering regrets for what he had said earlier: his impulsive query as to what would happen if the *Laurentia*, with US citizens aboard, should be sunk. Perhaps the King was seeing that simple remark as likely to be quoted against the British, insofar as he might be said to have spoken from the heart, to have obliquely uttered a secret hope that President Wilson might be forced into the war.

Mr Churchill went back to the duty captain and asked a question.

'Escorts. Is it too late, Captain?'

'There are no escorts available at Queenstown, sir. As for the Channel, there is thick fog from Plymouth round to Dover. Nothing can move from there at this moment. Of course, it may clear with the dawn.'

Perhaps. But probably much too late for any despatch of an escort vessel to be effective. Britain would be criticized for that; they had not taken the German threat seriously enough. Now Mr Churchill, a sinking feeling in his stomach, knew that to be only too true. He questioned his own motives, questioned Jacky Fisher's again. Then he stiffened: he must show no doubts before the naval officers in the War Room, or outside to the Cabinet, or the general public as represented by the press. If blame was to be cast, then it must be at the person most easily and effectively cast at: the Master of the *Laurentia*, Captain William Pacey. At any subsequent Court of Inquiry, much mud could be slung, the Master's capabilities – even his loyalties – called into question in open court.

Mr Churchill puffed quietly at his cigar and ruminated. A little later he fell asleep in a comfortable chair, catnapping. He remained asleep for some while; when he awoke the dawn was about to break. For many out at sea, it was to prove the last dawn of all.

22

MISS Greatorex had knocked at Livia Costello's cabin door. A bleary voice answered.

'Who it it?'

'Me,' Miss Greatorex said, and opened the door. She went in, stiffening herself for a nasty interview. The actress was lying on her bunk, smoking a gold-tipped Russian cigarette, a Balkan Sobranie. She was wearing her undergarments. Her eyes were bloodshot. On the table beside the bunk there was an open bottle of gin, half-empty; in her hand a glass, the rim red with lipstick.

'What do you want?'

'I want to talk to you, Mrs Costello.'

'I don't want to talk to you. Get out.'

'I'll not get out, not until – '

'I said, get out. If you don't, I'll ring for the night steward.' Livia rolled over, hand outstretched towards the bell-push. Miss Greatorex moved very fast: she grabbed the arm and twisted it, forcing it away from the bell-push. The actress screamed at her.

'You've assaulted me, you bitch! I'll – '

'Keep your voice down,' Miss Greatorex hissed at her. 'It's no assault and you know it. But if you call out I'll – I'll scratch your face to ribbons and you won't look very pretty afterwards! Oh, then it'll be an assault, I know, but I don't care. I just don't care. If you don't listen to me and do what I ask, my life's done for anyway. I – '

'I guess you're kind of beside yourself, aren't you?' Livia seemed to relax. She lay back in the bunk, sneering. She had a lunatic to deal with. Maybe a little humouring would help. Only she found humouring a difficult task, the more so with a woman. 'Why not ease down, and tell me what this is all about?'

Miss Greatorex was trembling. She knew she was unattractive. Flat chested, clumsy, not much conversation, no teeth currently. It was all such a contrast: even though Mrs Costello was raddled with past excesses, she was still good-looking, still, to use a not very nice word, sexy. And it wasn't fair. Miss Greatorex said so, a lifetime of unattractiveness finding vent.

'It's all very well for you and lots like you. Fame, money – men. You've been accustomed to lifting your little finger and they all come running. You've never lacked for – company, have you? You've had it all so easy. I haven't. I've had to work hard all my life. With children. Governess, then nanny when they found out I didn't know enough to teach . . . now I've got a job I like. A *life* I like. I'm not going to lose it because of you. I'm *not*!' She was crying now, and her nose and face had gone red.

Livia laughed. 'Quite a speech. Jealousy's a nasty little worm, isn't it?'

'I'm not *jealous*!' Miss Greatorex said brokenly. 'Jealousy doesn't come into it – '

'Like heck it doesn't. Why not come to the point of all this carry-on?'

'I will. It's Mr Matthews.'

'Oh-oh.'

'You're going to – to threaten him. Blackmail him. Threaten to lose him his job because of – '

'I get it. *You* want to get that guy into bed and he's given you the brush off?'

'I don't want to – to do what you suggest!' Miss Greatorex almost screamed. 'It's not that at all! For heaven's sake . . . did it *sound* like it?'

'Yes,' Livia said, 'it did. You want to protect the nasty little bugger, because – '

'*No, no no!* The point is, can't you see, if you lose him his job he's going to lose me mine . . . just as an act of revenge because of something I said to him – '

'What did you say to him?'

'I didn't say anything to him.' Miss Greatorex was getting very flustered, confusing things. 'I meant, what I said to you. *About* him. About what you'd been up to with Mr Matthews. He got to hear about that and now he's threatening me if I ever say it again – '

'Then just don't say it again. Easy, isn't it? To anyone other than a dolt.'

'You don't understand, do you? He said he'd silenced you. I don't believe he has. If you open your mouth to the Line because he's – he's walked out on you, then I'll be dismissed. He'll see to that. He said so. So I'm asking you to keep quiet – that's all.' Miss Greatorex stood before the actress, her chest heaving, tears streaming down her face, her body shaking as though it would never stop. 'I read the papers in New York. I believe you're trying to get a divorce from your husband. Isn't it in your own interest as well as mine, to keep quiet? I mean, I don't know about American law, but surely if you're trying to divorce anyone for their – their infidelity, you're expected to be faithful yourself?'

Livia laughed, a jeering sound. 'I guess you're dead right, you don't know America. Anyway, I'm not divorcing on account of Larry's infidelity as you call it. That bum can screw anyone he likes. I'm divorcing him because he's so goddam mean, so low he can crawl under a snake with a tall hat on his head. And because I just don't like the guy any more. All right? So I'll talk all I want, if I want. So just get the hell out of my cabin and let me get some sleep, right? I'm not going ashore in Liverpool looking a mess even if you are.'

Afterwards, Miss Greatorex saw that final remark as the very last straw. She had no ready response to it. She turned and stumbled out of the cabin, speechless. But she was thinking hard, her mind racing ahead of herself. Soon Mrs Costello would be sound asleep, drunk on gin. Miss Greatorex went to her own cabin. She had not been observed, she knew that. Not that it would matter any more. In her cabin she rootled around in her drawers until she found a long, thin, steel hatpin. She had never in fact worn it as such; no one aboard the *Laurentia* knew she possessed a hatpin. It had been given to her by an aunt years and years before with the sole object of repelling rape which the aunt had believed lurked round every corner in a working girl's life. She had, of course, never made any use of it; rape had never been threatened.

She slid the hatpin down her corsage. Then she sat down, her heart beating like a drum, and waited.

She waited for one hour precisely, until the ship was very quiet except for the throb of the engines and the wash of the sea past the hull. Then she opened her cabin door quietly and carefully and peered out. There might be a patrolling nightwatchman.

There was not. The alleyway was empty beneath the shaded police lights. Miss Greatorex padded along, wearing her bedroom slippers. She was breathing fast, her eyes were blazing, she was very determined. She would burst in – she blenched when for the first time she realized that the door might be locked this time – but if it wasn't she would burst in and it wouldn't, or shouldn't, take very long. Miss Costello would be drugged with drink and wouldn't react fast if at all. If the door was locked, then she might have to bang and that would be risky, bringing a nightwatchman along to see what was going on. Moving along the alleyway, Miss Greatorex prayed that the door might not be locked.

'Starboard ten, Mr Main.'

'Starboard ten, sir.' The order was repeated by Main to the quartermaster.

'Steady her on ten degrees north of east, Mr Main.'

'Ten north of east, sir.' The First Officer was now at the binnacle, watching the moving needle of the steering compass. As the needle swung close to eighty degrees, he said, 'Steady.'

'Steady, sir. Course, oh-seven-nine, sir.'

'Steer oh-eight-oh.'

'Steer oh-eight-oh, sir.' At the wheel, Quartermaster Hendry brought the spokes over a little to port to check the swing. The *Laurentia* steadied on her new course, heading now direct for the Fastnet Rock, last but one leg of her voyage. The alteration had been made whilst the ship was heading on the mean course of the zig-zag; the alteration made, the zig-zag pattern was resumed around the new course.

The wheelhouse was very silent in the night's darkness. No lights burned other than the shaded binnacle light to enable the quartermaster to read the course. When the fog had cleared Pacey had ordered the navigation lights to be extinguished – the red on the port side, green on the starboard, the two masthead lights, the one on the mainmast set higher than that on the foremast in indication that they were carried on a vessel of more than ordinary length.

There would be no visual assistance given to any lurking periscopes. And now, because the *Laurentia* carried no warning lights, there was a need for extra vigilance. There had been no Admiralty order to steam without lights in the danger zone; Pacey was taking that upon himself. If anything went wrong, if there was a collision, then he would be at fault – he and no one else. He was prepared to take that risk. He took it in the names of the women and children for whom he was solely responsible. The risks from U-boats, in his opinion, greatly outweighed any real risk of collision.

Pacey walked the bridge, keeping a sharp watch. The night air was cold; he shrugged himself deep into the turned-up collar of his bridge coat. He had taken the decision to hold to his ordered landfall, the Fastnet Rock and then the Old Head of Kinsale ... from there to St George's Channel and the turn up for Liverpool Bay. More than any other voyage in his life, Captain Pacey wished for the end of this one, the moment when he would ring down to the engine room, Finished with Engines.

He was very uneasy.

The door, Miss Greatorex found, was not locked. By now the beating of her heart, the dreadful flutter, seemed about to choke her. Once the thing was done, she too would be done for. She would climb the companionways to the after end of the main deck, where it was open to the elements, and she would throw herself into the sea.

Like the killing, that too would be quite easy. Just a quick movement and that would be that. There would be no time for regrets. There would be things she would regret, given the time. She had already run through them: walking in the dales of the North Riding of Yorkshire, along Wensleydale from Leyburn to West Witton, or perhaps the bus through to Bainbridge and Hawes, said to be the highest market town in

England. All the sheep, and in due season the little lambs gambolling on the roadway and making the bus slow down and stop. She had spent one or two leaves from the PanAtlantic Line not in Birkenhead but in the North Riding, and farther north in Westmorland, where once she had been to the Appleby Horse Fair, though she hadn't much enjoyed that – too many carts and traps and caravans, too many gypsies and farmers, too many tinkers, all very rough men. But the fells were splendid and the air was good, better in fact than sea air which always made one feel salty. She would miss all that, but it was over anyway. If the Line threw her out with a rotten reference that would preclude any return to nannying, then she would never be able to afford any holidays, never be able to afford even to live, since she had no other qualifications to offer an employer. She could see herself ending up in something like domestic service, a 'general' in some tradesman's house, a skivvy. That would be much worse than death.

She inched the door open, very quietly. She brought out the hatpin before she had opened the door very far. She saw that one light, quite a dim one, was still on. Well, that would be a help, of course. Then she became aware of very heavy breathing and a lot of creaking and what sounded like grunts, as though Mrs Costello were having a fit or was otherwise ill.

Miss Greatorex eased the door further until she could see. There was a heavy, gross body, a man, on top of Mrs Costello. She recognized the man when, hearing something, he looked round, his face red and angry.

Earl MacRae had made it at last.

In Germany, Admiral Von Neuburg remained awake throughout the night, the night before the dawn of glorious happenings out at sea. He had no need to be awake; as a retired officer, he was no longer concerned with the conduct of the war. But he felt involved through his son-in-law Klaus Eppler. Von Neuburg had, as a courtesy, been kept informed of the reported positions of the *Laurentia* as she ploughed across the Atlantic from the Ambrose Channel. Her estimated time of arrival was still a matter for some, but not much, guesswork. But the time of the torpedoing was still a matter entirely for *Kapitanleutnant* Eppler, and it could take place during the night, so Admiral Von Neuburg, once again in Wilhelmshavn to await U-120's return in triumph, kept awake, smoking his pipe and drinking schnapps. He had a good stomach for both.

His daughter Ilse stayed with him until just past midnight, then said she was going to bed.

'While your husband fights for the Fatherland, Ilse?'

She said, 'He's been doing that ever since the war started. I haven't kept awake since then.'

'But this is different. A historic moment, Ilse! Remember the commemorative medal, waiting to be issued.'

'I've not forgotten, father.'

Von Neuburg looked at her and shook his head sadly. 'I think you do not sufficiently honour Klaus, Ilse. I know the way you think of him . . . you have always belittled him. Is this going to continue after he returns with so much glory?'

She shrugged and said in a brittle tone, 'Really, I don't know. Perhaps not. But he will still be the same Klaus – won't he?'

Von Neuburg didn't answer directly. He sighed and said, 'Ilse, I believe Klaus is doing this not for the Fatherland alone, or the Emperor. He is doing it for you.'

'Killing women and children – for me?'

Von Neuburg raised his eyebrows: although he had his own reservations he found this a strange reaction on his daughter's part. He said, 'You must not think of it quite as that, Ilse. The *Laurentia* . . . she carries women and children, yes – but also she carries arms. It is believed she carries not only rifle ammunition and shells but also has secreted in her holds many bombs and heavy guns for use against our troops at the Front. That is what is believed . . . if I did not believe this, I would not condone the sinking of a passenger liner. No, you must not think of it along the lines you spoke of.'

Ilse made no comment. She shrugged and said, 'Good night, father.'

Admiral Von Neuburg wished her a good night and sat alone, waiting for the news to come through. It would probably come first, not from Klaus Eppler in his submarine, but from the British, who would be in much disarray.

And then, by the following morning, the flags would be fluttering along the Unter den Linden, and perhaps His Imperial Majesty would speak to his people from the balcony of his palace.

Miss Greatorex had turned and fled. Earl MacRae had lumbered off the bunk.

'She had a hatpin,' he said. 'I saw it.'

'A *hatpin*? You sure?'

'Sure I'm sure. So what do we do about a case of attempted murder?'

'Tell the Purser,' Livia said crisply. 'Let Matthews – and the Greatorex woman – sort that one out between them and the PanAtlantic Line!' It wouldn't be hushed up, if she had anything to do with it. Which she would.

This, Miss Greatorex realized. She had muffed it, though that hadn't been by any fault of hers. In any case, there was nothing left now, whether or not she had done what she'd intended. Her life was just as much over. So she would keep to her plan. She hurried up the companionways and reached the open deck unobserved. She made her way aft along the embarkation deck, beneath the outslung lifeboats on the falls from the boat deck. There was a creak of woodwork and of rope chafing against blocks as the liner rolled. This creak perhaps overlaid the soft sounds, the flap-flap of Miss Greatorex's bedroom slippers.

Anyway, she was not remarked. No one saw her go over the side. She left life as she had lived it since childhood, since her parents had died – alone and making absolutely no impression whatsoever. There was no report to the bridge. Something of a splash was observed by one of the lookouts, but Miss Greatorex had been a small woman so the splash was not large and the lookout put it down to the engine room discharge or perhaps a bucket of refuse, potato-peelings and such, from the galley. Unknowing, the liner steamed on for the Fastnet.

The dawn came. There was no fog now. It was a fine day, with a little wind, not very much. Enough, however, to act as a shield for periscopes, enough to disguise the spray from the raised lens that gave Klaus Eppler his view of shipping so that he could bring his command to her firing position.

As that dawn came up, Klaus Eppler left his station at the periscope within the U-boat's control room and went to his cabin space. He rummaged in a drawer beneath his bunk and brought out a photograph of Ilse taken beneath Berlin's Brandenburg Gate.

He kissed the photograph passionately but with half an eye on the curtain in case a member of his crew should draw it aside and witness softness in his Captain. Then he got down on his knees and offered up a prayer. He prayed for Ilse's safety in Germany and that she might come to love him more; he prayed for his Emperor and the Fatherland; and he prayed to God that the *Laurentia* should be brought conveniently within the range of his periscope; prayed that neither his motors nor his torpedo crews would let him down at the last moment.

It was not at dawn but at an early enough hour, before her breakfast, that Mary Pacey had walked from Victoria Road South in Southsea, along Marmion Road to St Jude's Church. There was no one else there; the vicar was still in bed. Mary Pacey knelt in her accustomed pew and, like Klaus Eppler, prayed. She knew approximately enough when the *Laurentia* was expected to arrive in Liverpool. She had enough vicarious knowledge of the sea, the North Atlantic route in particular, to make a good guess as to where her husband and his ship would be at that moment of prayer. He would be coming into the danger zone, the zone where so many British ships had been lost to the German torpedoes over the months of war.

Fervently she prayed for the liner's safety. For her husband. She prayed that nothing whatever might impede the great ship on her last leg home. She knew William Pacey so well; it was possible he would choose to go down with his ship in the long tradition of the sea. She hoped against hope that this would not be so, but she did not include it as a request in her prayers: William must make his own decision on that and she felt it would be an impertinence to put it to God, who might decide that such a course was for the best.

She was hungry now, but she stayed at what she thought of as her post while her husband stayed at his. It was the one way in which she could help. Her knees grew stiff but there was something urging her not to give up, that if she did then all would be lost for the *Laurentia*.

Old Mrs Holmes prayed at her bedside, with her grandson John in her mind. It would be so lovely to see him again; she had missed him so much. In Annapolis the Holmes parents also prayed. In New York's St Patrick's Cathedral Maria Pascopo lit a candle and prayed in her rapid Italian. Guido was so lovable, so kindly and so helpful to everyone with whom he came into contact. His loss would be the greatest agony to Maria, and she was sure the Blessed Virgin would understand that.

Many did not pray. Jonas Gorman, in Annapolis like the Holmeses, was one who did not. He went to work whistling; the *Laurentia* would soon berth and then Elizabeth would in effect be half-way home again. Prayer was very far from the mind of Larry Costello, waking up in the arms of a woman in New York; had he prayed at all, he would very likely have prayed for catastrophe leading to that desirable negation of alimony. He didn't give a hoot for Olivia.

Later that morning Fillmore MacKerrow was removed from his cell in Louisville, Kentucky, and taken to the electric chair. He was wired up, electrodes on wrists and ankles. The vital letter had not yet reached England and possibly never would. He did not become Sir Fillmore MacKerrow and he did not pray. He died laughing and jeering, and vanished in a long-drawn-out twitch and a small amount of blue smoke and electric crackles. The moment of death came to him in the moment that, almost due south of the Old Head of Kinsale, *Kapitanleutnant* Eppler, through his periscope, made his first sighting of a large four-funnelled liner wearing the colours of the PanAtlantic Line and steaming fast for home.

'Dirnecker!'

'*Ja, mein –* '

Eppler had stood back from the periscope. 'Check what I believe I have seen.'

The First Lieutenant took Eppler's place. He looked for a long time. Then he straightened. '*Ja, mein Kapitan*. It is the *Laurentia*.'

23

Two hours earlier, on the bridge, Pacey had brought down his binoculars. 'The Fastnet, Mr Arkwright. Landfall at last, and thank God for it!'

'Amen to that, sir. Cease the zig-zag?'

Pacey nodded. The time of landfall was noted in the deck log. In a little over two hours the Old Head of Kinsale would come up on the port bow. The Chief Officer scanned the horizons all around. He found nothing suspicious and no reports came in from the lookouts; the seas were clear and open, a bright sun and a flat sea beckoning them home. The green land of Ireland lay behind the rocky promontories, herald of England. In the saloons luncheon would soon be served: it would be a happy meal. Carefreeness was in the air now; they were so close to safety. There were some, not many, to whom the arrival would be far from happy: the prisoners, notably Frederick Jones facing a positive murder charge; and Leon Fielding for whom the world, as he had known it, could be about to come to an end. To Livia Costello, who feared now that she might in some way be connected with the disappearance, obviously overboard, of Miss Greatorex. There had been a lot of hoo-ha, as Livia put it, when no one had been able to find Miss Greatorex. . . .

When the word went round that a landfall had been made, Patrick Haggerty went on deck for a long look at Ireland. With him were Henry Sayers Grant and Senator Manderton. Haggerty lifted an arm and pointed.

'The land of freedom,' he said. 'Bane of the English, I guess. You'll never get the Irish down, never in a million years.'

'I wouldn't say that in London if I were you,' Grant said, and meant it.

'Nothing like the truth. But you're a diplomat. What are *you* going to say in London, when you meet King George?'

Grant said, 'Well, I think it's more to the point what are you going to say? To Asquith, and the Chancellor of the Exchequer? And Winston Churchill, come to that?'

Haggerty laughed. 'That stays a secret. For now, anyway. But I don't mind saying, Mr Ambassador – '

'Don't jump the gun, Patrick.'

'Ambassador in all but name, by now. What I was about to say . . . they're asking a lot – you know that. And I don't see why Uncle Sam should be put to the expense of bailing them out. I really don't. But – okay – I have to remember, and I do, what the President's wishes are.'

'Anything short of war,' Grant murmured. He was unsure of Haggerty: the man was straining his eyes to pick up a sight of the Irish coast. When he did, his perverted patriotism might come to the fore, could affect his judgment of the British. Or again it might not. Haggerty was an experienced man, a man with a solid record in banking and finance; when the chips were down his judgment would probably be sound enough and unswayed by what Grant considered irrelevancies. Changing the subject, Grant, turning to Manderton, made an enquiry about the senator's fact-finding mission. 'Any more success, Melvin?'

'Oh, sure, I guess I'll have plenty to report to Congress,' Manderton said sarcastically, 'They're goddam close, the limeys. Don't give much away.'

'Not to Americans, maybe. That's understandable. They're all standing together now. Like one big family. You've got to admire them, Senator. Stiff upper lips, that's what they say.'

'I'll take your word on that,' Senator Manderton said. While Grant carried on the conversation with Haggerty, Melvin Manderton brooded. He would need to inflate his report to Congress with his own impressions; he hadn't managed to get near enough hard fact by way of revealing conversations. The English, he'd found, were all war minded and critical of the way the US was holding off. Like Haggerty, Senator Manderton found no good reason why America should be expected to fill the begging bowls of Europe. Europe – it wasn't just Britain. There was that French general, all sky-blue uniform and stiff back, straight from his own begging mission to Washington and dropping remarks about the duty of the United States. A fop, and an arrogant one. He got under Senator Manderton's skin. Neither the British nor the French had done especially well in the fighting. Manderton, however, knew one thing: if ever the US did enter the war, it would all be over in five minutes. In his mind's eye Senator Manderton saw the Yankee divisions disembarking from the transports, singing and cheering, and later marching through the City of London with bayonets fixed, steel helmets on their heads, their leather-gaitered legs swinging along to the strains of a Souza march, and the girls throwing flowers and blessings on their saviours.

God Bless America.

Now Klaus Eppler was as motionless as a statue at his periscope. The submarine was very silent as all aboard waited for the orders. There was a very gentle rise and fall as the deep-water currents surged up to touch the cigar-shaped hull of U-120.

Eppler moved a little as his hands adjusted the set of the periscope, bringing the *Laurentia* into the dead centre of the cross wires that acted as the periscope's sights, lining up for the kill. In the for'ard torpedo compartment the crews stood by their tubes, fingers ready for the firing levers when Eppler should give the word. The tension was high, as was the expectancy. After sinking the *Laurentia*, U-120 would return to base, and that would be welcome. Wives and mothers and sweethearts beckoned and, glorious though duty was, the submariners were men with normal appetites and whom, for long periods, the sea deprived of female comforts. Now, at last, after a long patrol, home was close at hand.

As he watched the *Laurentia*, Klaus Eppler found his thoughts straying to Ilse in Wilhelmshavn. He suspected those other men, his fellow officers at the submarine base. But in the Fatherland military prowess, courage, the successful outcome of a great mission were all held in the very highest esteem, far above thoughts of love and dalliance. Ilse must surely bow to convention. It would be expected of her. She would respond. She was an Admiral's daughter and knew her duty.

There was a slight shake in Eppler's hands as he once again moved the periscope very slightly. There was a hoarseness in his voice as he passed the preliminary order.

'Stand by bow tubes.'

Earlier that morning as he closed the coast and the U-boat area Captain Pacey had ordered the cells to be evacuated. The two German nationals, Freitag and Prien, together with Craigson, Big Jake Ommaney and Frederick Jones had been brought up and locked into a deck store with a bosun's mate on guard outside. Big Jake Ommaney was cursing about pommie bastards and the proximity of poxy bloody Huns, which was the fault of the pommie bastards . . . Mr Jones sat with his head in his hands, feeling nothing but a terrible blankness: he was already dead and awaiting Judgment Day, when Maggie would be called from wherever she was to give evidence against him, though she might find this difficult with no teeth; her words would slur. But Mr Jones doubted if this would really help him much. God would already be aware of what he had done and Maggie's evidence would be merely corroborative. He was glad the actual hanging was over and he found himself saying so, aloud.

Big Jake Ommaney loomed over, a bulky silhouette against the electric light bulb in the deckhead.

'Shut yer row, pommie bastard. You're not bloody dead yet, mate.'

That penetrated. Mr Jones yelled something out, he didn't know what, he was in such a state, but whatever it was it brought a kick in his ribs from Big Jake Ommaney and then things came back to him. He still had to face the hangman. He stared, ashen faced, at the bulkhead opposite where he sat on the deck of the store. Now he saw visions, very vivid ones: a gallows, and a big man in a black mask, and a parson, and a coffin made of what looked like plywood or something cheap. And a man with a sack with the word QUICKLIME stencilled on it. And, very curiously, a loud flutter of wings from somewhere not actually in the vision. All those poor wretched seagulls, killed by eating Maggie's teeth, gathering to add their evidence against him.

Elmer Pousty was one of those who had gone up on deck to watch the shores of Britain come into view as the *Laurentia* held to her track for the Old Head of Kinsale. This was visible now, an immense rocky promontory, cold and bleak beneath the sky and its clouds, with rock-bound shores stretching to either side. Pousty was feeling the strong excitement of arrival in a foreign land, and he was eager to get into the war in his wound-ameliorating capacity. He too had visions, had had them for a long while: the gun flashes, the shell holes, the infantry attacks when the troops would go over the top of the trenches on the signal from their officer and storm out firing their bayonetted rifles across No Man's Land to the German lines. The barbed wire, the bodies hanging from it to be colandered by the other side, Germans as well as British. The screams and the blood and over all the terrible artillery bombardment and the whine and whistle of the shells in flight. Then the medical teams, the field ambulances, the first-aid parties and the stretcher bearers of whom he would be one. It meant a lot to Elmer Pousty that he would be one of a team of helpers, a non-combatant, doing good rather than killing. He would aid the Germans if the cookie crumbled that way; to him they were not the enemy. They were human lives caught up in a war brought about without their say-so, just like the Tommies. As an American citizen, Elmer Pousty would be a neutral and as such should not differentiate. He believed that the great majority of Germans had no desire at all to kill.

He was standing on the *Laurentia*'s port side, at the fore end of the promenade deck, just for'ard of the funnels and above Number One boiler room. Leon Fielding had not come with him: the singer was in his cabin, rocking Ming's empty pram. A slight beam wind, Pousty found, was tending to blow the engine-room uptakes straight down on his head, giving him a nasty taste in his mouth each time he breathed. He shifted over to starboard.

'Almost there, Emmy. Nothing to worry about now.'

'No, Jeffrey. Except the boys.'

'Well, we're always worried about them.' Rickards spoke a little tetchily: to speak of lieutenant-colonels, fighting on the Western Front, as boys always seemed totally ridiculous to him, but women were women, mothers even more so. There was no accounting and no arguing: boys they remained. He went on, 'I daresay there'll be letters when we get in. It's you I'm more concerned about. As soon as we get to London I'm having a better opinion than Fellowes', Emmy.'

'Yes, Jeffrey.'

He asked, 'Do you want to go up on deck? Fresh air – do you good. There's been too much sitting around – perhaps that's it. H'm?'

'Yes, Jeffrey,' she said again.

Rickards clicked his tongue. Emmy was getting like a parrot, he thought. 'Yes, Jeffrey,' was about all she said these days. Either that or 'No, Jeffrey'. He bent and gave her an arm and assisted her along the alleyway and up to the first-class lounge, where she could sit comfortably and look out across the open deck to the Irish coast. Rickards reflected on Ireland: he'd served there years ago, in the Curragh garrison. The place had always been troublesome, the British not popular even then. Yet there had been no more loyal soldiers of the Queen than the regiments recruited in Ireland: Royal Dublin Fusiliers, Connaught Rangers, Munsters, Leinsters, Royal Irish Rifles . . . likewise the policemen of the Royal Irish Constabulary, grand fellows all of them, mostly Catholics of course, but never resentful of Protestant officers, unlike the Catholic peasantry who couldn't abide the Protestant Ascendancy who were the landowners . . .

A shadow came across his thoughts. Lady Barlow, with Eustace in tow.

She stopped and said, 'Good morning, *Mr* Rickards.'

Ever a gentleman, Rickards clambered to his feet. 'Good morning, Lady Barlow.' He said nothing further; his face was hard, remembering the proposition the woman had put to his wife, remembering how upset Emmy had been and still was.

'Do sit down,' Lady Barlow said frigidly.

'I prefer to stand.'

'I see. So I go quicker.'

He shrugged. 'If the cap fits, wear it.'

She drew herself up. 'Thank you for being rude. Just because you think you're still riding high like you used to. Well, you aren't, are you? You 'aven't got a bean in the world, I shouldn't wonder, looking at you. Well, I just dropped by to say don't bother to put in a word for my son at the Foreign Office. We don't need your help. Wouldn't be worth a toss any road, would it?'

She flounced away. Rickards, words tumbling up but not uttered, felt physically sick. No point in bandying insults. He looked down at his wife: she was crying. He said gently, 'Oh, don't, Emmy. Don't pay any attention. We'll never see her again after we disembark.' Then he became aware that Eustace Barlow was by his side, looking highly embarrassed.

'Well, Mr Barlow, what is it?'

'My mother. . . .' The man was almost tying himself into a knot, hands twisting together. 'Please don't take it badly. She . . . she's awf'lly difficult sometimes, as I should know. May I apologize on her behalf . . . to you and Lady – '

'*Eustace!*' The shout rang through the lounge, causing heads to turn. 'Come here at once!'

'Awf'lly sorry, sir,' Eustace said to Rickards. 'Have to go, don't you know.'

He went.

Rickards said, 'Ha.'

The Descartes children were being a nuisance. The packing left to their parents, they were running wild about the decks, indulging in some sort of chasing game, the last aboard ship. They wove in and out of groups of adult passengers, collecting other children on the way, all full of high spirits as the thought of a new country began to take on the shape of reality. They congregated eventually around Elmer Pousty in his position on the starboard side of the promenade deck, laughing and shouting.

Bosun MacFarlane came along and spoke to Pousty. 'Being little pests, are they, sir? If you say the word – '

'No, it's quite all right, thanks, I can cope. Just high spirits, I guess.' MacFarlane nodded and moved away: he had work to do and if an adult passenger was prepared to put up with the children, whom MacFarlane considered to be beyond parental control – a proposition proved many times during the voyage – and keep them out of his way, well, fair enough. Meanwhile Pousty, known by this time as the funny singer's self-appointed guardian, was being peppered with questions.

'How's the dog, Mr Pousty?'

'Is Mr Fielding soft in the head, Mr Pousty?'

'Are you going to join in the war, Mr Pousty?'

He answered the last one. 'Yes, I am – '

'No you aren't.' This was a chorus.

'Oh yes, I am. As a stretcher-bearer – '

'*Stretcher-bearer!*' They'd known this already, of course. They baited him. 'That's not fighting, is it, Mr Pousty? That's for softies. Are you a conchie, Mr Pousty?'

He answered that one too. 'Yes, I am. I don't believe in killing, I don't believe in war, but if I can help war's victims, then I'm happy.'

There were more expressions of assumed horror and someone mentioned white feathers, but Elmer Pousty, as a Quaker, was used to this sort of thing from certain circles and he remained patient and smiling, his kindly face untroubled by childish tormenting. They stayed with him in a bunch; stayed there above Number One boiler room and the adjacent cargo hold which, as it happened, lay in the dead centre of *Kapitanleutnant* Eppler's periscope sights.

'It will not now be long, *chérie*,' General de Gard said, adjusting the set of his uniform tunic before the long mirror in his stateroom. 'For a little time apart, and then – '

'I still don't see why we shouldn't meet in London, François.'

'It would not be tactful – I have told you this. It is necessary for me to preserve the conventions while I am in London. I have to meet Mr Asquith and Mr Churchill. I expect also to be granted an audience with His Majesty King George. It is well known that Her Majesty Queen Mary holds strict views on – on these matters.'

Adeline grinned at the General's reflection. 'What matters, François?'

'You know very well,' he said stiffly. He was, she thought, a curious man, full of contradictions. No mean lover, and certainly no inexperienced one either, there was a strong streak of prudery. Or if not prudery, then perhaps it was self-preservation. Scandal would not do, even in the midst of war.

Mischievously she said, 'Call a spade a spade, François. Adultery. All right, I won't say it again . . . not till we get to Paris. You're really serious about Paris, are you?'

'Oh, yes, *chérie*.'

'I hope so,' she said. She sounded suddenly a little dubious, a little afraid. There would of course be other women in Paris and she was beginning to feel dependent on François de Gard. She didn't want to have to spend too long with her dead husband's parents in Stratford-on-Avon. They would be as dull as ditchwater. Stratford-on-Avon would be, certainly. Paris beckoned strongly. The hotels, the salons, the cafés, the Seine and its bridges, the whole life and ambience of a capital city of romance and passion, a city where assignations and all that went with them were an accepted part of life and a General of France who might shortly be in action on the Western Front would be expected to have a mistress to buoy him up on his path of duty . . .

Below in the power house of the ship Chief Engineer Hackett had made a tour of his engine spaces and boiler rooms. Soon, in Liverpool, the *Laurentia* would be boarded by the Line's Superintending Chief Engineer and everything would be laid open for inspection. Hackett wished to have everything on the top line; his reputation depended on no faults being found other than the various items he had noted down as needing dockyard attention, notably, of course, the trouble with the low pressure boiler and the difficulty that might follow upon an order from the bridge to put his engines full astern.

He was accompanied by his senior second engineer as he carried out that final, pre-arrival inspection. Once this was completed, he would have paperwork to do in the engineers' office, and then he would be needed on the starting platform as the liner proceeded on the final leg up St George's Channel where there was always a great number of vessels around, coming down from Belfast Lough to the Bristol Channel or into Milford Haven. Sudden engine movements might well be required and he liked to be there in pilotage waters, in the same way as the Captain would be on the bridge.

With the senior second engineer, the two of them discussing the low pressure boilers, Mr Hackett entered Number One boiler room beneath where Elmer Pousty was still being the good-natured butt of the Descartes children and others.

Alva Lundkvist was keeping Olof below in the warmth of their cabin. He was very peaky; Dr Fellowes didn't appear to have done any good and had shown little sympathy. Alva would be glad to disembark and get to London, and seek the opinion of a specialist: she knew about Harley Street where all the best medical men had their consulting rooms. Then, advice having been taken, she would go across to Sweden if the war permitted. As the voyage ran down towards its final stages, she was feeling the blank in her life more than ever: Torsten had been so much looking forward to spending some time in England, and in going north to Scotland and its beautiful highlands and lochs, though Alva herself didn't believe they would be as beautiful as those in Sweden and Norway.

There was a knock at her cabin door.

'Yes?' she said.

It was Sister Perpetua. 'Good morning, Mrs Lundkvist. I was wondering – did you want any help at all? Packing – or anything else?'

Alva shook her head. 'Thank you, it is very kind, but no, I shall manage.'

'You're sure?' Sister Perpetua crinkled the seamed flesh around her eyes: the Swedish woman didn't look well, she was a bag of nerves and no wonder, all she had been through and more to come when her husband's murderer was brought to trial – and before that the police investigation. 'Will you have to stay a while in Liverpool?'

'I do not know. I think not. The Captain – he will do what he can.'

'If you do, then I can stay with you. I can arrange that with my Order. And if you go straight to London, I can go with you if that's of any help.'

'It is very kind,' Alva said again. Then she broke down. Sister Perpetua went to her and enfolded her in her arms, comfortingly. She said, 'My dear, I shall stay with you. You'll have the little boy to think of. I'll be with you.'

Purser Matthews and his staff were busy on a number of matters pertaining to the ship's business: Portage Bill, crew's wages, detailed lists of passengers for the Customs and Immigration authorities, the handing back of and obtaining signatures for the valuables deposited in safe custody for the duration of the voyage, balancing the cash for the voyage account . . . the paperwork was always immense. He didn't welcome the advent of the Reverend Divine.

'Yes, Mr Divine, what can I do for you?'

The Reverend Divine, as batlike as ever, coughed. 'An embarrassing mission, I fear, Purser. It's Mrs Costello. I fear she has drink taken – '

'Not unusual.' There was a small knot of fear in Matthews' stomach: those in drink, as he well knew, could come out with indiscretions. 'She's not my problem, Mr Divine, but if I were you I wouldn't worry about her. She'll be sober enough when the time comes to disembark.'

'Perhaps, yes.' They were in Matthews' private office, leading off the main passenger office; even so, the Reverend Divine lowered his voice and moved closer. 'The lady has talked to me. Told me of her – troubles perhaps I might put it. And I believe she intends to, as it were, spread those troubles. Do you follow? Just a word of warning. You are a man with a career. The lady is a person who . . . is unworthy. You will, I know, respect my confidence.'

Hoarsely Matthews asked, 'What am I supposed to do about it?'

The Reverend Divine shrugged. 'Why, I'm afraid that is up to you. I merely – '

He saw Matthews' expression; the Purser was staring past him. He turned. The door had opened and Livia Costello stood there, swaying as she clutched at the doorpost.

'You slimy old ratbag,' she said. The Reverend Divine edged past her and went out of the door, closing it behind him. Really, they had both asked for it.

* * *

'Not far now, Elizabeth.'

'No. Not far.'

'You'll be going back to the States – to Annapolis?'

She nodded. 'Yes, John, I will.'

'This guy . . . Jonas Gorman. You really love him?'

'Yes, I do.' Impulsively she laid a hand on his arm. 'I'm sorry, John. I know how you feel. I've enjoyed the voyage, thanks to you. You've been a help at a difficult time. But it's no use and never was really. I'm older than you . . . and you have a war to fight. You're keen to get in on that – aren't you?'

'Yes,' he said. He was; he still had the spirit of Sir Christopher Cradock and his other naval heroes. Quite soon now he might be at sea; in the meantime he had to go and see his grandmother down in Worthing, not far from London by the train. His mind was already beginning to project ahead, away from what he was forced to see as a shipboard romance. No point in self-pity . . . he swallowed; there was a lump in his throat. He said, 'When you get back to Annapolis . . . would you drop by my mum and dad?'

'Of course I will,' she said. She squeezed his hand. 'That's a promise. All right now?'

'All right now,' he said.

The time was 1426. The range was 2000 yards.

'Fire one,' *Kapitanleutnant* Eppler said calmly. U-120 lurched a little as, the torpedo fired, some of the weight came off the bow section. There had been a sort of *whumpf* of sound and a slight check in the boat's way and that was all. Eppler continued looking through his periscope, watching his unsuspecting target. He had considered giving a warning, so that the British could get their boats away and save lives; but had decided, after consulting with First Lieutenant Dirnecker, who had not disguised his disapproval of any warning, not to. He was somewhat too close to the Irish coast and the naval base at Queenstown to show such chivalry, Dirnecker had said.

Eppler watched the torpedo hit.

The torpedo trail had been spotted, too late, by the *Laurentia*'s lookouts. Too late, the siren blasted out its order to all passengers to muster at their boat stations. Eppler's torpedo struck as Pacey went fast for the starboard side. There was an immense explosion below him, right on the point of aim that had been Number One boiler room. There was thick smoke, and the red lick of fire. The *Laurentia* gave a lurch, her head going down perceptibly as the water entered her hull. In ten seconds by Pacey's reckoning a fifteen degree list to starboard had developed.

Pacey shouted, 'Close all watertight doors. Carpenter to check round for'ard . . . stand by all lifeboats!'

Then, looking aft, he faced the reality of getting the boats away: all the port side boats had taken a swing inboard and could never be got away. Those to starboard were swinging outwards from the falls, and it would take time, too much time perhaps, to grapple them in for embarkation.

Despair gripped Pacey's heart as he realized that his ship was doomed and with it undoubtedly many of his passengers.

There had been a sustained cheer throughout U-120, men shook hands with one another, slapped each other on the back. Someone began singing *Deutschland Uber Alles* and there was another resounding cheer, this time for the Kaiser.

Eppler ordered, 'Down periscope.' He watched as the great shaft descended into its bed beneath the control-room flat, bringing with it a drip of water.

'Take her down, Dirnecker,' Eppler said. The speed of the electric motors was increased and U-120's nose took a downward slant as the hydroplanes were manipulated in accordance with Dirnecker's orders. Eppler went to the chart table aft of the periscope housing. The various courses for Wilhelmshavn had already been pencilled in.

Eppler said, 'Port twenty. We go home.'

Unremarked – unseen, unheard – U-120 slunk away beneath the surface, heading for deeper water, putting distance between herself and the Old Head of Kinsale, heading out into the Atlantic until she was far enough away from the British coasts to turn north and then east across the Orkneys to make the passage of the German Ocean to her base, thus avoiding the English Channel and the torpedo-boat destroyers of the Dover Patrol.

24

THE confusion was total. In the shattered boiler room Chief Engineer Hackett and his senior second engineer died instantly, their bodies fragmented by the explosion itself and by the eruption of the boilers. In the stokeholds the enormous furnaces spilled out their fires until, in the section closest to the hole in the liner's side, the inrush of the sea doused them. From split engine room pipes, superheated steam came out under pressure, flaying the skin from many of the engineers and greasers before they too died in screaming agony.

On the bridge, Pacey had realized that too much strain was coming on the transverse bulkheads below, on account of the ship's way through the water. He passed the order for the engines to be put to full astern to relieve the strain. Below, the senior third engineer put steam through to the low pressure turbines; and what Chief Engineer Hackett had feared now happened: the blow-back took place. On the boat deck a condenser top was blown away as the result of a main steam pipe fracturing. In an attempt to take off the steam pressure on the astern turbines, the senior third engineer went back to full ahead without orders from the bridge.

Pacey, looking aft, saw a great head of steam coming out like a cloud between two of the funnels. With way still on the ship Pacey used his megaphone to bellow orders to the deck officers.

'No attempt is to be made to launch the boats until the way is off the ship!'

Chief Officer Arkwright responded. 'Aye, aye, sir. We've got an unhandy list . . . I suggest we balance by flooding the trim tanks, port side – '

'Very well, Mr Arkwright, see to that, though we'll lose some of the buoyancy.'

Arkwright saluted in acknowledgement and ran to pass the order. This was never carried out: the men responsible for the flooding valves were no longer at their stations, having made for the boats without orders. The angle of list increased to starboard. As the way came off, Pacey summed up the situation: the *Laurentia* was done for, was almost at the point of capsizing unless, in the comparatively shallow water, her bow took the bottom as it drove farther and farther down. The sea was coming fast up the fo'c'sle and foredeck, water was pouring in through the hatches and the ports on the lower accommodation decks. It was time now to try to launch the lifeboats. Pacey called for Staff Captain Morgan; but Morgan was dead. Having gone below at the double to assess the damage, he had missed his footing on a twisted ladder and had dropped through two decks to break his neck on a fractured steel beam and fall helplessly into the water surging into the hull.

On the promenade deck above where the torpedo had hit, the initial blast had gone upwards. When two of the Descartes children, a boy and a girl not yet ten years of age, were blown along the deck and over the side, Elmer Pousty dived in at once. Just as he did so there was another explosion below, for'ard of Number One funnel: Pousty died in the blast, as did the two children.

On the bridge Pacey took the reports as they came in. The fires were not spreading thanks to the inrush of water, but that was now of secondary importance: the second explosion had destroyed the bulkheads of certain watertight compartments and the flooding was increasing fast. There was no hope, never had been, of saving her by use of the pumps.

Callander, senior second officer, was standing by the Captain, waiting for the order he knew must come, the only order that was left to give. Pacey said, 'That second explosion, Mr Callander.'

'Yes, sir?'

'Another torpedo?'

'I don't think so, sir. It seemed to come from inside the ship.'

Pacey nodded, his face white and strained. 'I thought so too. The explosive cargo?'

'Yes, sir, I believe so.'

Pacey nodded again. More reports came in, of the shattered boilers, the steam-filled engine spaces, the encroaching water. From the wireless room the Mayday call had already gone out. There was nothing more to do now other than to save as many lives as possible. The *Laurentia*'s life had ended and Captain Pacey sounded the death knell.

'Abandon ship, Mr Callander. Go to your boat station at once. And may God go with you – and with us all.'

Callander saluted and turned away. As he made for the ladder from the bridge, a figure came up at the rush, blood pouring from a gash on his head: Mullins, Captain's Steward, who would stand by Pacey until the end.

Now the decks were a shambles, passengers milling about, many of the women crying, all looking lost. Members of the crew did their best to sort them out to their proper stations while the liner's stern lifted gradually into the air, water dripping from the plates, the four immense screws turning still under what power was left in the engine room. Chief

Officer Arkwright was shouting orders; no one took any notice, no one seemed even to hear. Despite all Pacey's efforts to improve the boat drill by daily musters, chaos was now the order of the day. There was muddle and in some cases inefficiency; numbers of passengers appeared ignorant of how to tie on their lifejackets, though this was due largely to panic as the ship went into her death throes. An assistant clerk from Purser Matthews' office seemed reluctant to take charge of his boat station, unable to project his voice above the hubbub and the screams of the women. It was a woman who took over from him: of all unlikely people, Lady Barlow.

'You're a nincompoop, young man. Just you leave it to me.' She yelled at the passengers: 'Come along, you and you and you, *get in the bloody boat!*' Women and children first, she counted them in and when the boat seemed filled she got in herself and shouted at the seaman in charge of the falls. 'If you're the man that does the lowering, get on with it!'

The filled lifeboat was lowered with a jerk. When below the embarkation deck, something happened. The after fall jammed around the blocks, the for'ard fall continued to run out, the boat's weight taking charge from the seaman who should have been in control. The boat came up-and-down and spilled the occupants out. The bodies went down to take the water, helpless, doing their best to strike out and away from the ship's side as the bows went deeper and deeper, the sea rising up along the fo'c'sle plating to wash against the central superstructure. Right aft, the Reverend Divine tended a line, lowering Sister Perpetua into the water from the uplifted stern so that she could, as he hoped, embark aboard a lifeboat that had been got away safely but contained only three persons. He scarcely heard the panic-stricken, warning yells from beneath but continued lowering the nun until a high scream of agony came up. He looked over the stern then. He had lowered Sister Perpetua on to the still-moving propellers, and she was little more than a quivering lump of red meat.

In the water, scores of men and women waved their arms and called out for rescue. Floating as the liner went further down by the head and the foremost funnel took the water, Senator Manderton felt a strong pull, a kind of suction, and was then drawn straight into the funnel, his body pushed by the inrush of water down and down until an underwater explosion ejected his lifeless body back to the sea. On the boat deck, where he had gone since it seemed to him logical – the boat deck, or at any rate its after end, being the furthest point from the sea – Leon Fielding lugged his perambulator in panic-stricken circles, looking unavailingly for Elmer Pousty and thinking of his wife in New York, and poor little Ming. With the further tilt of the deck, he lost his footing. The perambulator took off and he slid behind it on his stomach, and then shot through a gap in the guardrail where a lowered lifeboat had been. He went over the side, hit the water and knocked himself out. He was grappled by Henry Sayers Grant, who pulled him aboard his boat to lie half-dead on the bottom boards. The heavy lifeboat, now being pulled urgently by its crew away from the whirlpool that would be caused when the great ship went down finally, hit Patrick Haggerty fair and square from behind as he swam. Unjacketed, Haggerty with his precious briefcase stuffed with financial detail and closely argued policies on loans, sank and was not seen again. A little later a corpse drifted across Leon Fielding's boat and Grant recognized it as that of Eustace Barlow. Hanging onto the lifejacket was a small man, one whom Grant didn't recognize. He directed the coxswain's attention to this man, and the lifeboat was pulled towards him and he was assisted aboard.

'Thank you, thank you so much, *signor*,' Guido Pascopo said, tears streaming down his face when he thought of the anguish Maria in New York would be going through until she had the word that he had been saved.

Precisely what Mrs Rickards had feared had come about: the lifeboat to which they had been allocated had been filled to capacity and beyond. Women and children first – indeed they were mostly women and children, some of them who should not have been at that particular station. The officer in charge could manage just one more.

'Emmy.'

'No. I shall not go without you. We've always been together, always.'

'Please, Emmy. I shall be all right, I promise you.'

'I'm not going, I tell you!'

It looked like being a long argument. Disapproval came from the people already embarked: somebody had better make up his or her mind. Livia Costello was the most vociferous. The shock of events had sobered her to a very present realization of her plight. She'd had to fight for a place in the boat and she was quite determined the fight wasn't going to be in vain.

'For Christ's sake,' she said in a shrill tone. 'Those two are goddam *old*, too goddam old to be given space. Sink or swim, what the goddam *hell* does it matter?'

One of the other occupants of the lifeboat rounded on her, told her to shut up. But she had made a point and it stuck with the others. The boat's officer said urgently that he would wait no longer. Rickards did his best but his wife hung on to a stanchion like a limpet. The boat, the officer repeated, could take one more only. The officer himself was starting to panic. He gave the order as the two old people still dithered; and the boat was lowered at once from the embarkation deck.

'Now see what you've done, Emmy.'

'They *could* have taken one more!'

'No. The feller was right. There's a point when you can't take any more, you risk the lives of all the others. Can't be helped, Emmy. Let's see if we can find another boat.'

They moved away, slowly: she was very stiff and so was he, far too old for sinking ships. Eighteen minutes after the first explosion the *Laurentia* began to go down very fast, her bows sliding finally beneath the sea, the funnels breaking away, the stern standing clear of the water for what seemed a long time, absolutely motionless, and silent but for the cries of the swimmers and large bubbles of air that kept coming to the surface and bursting. Then, after another internal explosion, she plunged amid a great cloud of steam. The liner's end took the Rickardses with her, a shared death. They had fallen as the angle increased and had become trapped in some gear trailing across the deck from one of the falls, and they had drowned.

So had John Holmes. He had dived overboard after seeing Elizabeth Kent safely into a lifeboat, one that as in the case of the Rickardses could take no more weight; swimming towards an inflatable raft he had been seized with a sudden stomach cramp, and had gone down like a stone, bent double in helpless agony. As he went, Lady Barlow, floundering in billows of undergarments, could be heard calling out for news of her son's whereabouts. Eustace had been one of those flung from the upended lifeboat, and the shock had proved that his heart condition had not been entirely imaginary.

All the men from the cells were safe aboard an inflatable life raft, still under guard by armed seamen. Earlier, orders from Staff Captain Morgan had ensured that they were given more than a fair chance of survival. It was never to be said that prisoners' lives had been set at risk and lost thereby: even the two Germans had to be given their chance. The rifles of the armed guards were for their protection against angry passengers as well as for ensuring that they had no opportunity of escape when the Irish coast was reached. Frederick Jones sat and shivered. He, who would have welcomed a quick end to his life, was to be saved for the hangman's noose. Big Jake Ommaney was silent but watchful, waiting his chance for a getaway in the confusion of rescue. Craigson, tears streaming down his face, looked out for his wife and son but found no sign of them. The body of Earl MacRae floated past, eyes staring, blood welling into the water from a shattered skull. Not far away was the body of Bosun MacFarlane, who had died trying to protect MacRae from a falling spar that in the end had killed them both.

Pacey remained on the bridge until the last moment and would have stayed with his ship as she went down had he not been swept away on the rising waters as they encroached over the bridge and filled the useless wheelhouse. Earlier, he had ordered both Mullins and Quartermaster Hendry to leave the ship and save themselves.

'An order,' he'd said brusquely, seeing their hesitation.

'No, sir.' This was Steward Mullins. 'I'm staying by you, sir.'

'I repeat the order to both of you.'

'We're disobeying it, sir.' Mullins gave a tight grin. 'A case of mutiny you might say, sir!'

'I'll have you hanged, drawn and quartered, Mullins.'

'Aye, aye, sir.'

Pacey gave it up; there was no point in trying to enforce the unenforceable. He shook each of them by the hand, wordless now. There were tears in the eyes of all three. They had been shipmates for many years, they were seamen of the old tradition. Pacey was feeling in his bones, in the soles of his feet, to be more precise, as the deck shuddered beneath him, the poignancy of the end of a great ship committed to his charge. As the water came closer, an inexorable rise, he lifted his binoculars and stared towards the distant Irish coast and the great eminence of the Old Head of Kinsale.

'Where in hell's the rescue ships?' he asked savagely.

There was no answer to that. The sea stood empty of succour. It was as though no one ashore cared. Pacey saw that a mere half-dozen lifeboats were afloat – six, out of forty-eight, floating on a dead calm sea. In some of them were babies in wicker baskets – Moses baskets from the ship's nursery in which they had been put to sleep after their lunch. As the rising waters swept Pacey and Mullins off their feet with Quartermaster Hendry there was a huge rumble from the innards of the liner as the boiler rooms were shattered by the collapse of the bulkheads under pressure. The whole area seemed to be covered by a cloud of escaping steam, beneath which the *Laurentia* slid finally away beneath the surface.

25

At 1420 Admiral Hood in Queenstown had been informed of the Mayday call from the *Laurentia*, giving her position south of the Old Head of Kinsale. Hood reacted at once; the light cruiser *Juno* was ordered to proceed immediately to the scene – having entered the port only an hour or so earlier, she still had steam on her main engines.

Soon after this, a report was received that the *Laurentia* had gone down. With all urgency, Hood gave orders for all possible small craft to put to sea and close the liner's given position. He then reported to the Admiralty, and Lord Fisher was informed personally. He was told that a full summary would be made by wireless once the *Juno* had reached the scene. Fisher stared.

'The *Juno*? Is she at sea?'

'Yes, sir – '

'Then she is to be recalled immediately!' Fisher stormed. 'She'll be nothing more than damn bait for another damn torpedo! I cannot and will not afford the loss! *I have not got the cruisers to spare!* The rescue is to be left to the small craft. See to that immediately, and see to it that the *Juno* is sent the recall.'

The *Juno* was seen by the survivors in the water just as she received the recall from the Admiralty. She turned away in obedience to orders, heading back into Queenstown.

Pacey watched in amazement, scarcely able to believe what he was seeing as he floated in the water, supported by his cork lifejacket and by Mullins and Hendry. His thoughts rioted in a welter of bitterness and disbelief. Right from the start of the voyage, from the moment of clearing away from New York, no one in authority had cared a jot for the *Laurentia* and her passengers. No one at all. He, his ship, his passengers, his crew – all had been just simply left to it, with no proper instructions, no proper advice of any sort. Who was to blame? Well, he would do his utmost to find out and try to pin the responsibility where it belonged. But could he hope to succeed? There would be a very heavy official smoke-screen undoubtedly. That was the way things went: it was usual for the man on the spot to be landed with the blame. But Pacey's conscience was clear.

It was almost two hours later that the first of the small craft came in amongst the survivors. And after the next day's dawn the picking over of the bodies began along the Irish coast. Two hundred corpses were the start. From Garretstown Strand, Courtmacsherry Bay, Schull, Bantry and all along the Kerry coast, were yielded up the dead and the financial rewards that they represented. Over the following days the sad harvest continued along the wild and rocky coasts around the Old Head of Kinsale: 761 survivors of the sinking had been picked up by the little craft of the rescue operation, an operation that had taken around seven hours to complete. A number of those who had survived the actual sinking died on the way inshore: the long exposure had been hard on the elderly. One who succumbed aboard one of the small boats was Lady Barlow, wrapped in grief for her son who had not been seen after the upending of the lifeboat, other than as a floating corpse by Leon Fielding who himself lived on, somewhat miraculously, to face his terror of a charge on an unpleasant matter, not knowing then that the Craigson boy was dead. And, curiously, it was while he was being borne to safety across that bloody sea that it came back into Fielding's mind why he had crossed the Atlantic to Great Britain. How *could* he have forgotten? It had been his war effort: he would sing to the troops on the Western Front, hold front-line concerts to bring cheer to the brave boys facing shot and shell in the dreadful Flanders mud. Old he might be; but surely the War Office would be able to make use of his services in this hour of need. Anyway, it was his intention to try. Or had been; things were different now: with that appalling case hanging over him he was done for. The troops wouldn't want to hear an old man who'd been charged with that sort of crime. The War Office would cold-shoulder him. Lord Kitchener, Secretary of State for War, would see to that. But by the time he reached the Irish coast, his mind had clouded over again.

Another who lived was Alva Lundkvist, in misery and despair because she had now lost Olof who had shivered himself to death in the sea before the approach of the rescue fleet, joining his father whose corpse had gone down with the ship. Among the corpses that were to be washed up, to be found by the scavengers, were those of Dr Fellowes and the Reverend Divine, who had joined forces in doing what they could to keep up the spirits of the other survivors but had become exhausted and had sunk below the water before rescue could reach them. Among them also was General François de Gard, whose stiff neck had been broken when he had jumped overboard and had taken the water badly, crashing onto a baulk of timber broken away in the explosion. Adeline Scott-Mason, grieving for the lost hopes of Paris, was among those rescued. She was now faced with a visit to her parents-in-law. . . .

Purser Matthews survived, fearful when he came ashore of what Livia

Costello might yet do to his career, not then knowing whether or not she was to be one of the 1201 persons, men, women and children, who were to be reported drowned. Possibly she would be; her constitution, thanks perhaps to so many years of gin, would not be of the strongest even if she had got away from the ship.

Once the scavengers had picked up the corpses and deposited them in the backs of their side-cars, that the English called jaunting cars, and identifications were made, there was sorrow in Worthing. The telegram was brought to old Mrs Holmes by Milly, herself in tears when it was opened.

Mrs Holmes stared into space, her face ashen. 'Everything had been ready, Milly.'

'Yes'm. Oh, I'm ever so sorry, 'm!'

Mrs Holmes stood up, straight as a ramrod. 'Dry your eyes, Milly, you're a mess.'

'Yes'm. . . .'

'Life must go on. We must – just carry on, that's all, as Master John would have done. We shall be proud of him – coming over to fight. And we must think of his parents more than of ourselves.' She went over to the window, gazed across the peace of St Botolph's Road, in the direction of the railway station where she had so hoped to welcome John back to England. So many plans had been made, perhaps a stupid thing to do in wartime. And after all there *was* a war on, and she must never weaken.

Mr Churchill was in conversation with Prime Minister Asquith when word came in that the body of Patrick Haggerty, banker from New York, had been recovered from the mudflats at Courtmacsherry Bay. It had been valued, Mr Asquith said, at no less than one thousand pounds sterling payable by the United States Government. Churchill had smiled at that.

'So somebody's gain, Prime Minister, is *not* exactly to be our loss!'

Asquith looked bewildered. 'I don't follow, Winston.'

Churchill waved his cigar. 'The Almighty is on our side, as I confess I have always believed. If Haggerty had lived, then I'm convinced we would never have got that loan. Now, however . . . with America in a more receptive mood after the deaths of her own citizens, I believe they'll send over a man who's more in tune with our own aspirations – and with our needs.' He puffed away at his cigar. 'Really quite a good result, though I suppose it ill befits me to say so.'

Asquith looked at the First Lord suspiciously and with a degree of wonderment: Winston Churchill's cherubic face held an impish grin . . . the Prime Minister found himself speculating on many things as he tried to read the message of that grin and to match Mr Churchill's apparent confidence as to better auguries to come from the United States. Did Churchill really believe that America would now not only grant the loan but also immediately enter the war? Asquith was by no means convinced of the latter proposition. President Wilson was too dedicated to peace to make a quick decision.

In any case, as events turned out, Churchill was no longer in office when history took a step forward: a few days after that conversation he was forced to resign as First Lord: he had failed in the end to survive the disaster of the Dardanelles. And at about the same time Lord Fisher of Kilverstone, Admiral of the Fleet, resigned his office of First Sea Lord, not long afterwards suffering what amounted to a brainstorm, the lead-in to which over the last few weeks could have been responsible for some of his actions and inactions. So two careers had foundered, largely upon the rocks of mutual enmity after a one-time close friendship and perhaps also to some extent upon the loss of the *Laurentia* and the hundreds, including 139 United States citizens, who had died with her. Nevertheless, the two men's spite was to linger on in official circles to infect the Inquiry into the liner's last voyage.

In London on the night of the liner's sinking Ambassador Page, soon to be relieved by Henry Sayers Grant, had planned a dinner party. Not knowing the full extent of the tragedy until just before the arrival of the guests, Page decided not to cancel the affair. Throughout the meal there was a constant flow of telegrams. The list of American dead grew. It was taken for granted that the United States would now enter the war, with her immense potential the best hope of victory for the Allies. In Berlin and Brussels the American ambassadors began the process of closure of their embassies, not waiting for the word from the State Department. In Washington President Wilson had taken himself off into his garden, where he had cried: his long hope of peace seemed to be shattered. He had then arranged a game of golf.

Next day the world's press had reacted in its different ways.

The *New York Times*: 'Few of liner's 1273 Victims Found,' it proclaimed, quoting figures that had not then been finalized. '120 Americans dead.' Figures again incomplete. 'Sinking of the *Laurentia* is Defended by Germany; President Sees Need of Firm and Deliberate Action.'

The *New York World*: 'Modern history affords no such example of a great nation running amok and calling it military necessity.'

Le Petit Journal: 'It will have no other effect than to strengthen humanity in waging a relentless war to the death and to round up the enemy as one rounds up a beast escaped from a menagerie. . . .'

The *Daily Mail*, London: 'British and American Babies Murdered by the Kaiser.'

Frankfurter Zeitung: 'An extraordinary success.'

And there were other sources, hidden ones: a pre-resignation marginal notation by Lord Fisher on a memorandum from Captain Richard Webb, RN, of the Admiralty's Trade Division stated: 'I trust Captain Pacey is arrested the moment the Inquiry ends, *no matter what the finding.*'

And a note from Captain Webb was later delivered to Lord Mersey, Commissioner for Wrecks, who was to conduct the Inquiry, this note stating unequivocally that the Admiralty 'deemed it to be politically expedient' that the Master of the *Laurentia* be held responsible for her loss.

Meanwhile the censoring officers at the Admiralty were kept busy: total concealment was in the air. Admiral Hood in Queenstown was sent instructions that he was to make a discreet selection of bodies for the inquest, taking care not to offer up too many injured by explosion since such might tend to reveal the nature of the *Laurentia*'s war cargo. And it was announced to the press that the *Juno* had not been recalled from the rescue: a statement was issued to the effect that she had been intercepted in her mercy mission by another U-boat that had mounted an attack on her.

Livia Costello was not among the American dead. Landed with other survivors from the boats, she was in a hospital ward in Queenstown where she was drying out both externally and internally. She badly wanted a drink but none was forthcoming. She lay with her teeth chattering and her face haggard, drawn and pale. Her thoughts rioted: thoughts about Larry in New York, about Purser Matthews who could be alive and could be dead. Larry, the louse, would be furious when he got the news she was one of the survivors. She would have bet any money that had she been among the dead he would have thrown a party to celebrate the fact. He was going to be baulked of that, anyway, if she pulled through – which currently she didn't feel was on the cards. And for now alimony would loom large in Larry's mind. He would be good and mad.

A nun approached, a nun of a nursing order looking not unlike Sister Perpetua. Livia stirred herself, asked for a drink.

'Gin,' she said, 'For Christ's sake.'

The nun disregarded the blasphemy: the sick were the sick, and the survivors from such a tragedy must not be blamed for loosening their tongues. But there would, she said, be no gin.

'Now look, Sister.' Livia heaved herself up on one arm. 'I need it. I'll die without it. That's how I feel.'

'It'll be up to the doctor when he comes on his rounds next. And you are not going to die. But your resistance has been lowered and you must have time – '

'My resistance is quite OK, you silly bitch. All I need is a drink, goddammit!'

'That'll be quite enough of such talk, thank you.' The sister moved away, head in the air. The rustle of her habit seemed to express her indignation. Livia gave way to tears; sobs racked her thin body and she lay in a pit of utter misery. She had been deserted by everyone. She no longer cared about anything. She should have died; God, if He was in the least merciful and caring, should have seen to that. That was, if there was a God.

What was she going to do?

There was, or there might be, Ralph Matthews for what he was worth. He was a bum, not to put too fine a point on it, but Larry had accustomed her to bums. At sea he had been a port in a storm, as she had told herself when the affair had started. Well, he could be again. Maybe. With just some urging in the right direction. He'd given her the brush-off and it had appeared very final, that was true. But he wouldn't want to have a complaint laid against him to the Line. He might be amenable . . . at the least she might be able to get some much needed cash out of him. Alimony would take time, much legal and expensive time, to sort out. She knew her own nose was not entirely clean, and there was the fate of the Greatorex woman that might prove a source of awkward questions but she, Livia, had not in fact been responsible for her death so they couldn't really pin anything on her.

When the doctor came round there was still no gin.

Captain Pacey had been warned to be ready to appear as a witness at the Court of Inquiry to be convened the next month. Before the Inquiry opened and after he had attended some preliminary sessions in London with the lawyers who would represent himself and the Line, he was able to get away for a few days. He sent a telegram to Mary in Southsea and two hours later she was on the platform of the railway station to meet him. They went home in a cab, saying little but holding hands in mutual sorrow. Pacey was on the verge of total exhaustion; it had been an unusually stressful voyage quite apart from its terrible end: Fielding and the charge against him, the man Frederick Jones, the Australian Ommaney, the apparent suicide of Miss Greatorex and so many other difficulties . . . of course to cope with such was what was expected of any shipmaster and it was those bitter thoughts that filled Pacey's mind, thoughts about the abandonment, as he saw it, of his ship by the Admiralty who had allowed her to sail into dangerous waters without the warship escort promised by Sir Courtenay Bennett in New York and without precise, or indeed any, wartime instructions.

At home he was able to relax and recover a little; then came the recall from leave, more long hours with the lawyers and their warnings that every effort was likely to be made by the Admiralty to pin the whole blame upon him alone, and finally the ordeal of the Inquiry itself. This, in the event, was to drag on for more than a month.

For Captain Pacey it was a time of nightmare. The dry-as-dust atmosphere of the courtroom, the pallid faces of the learned counsel and the clerks, the very appearance of the presiding Lord Mersey with his Assessors – an admiral, a lieutenant-commander RN and two Merchant Service captains – he found it daunting. It was in his mind that Lord Mersey, at the Inquiry into the loss of the *Titanic*, had roundly castigated the Master of the SS *Californian* for failure to go to the *Titanic*'s aid . . . and daunting also was Sir Edward Carson, the Attorney-General, appearing in the Admiralty's interest; daunting too were the piles of paper on the many tables that filled the courtroom, documents that might lead to the suspension or cancellation of his certificate of competency as a Master Mariner. Or worse, as desired by the Admiralty: the whole blame for the catastrophe, the loss by default of so very many innocent lives, including so many Americans. Over the years Pacey had made many friends in New York. If the blame was held to be his, then his own life would be over too. It would be an insupportable burden.

The proceedings opened with the various depositions and the establishment of identities, all the formal processes of any Court of Inquiry. The case for the Board of Trade was put by Sir Frederick Smith, the Solicitor-General; Butler Aspinall, a King's Counsel of distinction, was to represent Pacey and the Line. Pacey was scarcely able to take it all in. He was no lawyer; he was a man of action, a seaman to his fingertips, a shipmaster well able to command obedience, well able to inspire confidence and respect and the concept of service to the Line; but he was no fusty lawyer. The law at times seemed hostile to a Master Mariner trying to tell the simple truth about what had happened, about a voyage that had ended so disastrously – the simple truth to combat the expressed opinions, ready-made, out-of-court opinions that were to become all too obvious as the Inquiry progressed and Pacey recognized blatant lies told against him. It became crystal-clear that Winston Churchill and Lord Fisher were determined behind the scenes that Lord Mersey should find him guilty of criminal negligence in that he had failed to use the zig-zag during his final approach to the Irish coast and to increase his speed at a critical time, as well as to prove that he had failed to act upon Admiralty instructions that he had never, in fact, received.

The early proceedings were straightforward and Pacey had everything clear in his mind at that stage as he answered the questions: questions as to the number and condition of his lifeboats, whether or not the correct drills had been carried out and at the proper times, whether all passengers had attended boat drill and been properly instructed in the use of lifejackets and in their required actions should the vessel have to be abandoned; the state of the engines, the nature of the cargo as per manifest – which did not indicate in fact the nature of the war materials carried – the number of his crew possessing lifeboat certificates enabling them to take charge of the lowering of boats and their handling when away from the ship.

When all of that was out of the way there were navigational and ship-handling questions, but later in the proceedings the questions became more personal, more hostile in Pacey's view. He found, as the long days of cross-examination went on, that Sir Edward Carson was able to make the truth sound like lies.

Carson: 'Will you please tell us again your qualifications, Captain Pacey?'

'I am a Master Mariner . . . I have an Extra Master's certificate.'

'I see. And you became a master in sail?'

'Yes.'

'A seaman, an officer, of much experience?'

'Yes.'

'But not, I suggest, in war?'

'Not in war, no.'

'Then it would be true, would it not, to say that you might perhaps . . . make mistaken decisions when events developed beyond your capacity to cope?'

'No. I don't think so.'

'You don't *think* so?' Carson's eyebrows had gone up. 'You seem uncertain, Captain Pacey. Tell me, why are you uncertain?'

'I find that a difficult question to answer,' Pacey replied, not adding *without losing my temper.*

'Very well then, we shall leave it for the moment. But we have already established that you have no experience of wartime conditions, have we not?'

'No, that's not entirely – '

'Thank you, Captain Pacey, that will be all for now.' Carson gathered his gown about his body and sat down with a long-suffering look towards Lord Mersey.

And again later:

Carson: 'Was there, perhaps, some panic as the ship was hit and there was an explosion? Some of your crew were not quite up to it?'

'I have a very good crew. Many of them are – were – men who had done their time in the sailing ships, as I have myself. I had the fullest trust in them.'

'Because they had shared your past experiences?'

'I did not let that sway me. They were good men, that is all.'

'Well, never mind, Captain Pacey. You have not in fact answered my original question – yet it leads to an interesting further question.' Carson rustled a sheaf of papers. 'You would call these men shellbacks? Yourself as well?'

'No, I would not.'

'Oh? But the term shellback, surely, is a very usual way of describing such men?'

'Perhaps. But I believe you mean it – you employ it – in a derogatory sense.'

'Ah, I see. To describe men with, perhaps . . .' again Carson rustled his papers, then waved them in a circle, 'with blinkered minds, set minds no longer receptive to te present day but anchored to the past? That is what you mean, Captain Pacey?'

Pacey's answer was brief and angry. 'It is what *you* mean, Sir Edward.'

There was a smirk now on Carson's face. Pacey grew angrier. He felt that somehow or other a point had been scored against him. The question was set aside and Carson went off on another tack. 'Was there any evidence of *cowardice* on the part of any of your crew, Captain Pacey? Cowardice that may have led to a larger loss of life than would otherwise have been the case?'

'No.' Pacey was firm. 'None at all.'

'That you could see?'

'I said there was none. I repeat that statement.'

'I see. But, of course, it is an incontrovertible *fact* that you couldn't be everywhere at once, could you, and that is quite understandable.' A pause, a long one, with Carson taking a firm grip on the two sides of his gown. There was a dead silence in the courtroom as though all present – witnesses, survivors together with supporting friends and relatives, lawyers and their clerks, Lord Mersey himself – knew what was coming next. 'Cowardice, Captain Pacey. An interesting and emotive word, is it not? And is it not in the tradition of the sea that the captain goes down with his ship?'

'Are you accusing me – '

'If the cap fits, Captain Pacey . . . but please answer the question.'

Pacey was shaking with barely suppressed anger and humiliation. But he managed to answer, 'It has been held so, yes.'

'Very often, I believe. Captain Smith of the *Titanic* for one.'

Pacey made no response to that. Carson went on, 'Why did you not follow that tradition yourself, Captain Pacey?'

'Because I suppose – '

'You suppose? Are you not certain?'

Pacey swallowed. 'Because I believed I might be of more use to my country in time of war alive than dead.' He didn't add that he might have remained if the sea itself hadn't removed him. Carson would have twisted that; and what he might have done was scarcely evidence, he supposed.

'So you would insist it was not from cowardice . . . that is all, Captain Pacey, thank you.'

It was more than a nightmare. Pacey sweated into his heavy clothes as he was dragged through the legal mud, seeing quite clearly what they meant to do to him. He became bogged down, began to give confused answers when the questioning moved onto orders received or not received from the naval authorities. The intention was, of course, to set traps, to get him to contradict himself. Or incriminate himself.

There was, for instance, a muddle in his evidence over whether or not he had seen, during his final approach to the Old Head of Kinsale, a zig-zag order from the Admiralty: it all had a different ring to it when it was put to him by Lord Carson, a lawyer with no knowledge of the sea or seamen, a man who had never been accustomed to the making of instant decisions that affected men's lives for good or ill, a man with all the time in the world to make his legal decisions and to prime traps for the men at the sharp end of events. In this muddled state Pacey was flustered into agreeing that indeed he must have seen such an order, though later reflection showed him that he had never in fact received it at all. Although he had used the zig-zag earlier, he agreed that he had not been zig-zagging when the U-boat had attacked. Believing, as a result of virtually no information from the naval authorities, that he was nearing a clear area, he had seen no need to extend his final approach with a zig-zag, which of itself would have kept him longer at sea when he was nearly home. He was quizzed as to the readiness of his ship's organization to cope with emergencies and again as to his own competence in a war situation. He answered everything confusedly but honestly; and he was patently a truthful man. He insisted that the only recent information he had had was the report two evenings before of a solitary U-boat steering away from the area of his approach. That, and nothing else: no warning of another U-boat in the vicinity. That being so, he had honestly believed his course and speed to be entirely safe.

The Inquiry ended after four terrible weeks on 17 July. Lord

306

Mersey's summing up was as fair as he had himself been throughout Pacey's ordeal; and Pacey had been well served by the defending counsel, a counsel with whom Lord Mersey had had a protracted conversation in the course of which Mersey expressed the view that Pacey had been a truthful witness, confused though his evidence might at times have been, throughout the Inquiry. And he found that Captain Pacey had been entirely prudent in his actions and in his assessment of the developing situation as he honestly saw it and had been by no means negligent. Captain Pacey had no case to answer. Apart from this, no conclusions were come to. Other than for Pacey, it was an unsatisfactory ending; but it was a clear defeat for the intentions of Churchill, of Fisher, and of the Board of Admiralty.

Captain Pacey had left Central Buildings in Westminster in a turbulent frame of mind. So many innuendoes, so many outright accusations – never mind Lord Mersey's stand in his favour, all this stuck in his throat. The manoeuvrings of the Admiralty to secure a finding against him, to have him blamed wholly for the tragedy with no admissions on their own part of incompetence and untruths, were no less galling and embittering for having been frustrated. But what could be done about it? The answer was, nothing at all. Pacey wished to go back to sea in command as soon as possible; with the Inquiry not finding against him, he would do so – he had been assured of that by the Chairman of the Line. To stir up muddy waters now would help no one. His name had been cleared; best leave it at that and be thankful. In any case he had no fire of spirit left with which to fight an Admiralty that was never likely to admit intrigue and deception.

The young woman who presented him with the white feather had obviously read the newspapers diligently: the passage about cowardice, and the leaving of his ship as she went down. The young woman rankled, made him want to give her a tongue-lashing that she would remember. But he didn't do this. Why bother? She would conclude only that her shaft had gone home. He wouldn't give her the satisfaction of that.

The taxi took him to Waterloo and he went home to Mary.

The crew of U-120 received their acclamation as had been expected. There were immense, cheering crowds outside the Wilhelmshavn base. *Kapitanleutnant* Eppler was met by Ilse and his father-in-law, Admiral von Neuburg, and by his own father. Eppler senior, the lowly ministry clerk, shook his son's hand and offered his congratulations as was expected of him; but the look in his father's eyes went straight to Klaus Eppler's heart. It was as though he had destroyed something precious that had been between them, that he had destroyed much more than a great liner. But his father was pushed into the background by the congratulations of Admiral von Neuburg, who had overcome all his own reservations. It had been, the Admiral said, a most notable success, a tremendous blow against England, now seen by all the world to be impotent, unable to protect her merchant shipping. It would have the effect of keeping British and Allied vessels off the seas, and the result of that would be starvation for the British. That night a great reception was held for the officers of U-120 and many adulatory speeches were made. *Kapitanleutnant* Klaus Eppler would in due course be received by his Kaiser and decorated. The reception ended with the most fervent singing of *Deutschland Uber Alles* preceded by many other patriotic songs.

Afterwards, in the early hours, Admiral von Neuburg left his daughter and son-in-law in their apartment in the town and they were alone together.

'You are pleased with me, Ilse?' Klaus asked diffidently.

'Oh yes,' she said in a tone of indifference. She gave him an enigmatic smile but no further answer to his question. She said, 'I am tired, Klaus. We shall go to bed.'

'And – ?'

She yawned. 'I am so tired, Klaus. Sometimes I believe that that is all you can think about.'